A Wind of Many Colors

By John H. Brown

Published by MAJEC

Cover By Elizabeth Kruse

Library of Congress Cataloging Control Number: 2007929365

I S B N
978-0-9793160-0-5

Printed in the United States Of America
First Edition

Printed by
The Covington Group
Kansas City, Missouri

A Wind of Many Colors

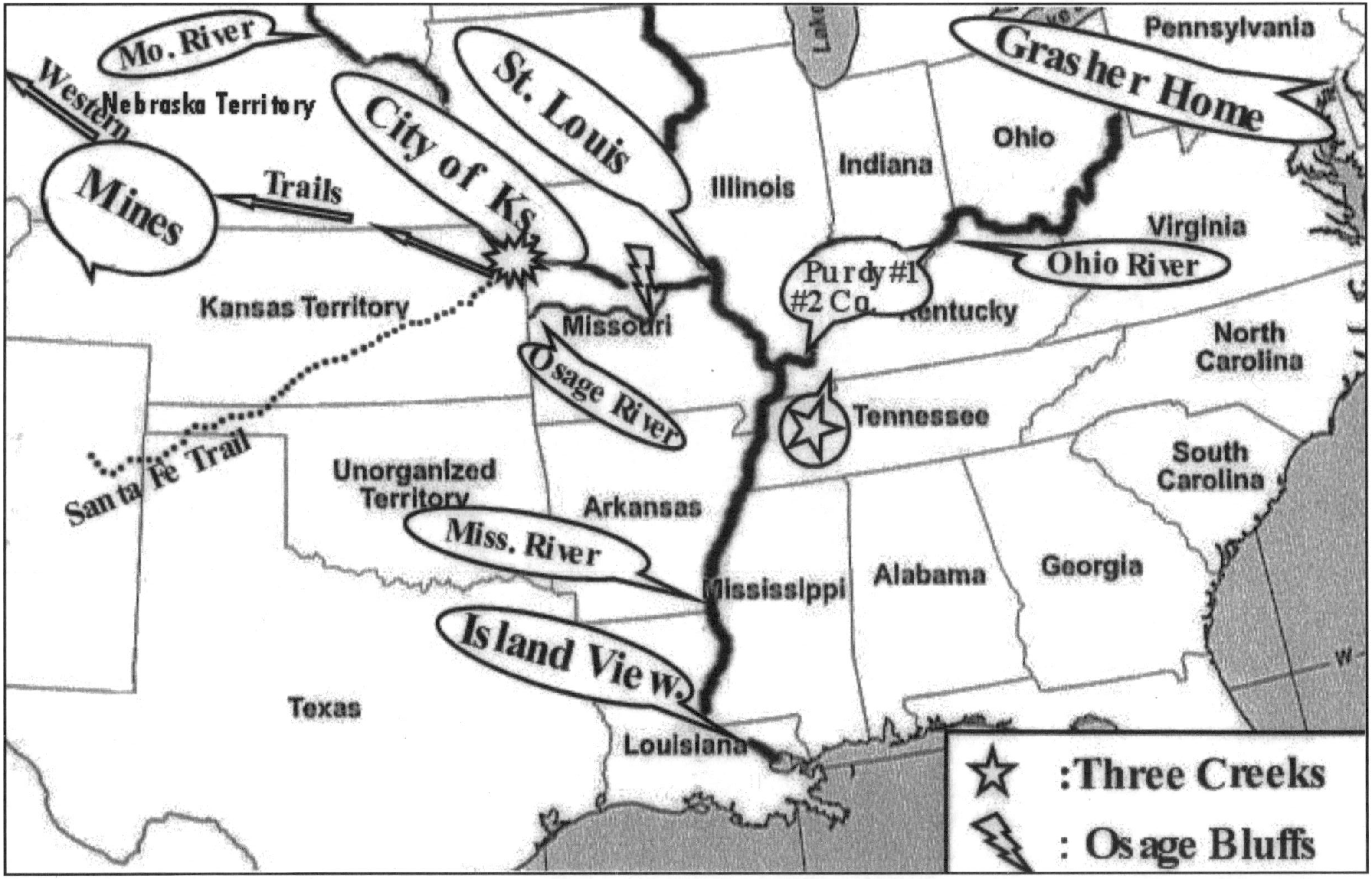
Mo. River
Western
Nebraska Territory
Mines
Trails
City of Ks
St. Louis
Kansas Territory
Santa Fe Trail
Unorganized Territory
Texas
Missouri
Osage River
Arkansas
Miss. River
Island View.
Louisiana
Mississippi
Illinois
Indiana
Ohio
Purdy #1 #2 Co.
Kentucky
Tennessee
Alabama
Georgia
Pennsylvania
Grasher Home
Virginia
Ohio River
North Carolina
South Carolina
:Three Creeks
: Osage Bluffs

Dedication

A Wind of Many Colors is in tribute to those of our bloodlines that came before my wife, Margaret Ann Correll Brown and me. They were an interesting lot of hard working Christian middle class who, by today's standards, may be thought of as having been poor. Most of us did not realize we were poor until we were adults, for our blood kin always made room in their lives for us. Certainly there were some characters, an outlaw or two, and a crazy one now and then in our lines I suppose. Still, they were the foundation of America. And we still are.

Special thanks to,
Dr. Neita Geilker,
The Grammar Guru of Kansas City

And

Elizabeth Kruse
Cover Artist

Dedicated to
Margaret Ann Correll Brown
my help-mate, lover, and wife of nearly 50 years

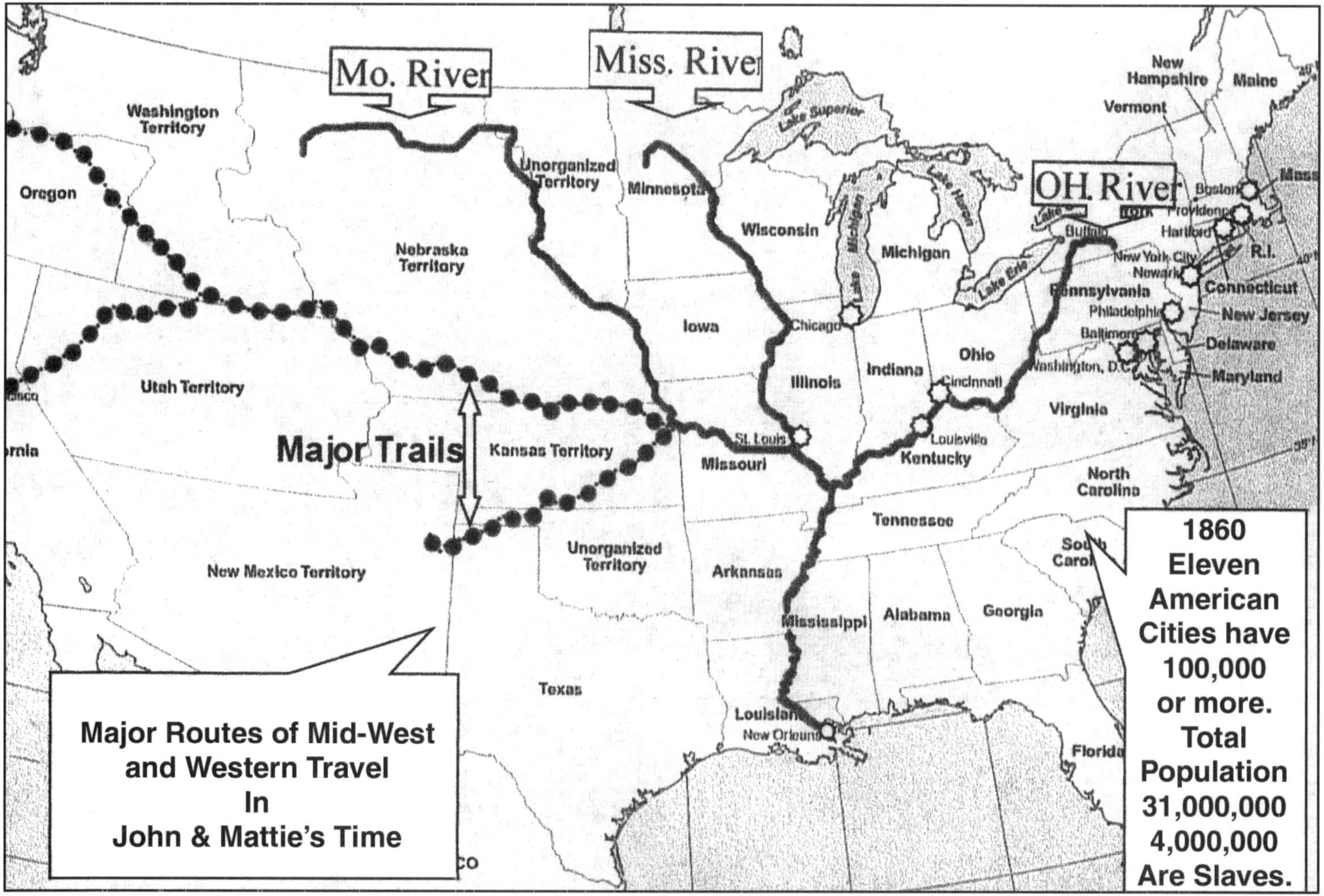
Mo. River
Miss. River
OH. River
Major Trails
Washington Territory
Oregon
Nebraska Territory
Unorganized Territory
Minnesota
Wisconsin
Michigan
Lake Superior
Lake Michigan
Lake Huron
Lake Erie
Iowa
Chicago
Illinois
Indiana
Ohio
Cincinnati
Louisville
Kentucky
St. Louis
Missouri
Utah Territory
Kansas Territory
New Mexico Territory
Unorganized Territory
Arkansas
Tennessee
Mississippi
Alabama
Georgia
Louisiana
New Orleans
Texas
Florida
Virginia
North Carolina
Washington, D.C.
Baltimore
Philadelphia
Pennsylvania
New York City
Newark
Buffalo
Connecticut
New Jersey
Delaware
Maryland
R.I.
Hartford
Providence
Boston
New Hampshire
Vermont
Maine
1860
Eleven
American
Cities have
100,000
or more.
Total
Population
31,000,000
4,000,000
Are Slaves.
Major Routes of Mid-West
and Western Travel
In
John & Mattie's Time

Author's Comments

Much of this story is based on yarns of my family, plus a lifelong fascination with those times leading up to the Civil War, in which my ancestors fought and died for both sides. One of my Missouri great grandmothers, Belle Bay Brown, traced her noble Scot ancestry through Kentucky, back to the Cumberland Gap, up the Shenandoah Valley to a second son who would have received neither title nor money. He sailed for America to make it on his own, and their story is woven into this book. My father-in-law was an older man when my wife was born as was his mother at his birth, thus making my wife's grandmother, Amanda Hankins-Correll an interesting nub on our family tree. She was found as a four-year-old, wandering along a frontier creek bank clutching her bloody rag doll, the sole survivor of a bloody Indian attack. America is a land of such stories.

A Wind of Many Colors is a swashbuckling 1840-60's love story between John Purdy, a man primarily of Irish descent, and Mattie, his beautiful German wife. This family saga is set amongst a group of robust and rambunctious characters in an America that was certainly a different place than now. The story reaches wonderfully back to catch a flavor of the main characters' ancestors, plus the social forces that made our characters as they were at story time.

Perhaps nowhere on earth could have been more different than the American east coast, just prior to the Revolutionary War. John Purdy's grandfather, Paul Purdy, was barely 14 when he and his uncle's family walked down the Shenandoah Valley to pass through the Cumberland Gap. They came with the Lincolns who brought their son, Mordecia, who was Paul's 14-year-old best friend. As Mordecia's younger brother Tom watched, their father was killed by savages in the Gap. Mordecia bravely grabbed a rifle and fired at the Indians as young Tom stood transfixed by his father's body. Young Tom lived and would honor their father one day by giving his firstborn son their father's name, Abraham Lincoln.

Not many years after Paul Purdy came through the Gap, Virginia's de Falcos' ancestors brought servants and plenty of gold as they sailed regally into Orleans Bay, at a place called New Spain. This was about the same time that Mattie's grandfather, and his best friend, a Catholic, escaped the German chaos. They indenturing themselves to a sea captain, who would bond them for years to men yet unknown. In return for some of their very best years these young men received passage to a new shore called, America. Many of us, if not most of us, had such ancestors who paid an incredible price for our ticket here.

One has but to look down over the Cumberland Gap from several different spots to come to realize that Daniel Boone must have truly been a human GPS. Thanks to his genius, a good part of the story takes place in "Three Creeks, Kentucky" which could be any one of a half dozen western Kentucky settlements that became contemporary towns. A good number of you will say, "He's talking about back home."

The character of Mattie Purdy was inspired by the wife of my father's kinsman. She was five times more sensual in real life than Marilyn Monroe tried to be on the screen. Men made over her so that from about the ages of 18 through 40 the only public place she generally would be seen was at a family gathering or perhaps a funeral. Our kinsman's wife was a chaste and honorable woman; however, as a young lad she certainly helped awaken in me the difference between us as men,—and us as women.

Virginia de Falco's plantation model is that of a Scotswoman by the name of Francis Wright who came to Memphis in 1825 and bought slaves by the hundred. Francis was ahead of her time and in 1828 she was run off of her 2000 acre plantation, Nashoba, and out of the South by the more traditional slave owners. To gain a clearer understanding of the peculiar institution of slavery, I heartily recommend Fleischner's exquisitely documented, *Mrs. Lincoln and Mrs. Keckly.* Therein she describes no less a personage than Thomas Jefferson writing, wherein he admonishing all; "A child raised every two years is of more profit than of the best laboring man." (pg. 28) She also describes the weighing of slave children to be sold by the pound (pg. 43) and in a few more pages she relates the flogging of such a child's mother "for she would not put on a happy face." Laws pertaining to slavery varied extensively in different parts of the country and it is impossible to be exacting except to say that slaves had it hard, wherever they were. All examples used here were true at some point in time for a major jurisdiction.

"Junior" and family were real. He terrorized me all through 3rd grade.

In preparing to write this book I have stood at every major location referred to, (see map) and tried to imagine how it might have been. It's hard, if not impossible. There are more cities currently with 100,000 population in the state of Virginia than there were in all our land (11) in 1860 when the Civil War started. Washington D.C. was a town of 60,000 then, with 11,000 free blacks and 1200 slaves. In twenty short years (1840-60), St. Louis, Missouri, exploded from a small western village to a major city of 160,000 and to become what was arguably the most sophisticated place in all of the land.

Cost comparison or the value of a dollar is impossible to calculate with a simple formula. Things were different. For example, a modern day home's most expensive rooms are the kitchen and the baths. A fine home in 1850 required a stove and an icebox, but no appliances nor a heating and air contractor, or plumbers, for most locations did not provide a gas line, water line or sewer. Homes were taxed on the number of rooms so there were normally no closets; therefore, homes with those specifications could obviously be built quite inexpensively even today. Land was cheap, and pre Civil War $1 an acre Ozark hill country now brings $1,000 an acre for recreational purpose, yet wages are not 1,000 times higher. Some had thousands of dollars but the working man had to get by on one or two dollars a day. For a better appreciation of this story I suggest the reader think in terms of 20 or 25 times the values discussed in the book as the present day value. When John offers Virginia $3,000 for her slave he is talking at least $50,000 of our money.

The absolute truth is sometimes hard to glean. For example; it is unquestioned that Francis Chouteau was among the first white settlers ever in Kansas City, and his wife, Bernice, is known as our city's mother. One authoritative source tells of his death in a barroom, while another equally authoritative source reports of his tragic trampling by a group of half-tame horses. One source tells of the Alexander Majors holding parties in their fine new home at Christmas time 1860, while yet another suggests that this was his daughter's doing, for by then he may have moved to Nebraska City to be closer at hand to organize the Pony Express. Alexander Majors' home still stands down on State Line Road and there have been few enterprises ever in Kansas City to match the Waddell, Majors and Russell pre-Civil War freighting empire. Majors' strength of character, community involvement, and decency are well documented. At any rate, the documentation concerning the "Kansas Bogus Government" seems substantial enough. This was the first governmental body that claimed authority in the Kansas Territory and gained its name from little irregularities. Such as the 1628 votes cast by the 42 legal residents of Oxford Township.

The City of Kansas' close by Kaw riverbank divorce-mill is well documented, and after the Civil War, in 1869, wild and wooly Kansas City became home to Annie Chamber's palace of pleasure, probably the finest brothel ever on American soil. Annie stood well over six foot tall and was a very beautiful woman. She was abused by both father and husband, then found the City of Kansas divorce mill and became a "Fallen Angel." Naturally enough, Annie's was staffed with extraordinarily beautiful talent, fresh up from the riverbank. It is worth noting that later in life Annie had a religious experience and her donated fortune was the beginning of our City Union Mission, originally a haven for men down on their luck.

Men on horseback could cover surprising distances in a short amount of time. Bill Cody (later known as Buffalo Bill,) a faithful employee of Alexander Majors and rider for their ill-fated Pony Express, by happenstance once covered 384 miles on horseback without taking time for an appreciable rest. Bright moonlight and the fact that a fresh already saddled horse was waiting for him about every fifteen miles allowed him to accomplish his unplanned feat in about 24 hrs. Nonetheless, it was the rivers that were the interstate routes and the West would never have been the same without the steamboats which plied the rivers getting our ancestors upstream west; "to get started West." In pre-Civil War days over 60 steamboats made hundreds of *scheduled* stops each year in Kansas City and a few of them, especially those over on the Mississippi River, had cabin class accommodations that put the finest hotels to shame. The Arabia Steamboat Museum in Kansas City is worth the trip here.

Conditions over the Santa Fe Trail, and out across Nebraska to Gregory's Gulch are depicted accurately. There never has been, nor probably will ever be, another spot like the "richest square mile in the world" with its 17,000 mines crammed onto this tiny bit of the Kansas Territory's eastern slopes.

Some of the most spectacular Osage River bluffs are at approximately the two-mile marker of the Lake of the Ozarks, their tops now towering over water about 100 feet deep. When I was a lad the lake was an undeveloped fishing hole with 1200 miles of shoreline, and there was a charred foundation and some fireplace stones at a remote spot on these bluff tops. An incident similar to what I depict was reputed to have taken place there.

Our family owns hundreds and hundreds of acres of those Ozark hills, close by this spot. Some are spectacular, with an occasional high black-rock mesa (officially they are called glades) surrounded by sporadic clumps of cedar, where one has an expansive birds-eye view of wooded hills, creeks and valleys. Often, as our family rides to a high black-rock mesa, we meander about to count the various kinds of wildflowers in the creek bottoms along the way. Or we cool off in the mouth of a cave or watch water tumble from a mysterious source. Sometimes I stop by one of the pioneer cemeteries or just stand and meditate at one of the Indian thong trees. One cannot help but to wonder at the pluck of those who came before us.

I have taken what advantage I could from the work of many others, and have taken their works at face value. My thoughts have formed over so many years that I am fearful I may have forgotten what may have been the original source; hence, I cannot possibly give others all the credit they are due. I do list some excellent resources which I have shamelessly pillaged.

At any rate, many things in this book actually happened while every single thing in this book could have. My job is to make you wonder where the fiction begins.

Enjoy.

John

Western Kentucky, 1859

America the Beautiful is, and was. Particularly in the spring of 1859, along Bluff Road where the road meandered through the most pleasant of landscapes. The spectacular panorama from up on top of the bluffs, which lent their name, included a breath-catching view of the roaring river far below. As the river charged past the bluff's base, it squeezed though some narrow rock gorges which had enough fall to make the water foam vigorously; however, Bluff Road then wound down to water-level, at a place where the clear water sparkled as it flowed gently through wide and shallow places. Then, for the next several miles, it meandered among a plethora of seasonal wildflowers that lined the gardens and fields dotting the flats between the riverbanks and the Kentucky hills. Occasionally the road was forced precariously close to the river as a hill closed in to crowd one bank or the other. Bluff Road continued on far past its fork onto Three Creeks Road, which ran at a right angle through a low pass in gently undulating hills. From this junction Three Creeks Road made its way easterly up and over to the next watershed, to traverse the equally charming Three Creeks Valley.

Both Three Creeks Road and Bluff Road were joined time after time by trails leading out of the hills on both sides of the creeks and the river. These secondary trails had but limited use by their two, three or even four families each. An occasional one of their homes peeked through the trees. Both of these fertile valleys embraced numerous plots of wheat, pumpkins, squash, and a great variety of other garden produce. Most of these flat valley acres were devoted to corn, for cornmeal and "corn extract" were by far the locals' major crops. The few homes one could spot in the foothills were similar, a better class of cabin built with two separate rooms of well-chinked squared logs and a fireplace at each end. The popular design included a dog-trot (breeze-way) between its two rooms, a porch completely across the front, then with an attic and shake shingle roof over the entire structure. Some homes consisted of a great deal of new added to the old, while others were entirely of recent vintage. One of the two rooms typically served as the kitchen, eating, and living space while the other served as the adults' bedroom and perhaps a place for the family's valuables. Often the second room's most notable contents, in addition to a bed with corn shuck mattress and the baby's bed, were precious seed for the next season, dried foodstuff, plus corn and wheat to be ground into meal. The spacious attic was accessed by a ladder in the breezeway and stretched over the top of both rooms, plus the dogtrot and porch. Typically, it served as bed space for three to thirteen children.

Nearly half of these home sites had a small separate smokehouse to store cured meat and other such necessities; however, a three-sided shed to shelter the family's animals close by was standard. The owners were justifiably proud of their improvements, for these homes were decidedly better than typical western Kentucky hill-people lived in. On casual observance, one would think these homes had been scattered haphazardly about; however, this is cave and spring country, and these were smart people. They always built close to a good spring, which often as not, was close by the cave or overhang where their ancestors had survived during their first winter in Kentucky.

This fine afternoon, as if by magic, two men and three mules appeared single file from a great clump of hillside brush. The men were careful to leave no tracks on the creek's rock bottom, or any other evidence they had ever been there, as they followed the creek bed over to Bluff Road. The cave they emerged from was precisely what gave Kentucky its name of "The Cave State," and, as is common-place, this cave was especially well concealed. The dry creek bed leading to the hillside made a fishhook shaped bend into its mouth, effectively hiding the opening unless one was standing right in it. Additionally there was the profusion of brush which made the cave entrance completely invisible. The two scruffy looking mule riders gained Bluff Road, then plodded along leading the third mule which bore only a saddle. The mule riders carried side arms plus each had a rifle in their scabbard with one piece being a huge "bench rifle." At the junction they turned east onto Three Creeks Road, which climbed up through its slot in the rolling hills, to the next watershed and its settlement.

The village of Three Creeks obviously drew its name from the local creeks and boasted houses that were decidedly upscale from the nearby countryside. Nearly all of these homes were considerably larger than the riverside and valley ones, plus they were constructed mostly of sawed lumber. The three, clear-water, name-sake creeks originated way high in the hills to then merge into one major creek just upstream and gurgle merrily past the spot where the settlement now perched on its bank. Several homes plus the combination church-school with its attached shelter house sat facing the creek from the opposite side of the road. The roofed shelter's open space was frequently used for overflow crowds at church, picnics or weddings, and made a great place for the school children to play in inclement weather.

The smallest two homes sat either side of the church-school, one was a parsonage, the other for a schoolteacher. Dody's Tavern, which was large and extremely nice for a country tavern, also sat on the side of the road away from the creek on down the road past the school. Stables for Dody's overnight guests and to provide shelter for horses the children rode to school sat behind the church-school and tavern. The school playground was also on the side away from the creek; however, Dody maintained a manicured park-like creek bank area for sitting, strolling and fishing straight across the road from their tavern.

The entire strip of land between the road and the creek was dominated by the Purdy home, the Purdy Mercantile Store, their stables, Dody Park and the Purdy grinding mill setting at the very edge of the creek bank further down the hill. The Purdy home was definitely a showplace; however, it was the store that was most remarkable. The unaware were always amazed at how a small settlement and community could support such an enterprise. The Purdy Mercantile building had been expertly added onto time and again, but with careful observation one could pick out phase one, then two, then three and then four.

The scruffy looking mule riders rode up and dismounted a safe distance from the store, then the chap who had been leading the third mule tied its halter strap to the mule he had been riding. It was past any normal closing time, so the duo was surprised to see lights in the place. The smaller of the pair slipped over and took up a guard position beside the store's front door. The other, a full-chested stout looking fellow, took a moment to prepare for their venture by taking a stiff snort from the jug that hung from his saddle. Sledge, the stout looking whiskey drinking fellow, took his time peeking about to determine that the barber was not in his shop space, the seamstresses were not working late on a dress, nor were any of the other concessionaires still at their stations.

Suddenly Sledge's eyes flew wide open! This was going to be a lot easier than he or his partner Johnson could have imagined. They had talked about the various schemes they might use to lure her out of the house and away from the others who would normally be around tonight. All of that planning had been unnecessary, for there she was! Alone!

Mattie Purdy was tidying up a few things as she waited for their customer, who was coming in with his son to pick up their new steel moldboard plow. She seldom worked in the store anymore; however, her husband, John, had taken the general manager and their dozen or so employees over to the house, to introduce them to their new pay plan. John was both impatient and excited to hold this meeting, for his generous plan included an 1859 version of profit sharing. When it became apparent the plow customer was running late, she readily volunteered to come over to the store, to wait around.

Mattie, a blue-eyed honey blond, stood a statuesque five feet eight and one half inches tall and was truly a magnificent specimen of the female of the species.

She was city born.

And city bred.

And astonishingly beautiful.

Considering her sophisticated upbringing, it was more than a bit surprising that, as opposed to looking down on their neighbors, Mattie continuously marveled at them. At how a man and a woman could live in this country and be mother and father, farmer, housekeeper, hunter, fisherman, cook, weaver, soap-maker, carpenter, stone mason, poulterer, stockman, butcher, leather-tanner, shoe-maker, harness-maker, ammunition-maker, gardener, fruit-grower, bee-keeper, wine-maker, food-preserver, canner, and nurse, be great musicians and teach their kids to be God fearing people — all while making their excellent corn whiskey. Both Mattie and her husband, John Purdy, loved and respected these people and for years they had been, and currently were, of incredible help to many of them in achieving their more prosperous lifestyle. John Purdy was truly a business visionary and Mattie was everybody's sweetheart. Nobody knew anybody as respected as John.

Nor more loved than Mattie.

Embolden by his whiskey, Sledge became impatient with his long time partner, Johnson, causing Johnson to query Sledge for about the umpteenth time:

"You shore about this thing?"

"I done told you a thousand time what I got to do. Hell, even when I'm with old Sadie, I think about nuthin but this woman. If your scart, get on outta here. I'll take keer of it by myself."

"Naw, we been partners way too long to let you go it by yourself. Sides. Thayed catch you sure."

"We'll get her back to the cave fore anybody knows we been here."

Johnson was still not completely sold:

"If they catch us, it'll be rough."

Sledge attempted to settle Johnson down:

"Ain't nobody gonna catch us. Nobody I ever talked to knows about that cave nor where it is. We'll hide her in there for a day or two then quick be deep in the hills of Missouri, and ain't nobody from ta here ever comes over ta thar."

Sledge was past just being impatient by now. He had dreamed and schemed about Mattie Purdy from the first time he caught a glimpse of her on one of the pairs' infrequent trips through Three Creeks. She was a prize beyond description. He could conceive no greater contrast or pleasure than the beautiful, well-groomed, sweet-smelling Mattie Purdy. Especially when compared to the rough and unkempt Mississippi River women who regularly took care of his needs.

Johnson and Sledge were hunters by trade and knew full well that just plain luck often determined the results of any hunt. Fortune was smiling upon them right this minute, and so, as Sledge gazed through the window and observed his prey, he smiled back through his filthy tobacco stained teeth. This was going to be much easier than either had anticipated, for she was unexpectedly vulnerable tonight. All of their schemes were wasted. She was in there, just waiting.

When Sledge walked in, Mattie was genuinely surprised to see a customer at this hour. Nonetheless, she queried brightly:

"Hello. May I be of help?"

Sledge looked about to make absolutely certain they were alone. He was delighted. Turning to Mattie, he pointed to an assortment of their best men's hats.

"Yes. I need a new hat. How much are these?"

"The lower ones are three or four dollars. Those up there are as much as eight."

He pointed to the very top.

"Can I see that one?"

The Three Creeks Purdy Mercantile building was so crammed with merchandise (again) that Purdy had taken to constructing extra-high shelves. The staff used stepladders on wheels to retrieve the higher goods, typically the high priced lightweight stuff.

Mattie was somewhat taken aback when her crudely dressed prospect expressed interest in such an expensive hat, but she willingly pushed a ladder over to climb up and fetch it. When she stepped back down he had positioned himself such that she unwittingly backed down right into him. He greedily reached under her armpits and grabbed both hands full, and as he held firmly onto her bosom he forced himself against her bottom. He made her well aware of his condition, and then gave the wheeled ladder a push with his foot. Between being caught off guard, the ladder rolling from under her one foot, and his hungry grasping, Mattie couldn't regain herself. As she struggled to gain her balance, she wound up pressing against him and was distressed at the manner he stuck to her backside like glue. Her eyes darted here and there.

Except for the man grasping at her and the scuffy chap who came in with him, there was no one else about. As Sledge nearly squeezed the breath out of her in his bear-hug, the second man stopped pacing and watching everywhere, to charge in their direction.

Eastern Pennsylvania, 1840

John and Mattie's Story Begins

Mattie Grasher was trying very hard not to be impatient with Ory today. But Really! He knew full well she was in a tizzy of a rush to get home from her violin lesson! Ory, doggedly insisting on being the very responsible type that he actually was, kept the mares to a respectable trot. The last thing Ory intended to do was to scare somebody or, worst yet, for her father to hear that he had been careening around city streets in a dangerous or disrespectful manner. Besides, as the Grashers' groomsman, driver, gardener, and handy man, Ory Winkler would also have to answer to his wife Thelma, their housekeeper and phenomenal cook. The couple had the two most coveted jobs of their kind in the entire state of Pennsylvania and he was not about to jeopardize that.

The carriage was hardly at a stop when Mattie jumped out and hustled up the front walk to let herself in the beautifully carved front doors. Even in her haste she took time to properly store her marvelous 100-year-old violin in its proper place. Her father had never shared with her what he had paid for it; instead he simply insisted that she never carry it on the streets when out by herself. He had also smiled mischievously this morning as he speculated that if John Purdy was anything like his older brother, or his father, that this should certainly be a very fun and stimulating week.

Lewis Grasher generally arranged for his business guests to stay at a nice hotel at his expense and had them out to his home for dinner a time or two during their visit. The Purdys, on the other hand, were very special people and were invited to be house guests during their entire stay. Mattie took a quick look in the mirror and stepped down the hall to the library, where the new arrivals were having a spot and loosening up from their travels. When she popped into the library they were discussing the fact that the country was going railroad crazy and Pennsylvania would soon have 750 miles of railroad track. If the voyagers were carrying the right kind of money it cost somewhere between 3 and 4 cents a mile to travel on a steamboat, the two stagecoaches, or any one of the half dozen different railroads they had taken to get there.

Grasher stood and warmly welcomed his daughter and then taking her arm he began presenting her to their guests. As John Purdy stood and watched this gorgeous creature being reacquainted with his father, a strange thing happened. Someone let a double handful of butterflies loose in his stomach and they ganged up, forced his breath to catch. Try as he might, it would go neither in, nor out. As he was anxiously trying to get his breathing started again, Mr. Grasher brought her over to him, and for some inexplicable reason, at exactly the wrong moment he completely forgot his own name. John stood awkwardly mumbling and stammering incoherently, which totally embarrassed her as well as him. Mattie quickly realized full well that it was all her fault. She had inadvertently turned her smile up to “full dazzle” and, for about the last year or so, no virile young man could stand that kind of pressure.

John had accompanied his father as a part of his business education on the long trip east all the way from Paducah, Kentucky, where his father's branch of Purdy Mercantile thrived. Their part of the firm was strategically located in western Kentucky at the confluence of the Ohio and Tennessee Rivers, which is also just a few miles upstream from where the Ohio joins the Mississippi. Lewis Grasher was an extremely successful importer-supplier and both a merchandise source to the Purdy Mercantile Company and a dear friend of John's father, as their fathers had been.

Mattie's mother, Edith Grasher, had died when Mattie was eight and she was subsequently raised by her father and a striking silver-haired older widow named Effie Purvis. The widow Purvis was truly a consolation gift from God as she had finished raising nine of her own including six girls. Mrs. Purvis was well enough off financially but wanted something to occupy her time and had wisely chosen not to live with any one of her own children just yet. Reluctant to live alone, the new widow gladly moved in and took over managing the Grasher household after nine-year-old Mattie had returned from a miserable year at a classy girls boarding school full of "prissy snots."

Mrs. Purvis' greatest joy in life had been teaching her girls to be ladies, and having run out of daughters, she now truly enjoyed being Mattie's confidante. Mature beyond her years, the almost sixteen-year-old Mattie had far more in common with her father's business guests than with people her own age. She much preferred to act as hostess to the company of adults, who in turn always enjoyed her marvelous sense of humor and radiant beauty.

Mattie wanted to be a Mrs. Purvis. The older woman simply sparkled and her children and their families came to see her quite frequently because they wanted to, not because of any sense of duty. She was way ahead of her time for she had collected a list of foods that she had determined helped women have healthy babies, and crammed as much spinach, blackstrap molasses, sardines and milk as she could get down any woman she knew in that condition. She also insisted the family women bind their breasts in a supportive linen wrap that went up over their shoulders so they didn't have "belly floppers" and taught them to do "a feminine exercise" to get their bodies back in shape after childbirth. Effie Purvis' daughters and daughters-in-law all considered her their very best friend, and she in turn was a living example of the blessing that a good marriage and large family could be.

It was obviously Mrs. Purvis who taught Mattie about men and how to judge them, advising her they all be given three "shots" except any man whose grandfather wore satin britches. He only got one. It was also Mrs. Purvis who, at the appropriate time, would give Mattie keen insight as to how to please her man in the marriage bed. To the cook Thelma's wonder, Mrs. Purvis and Mattie also spent hours in the kitchen and now as she approached 16, Mattie was an excellent cook, who could also just happen to sew a fine seam. Music, dance and an appreciation for the other arts were also provided by a constant stream of most excellent tutors. Mr. Rufus Julliard, her violin instructor, was by far the best the area had to offer and he consistently insisted that Mattie Grasher should be sent abroad, where talent of her scope could be fully honed. On the other hand, neither she nor her father had stage ambitions for her, and Mattie played for family and friends' enjoyment plus personal satisfaction.

Mattie was immediately attracted to this unpretentious Kentucky boy, and in turn John was awesomely infatuated with this delightful, mature-beyond-her-years, radiant beauty. In point of fact the young people were quite seriously attracted to each other as was most obvious from that awkward moment when their eyes first met. Mattie's father soon cautioned John privately that he felt she was way too young to be getting serious about any man, and he would insist on her being no less than 18 years old, instead of almost 16: "Why she is still just a growing youngster, John. She still is a kid even if she is over five feet seven and as tall as many men. She still has another inch or two to go."

John Purdy was not really a boy; he was a 20-year-old, six-foot-two, 200-pound man, built exactly like the good athlete that he was. At a time when the average chap stood well less than five foot eight, this big fellow was noticeable by his size. He was also wealthy, quite handsome, smart as a whip, well educated, a good banjo player, and a gifted conversationalist. This combination made him quite an interesting "hunk" to be around, therefore, it came as no great surprise that some number of women or girls had made themselves quite available to him. When John was at a very impressionable age, one of his friends "got lucky," then became horribly infected, and in turn paid an exceptional price for his moment of indiscretion. John additionally had more than one acquaintance find themselves infected when fooling around while in college, and even more recently, a couple of his Kentucky card playing buddies had taken disease home to their wives. He had resisted temptation mostly because he held himself to a very high standard, and to some lesser degree because he was concerned about the risk.

John made Mattie a promise:
"I will keep myself clean and I will wait for you."
He did.

John saved his time and money to go back for visits at every opportunity that time would permit. He worked hard in his father's branch of the family firm, and for that reason alone John and Mattie's times together were precious. That says nothing of the $60 for each exhausting trip. In the 1840s, $60 was two or three months wages for a working man, a very substantial amount even for a wealthy young man. Making the quickest time east was somewhat complicated, for the boats moved very slowly going upstream. It also took several different kinds of money and travel modes going that way. Fortunately he could take trains over to catch one of the various steamboats moving downstream on the Ohio, which made for excellent time going home. He spent little time off, or money, for anything else.

On his third such visit to be with Mattie for her 17th birthday, Mr. Grasher told him about an ugly scene at a social event where two men came to blows over who got the next dance with Mattie and how she came home crying. He was equally infuriated and disgusted, because they were both married men: "Mrs. Purvis is wonderful, but oh how I wish my Edith were here to give Mattie advice."

He handed John a glass of wine and rambled on, somewhat philosophically:

"As you well know, John, there is still a financial crisis in this country, mostly because there seems to be one set of laws for bankers and one for everybody else. Anyone who can get a state bank permit and license can then print all of the worthless paper money they have the guts to print. You and your father better keep hanging on to as much gold as you can. I am here to tell you there is another money crisis coming, the likes of which we have never seen. Much of my money is tied up in accounts, with Purdy Mercantile being one of my few customers that has their bill paid in full. President Jackson foolishly withdrew all government funds from Second Bank, and that is where all the monies came from that had been funding the boom in construction of railroads and canals. Until recently the government has been fueling this speculative fever all along by releasing millions of cheap acres in places like Michigan and Missouri. Now, the land speculators are just bewildered, but they are all still sitting out there waiting for the bigger fool to show up. Farm debt was growing at an uncontrollable rate so the government has brought it to a grinding halt by demanding 'Specie Circular' for all land purchases. Gold or silver.

I believe the whole thing is going to come crashing down again, for you can mark my words, John, there is not that much gold or silver in the country. There is very little confidence in these eastern banks on the bank notes of the small country banks out where you are, or down south either. Except for The Citizens Bank of Louisiana, these eastern banks discount every other bank's money substantially, or won't even redeem their paper at all. We're going to have a bank panic which will make the one we had in 1819 seem mild and the depression of the 1820's will seem like a mild slow down. My main European bank went broke on American credit and the only other two I use are very skittish. I have boatloads of merchandise stacked up all over Europe because of all of this mess, and I absolutely have to get over there to try and straighten things out. I have good managers in place for the firm, but there is another problem. Mrs. Purvis is getting on in years and starting to get a bit frail. It's not fair to make her completely responsible while I am gone. It is a very hard trip this time of year and the places I need to go are not fun, and for that matter some of them are probably not even safe for a young woman like Mattie. We expect to be gone for quite some time. Who knows? Maybe the best part of a year."

John's heart sank.

Then Grasher dropped the bomb: "I can think of no man I would rather have as a son-in-law or be a part of my family than you, or your father's son. I would be proud of having your bloodline in my family, John. She is still younger than I had hoped, and I will miss her desperately, but it is her decision. If Mattie wants to, instead of going with me, you two can get married and she may go back to Kentucky with you."

It is impossible to hide a jubilant heart from the face.

Mattie had known from the very moment his eyes twinkled as he sat chuckling at the thought of his grandfather in satin pants, this was the real thing. Other men had always seemed to look upon her as a flower they had a duty to pluck; however, big strapping John Purdy always seemed to look upon her as a treasure he must protect. She in turn loved him unconditionally. After an intimate wedding, the two happiest people in the world headed back to Kentucky.

It was small wonder that after meeting Mattie, John never had eyes for any other woman. She was beautiful by any measure, and no matter how modestly she dressed or how ladylike she conducted herself, young Mattie Grasher simply could not keep the men's attention turned away. Mattie had no conscious intent to be so; however, starting as a young teenager she was sensual to the nth degree. Even in a loosely fitted dress, her well-shaped ample bosom couldn't be ignored, and one had to be blind not to take note of the rest of her fine figure with small flat stomach and nicely rounded bottom set atop those long straight legs. She had the honey blond hair and brilliant blue eyes of her German ancestors, set perfectly with just a bit of a turned up petite little nose. Her lips were the color of a ripe strawberry and curved up at each corner like a bird's wings in flight. The shape of her soft red lips held a perpetual smile, which set off her white even teeth, with the beautifully sculpted curve of her jaw defining a strong feminine chin. All of this was flawlessly wrapped in an absolutely radiant peaches and cream complexion.

As beautiful as Mattie looked with her ever-present smile, she was even more beautiful on the inside. She seldom had a frown and, when she felt secure, she was as full of mischief as a puppy. Mattie eagerly welcomed the chance to move away from the city where it seemed, married or not, every man she met soon made his advance. Furthermore, as contrasted with the other young men she knew, the handsome John Purdy made them all look like spoiled little boys. And what's more, the "spoiled little boys" seemed to always want to touch and feel and had only that one thing on their mind. Mattie could not yet fully comprehend why she seemed to bring the male human animal so quickly on point, but she knew that she did no matter how she tried to not to. Jealous types might say she acted standoffish and was aloof; however, her real intent was simply not to be noticed, by the men anyway.

An impossible task.

Twelve wonderful years after John brought Mattie back to Kentucky, Mrs. French, the incredibly competent midwife, returned and bustled about again. It was her fourth trip and always the same except this time she brought her daughter, who by now was an accomplished assistant.

"One more big push, honey, jus one more big push! That's it! That's it! You did it, girl, you did it! It's another fine looking boy."

With practiced hands, Mrs. French cleaned up the baby and placed it on Mattie's bosom, whose first reaction had been what one might expect: "Why not a girl this time. When am I ever going to get my girl?"

Then Mattie nuzzled her newborn and began to count fingers and toes. She smiled up at Mrs. French.

"Well he looks perfect, and after all, with three other boys we know just what to expect."

Summarily, Harvey Purdy was welcomed into a world full of love, and with a few lusty cries to announce to Mrs. French he was just fine, he went to his mother's bosom, and then to sleep.

Once again, at the proper time after she and her daughter had everything in order and ready for company, Mrs. French ushered John Purdy in to meet a brand new son. After Dad had a chance to get acquainted, she summoned the rest of the family. The other boys, Hiram and Henry, were brought in and stood about their mother's bed. Trisha, the middle aged widow who had moved in with the Purdys some years back, held little Harold up on her hip as they all stood close by.

The Purdy boys were about ten, six, and not yet three at the time, and they all reckoned another brother would be just swell. Mattie had smiled a mother's smile as she realized these boys all looked just like the stacked Russian dolls her own mother had given her for the last Christmas they had together, that year when Mattie was eight. As her boys lined up by each other, they too looked identical except for size.

Well, she had a four-piece set now.

Mrs. French had relaxed and marveled for a moment: "Mattie, four boys in 10 years ain't no record, but it's pretty good, even for me and I helped bring over 300 comings into these valleys. And you look so fine. Why you looks like a young girl ought to be getting ready for a dance stead of a mothering four boys."

Mattie had always been very grateful Mrs. French was there. She was simply the best one could hope for at a time like this, so John had ridden well into the night to get her and bring her back. In the meantime, John had left Mattie in the hands of Trisha while he was gone, and although Trisha was steady as a rock, Mrs. French was legend.

Mattie was tired but continued to hold on to John's hand for a while. Finally she acquiesced: "Shoo all of you, I need some rest."

He kissed her and turned to go.

She flashed her tired but dazzling smile, and then as she settled all tuckered out into her pillow she had made John a promise: "John, we'll get that girl yet."

John continuously marveled at his beautiful wife. Take now for instance. He knew full well few women would talk about having another baby, right after she just had one.

By then John Purdy was quite an accomplished merchant. He ran the mercantile store at Three Creeks, Kentucky, and was by all accounts a respected, successful and honest man. Those who knew him well also called him a visionary. Three Creeks was in the middle of nowhere and in the middle of everywhere. About the same time John met Mattie, a good customer had purchased more goods than he could haul home, so Purdy Sr. had dispatched young John out of Paducah with a second wagon to help the customer, a Mr. Simpson. Two of Simpson's slaves drove the loaded wagons and John rode in a buggy with Simpson. The wagons followed along behind as the faster buggy casually wandered about, and Mr. Simpson confirmed many of the stories John's grandfather had told him. Simpson also carefully pointed out to young John all the trails and places where people currently lived in those parts. Simpson was familiar with the territory and knew many of the stories John had heard at his Grandfather Purdy's knee.

In 1750 an explorer by the name of Dr. Thomas Walker and then a land promoter by the name of Richard Henderson both "rediscovered" a low valley in the Appalachian ridge at an elevation of only 1665 feet. In places this valley is narrower than a city side street and runs along where Kentucky, Tennessee and (current) West Virginia touch corners. Grandfather Paul had once mesmerized young John, telling him of the

Indians and the places where gazing up the mountains on either side of the trail was simply terrifying. At Grandfather Purdy's first passage, the trail was far too narrow for a wagon, and could only be passed on foot or horseback.

The Indians had known about the gap for centuries, and the white man also found it in his very early days. Nonetheless, the mountains had always served as a pretty effective 600-mile wall between red man and white. Twenty five years after the land agent's "rediscovery," Daniel Boone and 30 other woodsmen blazed a trail all of the way to Louisville through this valley that is known today as the Cumberland Gap. Boone's wife and baby daughter were the first white females to gaze upon this part of Kentucky. Boone was an extraordinary man, having a photographic memory and an amazing ability to know exactly where he was and if he had ever been there before. It was common for him to describe the countryside they were approaching even though it had been a couple of years since he had been there, and it was this extraordinary ability that allowed him to mark the Cumberland Trail.

Before Boone blazed the way, there was but an odd bunch of rebels and loyalists in the area who had either used up their last chance elsewhere, or had simply chosen not to fight each other by moving here. Until Boone marked the way, America had practically stopped east of these mountains, but now, in Grandfather Paul Purdy's time, the country suddenly seemed limitless and there for the taking.

When John's grandfather Paul was a 12-year-old lad in Ireland, he had lain listening to his mother and father talk all night long. He could not understand their words, but he could tell it was an emotional conversation. At daybreak his father had come to his bedside and given him a bag which contained some clothes and a few of his favorite things. His father had then uncovered the hiding place and given him every last coin of the family's money. His mother's eyes were red and swollen from crying all night, but she tried to be brave as they walked him to the docks. His father's youngest brother and his wife's passage had been paid by a combination of government, charitable organization, and church funds. They were waiting there to board with papers for three; however, she was still heavy with child; therefore, Paul could use the papers of his unborn cousin to board the boat. He followed his uncle aboard and turned to look back at his parents. His mother leaned into his father who stood ram-rod stiff as they waved continuously to him as the boat cast off with the morning's tide. Paul stood at the rail and waved back until they were completely out of sight. He never saw them again.

Thus, in the 1770s, John's grandfather Paul by now a 14-year-old Scots-Irish lad, along with his uncles' family and thousands more of their countrymen, wound up searching for a better life by heading through the gap.

In spite of bloody Indian resistance, between 1780 and 1810 some 200,000 to 300,000 white people followed Boone's new trail into the unsettled areas of Tennessee and Kentucky. In the early years Boone's own son was killed by the savages as the lad stood by his father's side, and in a similar scene young Paul Purdy sat with his friend Mordecai, and Mordecai's younger brother Tom, who had also been standing close by their father. This time it was the father who was killed by the Indians. The kid brother Tom would one day honor their fallen father by giving his own son their father's name, Abraham Lincoln.

(By the mid 1850s the Lincoln family and the Purdy family had all but lost track of each other; however, one of John's well-to-do uncles had renewed these family acquaintances. This uncle was a substantial investor in the Chicago-Rock Island Railroad during 1856 when the Railroad chose to open the first bridge across the Mississippi River. Americans were once again moving the West farther west, this time by connecting the Chicago-Rock Island railroad to the state of Iowa, at Davenport. The railroad hired the Illinois attorney, Abraham Lincoln, to join the industry's team in defending the railroad's right to build such a bridge, against the steamboat industry's strenuous objections. The steamboat interests claimed safety as their objection; however, it was a thinly-veiled effort to maintain their shipping monopoly in the area. Mostly due to Lincoln's marvelous oratorical skills, the case eventually was heard in the Supreme Court. Witnessing the process, John's uncle became an admirer of Lincoln and interested in his political career.)

At any rate, in those early years of Boone's trail, many thousands of people such as the Purdys and the Lincolns turned, immediately after they got through the Cumberland, to become "highlanders." These fiercely independent and industrious folk brought their brood stock, tools, seed and whiskey to this, the new frontier. Others of their ilk pushed on towards the great Mississippi River. Soon, western Kentucky in the area of Three Creeks had also developed into a land of innumerable proud and independent small farmers. It still is.

Among the other things John Purdy got from the Purdy side of the family was a genetic make up which contained a goodly amount of "grit" from this sturdy Scots-Irish stock. There were five major early waves of Irish immigrants into America, brought about by five various circumstances: 1717-18 (drought), 1725-29 (religion and poverty), 1740-41 (potato famine), 1754-55 (drought and new land available in America), and 1771-76 (land-lease disputes wherein Purdy's family was thrown off the land.) John's grandfather, the 14-year-old Paul Purdy, came to America and then to the gap in 1775, in an early enough wave of highlanders to also be known as an overmountainers. These overmountainers were hardy Scots-Irish highlanders who had braved it all, including hostile Indians, to settle immediately west of the Cumberland Gap. By age 16, John's grandfather, Paul Purdy, had become an accomplished Indian fighter having gone hand to hand with them more than once after they had fired burning arrows into the white men's homes and their inadequate forts. By age 17, Paul Purdy was considered indispensable when such trouble arose.

It is accepted that the American Revolutionary War was a dispute between the Scots-Irish and the Crown, especially down in Appalachia. It is also generally agreed that no battle in that war was more precipitous than Stone Mountain, Georgia, between the overmountainers and the American-born loyalist Redcoats. Colonial Patrick Ferguson, inventor of the first British breech loading rifle, served directly under the command of Cornwallis. He was one of the few if not the only true Brit in this battle. Ferguson sent word for the overmountainers: "Desist from your opposition to British arms, or I will send my legions over the mountains and hang your leaders and lay the country waste by fire and sword." His message had just the opposite effect. To a person they were outraged! Besides being fighting mad, they had already had bully well enough of the Crown back home.

The overmountain men gathered together a rag-tag group that looked like anything but an army at a place called Sycamore Shoals. The group marched overland for ten days to Stone Mountain where they completely routed the loyal forces. The overmountian women had helped them clean their rifles, sent along plenty of food, and admonished them to "come back having made this a better place to live than we left, or come back dead." The battle lasted only 65 minutes, and when the Redcoats begged for a ceasefire, the overmountain men later drew criticism, for they did not realize the significance of the Redcoats' white flag. The British loyalists foolishly took their classic military stand in an open field while the overmountain men used the same tactics they had learned to use with the Indians and fought from behind rocks and trees and lying in the grass or a hole in the ground. The Redcoats were killed by a ratio of 10-1 (225 to 29); the rest were wounded or captured. At least two men swore that it was Grandfather Purdy who shot Colonel Ferguson dead off his horse. There was undisputed testimony that Purdy got way more than his fair share of Redcoats that day.

Young Paul Purdy marched home to continue helping wrest the land from the Cherokee and in due course married the girl next door. Their first springtime together she presented him with a son, and now with his very own wife and baby, Paul Purdy was as happy and content as any young man of his time. He no longer need borrow a family; he had his very own. For the first time in America he felt like he belonged to someone, and someone belonged to him. The following springtime tragedy struck, and both mother and baby died from the "burning vomit." It was another full century before people came to realize that the family milk cow became a walking vessel of poison if she ate the all-too-common plant, *Eupatorium rugosum,* known locally as white snakeroot. Today there are signs in the same area with a picture of this plant and the admonition: "Know this plant or die." Purdy had been so loving and considerate that he saved all of their scarce milk for his pretty young wife that he so adored and their beautiful baby.

At any rate, the inconsolable Paul Purdy wandered about far and wide making his living with his wits, his fists and his long rifle, until he found himself in midwestern Kentucky. He elected to linger for awhile at the falls at Louisville which had fairly well stopped the West from moving west down the Ohio. The river falls 26 feet in a bit over two miles there, and that perilous stretch of shallow river with its prehistoric coral-shelf bottom had effectively stopped westerly river traffic. Few men had the skill, or the guts, to take a heavy boat past this obstacle and Paul was a natural at it. Traveler after traveler hired Paul Purdy to take their heavy boats down these three miles of hazardous river, and sometimes they helped; but most often they and all of their passengers followed safely along the bank. Later on, Paul Purdy was one of many who helped devise a safe canal around this stretch of the Ohio.

Then, by happenstance, he stopped a robbery in progress at a general store in Louisville, where the owner was so appreciative he gave Purdy a job which proved to be a major turning point in his life. Surprisingly, Grandfather Purdy had a gift for the mercantile business, and as his employer grew older, he wound up pretty much running the place in his stead. When the older man died, Paul and his young bride, Ella, bought out his employer's widow.

Grandfather Paul was in his early 40s at the time he married John's grandmother, Ella, who was then less than half his age. Now, in 1859 she was a sprightly widow of 77 who weighed in at a bit over 107 pounds. Hers is an interesting story unto itself. She was orphaned twice. The first time she was taken in by a loving family who treated her as one of their own. The second time, Ella was found wandering along a creek clutching a bloody rag doll. She was four or maybe five at the time, and the only survivor of her settlement from an attack by a group of renegade Indians. The neighboring settlement took her in again; however, this time she was passed from family to family and somewhat scorned, for she was the product of a French trapper and an Indian maid. The locals reasoned it was because the Indians knew about the "Injin blood" in her that they had spared her. When Grandfather Purdy met Ella, she had an unheated place to stay and was getting the table scraps to eat for working long hours as a chore girl at the tavern where he stayed for a while. He treated her kindly and gave a couple of men a pretty good thumping for treating her cruelly. She in turn asked him to marry her.

They were the right people at the right time doing the right thing. When the canal made river traffic safe, Louisville exploded into a bustling river city, and Purdy Mercantile exploded in resounding success. Over time, Ella presented Grandfather Paul two daughters and then their only son, John's father. Paul and Ella had 38 good years together and no man ever went to his grave having had a more devoted companion.

From the late 1840s, and with the help of two hired servants, Grandmother Ella maintained her own fine home in Louisville plus another small but nice one in Paducah. She was a regular on the boats up and down the Ohio, and the Purdy home office was generally considered wherever she happened to be. It was most often Louisville in winter and Paducah come spring. She insisted that the firm set a stipend aside each year for her two daughters and that these funds be kept in hers and the girls' names. Their husbands, "fine men that they are," who now ran the original Purdy Mercantile enterprise, would never get their hands on this particular money. She considered John to be the most responsible and exacting of her grandchildren and after she passed he was to be the legal guardian of these funds. Grandmother Ella's instructions were simple: "It's okay for them or their children to have wants, but none of them should ever have needs."

Grandmother Ella Purdy was dumb like a fox and sharp like a razor, soft and cuddly to a hurt grandchild, but prickly as a porcupine to any one she considered unkind. She had good taste and sharp eyes and was considered to be the very best judge available anywhere around of fine sewing and cooking —and fine whiskey. Her two daughters had married into the very fabric of the Louisville well-to-do, but even they could not get their mother to give up her pipe.

As Simpson had given Grandfather Paul's ambitious grandson, John, the history lesson that day, he had also started his pitch.

"Since old man Murphy died and his widow closed the little shop they had in their house, there is simply no place to buy anything at all. A real store right here where these three creeks come together like toes on a chicken's foot could not keep stuff on the shelf. I own much of this land and, by the way, all we locals call this place Chicken Foot."

Mr. Simpson continued trotting the buggy about taking John on a pretty fair tour before his return home, and it was truly amazing how many people were close at hand. All of the roads and trails seemed to converge not far from "Chicken Foot." Simpson knew every one around, and to a person they agreed! The community would certainly appreciate and frequent a good store there.

Simpson offered to sell a generous irregular portion of land just downstream from where the creeks came together for a dollar. The land he offered was nearly one half mile long, with the main creek being the east property line. There was but one proviso: anyone who needed water could always have water from their side too. The reason for the length of the property was so it would include a perfect garden spot of rich bottom soil down in the valley. An interesting small cave-like overhang in the hillside, quite close to the purposed garden spot, always had cool air blowing from a few cracks in the back rocks. These rocks were really a false back concealing yet another room on farther back. The back room of the cave would make a great place for children to play, to cool off on a hot summer day, or to take refuge from a sudden shower.

Upon his return to Paducah, John convinced his father to allow him to open his own branch of Purdy Mercantile over at Chicken Foot. His father agreed for three very good reasons.

First; he too saw quite an opportunity.

Second; that is exactly why there was a store in Paducah. When John was just a baby his own father had convinced his grandparents, Paul and Ella, to allow him his own store, and his father had succeeded over in the new town of Paducah beyond anyone's wildest expectations.

Third; John's older brother was definitely the heir apparent to the big office in Paducah. Brother Paul was obviously named after their grandfather, and once had been called Paul Junior, but now preferred to be known as PJ. Brother PJ was an outstanding business man, and fair to his siblings, but he was also definitely first born in fact, and first born in spirit. Just as his father had before him, John chaffed for an opportunity to run his own show and pled his case to the board quite effectively.

John's father laughed:

"The Purdy 'Chicken Foot Store' doesn't have a very good ring to it, son."

Grandmother Ella kind of liked "Chicken Foot," but they decided to officially name the place Three Creeks.

Mr. Simpson had willingly hired out four of his slaves, who were excellent woodsmen, to fell trees and to hew and shape the logs to fit the building plans. The slaves enjoyed working for John and went him one better, preparing enough round logs for a fair-sized barn that was to be built further down the hill. The newly-wed Mattie and John stayed with the Simpsons and tried to be generally helpful for a couple of weeks before the house (store) raising. The store would be of hewed logs; however, the living quarters, which were attached to the east, or creek side, would be of sawed lumber with some very nice windows and doors. City-bred Mattie was absolutely wide-eyed and amazed. She brought the slaves cool cider and watched by the hour as they used their axe handles to measure each log and then used a pattern to form the notches. Soon she knew each of these excellent craftsmen and their equipment by name. These men were truly professionals with the felling axe, broad axe, adz, fro, wooden maul, crosscut saw, auger, drawknife, chisel, jack-plane and hammer. Per Mattie's request they finished their assignment by making beautiful indoor shutters, to be fit in the young couple's bedroom.

Everyone within miles had come to help at the house (store) raising that Simpson organized, and in appreciation for everyone's help the Purdys presented their new neighbors with some very nice favors. A fine knife complete with scabbard in a gift box marked with a large letter "P" for the men, while the ladies' box contained the finest hand mirror any of them had ever seen. John had a lot of fun because he related Grandmother Ella's superstition of not giving away anything with a sharp edge, for fear it would cut the friendship. He insisted on trading the men their knife gift for the least valuable thing they had in their pocket. In addition to some small coins, he received bent nails, balls of fuzz, loose pieces of thread and odd buttons. Everyone had a marvelous time the day of completion, celebrating with a feast few would ever forget. There was chicken and ham, venison and beef, potatoes, gravy, slaw, sauces, beets, cobbler, tarts, pickles, breads, wine jelly, cakes, coffee, tea, and on and on.

Mattie was the perfect hostess, finding Mrs. Ledbetter (whose thighs were bigger around than Mattie's waist) a stool for her sore foot while also helping care for one the many Sumpter children. (All the while Mrs.

Sumpter kept remarking loudly those young people should make fine looking babies, and she certainly hoped he was getting Mattie started.) Mattie hovered over the food tables as well, making certain everyone had something to drink. John was a pretty good five finger banjo picker and along with several fiddle players they started with "Turkey in the Straw" and "You are my Redwing" and went from there. At the end of day there was a definite buzz in the crowd as Mattie took her prize violin from its case. In those days in these parts, a woman who played the fiddle or banjo was considered fresh, or loose, or maybe even immoral. But as Mattie drew her bow, everybody soon realized this was really quite different. Just because one might live in a log hut papered inside with newspaper, did not mean one could not appreciate talent. It became respectfully still as they all sat in quiet awe of a special talent well honed. The Allegro movement of Sonata in E minor f 16 no 1 filled the air, and for the first of many times to follow the wondrous sounds of a classical violin masterpiece filled the hills and valleys at this place called Three Creeks.

With a good stock of bulk cloth, men's brogans, ladies walking shoes, blankets, shirts, caps, pipes, crackers, vanilla, coffee, tea, sugar, kettles, files, locks, guns, ammunition, wood working tools, (of which Mattie was the foregone expert) and all of the other necessities for family life, the Three Creeks store was a success from day one.

The store sat on the main branch or the "leg" of the three streams. Towards the top of the slope the creek divided into three, with the big stream coming on straight, having been fed both from the one wandering in from a sort of northerly direction, and the one wandering in from one more or less southerly. The water flowed by the store and a short ways further down the valley it then picked up speed as it went down a sharp drop. It was not quite a waterfall, but hill enough to make the water gurgle and foam vigorously for about one hundred yards before it then quieted down and went by the garden spot and cave. Most assuredly there was a spring or artesian well in the main creek up by the store because there was a consistent good water flow. It was also always near ice cold, making it quite delightful to drink and a great place to store perishables. John hollowed out a rock-lined hole connected by a sturdy rock walkway for a place to keep butter and eggs and such.

John and Mattie started their new business as well as their family on the banks of Three Creeks, among the hard working and honest locals who continued to call the place Chicken Foot. To those who got there first, Purdy's Mercantile would always be "The Chicken Foot Store."

In but a few years John was known regionally as a business visionary, for as soon as the store opened he began teaching the neighbors how to make cash crops from ordinary things such as toothbrushes with nicely carved handles and pig bristle brushes. He taught others to make and package a delightful tooth brushing powder made from hand pulverized charcoal, soda, chalk, orris root, lavender and peppermint oil. Three Creeks P&P (pig bristle and powder) became the tooth care of choice in the large German community that was tumbling into St. Louis, because John Purdy found this market. He regularly went with his neighbors to market, or took the neighborhood's products there and brought their cash back for them, taking only a modest amount for his efforts. He commenced providing many of the neighbors with charred barrels, and at a time when no bank would consider loaning money to many of the locals, he advanced them credit against their product at very moderate interest rates. Now, instead of selling their "corn extract" at once, as hard-scrapple economics had previously compelled them to do, they could afford to age their whiskey which could be sold years later at a great premium. In about six years, thanks to John Purdy, Three Creeks Kentucky Bourbon became a discriminating choice in fine establishments everywhere.

Most of the cash in-flow from these, as well as a great many other such ventures spawned in John Purdy's mind, quickly found its way across the counter at Purdy Mercantile. Three Creeks became a flourishing community and neighbors far and near recognized the Chicken Foot Store, and John Purdy in particular, as the very reason for their own more prosperous life styles. And heartily applauded the Purdys' resounding financial success.

Until she was a young matron with family, Mattie had taken to dressing as commonly as a kitchen maid unless John was about. Now, 17 years into being the "First Lady of Three Creeks," with both a husband and a family of boys, she was finally comfortable with being a magnificently beautiful, well-dressed woman. She and John knew every man, woman and child in the area. The women trusted her around their men and even the men who were simply casual acquaintances knew to conduct themselves as gentleman around Mr. John's stunning wife. As the neighbors and regular customers all held the Purdys in the highest respect, it was only men strangers that made Mattie uncomfortable. Even if there were numerous other people nearby, strange men always wanted to touch and feel and get very familiar, very quickly. Mattie tried hard not to be stand-offish, yet it seemed she could never let her guard down.

To that point, a particular boorish pair of hunters, a Mr. Johnson and a Mr. Sledge, terrified Mattie one early evening as she waited at the store for a customer. The two showed up late at the store and created a scene Mattie was not soon apt to forget. She had climbed a ladder to reach a hat for the one named Sledge, and she would swear he had kicked the ladder so she would fall into his grasp. As Sledge stood fondling her in a bear-hug, she had brought her hard-heeled shoe down smartly enough on his archway to hurt and surprise such that he momentarily relaxed his hold a bit. She had twisted about in his arms with a hat blocking tool in her hand and as the man named Johnson rushed over, she had smacked him smartly up on the side of his head. At about that very same moment Trisha had stepped in from a side room, and their customer and his son, plus another neighbor, also walked in. Mr. Sledge tried to explain himself away by insisting he thought she was taking a fall; however, Mattie did not buy one bit of his flimsy excuse. She did apologize to Johnson for putting a knot on his head.

In any event, a popular young couple was being wed that weekend and the bride's family had Dody's tavern overflowing. As was common place, the Purdy's opened up their lovely home to guests and so the groom and his five brothers were in and out of the house for the next couple of days. Mattie was delighted to be completely surrounded by men she trusted, for she caught an occasional glimpse of Johnson and Sledge, who were still close at hand. Women not half so attractive as Mattie had to continuously put up with men trying to get a first-hand feel, or worse, and certainly she had had far more than her share of such behavior. It didn't take a woman's intuition to tell her they were up to no good; however, as the wedding festivities continued Mattie decided maybe she was making more of the ordeal than it warranted, and best she turn her full attention to practicing the violin pieces they had requested she play.

It was a decision she would live to regret.

There was never a better timeframe than 1840 through 1859 to be living in the hillsides around Three Creeks. Except, that is, the summer Henry was four. That was a very hard year for everyone near and far. Family after family carried water from the creek and even though what sparse rain there was seemed to come at Three Creeks, few raised anything more than they would need for a mild winter. In the old Chickasaw Indian river country, which was a full three day trip for a loaded wagon, the few remaining Indians raised absolutely nothing that year. By then there were comparatively few Indians left east of the Mississippi as most were in the process of, or had been, settled on further west. There were, however, a few who had hidden out, and others who had quietly returned to a part of their homeland that was such that the white settlers did not covet it. That year the Chickasaws' pumpkins, squash and corn never made it, nor was hunting any good, and were it not for the fish many would have starved. (Mattie stopped saying that vegetarian was an Indian word that meant "poor hunter.")

The Indians never received a dime promised by the Jacksonian Democrats. Although the Indian removal treaties were signed in 1830, it was almost another ten years before any attempt was even started to resettle the Chickasaw. Jackson was far too busy trying to rein in the politicians in Washington who were intent on taking care of rich folk and strengthening the bonds of slavery. Few had noticed the small number of Chickasaw Indians who slipped back or were able to buy a small plot, or those who simply hid out to stay behind. At any rate, it was almost impossible for their village to survive on what was left of the poorest part of their old homeland. They were having a very, very hard winter. Without being prompted, John Purdy accumulated three large wagons of provisions and set off, along with some chosen neighbors, to the old Indian Territory.

In the middle of the third day several Indian braves materialized out of nowhere.

John held up his hand and quieried;

"Is Cousin of Piomingo here? I must see him."

Cousin of Piomingo was a much respected name in the tribe, a great warrior and some said a chief, who had led most of the group back to its present spot. Just the mention of his name brought instant attention, so John and his friends waited for about an hour, trying to relax under the uncomfortable and suspicious glare of the gaunt looking braves.

Presently a very large Indian appeared and John knew full well he was accepted as leader by the locals of the tribe, for his full headdress was a mantle of swan feathers. Obviously, he was in charge. Cousin of Piomiango did not admit to speaking English well; however, Mr. Simpson quickly managed to make him understand that the provisions in the wagons were his as a gift to his village from John Purdy; however, they wanted their teams and wagons back. After the chief acknowledged that he understood the food was theirs, but not the wagons or horses, he came and stood directly in front of John. Young athletic John at a full six feet two in prime shape and the older Indian who had stripped naked to the waist for this occasion were two very imposing figures indeed. Although he looked like he could use a good meal, the chief looked fierce. He also looked as though he could win a wrestling match with a full-grown grizzly bear.

John Purdy did not frighten easily, but he was certainly smart enough to know when to become concerned, and as he now stood watching, the splendid old Indian became very emotional. Neither John nor the others could read him well. It could be anger. Was he insulted? Could it be he wanted the horses too? Maybe it was a mistake for all of the whites' weapons to be secured out of sight and out of reach.

Chief, the cousin of Piomingo, suddenly grabbed John's left hand and simultaneously drew a knife from his waist. John Purdy stood frozen, wondering at his own judgment, getting mentally and physically prepared for anything. In one fluid motion the old Indian made a quick slice across his own thumb and in the same motion sliced John's. He then handed John the knife, handle first, and with his knife hand he held their bleeding thumbs together. The magnificent old Indian with his headdress of swan feathers turned about and spoke in a thundering voice to the Indians assembled. Then, one by one, each brave offered their chief and his new brother, John Purdy, their highest display of respect. The Chickasaw salute. The braves then unloaded the three wagons of foodstuff and handed the reins back to the white men. Chief, cousin of Piomingo, refused to take back the beautiful knife that he had carried at his waist for over forty years. The last recorded Indian incidents in the area were many years later: however, Three Creeks was never in fear of any mischief from the Chickasaws. Their respected leader had the blood of a Chickasaw Chief running in his veins.

The spring of 1849 proved Simpson was also a smart businessman, for the Glen Dodys paid a fairly substantial sum for the land across the road from Purdys' to build their comfortable tavern. The Dodys had two little girls, Marie and Mollie, and Mattie who acted more like their big sister than an adult was forever fixing their hair or prettying them up. And as always, strange men who happened to be in the tavern often simply stopped talking to stare for a while when Mattie Purdy happened by. She was simply breathtaking!

When the third Purdy boy was born, the Ballard sisters, Lillian and Dory, started to come and help with the heavy housekeeping and washing. They were a very proper middle-aged pair of spinster sisters who now lived by themselves within walking distance of the store. They had a milk cow and raised a big garden, along with some chickens and enough other livestock to make themselves fairly self sufficient. John overheard them talking about trying to make coffee from various kind of local nutshells, so he manufactured something for them to do at the store in return for a bit of coffee, sugar, dry goods and such. Soon they were also spending time helping Mattie, for life was a whole lot more entertaining for them in the active Purdy household than all by themselves down the road.

Trisha Blevens, a rather plain tall woman, moved in with the Purdys in 1850. She looked as though she had suffered much—-and she had. Trisha and her little family had always come in for Sunday Bible study, and when they missed one Sunday, John Purdy had ridden out to check on the family. He found her in a complete mental daze trying to dig graves for the remains of her husband and two little ones, who had all died from the dysentery. After gently scolding her for not alerting the community, he took the shovel from her hands and gathered up a few neighbors to complete the task at hand. On a bleak winter day he watched her say goodbye to literally everyone she loved, and not having the heart to leave her there, he bundled her up and took her home with him, where she had been every since. Trisha took to the boys and Mattie, soon loving the little Purdy men as much as life itself, and before long it was as if she had always been there. She became no end of help to Mattie and was always laughing at the boys' antics and Mattie's jokes. Each day about nightfall however, when she thought no one was looking, Trisha's face became the picture of sadness itself.

She was always up with breakfast ready and helped Mattie slow the boys down long enough to feed them at midday; however, she would only take Sunday and special occasion meals with the family at evening time. Trisha had a lovely place to stay in the old living quarters of the store, for by now the Purdys had moved into a spacious new home that connected to the store by a long covered walkway. The house had a complete wing which was a huge cleverly-done sleeping porch for the boys, plus a nice separate bedroom for the girl or two that Mattie wanted. There was also a gigantic great room for cooking and living, plus a vast parlor with room for the big piano Mattie hoped to get some day. The library, which also served as John's home office, was just off the entryway and a guest room faced it from the entryway's other side. The combination cook and washhouse was a separate little building and only used for cooking in hot weather. All of this was, of course, in addition to Mattie and John's comfortable bedroom with its two closets and cast iron stove. And which by design was as private and secluded as possible.

Mattie gave free music lessons to youngsters, was always first to help a neighbor, and would tackle the nastiest job that need be done; still, there may have been those who thought Mattie was spoiled for she had such a fine home and so much help.

"Why she is a kept woman."

If so, that was okay by John, He knew what the others could only suspect. He was also a well-kept man.

In 1850 John's kid brother, Henry, proudly announced he was bringing his new wife, Ruth, to Three Creeks, for he also wanted to run his own show. John was truly excited, for although Henry and he had fought as brothers do, they had become the greatest of friends since they were grown men. At the same time Henry announced their coming, he also announced that the place on the main creek where he and John had always thought would be perfect for a grinding mill, was going to get a grinding mill. There were over 50,000 grain mills in 1850s America, and a mill to grind grain into an even textured meal was the precursor to almost every real town that developed.

Henry's Three Creeks Mill was no ordinary mill. Locally made sandstone mill wheels were excellent for grinding corn and Henry included a large set of them; however, such stones made wheat hot in the grinding process, giving the flour an unpalatable taste. Brother Henry had examined the best mills within miles and miles, and then purchased a great set of three-foot by one-foot flint-stone millwheels imported from France. He installed them in addition to some locally made sandstone wheels in an unusual double millwheel configuration. If western Kentucky hillpeople were an expert on food of some sorts, it was cornbread, for they all ate it once or twice each day. With the coming of the Purdy Mill, excellent whole-wheat flour became available and the locals started focusing on growing wheat along with their corn. Now, a very fine mill was part of the Purdy family business, and more importantly, Three Creeks was truly on the map. People far and wide showed up at the mill with wheat to be ground, and soon Three Creeks whole-wheat flour was in good demand in Paducah and as far away as St. Louis

The Purdy Mercantile Company's other two stores were also having great success in spite of the two financial crises that had recently gripped the east coast. John's older brother, PJ, was now totally in charge of the Paducah store's day to day, and by now John's younger sisters had both married well and both sons-in-law were heartily invited to join the business. After much discussion the brothers-in-law agreed to join the firm and open a steamboat supply division.

In 1855, the neighbors started talking about a school and much to the Purdy boys dismay. Mr. Brown, a man of letters, was hired to come to Three Creeks. Brown only agreed to come after he had made a census of the neighborhood and was assured that all of the girls of appropriate age would be sent as well, for there were still communities that thought education was wasted on women.

One fine day all the neighbors met and by the end of the week a schoolhouse stood where one had not been before, complete with a small cottage for Mr. Brown. The Purdy boys, the Dody girls, and the rest of the close-by kids reckoned this was a pretty black day at Three Creeks. It took the Purdy boys approximately one month to tire of school as they much preferred the relaxed atmosphere of learning the three Rs at their mother's knee. Mom had even made the joke of the day a part of the learning experience; however, there was no doubt that Mr. Brown was very learned with a great many book-learned lessons to offer. Plus he told spellbinding stories about his travels. He scoffed at the once popular "blab school" concept where students were made to recite their lessons in a loud voice, all at the same time. A good blab-schoolteacher could make his school heard a half a mile away. In reality Brown was an excellent teacher with a good sense of humor, but he was also quite demanding of his students and pushed them to their very limits a good deal of the time. At first he was very reserved around the other adults, and as he and John became better acquainted they continued to maintain a rather formal relationship, even though they found each other good company. Among other things they marveled at how nearly they were to being exactly the same size.

What made school even worse for the Purdy boys, starting in 1857, was Junior Tuttoor. His mother, father and he had moved into an old shack down by one of the creeks and so he now came to the Three Creeks School. There is only one word to describe Junior Tuttoor: bully. He had no interest in learning and his only real purpose in coming was to lie in wait after school to grab one of the smaller boys and rough him up pretty good. This always happened away from school property where Mr. Brown's authority could be challenged. Mr. Brown was not a man to fool with and he would thoroughly admonish Junior, but his admonitions were always ignored and publicly challenged and dismissed by Tuttoor.

Teacher Brown's hands seemed to be tied and to be truthful, Tuttoor always seemed on the edge of becoming violent, which Mr. Brown obviously preferred to avoid. Simply put, Tuttoor was a bully too.

Tuttoor was a strange man who carried a false sense of importance and bragged to everyone what a tough mean man he was, insisting to all who would listen that any man who really knew him knew enough to be afraid. When he had any money at all he spent it drinking whiskey at the Dody tavern, and if by happenstance he saw Mattie there he sat and leered at her. And always he muttered quite loudly to anyone within earshot:

"No man should have that to himself!"

Tuttoor always kept a blacksnake whip close at hand and when being confrontational he would unfurl it and crack it with menacing gusto. Tuttoor set the standard for Tuttoor Junior who was continually taught that to be a real man everyone must be afraid of you. Junior often saw this at home where his father frequently gave Mrs. Tuttoor a thump or a smack with his fist, if she did not move fast enough to suit. Or if his cornbread was not crisp enough for his delicate taste.

Junior took turns on the Purdy boys. None of them was even a close match as Junior was older and as big as most grown men. Both older Purdy boys, Hiram now going on 15, and Henry going on 12, each in turn came home after school with bloody noses, black eyes and sprained elbows where Junior had twisted their arms. Along with the cuts and bruises where he had thrown them into the gravel, their puffy faces made the boys a sight. After Junior had worked over little Harold who was not yet 9 and about one third his size, John Purdy saddled up his beautiful stallion, Star, and rode out to the Tuttoor shack. He presented himself in a business like manner and started a conversation about how the school needed to be a safe place for children to go. They really needed to feel safe there in order to learn, and Mr. Brown was now at his wits end on how to maintain a learning atmosphere, without fighting with Junior himself.

Tuttoor was in his glory. The most influential man anywhere around was asking his favor! He stretched his hands up and clasped his hands behind his head for a while, just to show that he was in charge here.

Tuttoor then took his ever-present blacksnake whip from off the small porch where he had placed it when he saw Purdy approaching:

"What gives you the right to come to my home and tell me how to raise my son?"

Then he snapped the air.

KAA WHACKOOO!!

"You know my father taught me how to use one of these. I can take an earlobe off a man at 20 feet, or I can simply take out a little chunk of flesh off his back or lay it wide open. I would give a man like you his choice. What do you reckon you would prefer given the choice?"

CRACK O POP!!

"My daddy was the best there ever was with one of these. He was the best. But I am pretty damn good. I can whip a man where it doesn't leave a lasting mark or where there will be a scar for life everywhere I hit him. I can put my mark on a man's back in as good and regular a pattern as a checker board."

John gave it one last shot:

"Mr. Tuttoor, that is very impressive but this is not about you and me, its about your son who is as big as a full grown man and still going to the school. He makes life miserable for the little guys. You simply must control him."

With that, John mounted Star and swung him about. Tuttoor snapped his whip in John's direction and it popped loudly within a whisker of his ear. Purdy whirled Star back about and looked Tuttoor straight in the face. Struggling to keep himself from doing Tuttoor bodily harm, John Purdy was speechless! He decided best he leave right now so he whirled Star about again and urged him away in a gallop. John knew full well he and Tuttoor would meet again soon, but right now it would be best for all if he were away from this dreadful man.

John Purdy had one sure-fire cure for clearing his mind, his magnificent steed. His friends the Chickasaw had taught him much about Indian horsemanship and he learned to ride his magnificent animal Indian fashion without bridle or saddle. With voice, hand or leg movements or simply shifting his weight, Star could read John's mind, and they became as one. Right now there was no place to leave his fine saddle, so he simply removed the bridle and hung it from the saddle horn and urged Star home with his knees. The animal knew if he behaved well there was a least an apple waiting at the door, so he ran like the wind as John firmly held on to his hat.

Tuttoor felt like God. He was the man. Men should shudder when they tried his patience and even though Purdy liked to act self-assured and put on that brave act, he was convinced that deep inside John Purdy was scared to death of him. What power. What a great feeling. He felt the urge of his loins and hollered at his woman.

"Woman, get in here."

She appeared cowering like a whipped dog. So he took her like a dog. He was supreme.

After his animal-like performance his mind wandered to John Purdy and his beautiful woman. Sooner or later he would have to get better acquainted with the fair Mrs. Purdy.

Life at three Creeks was very good and Mattie now considered the biggest miracle in the Bible the instance where Joshua told his son to stand still, and he did! The closest thing to violence at the Purdy house hold was when Mattie would pop the end of her tea towel at the behind of one of her boys who would be snitching cookies ahead of time.

Harvey was hiding behind the door peeking around a corner.

Mattie spotted him and her eyes simply danced:

"A duck came into the store and wanted to buy some salve. I told him it would be a dime." She giggled.

"He told me just to put it on his bill!"

She continued to query little Harvey, her only audience for the moment.

"Did you hear about the dog who limped into the Dody tavern?"

"He was looking for the man who shot his paw!"

Then she practically collapsed laughing at her own humor and Harvey laughed at his mother more than at her jokes, as he raced out of her kitchen with not one but two cookies for his efforts. Soon he was peeking back around the corner and Mattie, smiling at the twinkle now in his eyes, picked up two more cookies.

"You got the wrong two. These are the ones with your name on them but they are going to cost you. The price is one smurzle and two buckets of water."

Harvey danced over to his mother and she sat down and held him on her lap. She bent down and stuck her mouth in the small of his neck and blew a "smurzle" which blubbered and tickled his neck until he screamed with delight. Mattie's boys loved this show of affection from their mom, and she held them on her lap until they were practically grown men. He turned his head up and got his mouth right on her neck under her jaw, and blew burbles of air, then jumped up and grabbed the two cookies as he raced for the door.

"Hey, you! Don't forget the rest of our deal."

Harvey was soon out the door after two buckets of water for his mother's bath, having once again successfully dodged a playful little swack of the tea towel at his back side.

That Same Summer

Four hundred miles south of Three Creeks, in the Louisiana cotton country on the western Mississippi riverbanks, there was nothing playful going on. Poor little Tizzy screamed in bona fide terror and genuine pain, all the while Mr. Coopert, the white overseer at the Island view plantation, was just loving it.

"It" this time was taking a peach tree switch and blistering the wench. He had made her hold her dress up and bare her bottom where he could get at her, and now she stood bent way over facing the ground with her head in a vice-like grip between the legs of one of the turncoat slaves. Coopert was laying "it" on but good, raising a whelp with ever strike. He knew better than to get the big whip as Tizzy was pregnant and he did not want her to abort — the more slaves on the plantation the better. Right now the issue was getting the crop in, and morning sick or not, this little wench had to pick her share by nightfall even though she threw up again as the whipping continued. The miserable Tizzy was little more than a child herself.

Her mother, having watched the whipping from a safe distance, now came over and held Tizzy from falling down by hugging her up close:

"Honey, you just morning sick, and this part goes away long for the baby shows up."

Tizzy's sack had very little cotton in it and was getting dreadfully little more, for poor little Tizzy just kept retching and retching. Shortly after Coopert moved on to check after the others, a huge Negro man who appeared to be in his mid 20s materialized. He knelt and also put his arms around the sobbing Tizzy for but a moment, then he put some cotton out of his sack into hers.

Bos was a magnificent specimen of a man. He had short cropped hair and beautiful close even teeth, stood almost six and one half feet tall with a barrel for a chest and small hips set on top of legs that were like two sturdy oak trees. It was more than quite obvious that in a fair fight he could whip a whole squad of Cooperts and he often prayed: "Some day God, give me Coopert." As it was, Bos knew any Negro who laid a hand on a white was as good as dead, or worse. As he turned to move on, Bos handed Tizzy's tearful mother some salve he kept secreted away so that she could now carefully rub some on her child's stripes. Bos had slept at the end of a row to start picking at the very first break of light in order that he might have more cotton than was required of him. He damned his luck for not getting to Tizzy before Coopert, and he damned Coopert.

He bent his back and kept picking.

The Island View Plantation was as close to hell on earth for slaves as anywhere in the South ever was. By the 1850s most plantation owners now found it simply good business to treat their slaves pretty well, and besides that, the owner community looked down very seriously on anyone who abused their slaves. Punishment without goodly cause, or excessive punishment, was generally not tolerated from any overseer. Except here on Island View.

The plantation was enormous, with the celebrated mansion that covered well over an acre by itself having once been the very showplace of the South. At 55,000 square feet the mansion included an amazing library which contained some rare handwritten volumes, plus four galleries full of treasures, seven staircases and a three-story-tall ballroom with one full wall of glass. There were more than 50 additional rooms. The plantation got its name from its position on a bend in the river where one could see "The Island" from either up or down the Mississippi River. The island was not large and could be quite pretty. Once there had been picnics and social affairs where guests were gently brought over by a skiff to join others who came by boats that tied off on the island's riverside dock. Having a cool drink out on this shady island, as the third largest river in the world gently flowed by, was indeed a very pleasant way to spend a hot afternoon. Now, although the dock was still usable and some old picnic furniture was scattered about, the island was practically abandoned and turned back to nature. Any view of the mansion was now virtually obscured from the island by the unkempt brush that grew out of control under a great canopy of pecan trees. Thanks to the virtually maintenance-free design of the old world craftsmen, the mansion itself was still reasonably neat, excepting for the huge yard with a chipped marble lane that ran down to the river. Of late it seemed there was simply not the interest, time, or willingness to expend the effort to maintain the grounds or the rest of the outbuildings as they had been but a few years back.

When coming up from the river, the great house was the first one would see of a great many buildings scattered about. Close by of course, was the kitchen building where meals were prepared, a round mostly underground icehouse, a laundry house and a smokehouse. Farther out back there were many additional buildings including a sewing house, a weaving house, a candle making house, and a carriage house. Then came the carpentry shop, harness shop, shoemaking shop, granaries, barns and stables. Most of these outbuildings were in various stages of disrepair and saw a minimum of activity except for those services required for the big house. The field slaves were poorly provided for indeed. Yet farther on back positioned closer to the original fields were the slave quarters which once had been quite adequate, but were now in total disrepair and seemingly always surrounded by either mud or dust. Most animals in the South enjoyed better living quarters than these poor souls.

In the early days, Island View was staffed with redemptory indentured workers, those hard-toiling people who could not afford a ticket to the new world and simply sold themselves into servitude for a period of years. It was six months to a years' wages per person for passage, and few ordinary men could save enough to bring themselves, let alone their family. In return for several years toil for themselves plus their wives and children, they had taken the opportunity to immigrate along with a great many non-volunteers whose family, often as not, had sold them to pay off a debt. The first two generations of owners were in the main God-fearing benevolent people, and treated such servants reasonably well. In those earlier years Island View was a pretty good place to be, and many people learned their trade in one of these shops while they lived for a while in these well maintained quarters, before moving on to full citizenship. The number of people willing to sell themselves into servitude slavery diminished, and cholera and yellow fever each took their tolls; therefore, by necessity, Island View became staffed with Negroes brought in by the slavers.

African slaves were brought into America in unbelievable conditions, stowed below on ships' decks with clearance as low 16 inches between those decks. Even children could not roll over as there was no room to give way. Several hundred of these poor creatures would be crammed in, generally manacled or shackled to each other. Often they were being shipped to given individuals and were branded with a hot iron to show their new owner's mark. Many of those died in route of infection from the brandings, if not from dysentery or lack of food or water. The Velos, a slave ship with a generous 33 inches of clearance between the holding deck and the main deck, once left the coast of Africa with 562 slaves crammed into the holding deck area. In 17 days she reported throwing 55 bodies overboard plus the ship's log noted several others who had jumped into the sea when they found the opportunity to do so. Those poor souls may well have been the lucky ones.

England outlawed the slave trade in 1807, and America in 1808; however, the slave traffic remained brisk for years in many places such as Cuba and Brazil. Finally an agreement between America and England created a blockade of the African coast in 1842, but for years a trickle of vagabond slave ships continued to make it to the lower Mississippi. The last recorded one, the Clothide, was caught close to Mobile bay in 1857. A great many of the poor creatures from earlier such ships wound up at Island View plantation which seemed always to have a need for more of them. Well over 400 adult workers once manned the fields and maintained this vast property to create, for the owners at least, an Island View Plantation that was indeed a glorious place. Over time the management skills required to run such an enterprise simply were not there; hence, as opposed to sound business practices, for the last twelve years, decisions were being made based on the worst of all qualifications. Birthright.

Gotfield Dinkins, the current owner in 1859, was a classic example of being "born to it." Although Master supposedly owned the plantation, it actually belonged half to him and half to Missus. Their grandfather, Enrique de Falco, had no surviving sons, and originally willed his two daughters, Elizabeth and Marybeth, one half of the estate each. Both daughters dutifully married men their father had selected and he then controlled the two couples' very existence. De Falco had, of course, required each groom to sign a prenuptial agreement, written by a brilliant young attorney by the name of Rawson.

Then things got complicated. When America purchased Louisiana from France in 1803, it was ruled by the Napoleonic code, and the first thing the new territorial governor, William Claiborne, did was to impose his version of English common law on the state. This then became the law that would control the conservation of an estate. Lawyer Rawson and his father had a client who had bequeathed his daughter a fine plantation in the late 1830s. She died young, well before any one of her sons came of age. Under these laws, her husband claimed and gained full control of the property and immediately began disposing of it and the slaves as well.

American Common Law from the time of the Louisiana Purchase was "*femme sole*" and allowed an unwed female of age to own about anything; however, at marriage the rule of "*femme converte*" took precedence. For all intents and purposes, at least from this body of law's point of view, at marriage a woman ceased to exist. Without a pre-nuptial document, any man immediately became principle owner of his lady's property upon the signing of the wedding license. Thereafter, even with an excellent lawyer and pre-nuptial planning, the best a woman could hope for in the event of a subsequent divorce was to regain perhaps one third of the holdings she had held as "femme sole." With these unfamiliar laws in effect concerning a female's estate, even with the best of pre-nuptial agreements Rawson and son advised that it was anybody's guess, for these laws were based on case history as opposed to a code.

Neither of de Falco's daughters had been close at hand for years. Elizabeth died young and sister, Marybeth, simply disappeared. Marybeth had a son who was named, Gotfield, after her husband who had also vanished just prior to her own disappearance. Daughter Elizabeth, who died young, had a girl named Virginia. Since one daughter was dead and the other had disappeared Grandfather de Falco subsequently willed his only two grandchildren, Gotfield and Virginia, each a fifty percent undivided interest in all holdings. Effectively this meant that after he passed, even if they were of age, neither of them could give clear bill of sale to a doorknob without the other's consent. In the years just before he died, Grandfather de Falco had truly become a tyrant, controlling nearly all of the money and manipulating the family members by temper, conceit or threat of the withdrawal of status.

When Gotfield's father disappeared sister Elizabeth and her husband Edwin were still alive. Gotfield's mother, Marybeth had propositioned her sister and brother-in-law.

"How much money can you two come up with?"

They told her truthfully. It was a fairly substantial sum, for most people anyway.

"I will take that for any claim I might ever have on my half of Island View."

Elizabeth and Edwin had both protested.

"That is not a fraction of the value of one half of Island View, not even considering the slaves."

Marybeth took the money, presented them with a comprehensive bill of sale, packed, and had the household servants put her on a passing boat. She was never seen again. This meant of course that Marybeth abandoned 10 year old Gotfield II and had never met her grandsons. At any rate, Elizabeth and Edwin, who was ten years older than she, reputedly drank themselves to death, although it was pretty much accepted by insiders that he had died of syphilis.

Facing the legal uncertainties, in order to insure keeping the ownership of the property concentrated, and to assure the conservation of the Island View estate, de Falco ultimately had resorted to extreme measures. He demanded that his grandchildren-cousins marry. At the time Gotfield was 23, and Virginia not quite 16. Marriage of first cousins was not all that uncommon and, as Virginia's parents had both died earlier on plus Gotfield had also been raised by his grandfather, there was really no one to object to his matrimonial engineering. Even though the couple cared little for each other, Grandfather de Falco practically conducted mating rituals until Virginia became pregnant. At the time of his death, Grandfather de Falco assumed that Gotfield and Virginia's four-year-old twins, Fredrick and Godfrey, were normal enough. The circumstance that made their great-grandfather most proud was the fact that he had it legally arranged so that it was virtually impossible for any owner to sell their holdings to an outsider, so long as de Falco blood ran in any veins.

Even the "uncivilized" know the risk of such a marriage arrangement. Indian tribes for example were often divided into five to seven clans with the mother determining the clan a brave belonged to. No brave could ever marry inside his own clan and it was a disgrace to even consider it, for the Indians knew very well the dangers of a concentrated gene pool.

In 1859, the entire family consisted of spousal cousins, Virginia and Gotfield, plus their twin sons, Fredrick and Godfrey.

The boys were not truly retarded, but they were truly slow of wit. Extremely slow. Currently, as they were now approaching 17, Virginia and Gotfield's twin boys were even harder to tell apart than when great grandfather de Falco passed when the boys were cute four year olds. Gotfield's father was a German named Dinkins (handpicked by de Falco to marry his daughter, Marybeth); however, the twins ignored that name, preferring to present themselves as a "de Falco" for the name was still a powerful one. Besides, neither had much else to offer except their birthright. Fredrick (Dinkins) de Falco and Godfrey (Dinkins) de Falco were small in stature made to look worse by bad posture. Both had very pimpled complexions, unattractive teeth and rather a strange look in the eye. The teenagers were continuously armed to a ridiculous level, and swaggering about.

A big branch of the family tree had come from the city of Toledo, Spain, which is well known throughout the world for the knives made by Jews, Moslems and Christians, who had lived there harmoniously throughout the 15th through the 17th centuries. Together they had a common goal of making the finest knives in the world. For two hundred years the inspectors never made a "passed" mark on any blade, for if one failed to pass their stringent standards the blade was promptly destroyed. This procedure assured every warrior or gentlemen fortunate enough to acquire one, that their blade would withstand any test. Sometimes these blades were beautiful creations, etched or inlaid with copper, silver or even gold. Sometimes these blades were the work of the devil himself. A Toledo tiger claw fits into the palm of the hand similar to a push dagger, but instead has three razor sharp hooked blades sticking out between the holder's fingers. No more sadistic weapon was ever used on the unfortunate or unsuspecting. The twins both treasured their personal selections of these gold inlaid family treasures, which they naturally enough had appropriated from one of the family's timeless collections.

Fredrick and Godfrey both truly thought that people were afraid to get friendly with them due to their great social position, superior wisdom, expert marksmanship and formidable fighting abilities. In reality they were slow of wit, boorish, clumsy and unattractive cheats. This resulted in their being completely ignored by all of the available young white women, which in turn resulted in their spending a good many evenings down in the slave quarters, where among other things they also drank way too much. Other white men avoided them as well, for they were well known to cheat at cards, and after only a few drinks their efforts at dealing from the bottom and such were easily spotted. Fredrick and Godfrey were seldom a part of any kind of a social event except when they invited themselves. They always, always made certain to invite themselves to the "nigger fights."

A few slave owners had their fighting niggers and the well known ones drew huge crowds, and often great sums were bet on the outcome of these fights. Sometimes the private fights were even better, for on occasion the winning fighter might even be set free and just as frequently the loser would be mutilated on the spot by his master. Each participant knew what was in store for both the winning and losing fighter; therefore, these were generally fierce and bloody fights as one might well imagine. Frequently the contestants were completely naked and there was plenty of eye gouging and biting, with winners and losers alike being minus ears or other body parts when the fight was over. Fredrick and Godfrey could hardly wait for the next one; however, after the twins failed to pay a substantial bet on such a private fight it seemed that now they never heard when there was to be such an event, until the fight was over. Those bloody private fights had become the highlight of their social life and now that they were no longer welcome, they really, really missed seeing the fighting "niggers."

Almost every plantation owner made the rounds each day to see what was happing; however, Gotfield could not actually ride the corners of the huge plantation, for he did not know exactly where they were. Gotfield had very little to do with his slow-witted sons either, and the highlight of togetherness for them was the coming of age of one of the slave girls. Simply put, Gotfield demanded first rights of each. He instructed Coopert to always keep close watch on the slave girls and when proper time came, that he be notified. Practically the only time Master ever came about his slaves was for this occasion and when the word came down to get a girl cleaned up, that meant two things. Get the girl in a tub and scrub her till she was raw and make certain the special room in one of the old abandoned buildings was clean. When Master was through he would welcome the boys to be number two and number three, and finally when they were through they would turn the girl back to whoever was waiting to take care of her. Sometimes it was her father who was waiting outside, although most often it was a couple of the slave women. Generally the girl's mother would have been taken far back away by some of the others so she could not hear her daughter cry for momma.

Because Bos was the best built slave on the plantation and could do the work of three ordinary men, he was designated to breed the women. The facts were that his legs were not the only part of him built like an oak tree, and Coopert would often watch as Bos, trying his best to be gentle, would perform as demanded. Since Coopert had been hired some 15 years back, as soon as Bos was old enough, Coopert had seen to it that practically every woman on the plantation was exposed to Bos' seed. It bares repeating; slaves could never be legally married; however, each master generally had some kind of an approval process for cohabitation. Currently at Island View they jumped over a broom together and repeated: "I marry you, I marry you, I marry you" three times together. The slave women always slept with these husbands causing Bos to often wonder which of the children might be his. Fatherhood brought him no joy whatsoever as Bos never had a special relationship with any of the babies, as the other men lived with them and assumed whatever fatherhood role a slave might enjoy.

Once, right after Coopert designated Bos as the breeder, he sent the woman on her way and Bos watched in stupefied amazement Coopert taking off his own clothes.

"Now do me." Coopert commanded.

As Coopert dressed and prepared to leave he spoke again.

"If you spill a word of this I will skin you alive, boil the meat off your bones and feed it to the dogs."

That was the first of many times Bos had to keep his mouth shut.

Bos was not stupid; in fact, he was quite bright, but he was ignorant, for his life experiences were very limited. He had only been off of Island View property twice, and although he had heard people talk about crazy, he was not certain he knew crazy when he saw it. Bos' religious training was also very limited, for church had been stopped on the plantation shortly after Coopert gained so much control. The slaves still had Invisible Church where they would go off in the woods for a secret service conducted by some of the older women, but there was no learned person to help them understand. Perhaps he thought, perhaps this man might be the devil the old women talked about.

Shortly after the first time Coopert had demanded personal service, Bos had decided to commit suicide; however, as the river water filled his lungs the will to survive overwhelmed him, and he came up sputtering. He thought of running away many times but he had seen two runaways slaves returned to Coopert and knew full well he preferred death to what the slaves were forced to witness on each of these occurrences. After he had abused the runaways unmercifully, Coopert both times had put each of them in a big barrel with long nails driven into it. Any slave Coopert thought might ever think of running away was forced to roll the barrel about. Bos was given a turn both times. When the bloody creatures were nearly dead and finally removed from the barrel, Coopert then set the slave catcher's dogs on them, which visciously tore the meat from their bones. The unfortunate souls were literally fed to the dogs. Bos frequently pondered his happenstance and figured he must be the most miserable slave in the world.

Missy was undoubtedly among the most beautiful of Negro girls, partially Jamaican, partially African and being as light skinned as she was, there was undoubtedly considerable white in the mix. With a beautiful face set off by close-cropped hair, high cheek bones, pretty white teeth, and a petite nose, she stood tall and slender. Coopert recognized the signs and sent word up to the big house and in very short order the word came back to get her ready. The room was cleaned, Missy was stripped, scrubbed, and led inside while her weeping mother was sent too far a way to hear. Gotfield and his two boys came down with glee and anticipation on their faces. Gotfield's nostrils were flared and his face was flushed when suddenly he gasped for air, then grabbing at his head he fell prostrate right on top of the terrified girl. During the confusion the frantic Missy ran out of the room crying for her mother, naked as the day she was born.

The twins were terribly bewildered as Gotfield was carried up to the big house and Missus was called out of her room. For the last few years, Virginia was seldom sober after mid-afternoon and she was just getting her buzz on for the day. Virginia did not seem overly concerned, although she seemed to comprehend quite well just what was going on. The stroke paralyzed both legs and one arm so that Gotfield could neither talk, walk nor control himself. After the doctor arrived and examined Gotfield, he pronounced that it was doubtful that Mister would ever get better. The twins were bewildered and quite slow to realize they were now the men in charge, but when they got their minds around the concept, they really liked it. Now they could participate first up at these sessions and do just about any other by God thing they wanted to. Life was good and going to get better.

The idea was born when the boys saw Amos and Ramos, Missy's twin half brothers, loading a wagon. The slave brothers were built about like Bos, being both big and strong for their age and handsome young men. Most wondered how Missy came to be such a beautiful slender girl, and could possibly have half brothers built so sturdily. The de Falco boys began to scheme. Twin slaves and twin owners were a pretty unusual thing they suspected; at least, it would make for an interesting fight. Each owner brother would pick a slave brother and the slave brothers would fight, with the wining owner brother gaining the right to be first with Sister Missy. What a great idea they had. They must not breath a word of this to Coopert or the Negro slave driver turncoats whom he had helping him boss the other slaves. None of them would want two beat-up slaves unable to work in the middle of the picking season. Other than that, Coopert could give a damn about what they did to their niggers. Fredrick and Godfrey decided the island would be a great place for the fight, for it was impossible to see from the great house; plus, if one of the slaves tried to run away they would have him cornered with no effort at all.

This was brilliant.

The boys decided that to insure a good fight they would offer the winner of the fight a coveted promotion to household slave. There were three classes of slaves in the South in those days, the field nigger being the lowest on the rung. They had little, worked harder and were punished more often and most severely. There were town slaves who were often craftsmen or shopkeepers and were given a stipend they must meet each week or month or year. Once they had paid their master the required stipend the rest of their earnings were theirs to keep. The highest ranking slaves were the household servants, who were often loved and treated as part of the family. They ate practically as well as the master, wore the master's hand-me-down clothes and were given what medical treatment that was available.

The winner of the fight would live a slave's dream.

The loser of the fight would be castrated.

The fight was to be at midmorning when it was cool, so everyone except the house servants would be in the field. Fredrick had told Coopert they needed Amos and Ramos to do some heavy lifting and instructed that they were to be left behind to do so. The slaves had been threatened with their very lives if they breathed a word about the boys' planned entertainment for themselves. In order to create as much of an illusion of authority as possible, Fredrick and Godfrey made certain their guns and daggers were prominently displayed this beautiful morning, and just the sight of the eagle claw daggers told the slaves what kind of a morning would be in store. All four of them made their way over to the island in the skiff, which was held by a rope fastened to both the island and the shore which also passed through an eye bolt on each end of the skiff and through a winch. One simply turned the crank on the winch whichever way one wanted to go. The slaves of course were made to turn the crank.

Bos was heartsick when the twins secretly told him they were to fight, for not only were they fine looking young negroes who undoubtedly would be scarred for life, one of them would never know the joy of manhood. The three of them talked most of a night and Bos shared with them that he had wanted to run away for a long time, and finally was now so heartsick he decided the time must have come. Bos knew that a runaway slave always took precedence over anything that could possibly take place at Island View, and that Coopert would immediately mount a great effort to find him. Horrible memories of the punishment dealt out to the other two as an example to the others when they were brought back, meant full well he would kill himself if they were about to catch him. He selected a sharp kitchen knife and rubbed his finger over the spot on his throat where he would stick it, for being on the butchering crew had taught him exactly the best spot to stick a knife for a quick kill. He put whatever else he could appropriate into a small bag but essentially he had nothing except what he wore. Fortunately Coopert kept him in better shoes than most of the others so he now had a fairly new pair that were just broken in. Other than that he would swipe some food from wherever he could for his run to the North.

Bos wondered where up north was, since everybody always talked about getting up north, but no one he knew had ever been there. All he knew was "they" say he had to get across the river, and over there the water generally runs south. "They" also say the river was easier to cross up a ways north of the plantatioin. He knew where the North Star was, so he would follow it for a few nights and then try to get to the Mississippi's other side. Bos remembered the slave catchers bragging that they caught the other two in broad daylight so he assumed his best chance would be to move north by night and hide by day. If the twins succeeded in their part, he would not let them down. No matter what,

Bos was determined to start his run at the best time to be as good of a diversion as he could possibly be.

The dreaded time was finally at hand. After the slaves stripped naked as ordered, the fighting area was designated: that being a small area where the island protruded towards shore. Fredrick and Godfrey then seated themselves at an old rickety picnic table from yesteryear that sort of closed off the fighting area. The moment came and the masters ordered that the fight began. There were of course to be no rules. Fredrick had drawn Amos as his fighter and that of course meant Ramos was fighting on behalf of Godfrey's interest. The twins squared off and almost at once Amos hit Ramos a mighty blow to his face that sent him stumbling flat towards the young masters' picnic bench.

"Look at the size of those arms, they are as big as my legs! That was a solid hit! That had to hurt!" Godfrey gleefully shouted.

"This will be great! Look! My man already drew blood!" Fredrick bragged.

"Get him! Get him back!" Ordered Godfrey.

The young masters could hardly contain themselves. Ramos stood up, blinking and wiping his eyes to get the dirt and sand out of them, as Amos quickly bounded up to challenge him again. Fredrick and Godfrey both reveled in getting to see the fight with these ringside seats, close enough to smell the fighters' sweat and feel their incredible fear. It was tremendously erotic!

Suddenly Amos and Ramos wheeled about and lunged at their masters. Amos grabbed Godfrey's head, and with one hand to his chin twisted until his neck gave a loud pop; continuing he twisted it completely around. At the same instant Ramos managed to pin Fredrick's arms to his sides in a strong bear hug. It was no contest for the strong young slave to hold the punk; however, Amos soon pounced on Fredrick as well, to grab his gun. Ramos moved his right biceps until he had it firmly around Fredrick's throat and then grasping both hands together he began to flex his arm muscles. Fredrick struggled just a bit, his face turning purple as the life was choked out of him.

It took but a few moments.

After surveying the scene, neither naked young slave said a word. They simply held each other in a momentary embrace and then backed away to look knowingly into each others' face. Without another word Ramos hit Amos on the chin with all of his might, sending him crashing into the rocks. Amos skidded across the beach, causing him untold cuts and bruises as he fell naked into the gravel. The inseparable youngsters quietly began to give each other a most furious beating, kicking, biting and pounding until finally Ramos fell, unable to get up. Amos went over and held his beloved brother and then helped him stand up, steadying him as he wobbled about. Picking up their young masters' pistols, at the prearranged hand signal which they had practiced over and over, they fired simultaneously. One round into Godfrey's neck about where they thought it would be broken, the other straight into Fredrick's face. They then placed the pistols in the young masters' hands and stood quivering in their nakedness, surveying the scene.

Fredrick still seemed to look strange in the face from being choked, so they drug him a few feet over to the edge of the water and positioned him such as he might have fallen there, face down into the water. The brothers embraced again and Ramos held up his arm so Amos could hit him; he took a rock and broke at least two of Ramos ribs and watched him fall to writhe about the gravel in pain. Besides being bloody and holding one arm grotesquely, Amos' face was now swollen such that he could only see out of one eye.

As he lay writhing in pain, Ramos gasped:

"The hard part is coming up now."

"I knows. Pray!"

Amos made for shore.

Amos was in such bad shape he mostly crawled the entire length of the long unkempt lawn through the brush up to the big house. Although he hollered for help any number of times, he was not heard until he was at the back door. When Mammy came out to see what was up, she screamed at the sight of the naked young man who was now too bloody for anyone to recognize.

"My God, what happened?"

"The young massers, they make us fight."

"Who fight?"

"My brother and me."

"What happen?"

"The young massers they argue over who won de fight and day shot each other over it."

"Dey hurt bad?"

"I think dey both dead."

Mammy fainted.

One of the household slaves came racing into the field screaming:

"Come to the big house, Mr. Coopert, come to the big house, Missus needs you at the big house!"

Bos watched the hated overseer mount up and spur his mare towards the mansion, then the huge black man cast an anxious eye to the coming nightfall and the far distant rain clouds that were rolling in.

After taking a look at Amos, Coopert went over to the island where he saw both bodies plus poor Ramos still lying quivering in a naked bloody heap. Those two white boys never had any sense. He was actually very glad they were out of the way. With both them and Master out of the way, if there was ever a time for him to consolidate full control over Island View, it definitely was now. Virginia, the drunk, had not been down to the slave quarters in a good many years and was never around any of the operation of the plantation. She probably never even knew the factoring agent where they sold their crop or what constituted a fair price. He doubted if she even knew the banker's name. What an opportunity. He could now skim off even more than he had when Master took time to look things over a bit from time to time.

Since Master never cared much at all about what happened at Island View except when one of the slave girls came of age, he had willingly let Coopert take on the business side of the operations. Naturally enough this made stealing from the plantation quite simple. Nowadays at the appropriate time Coopert took in a separate shipment of the finest quality hand worked cotton, and sold it independently of the rest through a second agent. These fine 250-pound bales of hand-worked brought twice what a 400-pound bale of machine-ginned would. This money went into a separate account at the other bank and quite naturally had his name on this "Island View" account. After he made friends with one of the bank officials who really enjoyed his caresses, Island View's name simply disappeared from the account. There was quite a substantial sum in this account and he considered it his own. He added to it every year in this manner, as well as adding the cash he received from renting some excellent cotton land they never needed anyway. He regularly inflated the plantation bills and kept the extra, accumulating yet another hefty sum in cash including some gold which he kept buried in a clever place.

Over the years Coopert had been very successful in making any other white overseer or employee's life so miserable, or appear to be so incompetent, that they never lasted long. Thus he was able to gain nearly complete control. He relied on about a dozen "turncoat" slaves to help him drive the rest, and saw to it that the turncoats lived enough better than the others to make the hatred the others felt toward them worthwhile. He actually entertained himself on weekends by punishing those the turncoats had put "on report." At any rate, as Coopert now stood surveying the scene, a malevolent sneer came over his face. He had recently felt absolutely confident that he could consolidate his hold on Island View. It obviously was time for him to make his move.

Coopert stood rubbing his hands together.

Yes Indeed!

The time was now!

When Coopert joined Virginia on the island, she was seated at the old picnic table, apparently in a daze; however, what she was really doing was burning every last detail of the horrific sight into her incredible memory. At this point she considered the most curious detail the fresh container of salt sitting on the shaky old table. Something about the scene was definitely amiss but she could not put her finger on it just yet. Virginia sat totally disgusted, as she mentally inventoried the weaponry. For their private show, each of her sons had brought their eagle claw dagger, a push dagger, a small sword, a razor sharp knife, a blacksnake whip and their newest pistol.

Coopert was very insistent that the white twins be moved immediately to the big house, and Virginia requested that Amos and Ramos be cared for there as well. While the white twins were being cleaned up, Virginia spent a moment getting herself together. This meant downing half of a large water glass full of straight warm whiskey. Then she began a most stern and demanding interrogation of the Negro twins.

"Tell me again why such a viscious fight? You two have not spoken to me clearly so that I might understand."

" What do vicious mean, Miz. Virginia?" Asked Amos.

"Why were you fighting so hard?"

"Cause the loser going to get —-He ging to get ahhhhh. Miz. Virginia, I can'ty talk like that and say dem words to no white lady."

"Yes you can, Amos, I am ordering you to."

"It ain't nice talk, Mam."

"Tell me!" She thundered.

Ramos spoke up:

"The loser goin to get castrated, Mam!"

"My God!" Virginia turned pale.

She knew her sons were not popular people, but now it really begin to sink in as to what they had truly become. They had even brought salt to rub into the wound.

"The winner was ..."

" Yes I got that part about being a house slave but tell me more clearly the young master's prize when his fighter won."

"Aw plese, Miz. Virginia, ask some of the womens about this caus we don't know nutten much about them coming down to have a ceremony to do girls an such an don know what it really like an can only talk filth to you cause we don't know abot that kind of thing." replied Amos.

Virginia stood up, brushed back her salt and pepper grey hair and marched straightaway the nearly a mile back to the slave quarters. The fresh air was feeling good to her face and lungs, but as she approached the quarters she covered her mouth with her hand and looked on in bewilderment. She had not been to the quarters in years, and was therefore completely unprepared for what greeted her there. The filth and squalor were overwhelming!

Some of the cabins had no doors, so one could readily see the lack of furniture or much of anything else except for children, some of whom were standing about completely naked. The stench from the outhouse that she walked by was so overwhelming that Virginia swallowed hard to keep from throwing up, and she had to lean against a tree to regain her composure. She stood there confounded. Could the land and showplace of her ancestors have come to this? Instead of a home for those who served them on this very land for which she and her cousin/husband had given up all hope of happiness, the quarters were now nothing more than miserable looking stables unfit for animals.

She accostèd two Negro women, one of whom she recognized, and demanded of them:

"Tell me about brutalizing young slave girls down here!"

"Why, Miz. Virginia!" remarked the one named Alma,

"We ain't seen you down here for some long time!"

"Tell me about so-called ceremonies on young slave girls down here!"

With apprehension, these two Negro women, as well as some of the others as they were summoned, gathered round. Finally the Negroes began to speak. As they continued to witness Virginia's manner they began to feel completely unthreatened and sent for Tizzy and Missy. Missy said very little; however, Tizzy described in great detail the day she was brutalized and how she was then tuned over to Bos until they were certain she was pregnant. She related how sick she was most mornings now, and showing Missus her switch marks, she related how life had become for her since she became of age. Most of the Island View slave girls were mothers well before age 15, grandmothers at 30 and would have buried half their numerous babies and likely be dead themselves by age 40.

Alma continued:

"You know, Mr. Coopert he make all us women do it with Bos while sometimes he watch us. Sometime he stay with Bos a long time after he call one us in too, and we alls wonder whut goin on. Now that Bos he be a kind darkie but he built so that he can't hep but hurt thay little uns even tho he try hard not to. Mr. Coopert he likes to watch it hurt. He wunts dey whole plantation full of slaves done built big and strong like Bos."

Then Tizzy's mother filled Virginia with a mighty rage.

"Bos and your boys, why dey make a good many of the babies we had in some time and you know Master and dem was about to do Missy when he had his spell, Miz. Virginia. Stead a doing her, he done grab his head and fall down rat on top o her."

Missy nodded her head in agreement, but was yet afraid to say much. As Virginia turned to go, the slave women were sorely afraid of Coopert's reaction, for he would say they had told far too much. Still they had simply done as the Missus had ordered. And after all, she had rank.

It was noon time, and as Virginia was starting to head back to the mansion some woman brought food and put in a trough and the little ones gathered around like hogs. Some of them stood stark naked, smashing food into their mouths with their dirty fingers while two very young black mothers looked on. The two younger women were holding fairly new babies which appeared to be mulattoes. As she looked on, it was as though someone hit Virginia very hard in the gut: these babies had de Falco blood in their veins.

They were her grandchildren.

When Virginia returned to the mansion she was so shaky that she went to her room and downed two huge gulps of whiskey. When she came down from her room she instructed that she immediately be taken back over to the island and be allowed to spend some alone time there.

Realization was setting in as to what a "Work of the Devil," Island View had become, and she sat trying to unravel the expression on Coopert's face while he had stood viewing her boys' bodies. It was true that her boys had been almost impossible to like from the age of eight or ten. Hell they were despicable. But they were after all given to her to love she supposed. Gotfield had spent as little time with them as he could, disappearing almost every afternoon to wherever. She winced as she marveled how father and sons apparently had but one common interest.

Virginia had once spent much of her time reading, constantly prowling the great library, and having many other books brought to her as well. More recently, she simply had crawled down into her whiskey bottle and stayed there. Early on she had been the best mother she knew how, but Gotfield undermined her every effort and encouraged the slow-witted twins to ignore her. Mostly, thanks to him, she was just some woman they refused to mind, or to respect, or take advice from. At her last birthday dinner that Mammy had so lovingly spread, the boys were so uncouth and disrespectful that she had retreated to her room in tears. As of late, she had paid them scant attention.

Comprehending what the boys had become and what they and Gotfield had brought upon themselves was now adding an immeasurable amount of disgust to an overwhelming feeling of anger. And guilt. As Virginia reviewed the picture in her mind for the hundredth time it finally hit her. Fredrick had been recently caught cheating at cards again, and the other chaps had nearly twisted his right thumb off. For over a month now he had been forced to try to shoot with his left hand. She could see the scene clearly. The pistol was definitely in his right hand.

As dusk approached she sat on the island like a rock, still with a million thoughts racing through her mind. She looked at the brush and could not help but think of how her grandfather would react to such slovenly upkeep. Ah yes, her grandfather.

Dear old Grandfather, Enrique de Falco, who had ranted and raved and how sad Gotfield had become when he had wanted to bring a young woman home to meet the family. She remembered it well. Grandfather had screamed and yelled and cursed:

"Hell, she is a nothing. A nothing do you hear me? How dare you, a de Falco cavort with such a bitch. Her mother was a common French whore. Do you hear me? She is the daughter of a whore! Don't you ever bring the likes of her here. You better damn well understand me! I will throw you off this plantation without a cent to your name."

Virginia continued to reflect:

Of how poor Gotfield did not have the nerve to stand.

For either himself — or the girl. Or against their marriage.

Of her grandfather's paranoia that she might let part of the plantation get out of family, because she was a woman.

Of his brilliant move to solve both of his problems.

Of a husband she had never even liked, let alone loved.

Of her wedding night which was nothing more than legalized rape.

Of sons being prepared to be buried.

Of that same unfortunate Gotfield, who was now unable to do anything, or say anything for that matter, except for those three words he repeated continually, over and over and over and over and over again:

"Damn Island View!"

"Damn Island View!"

"Damn Island View!"

Rain clouds were gathering in the distance as the sun started casting its longer shadows of the day. She looked once again over where the body was found lying face down in the water and realized that the more closely she looked in the longer evening shadows, the more obvious those telltale marks were. Yes, there were definitely marks in the sand and gravel showing that Fredrick's body had been dragged a short distance to the water's edge. She waved the signal to be picked up, and while waiting for the skiff to come back over she casually picked up a brushy piece of flotsam that had washed up on to the shore. As she carefully brushed away the only remaining clue, Virginia spoke softly to herself:

"Island View is already dammed!"

Mattie's wedding night had been a most pleasant dream compared to about anyone's, and especially when compared to Virginia de Falco's. In fact on their wedding night Mattie and John were completely inexperienced, and as he fumbled around trying to be gentle it was she who finally gave a sudden pelvic thrust to become the woman instead of the maid. She was quite surprised when John shuddered, suddenly arched his back and sort of exploded. It was over before it started and she was convinced that she had done something wrong. As John lay quietly beside her, she was concerned that he must be wondering about her abilities as a wife, so she got up and freshened herself. Thanks to Mrs. Purvis' special salve it had not hurt really all that bad, and she was determined to do better. John recovered from his dozing and came to attention quite quickly with Mattie sticking her tongue in his ear.

Mattie Purdy was every inch a lady for the entire world to see, but when she closed the door and shuttered the windows in her and John's bedroom, she became a totally different person. In all the years they had been married, he could scarce remember when they were enjoying total privacy that she had kissed him with her eyes open. Or her mouth shut. Once Mattie traded a barrel of books from a traveling man for some supplies he sorely needed and as she went through it looking for the ones the school could use she came upon a book of erotic drawings and stories. After she recovered, she begin to look at it from a different point of view, and rather than burn it she had secreted it away for further reference. When Mattie stepped into their bedroom at the end of the day she had always, always paid great attention to her personal hygiene and smelled of lilac or rosewater, her bedtime breath sweet from mint. She would let her beautiful hair down and unless it was quite cold she stepped completely out of her clothes. John loved to watch as she sat brushing her hair out to a beautiful sheen. He knew Mattie would soon take him to the place where eagles soar, and when he had no wings left to fly, with incredible timing she would bring herself to intensity and they would land and collapse in utter exhaustion. Together.

John Purdy thought he had married the most beautiful and imaginative woman in the world.

He was close.

Shortly after John's trip out to the Tuttoors' shack, Henry Purdy made a smart remark to Junior which was all the encouragement Junior ever needed to pound the snot out of someone smaller than he was. Junior immediately took off chasing Henry through the woods when suddenly his feet got tangled and he fell into a small brush pile. The big bully soon realized that he was tangled in a cleverly set snare and was thrashing about trying to get loose, when the three other Purdy boys suddenly appeared from nowhere. They brought a rope, and quick as a flash Junior was tied up snug. Earlier, before they had tricked Junior into their snare, the boys had all climbed up a birch tree and together managed to ride it to the ground, securing the top to a nearby stump. They released Junior from their snare and dragged the bound up bully to the birch tree, where they then fastened a short rope under his arms and to the birch's spring-loaded top. After pounding on him quite a bit, little Harvey came and smacked Junior on the nose as hard as he could, then spit in his face and urinated on his shoes. The Purdy boys all took turns spitting in Junior's face until they finally tired of that, so then quite ceremoniously Henry stood on the stump and recited some bible verses. They all held onto the knife together, and sawed on the rope holding the birch treetop down.

Swoosh.

Junior was forcefully yanked off the ground with a face full of spit and some very dirty shoes while the Purdy boys gathered around, giggling as they watched him swing to and fro just a bit off the ground.

"From now on you bully, if you take on one of us, you take on all of us," came the chorus!

For the next half hour Junior Tuttoor had plenty of time to think. The more Junior thought about what happened the more he thought it was kind of funny. In fact it was very funny. He laughed heartily at his own predicament for they had not really hurt him and he reckoned how he must be some kind of a sight dangling from that tree top. The four Purdy boys had all skipped away with their arms around each other and slapping each other on the back. Those brothers might fuss once in a while but they sure liked each other and would fight for each other too, whereas Junior could not remember anybody ever being on his side except his mother. It would be wonderful to have a brother or anybody else to be just a friend. Eventually Mr. Brown happened by on his prized Cayuse, a large horse for the breed, it stood a full 15 hands high and could easily pull the tree over to where Mr. Brown could cut Junior loose. The truth was that the worst part about today would be if his dad found out about him embarrassing the family name by getting beat by those littler guys. The truth also was that he envied them. He dallied around for a while hoping to God that his dad would be drunk or asleep and not know when he got home.

No such luck! His father had made one of his infrequent trips into Three Creeks today. Tuttoor heard people laughing about the incident and arrived home, pretty much out of control in a violent rage, just about the same time as the youngster showed up.

So he screamed out each time when his dad hit him for getting embarrassed by those Purdy kids, because his dad would only stop punching after he had caused enough pain to make him feel like he was "the man." After Tuttoor chastised his wimp of a son for being such a sissy, he sat drinking from his whiskey while he brooded. John Purdy must pay for this. Yes sir, him and that teacher Brown too, for they both had to be in on this plot to humiliate him. Brown could wait, but Purdy had to be tended to. He needed a plan to make that son of a bitch quake at the sound of his name. He would lay in wait. Yes. He would lay in wait. And Purdy's blond-headed woman could figure into the plan too. As Tuttoor was plotting the Purdys' fate, he either passed out or fell asleep.

After the incident John and his boys talked a long time. Little Harvey really felt sorry for Junior, insisting that all the big guy really needed was a friend. The next school day after swinging Junior from the tree, much to his amazement, six-year-old Harvey Purdy went up to Junior and asked him to play Shadow Jumping at morning recess.

Junior could not remember anyone ever asking him to play.

"Sure."

The small boy and the man-sized Junior frolicked for the short recess break and had a good time. At noon-break another of the Purdy boys choose Junior first to be on his team for playing "Annie Over."

Junior was always the last one chosen for anything, and never made to feel welcome. Now the most popular guys in school were welcoming him into their circle and he didn't know how to act. But he liked it a lot.

"Mom says it is warm enough we can go creek climbing soon," retorted Hiram.

"What's that?"

"We go down where the water runs fast down the hill and climb up the middle of the creek. It's a lot of fun. Even Mom comes."

"Your Mom goes swimming?"

"Yeah, she has her special swimming dress. Most of the rocks are smooth but its best to put something on your feet, because there are some sharp ones. Dad goes too sometimes."

Junior could not imagine his mother ever having played. Or his father.

"Sure, I'll come."

"I'll tell you when we're going."

Junior went home deep in thought. Having people all be scared of you wasn't really such a good deal and he wondered why his dad thought so. It was fun and he liked being accepted instead of being an outcast. Well anyway, he might get his mom alone and talk. There was no use talking to his dad.

Not long after that conversation the boys invited Junior to come over and eat lunch with them, and he had never witnessed such a lively fun mealtime. The beautiful Mrs. Purdy was just plain funny or silly, and at times both. Mattie put grease on everyone's hair and they all sat around looking like they had horns and talking like she thought a spook of some kind would sound. She also insisted the meat they were eating that day was actually jellied moose nose. Then there was the dessert pouch concept! Mrs. Purdy insisted that growing boys were equipped with a special part attached to the stomach called the dessert-pouch, and it was common for the stomach to be full but the dessert-pouch to be empty. If the stomach were well filled at breakfast, on occasion it was perfectly all right to only fill the dessert-pouch, and at such times she considered a cookie in each hand a balanced meal.

She had them all out at night one time, so they could stand looking at the moon from upside down between their legs, for when you look that way the moon is only half as big. Another time they all lay on the ground and ate their lunch off their chests while watching the clouds, with the first to spot a cloud that looked like an angel getting a special treat. As they were all getting in a circle with their heads together Mrs. Purdy was lying down beside him when her beautiful hair brushed his face, and he caught the whiff of lilac. It was then Junior decided that it surly must be she who was an angel, and soon he worshiped the very ground Mattie walked on.

School was out, and that summer the Purdys found odd chores for him to do at the mill or store and paid him a small stipend to have candy money. Instead he took every coin and gave it to his mother. Tuttoor seemed to take every opportunity to hit at Junior but the truth be told it took a lot to make Junior scream out, and he had quit crying long ago. Experience dictated that hollering out and acting whipped was simply the easy way to get past his stormy father. Junior could sound very real, for after all, the big teenager had heard his mother beg and scream often enough to know exactly how to fake it.

Down in Louisiana, the day right after the fighting incident, Virginia de Falco-Dinkins had another request: "Mr. Coopert, would you please gather your things and bring them to the big house? I would like for you to move in just down from Mister's room. I need you there."

Coopert was elated!

Ecstatic!

Overjoyed!

Euphoric!

A slave overseer was way, way down the social scale; however, a plantation executive manager who actually lived in the big house was a whole different matter. Such a position was socially a very prominent kind of thing, incredibly so at a plantation the likes of Island View. His dream of being elevated to the craved-for status of living in the big house had just come true, for in addition to the social ramifications, such a move fit into his plans perfectly. Even with all the confusion regarding the boys' deaths, he managed his move into the big house in less than an hour and was soon straightening up his things. He was assigned a beautiful but somewhat smaller suite right next to Gotfield, on the other side and down the hall from Miz. Virginia's bedroom. Coopert wondered briefly why he had not seen Bos all day, but in his excitement he quickly dismissed those thoughts and began to concentrate on how he might ingratiate himself more completely. (Weasel-in would be a more accurate term.) This was definitely the chance of his lifetime, and he would work it for all it was worth. After he seized full control, he would rule Island View with an iron hand. And that included the drunken bitch.

"Mr. Coopert, I need you to ride into town and bring the sheriff and any other officials you and he think need be involved with a thing like this. Under the circumstances I think a very private and quick burial would be best, but I am certain we need an approval of some sort."

"I will leave at once."

"Take a carriage. You will be more comfortable."

Coopert smiled to himself. This being a gentleman was going to be simply wonderful.

The next day at midmorning Mr. Davis, the high sheriff, Mr. Heacock, the magistrate, and young Mr. Rawson, the son of the lawyer who had represented Island View's interest for years returned with Coopert in the rainy misty drizzle. Virginia greeted them dressed in very appropriate mourning clothes, and as the group stood about offering their condolences she quickly cut to the heart of the matter.

"What must you do so that I might bury my sons? I have interviewed the slave boys and believe what they said to be true. Furthermore it seems to me they were both beat up so badly it would have been impossible for them to have been involved in any foul play."

Coopert chimed in:

"I know I am repeating myself, gentlemen, but I saw everything and as far as I am concerned I will swear it is self evident they killed each other. We need to bury these poor unfortunate souls."

"I wish you had not moved them and cleaned them up. It is hard for us to tell anything now. We at least need to see the Negroes," replied Sheriff Davis.

Virginia hung her head and looked at the floor:

"Sheriff, I simply could not allow them left out in the rain."

She then motioned to another household slave who opened a door.

Amos limped in as Ramos was carried in, bed and all.

"Good heavens!" Was the only audible remark.

The black twins were truly in an extremely sorry state, with each of them having eyes swollen shut, plus more facial cuts and bruises than one could count. Ramos' broken ribs were causing him great pain from having just been moved and also from having the bandages removed from the angry looking cuts and bruises on down his chest. Each had bite marks on various places with Amos' right thumb having been bitten quite severely. Neither Amos nor Ramos looked capable of swatting a fly.

"Gracious," remarked Rawson, "What a waste of money. These two will take months to completely heal, if they ever do. They may never be worth what they were."

The sheriff whistled softly:

" I see what you mean about these two. I have had one other case which I investigated where two men shot each other dead. That event was witnessed by several impeccable witnesses."

He turned to the Negro twins:

"Tell me what you saw and heard," demanded Davis.

"We dibent see much as we was on de ground a rasselen and a fightien and dey youn gentlemens were a arguing loud like, but we heard was juss wun shot." Replied Ramos through his swollen lips.

Amos painfully nodded his head, agreeing with his brother's assessment.

"What were they arguing about?"

"Which one o us was a winning dey fight, cause we couldn't either one get up off dey gravel right then."

Virginia chimed in:

"One of the household staff told me she heard what sounded like a shot but definitely did not hear two, Would you like me to bring her in? Sheriff this is very, very hard for me, to see my sons so. I sat with their bodies most of last night. By tomorrow we will need to burn incense and try to find flowers to mask the smell. When may I bury my sons?"

The two officials conferred for a short while as lawyer Rawson listened. Soon they pronounced:

"Our heartfelt sympathies. You may bury your sons."

Two graves had already been opened up in the cemetery where the previous generations of de Falcos were buried, and the small group of officials walked up the hill and stood quietly by as the only white witnesses. Except for Coopert of course, who held Virginia by the arm as she stood ram-rod stiff beside Gotfield's wheelchair. The household slaves gathered up close, however the field hands felt compelled to stand a respectful distance away as Master and Missus buried their sons. As the priest who had been called for struggled to say what could be said at a time like this, Virginia remained absolutely stoic. She could but help to wonder if any of her ancestors, in this or any other cemetery, were ever buried in such disgrace. As the boys were returned to the earth, Virginia and Gotfield watched the entire proceedings completely dry-eyed. The sheriff, and all of the slaves holding up the shelter from the misty rain for the white folk, found such lack of emotion most curious.

The next day Virginia arose early and fairly clear headed, as she had drunk moderately the previous day. Moderately for her anyway. She caught Coopert as he first left his quarters and asked that he spend the day with her, going over all of the records in Gotfield's office, "So that he might have a clearer picture of the business side of the enterprise." Coopert was again flattered beyond measure. Shortly thereafter they were pouring through the plantation's records in great detail, and as he obviously knew much more than she, Coopert was quite boastful as he enthusiastically explained every piece of information he already knew about such matters. He became more and more self assured as Virginia often sat gazing out the window at the gloomy drizzly day, seemingly quite preoccupied and completely disinterested.

By late afternoon they had been through banking records, sales records, expense records, per field records, per slave records, per gin records, supply costs per ton records, etc. As they went through each phase, Virginia casually reorganized the records in a more methodical order than they found them, so as she explained: "You might have a most complete and easily referenced file." Buyers, suppliers, shippers, bankers and such were all listed with the principal contact for each identified, discussed, evaluated, and then assigned with their own trustworthy code. Virginia wanted to know exactly which of them Coopert knew; how well he knew them; how well he could trust them; and which ones trusted him. He bragged about what relationships he had in any firm with a business connection to the enterprise of Island View. Virginia focused on those names which Coopert claimed as friends.

When Virginia was just a youngster, her grandfather took great pride in showing her off to anyone who would watch, for even though a southern lady was supposed to do naught but sit and look pretty, his granddaughter could cipher numbers in her head faster than anyone else he ever knew, even with pen in hand. At another time and another place she would have undoubtedly been Dr. Virginia doing math research at a major university. By the age of 10, she had figured out that if you multiply any number that ends in 5 by itself the answer always ends in 25. Then if you add one to the first number and multiply that you have the answer. For example 15 times 15 will end in 25. Add 1 to the 1 of 15 and multiply 1 by 2 and the answer is 2; therefore, 15 times 15 is 2 and

25, or 225. 35 times 35 works the same way, add 1 to the 3 and multiply 3 times 4. The answer is 1225. To divide some numbers, say 16 into 440, she would see at once that 4 would go into both numbers so she would divide 4 into 110 and come up with 2 and 30 left over. 30 divided by 4 is 7.5 which of course makes the answer 27.5. To multiply any number by 11 she simply added the outside two together and dropped that number in the middle; for example when multiplying 18 times 11, she would add the 1 and 8 and put the 9 in the middle and immediately know the answer to be 198. To divide by 5 she would take the number times 2 and move the decimal over one spot. Virginia had reasoned out all of these shortcut calculations on her own and could arrive at the answers to very complex issues in her head at approximately the same instant the problem was completely written down or described.

Before her grandfather began to look upon her as a threat to holding the estate in the family after her mother and father passed, she spent a great deal of time in his office. To keep his precocious granddaughter occupied, he would plant mistakes in his books for her to find and he never failed to be amazed at how quickly she could find a set of numbers that did not make sense. Even as a child she was astonishing, for she could tie facts together and find discrepancies far quicker than anyone else he ever knew. Frequently he would ask the youngster to check his numbers and accounting for the various fields production, yield per field hand and so on. One of Virginia's cherished memories was the full day her grandfather once spent with her to ride to the four corners of the plantation so she could see where all the numbers came from. She remembered every corner, fence row, field or stream.

After his session with Virginia, Coopert went down to the slave quarters to put in an appearance, but his mind was on this great opportunity to gain complete control of one of the largest land holdings in the south. He paid scant attention to who or what he saw. Virginia on the other hand took a great many of the records to her room and begin an intense, detailed and earnest search that lasted most of the night. Along towards dawn she picked up a scheme of the type that she was absolutely certain would be there. She now had a great many questions to be answered by those whom Coopert had so readily identified.

Virginia was again the first up the second day after the funerals, and woke up Mammy to make coffee and start packing for an overnight. Coopert was embarrassed that the Missus had risen before him yet again, and was taken aback when he was deluged with instructions for the next two days. As soon as Mammy had her packed, Virginia was leaving for town, and while she was to be away she specifically requested Coopert to spend as much of the day as possible with Master. She explained that on her way into town she intended to stop by a few neighbors and explain the boys' private funeral. He was to leave for town in time to join her early this evening for dinner, then they would stay at a local establishment where an early start on tomorrow had already been planned. As he mentally examined how he might take advantage of spending the night with Missus, several thoughts ran through his mind. Fantacizing that he might wind up having to be intimate with a woman, Coopert found that most distressing and was enormously relieved when he saw Mammy climbing into the carriage as well.

Spending time with Master was a tedious proposition for Coopert. All he did once they got him out of bed was to sit and slobber, as he waved his one arm about and hollered:

"Damn Island View!"

"Damn Island View!"

"Damn Island View!"

A young but mature household slave, Amanda, was normally responsible for those who helped Gotfield feed himself and tend to his personal hygiene; however, since Missus had put Mr. Coopert in charge today, Amanda and the others simply left the supplies and disappeared as instructed. Coopert was very uncomfortable in this situation and made excuses at late morning to go down to the slave quarters to make certain the day was being fully taken advantage of.

After checking that the turncoats had a vigorous day scheduled for every man, woman and child, his next inquiry was for Bos. He contemplated bragging about his new station and celebrating perhaps with some personal attention from the big man. However, he did not remember seeing him since he was called to the mansion to "take charge" after the incident. As he asked about Bos he became more and more alarmed as all of the other slaves were quite vague:

"Oh, I seed him not long back, he be around." Or "He say he bin aked to clean de stall ober younder" were the best responses offered, until Coopert got out the whip. With a few indiscriminate lashes here and there, he became convinced no one really had seen Bos since about the time of the incident. Coopert went back into Bos cabin to examine it more closely where he knelt down and felt the ashes in the fireplace; they were now both cold and damp. Obviously there had been no fire for some time. Both his old and his newer pairs of shoes were gone. His good shirt was gone! His molasses jar was gone! His butchering knife was gone!

Coopert's suspicions were confirmed:

Bos had run away!

Well now, by damn, the first stop in town now would be the slave catchers. Coopert knew some excellent ones that he had used before. Coopert was smoldering. After all of the special attention the giant black man had received. Both from him and all the women.

That ingrate! The rest of the slaves would watch as he skinned the big black alive.

Coopert spurred his mare back to the mansion to grab his clothes and head for town, intending to ride like a storm. Then it occurred to him: He was, after all, quite the gentleman now. Such conduct was completely uncalled for and quite unbecoming to one such as him living in the mansion and all. He should be ushered into town by carriage, to arrive smelling of spice rather than horse sweat. So Coopert relaxed and carefully went about selected the best of his wardrobe, avoiding of course his special coat, which had a fair-sized fortune of ill-gotten bank notes and gold coin carefully sewed behind the lining. He smiled broadly as his driver held the carriage door and then putting his hands behind his head Coopert settled back to enjoy his luxurious ride. Bos would just have to wait, but when he was brought home, he, Mr. Coopert of the big house, would mete out punishment the likes of which these niggers had not seen before. He relished that moment and eagerly looked forward to having whips, knifes, hot irons and such in his hands again.

He would need a bigger barrel this time.

Earlier that morning Virginia had ordered her carriage to town at the fastest pace possible. As the carriage bounced around, Mammy likened the ride to "bouncing around like an apple in a bucket of water back here." The first call was on Sheriff Davis' office. Davis was out, so Virginia asked for the chief under-sheriff and considered it a stroke of marvelous luck, that although it had been years since they had seen each other, Mr. Liger was an old acquaintance. She presented him with well-laid-out documentation of what she had found and explained exactly the scheme she suspected. Together they developed a plan and Virginia set out straight away for Cox's, the chief supplier of necessities for the plantation's every day functioning.

She knew the founder, the silver-haired older Mr. Cox.

After normal condolences appropriate to a lady dressed in mourning, Mr. Cox asked genuinely how he might be of service to such a long standing valued patron as the mistress of Island View.

"Mr. Cox, do you keep records of each concern you do business with going back over the last few years?"

"Of course, Mrs. Virginia, ever whit and tiddle."

"Wonderful. May I see your more recent copies of purchases by Island View? As you may well imagine I am pretty much by myself since Gotfield's stroke and the boys' incident. I must try to get as much information together as possible for a new manager I am about to appoint. In fact I may bring him by tomorrow or perhaps you might make me copies of some of those tickets now and save us some time. We have a very, very busy tomorrow planned."

"I can have copies of the last couple of years made for you while you wait if that would be of service."

"Excellent, but may I see this year's now?"

"Of course."

She soon became absolutely, totally certain.

It was a very clever scheme.

Under-sheriff Liger was interviewing his third bank employee when he hit pay dirt. One of the owner investors, a Mr. Swartz, was there and quite on top of things.

"Why yes, Mr. Liger, the overseer from Island View, a Mr. Coopert, comes in every now and again. He established a special working account for the plantation here some time back. I opened the account myself which was to be for special needs and not the day-to-day. It was a bit out of the ordinary for he put the plantation's name on the account with himself as the signatory. I remember it well. I had just bought into the bank and had become president and thought we might get their entire business, but that was 12 years ago and that's all we ever got. Opening a new account was a welcome and comfortable respite from all of my new and unfamiliar duties. I was going to speak to Mr. Dinkins about getting more Island View's business, but frankly I was afraid we would lose what we had. Our current local president, Mr. Flessing, runs this bank as we have several others now. I seldom see particulars on any of the accounts, just the totalized numbers."

"Is the account still active?"

"That is privileged information."

"Can you simply tell me if the account still exists?

"Since you represent the sheriff we will bend the rules a bit."

After some time Swartz came back looking quite puzzled:

"I know Coopert was in here not long ago because I saw him, but there is no Island View account."

"Let's keep looking."

"I will put some staff on it.

"Flessing is not here today and I am concerned that we have mismanaged an account."

It took only a short time for a staff member to come up with the signature card that matched the sample of Coopert's handwriting that Virginia had supplied. It was one of the bank's largest deposits. Interest payments to the owner of the account were specifically requested to be paid to the account holder. In gold.

Both the owner identification and signature lines of the account card read;

Cooper Tooter.

The next stop was to Planter's, the factoring agent that had brokered the plantation's crop since Virginia was a small child.

Mr. Norman, who was getting quite on in years and had turned the business over to his sons, came at once from his spacious back office when he was advised she was in the building. Taking her arm he ushered her back into its comfortable confines. Mr. Norman was pleased to see her but quite saddened to see her dressed in black, for although he knew about Gotfield's stroke, he was one of few who had not heard of the twins' incident.

"Virginia, I always think of you as a de Falco even though you did marry a Dinkins. Anyway, it distresses me greatly to see you dressed so. Why I remember you as a little girl and then as a beautiful young lady sitting in this very place. Your grandfather used to be so proud of how you could remember things and my, oh my, how you could work with numbers. You could tell us what maybe a third of a cent a pound would amount to on something like 16,778 pounds quicker than I could say scat. My how the time goes by. Can you still do that?"

"Yes, Mr. Norman. It would be $55, plus 92 and two thirds cents."

"Thunderation! Tell me how do you do that? Humor an old man."

"Well, you know that a full penny a pound would be 16,778 cents or $167 and 78 cents so you know it would only be a third of that, and three times $55 is $165 which would leave $2.78 left over and a third of $2.78 is 92 and two thirds cents so it adds to $55.92 and 2/3 cents."

"Virginia, you are amazing but you did not come here to do that. Please tell me what's happened."

She related the public version of the twins' incident and Gotfield's condition with a candor reserved only for those very few who have earned your complete trust.

"Mr. Norman, are you aware of any sales of Island View's crops through any other agency than your own?"

"Well, yes, child, I am, and I have always wondered what one of my sons did to have Gotfield take a piece of business to First Brokerage."

"How do you know about that"?

"The factoring agent over there, a Mr. Meiss, got quite mouthy with me one evening at an affair and bragged how he was getting the wonderful hand-worked bales and that he would soon get the rest. Such things are why I never drink much at all, especially around my clients or competitors."

Drink!

Virginia realized she had not had one today and suddenly craved one very badly. She started shaking and Mr. Norman gently held her hand and pointed to her black dress.

"Virginia, I can only imagine know how very difficult this must be for you child."

"Sometimes it is simply overwhelming and frankly right now I feel faint. Would you happen to have just a small spot of whiskey. I seldom drink at all, but somehow whiskey seems to help."

"Of course."

Virginia downed the glass like a sailor fresh on shore.

The next stop was the First Brokerage factoring office, and Mr. Meiss was very talkative.

"The hand-worked from Island View is the standard of the state."

When Virginia requested the Island View records, she offered promise that she would be recommending that her new manager split the business more evenly to include some of the machine ginned. Meiss produced what she needed and more. Liger then accompanied her back to the bank, and the case was made. Sales through First Brokerage matched many of the deposits to the Cooper Tooter account to the penny.

Virginia and Mammy were staying at Ligget's, the finest, most respected place available and with special accommodations for black servants. Virginia wanted no wagging tongues and had requested that the Liggets join her and Coopert, (or whatever his name really was) for dinner; however, they felt responsible to the rest of their guests. As Mammy had to eat at a place reserved for "her kind." they seated a minister and his wife at Virginia's table instead. A lady dining alone with a gentlemen employee in a place where rooms were available was a sure fuse to light up the gossips in town. Coopert was both surprised and relieved to find that he was staying overnight at the tavern down the road. He quickly decided to invite his dear friend over at the bank, Mr. Flessing, to spend some quality time and was quite disappointed to find that Flessing had been sent out of town on bank business again for tomorrow. Quite suddenly it seemed.

Morning brought sunshine and a scrumptious breakfast at Liggets. Virginia's faithful driver Daniel had the carriage freshly cleaned and polished from the wet roads. Gentleman Coopert steadied Lady Virginia and pompously swooped up the carriage steps, following almost too closely as she climbed aboard. Their first business appointment was to be at the Cox supply house but with an early quick stop by Sheriff Davis' office to pick up some papers relating to the boys' incident. Virginia asked Coopert to come in with her as she needed a witness to her signature.

As he arrogantly stepped inside the sheriff's office, Coopert's blood suddenly ran cold! His heart virtually stopped beating! He couldn't help from trembling nor scarce catch his breath. It took all Coopert had to keep from running for the door as he came face to face with the decidedly unfriendly welcoming committee. They were a distinguished group.

Sheriff Davis.

Under-sheriff Liger.

The magistrate.

Mr. Rawson.

Mr. Norman.

Mr. Cox.

Mr. Meiss.

Mr. Swartz.

Sheriff Davis broke the silence;

"Shall we call you Mr. Coopert or Mr. Tooter?"

"Well, ah, ahhh my father's name was Tooter."

"Why do you go by Coopert?"

"Well people made fun of Tooter, calling me Poooter Toooter or all sorts of things, so now I simply now use my first name Cooper and last initial."

"Mr. Tooter, do you have any idea why we are all here?"

"No."

"We seem to make you quite nervous. Are you certain you do not know why?"

"Well, Ahh no."

Mr. Swartz spoke up:

"It seems one of our people made a terrible mistake and let Island View's name disappear off of an account that you had personally set up for the plantation. Any account change such as that requires two people's involvement and must be initialed by the staff member who requests the change. In this case that did not happen. It appears the employee who made that change seems to know you quiet well and apparently you two have sort of an ahh special relationship. You are quite aware of all this of course?"

"Certainly not."

"I have been advised otherwise. At any rate yours is the only signature."

"Well Mr. Dinkins simply never got by to sign!"

"For such a huge amount? Surely you cannot mean that. That would be preposterous. At any rate it is quite obvious that this is the plantation's money, as we have the sales tickets from over at First Brokerage which match many of the deposits."

"Well of course it is the plantation's money."

"Mr. Tooter, this is fraud. Do you realize Mrs. Dinkins could put you in jail for the rest off your life for simply keeping the interest payments."

"No way! Why this, this is just, just an honest mistake. Yes! An honest mistake. We were to use those dollars for extraordinary plantation expenses. Why if Mister could talk he would tell you. He would tell you so. He could set this all straight."

"Since all of the money in the account is obviously theirs, and since Mr. Dinkins obviously cannot get by here, would you sign all of this money into a fresh Island View account with Mrs. Dinkins as the signatory?"

Just the thought of prison and what they did to his kind there terrified him. Tooter mentally reviewed his options, and not knowing what his friend Flessing at the bank may have reported, he could think of no other option. Trying desperately to keep his voice from trembling he replied meekly:

"Well — yes, of course."

"Sign here."

"One other thing, Mr. Tooter. We are well aware of your falsifying the bills from Mr. Cox's establishment and have asked Mrs. Dinkins what charges we are to press. You could get 20 just for that."

Virginia peered at Tooter with all of the distain and disgust one can manage with a look. She stuck the knife in deep and twisted.

"I had such great plans for you, Mr. Coopert, but as Mr. Tooter, I see you as a despicable common thief. It will take weeks of reviewing to see how much money you have pocketed for yourself, but I have asked Sheriff Davis and Mr. Cox to keep these records on file, to hire an accountant, and to calculate the final tally of your deceit. I am advised that I have years and years to file charges. Get back to Island View. You may keep your regular mount and saddle. Put your clothes and other personal possessions in a wagon and take a pair of the more common mules. Sheriff Davis will send an under-sheriff to escort you. I want you off my property by sundown, or you will spend the next 20 years in jail. If you ever try to give me or any of mine grief, or if something untimely befalls me, the sheriff and others will chase you to the ends of the earth and see you rot behind bars."

Virginia was shaky again, so she asked if there was anything else, thanked the gentlemen for their support and participation then practically fled. She gave specific instructions to Tooter's driver who was amazed at what he was to do. Then Virginia rushed to her own carriage where she grabbed whiskey and drank straight from the bottle.

Her driver Daniel handed her a note:

"A fine looking white haired gentleman asked me to pass this on to you Miz. Virginia."

It was on John Norman's expensive personalized note paper and read:

Please come by. I can help.
John

Virginia tried to pretend she did not know what this was all about but she would go by to be polite, and directed Daniel to take her carriage straight away to Norman's office. John Norman looked every bit the senior statesman as he sat watching, hoping she would stop by. He came immediately to lead her around to the private side entrance to his office where he directed her to sit with him on a sofa. He sat with her and took both of her hands into his and looked directly into her eyes. She saw wisdom, grace, kindness and concern in this face framed with the silver hair of another generation.

"Virginia, please do not think me forward, but I became quite concerned for you yesterday. I still am."

"Really?"

"Yes. I have three sons. Two of them have always been upright and fine citizens, but my third has had a serious problem with alcohol his entire adult life. We all help him fight the demon from time to time. Virginia, I know the alcoholic shakes when I see them."

She affirmed his thinking by nodded her head. His kindness broke the dam, and all of the strain and worry of these last days, no actually of the last 18 years, came flooding through. She leaned toward him and began to tremble, then completely collapsing onto the older man's shoulder, she begin to sob her very heart out.

She cried uncontrollably. She wept because there were such despicable men in the world as Tooter who stole from those who trusted them, and who could inflict such unimaginable pain on others and take pleasure in their screams; because there had been no such man as John Norman for her; because her mother died when she was young and she had no loving female council; because her grandfather had thought more of money than he did her future; because her cousin/husband was such a very weak person; because she had not given her sons the special care they needed; because Gotfield had led their sons into the darkness and they followed so readily; because she had spent so many loveless years in a mansion and was so very lonely; because she had given up any hope of happiness to maintain the family wealth; because those who were in their service and whom they were charged with caring for had become so abused; because the land of her ancestors had become a hell-hole of wickedness and evil; and because she knew the truth of what had happened on that island and must carry it to her grave.

As John Norman held her head to his shoulder, he gently stroked her premature salt and pepper grey hair and rocked to and fro, as he would if he were attempting to sooth a distraught child.

Virginia cried and cried and cried like one.

The sun began to cast its afternoon rays through the windows as she snuggled against him, completely wasted.

He patiently held her.

Finally, there were no more tears.

Just red and puffy eyes.
And the hiccups.
And shakes.
She was so very sad.
So very tired.
Right now she hated Island View.

She loathed what she had become.

Cooper Tooter sat in the carriage in a state of absolute shock. At breakfast he had held a fortune in his name, which long ago he had convinced himself was securely his. Now, before lunch and with but one signature, 80 percent of it had vanished. He tried to consol himself by concentrating on the treasure still sewed into his special coat and his cleverly buried box of gold. But still ....

There had been enough cash in that bank account to buy a fair sized plantation and enough slaves to keep him in style for life.

Gone.

How could he have become so unworried?

So unwise?

So smug?

So careless?

When he first arrived at Island View he had taken uncommon pains to cover his tracks, but it was so very easy and Gotfield Dinkins never paid any attention at all. Over time his special relationship with Mr. Flessing at the bank had lulled him into a false sense of infallibility. Now he could think of a hundred schemes more clever than the one he used, yet who would have thought about ... Oh damn it anyway! Now, with this annoying under-sheriff watching his every move, he would even have to leave his buried gold for some other time.

Cooper Tooter's chin quivered. Instead of soon becoming part of the landed gentry he was now to be summarily escorted off Island View property by sundown. Yesterday he had every intention of Island View becoming partially his, and with visions of plantation owners far and wide feeling so subservient to his position they would continually bow and scrape in his direction. Just this very morning he could feel the power he would exert over the others and the merchants as well. Gone. How complacent he had become to let the nitwits' mother, who had not even set foot in the slave quarters for years, trap a brilliant man such as he. What really galled was that even though he had seldom been around her, more than anything else Cooper Tooter considered Virginia nothing more than a drunk. Still, she had caught him like a rabbit in a snare. He was totally humiliated!

Under the watchful eyes of the annoying under-sheriff and some number of astonished slaves, Cooper Tooter selected a first-rate wagon and a common team of mules. Then he packed his belongings, taking great care to fold his special coat and place it in the bottom of an old trunk which he convinced the under-sheriff he might take. He then placed his whips along with some of his other "toys" on top of the coat in the trunk, and after packing whatever else he could convince the under-sheriff was his, he saddled up. Cooper Tooter was well mounted on a fine mare and fancy saddle but he had to trail old Mollie and Bigun, the pair of slow common old mules hitched to the wagon. Slow was the operative word. So, instead of being served a fine evening meal with a glass of excellent wine and retiring to his suite in probably the finest mansion in the South, he now simply had no idea where he might lay his head tonight.

Cooper Tooter wept openly as he was escorted off the land.

Once the story of his fraud got out, certainly no one in the South would hire him and Tooter had no real friends. Except for the chap at the bank, and he was not so certain of him right now. After some time passed he had every intention of coming back and interrogating Flessing quite thoroughly. That would prove to be a very interesting and enjoyable occurrence and he smiled for the first time today as he thought about his toys in the trunk.

Perhaps he could go into the business as a Gentleman Slave Catcher with his underlings first bringing the captured slaves to him, before returning them to their masters. He pulled out the newspaper ad that his slave catcher used that he still had in his pocket.

Bloodhounds

I have the Finest Dogs for Catching Slaves in the Area
They can take the trail Twelve to Sixteen Hours
After the Negro has passed and Catch them with ease

A pack of ten hounds would cost $1500 or so, and only two such packs would undoubtedly provide an adequate income. Just as importantly they would provide him a steady source of entertainment. He would of course not degrade himself by joining the chase. He would simply be waiting.

Cooper Tooter was no fool, and realized that for certain he would have to wait until memories faded and even then he would have to go into business quite some distance from Island View. Right now he could think of no better option, so he decided he might as well ferryboat across the river and go up to Kentucky where his brother was living after he too had been run out of the deep South. Thinking of his brother called to mind their father for a moment, and Tooter wondered if he might possibly still be alive. If so, he figured if the old man was able, he was still probably swinging his whip on some renegade slave ship out of Africa. Tooter had never known his father very well, although when he was home one time he gave his son some of his best tools—tongs made for crushing fingers and other nice gadgets. Unfortunately they did so much damage one could not use them on a valuable slave for they ruined that market value, but the tools certainly made him feel important. He smiled as he thought of them safely tucked away in the trunk.

As his thoughts turned to family he again thought of his only brother. Although his brother had hated the family name too, he had actually changed his name for a very good reason. He was now a Mr. Tuttoor and lived some place in western Kentucky.

At a place they called Three Creeks.

Bos felt compelled to move by night and made excellent time his first night out. He was a big, strong, tough man and made the miles fly by in the faint moonlight of early evening; before the clouds came in and his guiding star completely disappeared. He tried to continue moving on in the misty gloom, but kept running into obstacles or falling into ditches or creeks in the dark starless night. Bos became confused as to what direction was which.

Beyond the huge river front plantations was an area of smaller so called Oxford Farms. There farmers had wrested what acres they could from nature, and either by themselves or along with just a few slaves, they tried to make a living. Many of their homes were just shacks, with greased paper substituting for glass in the windows, and with some hogs and other critters lying around the front yards. Others were fairly nice with a very few being extra nice, sporting glass windows and well kept fences. Bos stayed as far from any one of these houses and cabins as he could and watched keenly for any signs of people or dogs, for any dog's bark sent his heart immediately to his throat. He remembered vividly having to watch as Coopert tortured the two separate runaway slaves that the dogs had caught, and finally when those dogs had torn the flesh from their bones.

Certainly Coopert must have hired the slave catchers and their bloodhounds to run him down by now, and for that reason alone he was grateful for the misty rain that was making his scent disappear. To that end he had also walked for a great part of his first night in streams, particularly where he could find one heading the way he thought he should be going. After having run into trees and falling into ditches innumerable times in the pitch black, Bos found himself a sturdy stick to tap his way like a blind person through the more difficult spots. Still he was beginning to feel hopeless as it seemed he was getting nowhere, so in desperation Bos decided that he must move by day and did so, giving any sign of civilization the widest possible berth. As Bos moved briskly through the next morning's mist he saw an isolated house with slave cabins to its rear and an outhouse way back. It was by far the largest and the best kept such house he had seen. It appeared at this distance to have the logs well chinked, glass in the windows, and with the hogs fenced away from the house and a large garden. He made his path a safe distance away but his mind, as always, made detailed notes. There was a wagon up on a jack with the wheel removed for repair and leaned against the long side of a building, which was the smokehouse where the family stored their cured meat no doubt. This reminded him smartly that he had only a small jar of molasses which he was stretching by dipping tender vegetation along with some raw field corn into the jar, and eating the entire thing.

As the day wore on, he came to streams and assumed some were running south, found trails that seemed to lead north and made a wide swath around the houses he came across. He kept relentlessly on the move and at dusk the next day he came across an overhang in the side of a creek bank where some fairly dry leaves had blown into it. He finished the last of his molasses with some flowers, ate some raw kernels of corn, and then crawled into the leaves to sleep fitfully until the rainy and misty dawn. He was up at daybreak, took his stick and moved on. Soon he came across his first civilization, a well kept house with slave cabins out back. It had a wagon up on a jack next to a smoke house with an outhouse way out back.

He was exactly where he had been the day before yesterday. After running his guts out so hard for so long, he was no further from Island View or Coopert.

Bos sat back against a tree and wept.

As he sat so very depressed looking at the house, a Negro man came out of one of the cabins and started harnessing two teams and hooking up wagons. Then a white man and woman plus their three children came out of the house, and the Negro's family, a woman and two children, appeared. They all boarded the wagons and waved goodbye to what appeared to be a colored woman who apparently was to be left behind. Bos had never known about owners who loved their slaves and treated them well. He would never have though that a master would work right along beside his slaves and nurse them when they were sick, or rejoice with them when they were happy. Or make certain their souls were saved and even feed them as well as they ate themselves.

Two dogs frisked about, following along as the teams moved out. So, after making certain he was downwind, Bos moved a bit closer to the road. He could just barely hear laughter and spirited conversation in the distance as the group started on their trip. All of the bigger kids were in the second wagon which followed all of the adults and the white baby in the first. Bos made a tactical decision. A Negro woman all by herself would be a minimal threat, and he was now wet, eaten up with insects and needed beans and pork fat or something of substance. Being certain the wagon had time to be a safe distance away Bos stole closer and closer to the buildings, until finally he was sitting on the ground with his back up against the wall outside an open window in the slave cabin. He caught a glimpse of her.

She was older.

"Old woman." he whispered loudly.

"Dat you, God?"

"No, dis no God."

"Yo shor? It be my time for long."

"No dis not God, dis a darkie."

"What darkie?"

"I come from a long ways."

"What long ways?"

"Down by de riber."

"What you want?"

"I hungry."

"How come your master he don't feed you?"

"Cause just cause."

"He know you hungry?"

"Probably don't care."

"You been bad?"

"Yes."

"You runnin?"

"Yes."

"Don't you come to me where I can see you cause I won't lie about it, cause de Lord would know."

"Can I have somethun to eat?"

"I guess dat don't hurt none. Keep yourself hid. I set it outside cause I don't want to see no runaway darkie. No sir. Dem slave catchers get it out o me when you be here and what you look like anyway."

"Yes mam."

"I used to live down by the riber."

"Yes mam."

"On a plantation right next door to de big Island View Plantation."

"Dat right?"

"Yes, I walk over there every day for over a year."

"Why?"

"Cause I had a baby and lots o milk, and dey had a baby over there whose mama got on poorly, didn't have no milk much, and he was a big one. I had way more than my George done need so I go over there a lot cause they didn't have no mama with extra right then so I go over there every day for a long time. I remember him so well, loved dat baby like he was my own and he be on the teat a long time. When he get off I go back a few times but he cried so when I leave they say, 'Which mamma you love?' After he got a few words when dey aked him he try to say both but it came out Bos. It so sweet they wound up a callin him Bos."

"I am called Bos and am a runnin from Island View."

The old woman literally burst out the door, looked him over for just a split second, swooped down and enveloped the huge man to her still ample bosom.

"Got to be my Bos! I'd know you if you be 100!"

This was the first time Bos had felt the touch of pure love since his mamma disappeared.

"What be your name, Mam?"

"They calls me Bessie."

"How come you be here now stead of down by Island View?"

"Well when my George be a little fellow Master Ben down there he need to sell some slaves and so he sell my man big George and little George and me. We all be sold to a Mr. Long down towards here and then when my George be a grown man de Master Farout here need some, and so he buy my little George and his wife and he say he only take em if I come too. That because my man big George he be gone now and lo Mr. Farout he paid pretty plenty for an old darkie like me."

When she stopped to catch a breath Bos asked,

"He a good master? Do you eat good?"

"Mr. Farout he de best master a darkie ever have, he so smart and his missus so smart and dey work so hard, why I tells him he need to take it more easy but he say we all got to earn our way cause the Lord be looking and he don't like no lazy folk. And sides that he say the best buy he make be me cause I makes de best gravy he done ever taste. He make me feel so good. You know he done had special shoes made up for me cause my old feet so knotty. He take two sticks and cut one just so for long and de other just right for wide. Then he put a walnut on the end of the short one and cut notches here they spose to cross. Then he take em to town and tell de shoemaker to make shoes to fit dis here. First time I ever wear shoes dat don't hurt. He say darkies that don't hurt and get some rest and eat good work a lot more and we have all got more good to look forwards to. He make good money on this place and be buying the one next door. Folk wonder how we get so much done around here."

"When he be back?"

"Day after tomorrow or maybe next day."

"Ain't you scared to be by yourself like this?"

"Old Bessie scared. Don't be silly. When you called out to me I had de shotgun right by me. Besides de Lord look out for old Bessie. We be friends."

"Master let you close to a gun?"

"All de time. I got my own."

"Where did the rest of em go?"

"Dey going to get some more slaves and to dey store."

"Why did de other slaves go too?"

"So to help along the way and to tell de new ones dis be a good place for a darkie to be and not be scared. He even take de dogs cause dey goin to camp out. Dey dogs good watch dogs. Yes sir, everbody earn their way here and took dey kids too, so old Bessie not have to watch out for em and to tell de new youngun he have plenty to play with. Yes sir, he bout de bestus man ever was. And Missus she look after them grandbabies of mine like they hers. She so smart she be better than any doctor old Bessie ever know about. If somebody says, 'Bessie, you want to be free?' I say no sir, dis Bessie happy where she done be at."

"Why you stay here and they all go?"

"Laws a mity somebody got to do the milken and feed the critters. Sides this old body don't need no jostling about in a wagon for no two or three days."

That night when she finally stopped talking, Bos slept in a house with a full stomach while Bessie just sat and looked upon him most of the night. Next day, after she had milked, Bos drank as much milk as he could hold again, and after an enormous breakfast she kept frying meat, boiling eggs and coming up with more and more food. She prepared as much as Bos could carry in his backpack which they had fashioned, and Bessie then did a pretty good job of making it waterproof to accommodate Bos' upcoming river crossing. He was a strong swimmer and planned on finding a place where the current would work with him, but he also took a rope to fix together a log float to use when he paddled across the huge river.

Bessie shared with him what she had heard of people on the other side of the river hanging quilts on their houses, with the North star pattern always hung with the North star pointing the way North. The flying geese pattern quilt also always had the flying geese flying towards freedom. Before he need go she went to the master's house and brought a toy he and Missus had fashioned for the children: a magnet and a magic needle.

"You rubs the needle on the magnet this way and then swap ends and rubs that way. After you rubs it both ways just like so, you puts the wood pieces on both ends and puts the needle into some quiet water. It always float about until this end point to de north, like this. Hee. Hee. Dem kids going to get in big trouble for losen dis, but Master he never raise a hand to nobody. But dey little dickens sure be tired of pullin weeds when he get through." She chuckled.

He embraced the old woman and prepared to go.

"Bessie," he asked; "how old am I?"

"You and little George be 24 now."

"I always wanted to know. Where be my mama?"

A storm cloud enveloped the old slave's face and she replied,"Somebody else have to tell you child. She be a good woman last we saw." Then she brightened:

"I'll talk to de Lord upstairs about you eber night."

Bos and Bessie were anxious that Farout and the others would be returning, so after getting well rested, on the second day, Bos headed north again. Now, better prepared and more confident than just about any runaway ever, he reasoned that, after all, this could not simply have been fate. God had to have a hand in this. And surely if anybody could keep God on his side, it would be God's friend, Bessie.

Cooper Tooter's mules, old Mollie and Bigun, had served Island View well for years and years, but now being well past their prime they moved at their very own pace. Nothing known to man would make them move more briskly. The fine mare that was Tooter's regular mount was eager to move on out, as was Tooter, and they were bored as they continually poked along and waited for the plodding mules to catch up. This gave Cooper Tooter plenty of time to review his situation. He had been forced to give back an enormous sum, but still had plenty of money to live well, and planned to start doing so by staying at the very best taverns along the way. Still, old Mollie and Bigun were so very slow and having gotten such a late start he found night fall long before the next public place. This put him in the disagreeable circumstance of having to look out for himself. As evening approached he spotted a cozy camp site with a group already preparing for the evening meal. He rode up, dismounted, and 'Hell o ed' the camp.

Steven Farout had just that day stopped at Cox's for supplies and provisions for the farm, plus his new family of slaves. The older Cox had positioned himself where he could watch the business transaction, for he enjoyed the game. Farout and his wife were both people of good character and sharp business practice, and they certainly knew full well how to get their money's worth. As always, there would be the two lists, one of "must have" and one of "would like to have," and they would simply leave some of the "like to have" if the deal was not good enough. Today the lists were exceptionally long due to the new slave family being with them, and the senior slave pair, George and Georgina, hovered about them. Farout had given each pair a very few discretionary dollars to spend, and they were making particularly careful choices. The new slaves, Sam and Sara, were bewildered because they had never had such choices to make before.

In the meantime the Farout's oldest had propositioned one of the clerks: "I would like to buy these treats for all of the children but my father only gave me enough money to buy for the others. If I bought for all of them would you please include one for me?"

Cox smiled to himself: a chip off the old block.

Farout had his lists priced out and sure enough he made a proposition:

"That is a lot of money, almost more than I have with me. But certainly if I give you $100 for all of this you would still have a fair amount of profit left, now would you not? Here."

Farout stuck out his handful of bills, for he well understood the allure of the sight and smell of money. He played his hand well, for it was a large amount and there was still profit enough to make the sale. Farout had already surmised as much, made the presumptive close, and moved as if to help the staff load his wagons. Cox admired his skill, for the man was good. Only after the deal was done he came out to visit; for given the chance, Farout would ask the boss man for even a better deal. Naturally enough Cox told Farout about the big scandal over at Island View and how Miz. Virginia had caught Tooter. Cox had marveled:

"She is a lot smarter lady than anybody except maybe her grandfather ever gave her credit for."

As the Farout party was about to leave, a young and ragged, barefoot street urchin came sneaking quietly in, and immediately one of the clerks produced some bread and meat which the child gobbled down as though she were starving.

Bonnie Farout inquired:

"What is this all about?"

The clerk explained:

"The child's father is dead and the mother unable to work, so we take turns seeing that she has something to eat at least once a day. She regularly comes in to warm herself by our fire when the weather has a chill.

Bonnie knelt down:

"Where are your shoes, child."

"I don't got none now times."

Bonnie took one of their new pans and asked if there might be some soap and water.

There was. Bonnie helped the child wash her feet.

"Please bring shoes to fit this child and three more pair of socks. Bring two dresses her size, perhaps just a bit large."

"Thank you. How much?"

Without a cringe the Farouts, who had spent just about everything, found enough more for a little girl they might well never see again.

Cox genuinely liked these people and felt good for them. The Farouts seemed to take great pleasure in being charitable. He walked out with them and gave Bonnie his arm as she climbed aboard the wagon to head to their farm, which they told him was now twice the size it used to be. He admired these people and knew they would camp out on their way home, spending no money for something as simple as a bed for the night.

"Hello, the camp."

"Hello, stranger, stop and refresh. My name Is Farout, what might be yours?"

"My name is Tooter, Cooper Tooter."

Steven Farout recognized the name immediately as the one that Mr. Cox told him that Coopert had used in his scheme over at the bank.

The Farouts had stretched a covering between their two wagons, making their party quite snug even against the mist or a rain. The campfire was nicely glowing already and everyone was anticipating the delicious hot stew and corn bread, which along with some pie, was to be the evening meal.

After dismounting Tooter came into their shelter and looked about. After some small talk he asked:

"You eat with your slaves?"

"Why without doubt. This one, Georgiana, is a great cook and made the most of what we are to eat tonight. She gets served first."

"You and your family sleep with your slaves?"

"Of course. George there will play some good banjo music before bed time then he will take the first watch."

"You trust a nigger to watch over your family and all that stuff in your wagons?"

"Absolutely. He would shoot anybody trying to harm me or mine."

"Shoot?"

"Certainly, George will have a shotgun and I will be close by with another."

As Mr. Coopert, the hated overseer at Island View, the thought of an armed slave was unsettling for there were many days when a slave would have shot him and taken the consequences, therefore Cooper Tooter could not conceive of arming a slave, and thought that it should be a capital offense to do so. This made him very uneasy. To his way of thinking slaves were to do all of the work and then to be used for whatever pleasure they might bring, whether it be in bed, fighting each other, or hearing them shriek in agonizing pain. This man was a menace to his way of thinking, and his kind needed to be dealt with. He decided, after sharing the Farout's delicious bounty, he would rather sleep to himself than to share their camp along with the Negros. Tooter thanked Bonnie Farout for her hospitality, saddled up and led his mules at their own pace on up the road a small distance. He made camp after a fashion and then sat brooding.

Yesterday he was a rich man living in a fine mansion, now he was without a roof over his head and there was some fanatic down the road treating slaves like people. He felt a strong responsibility to teach this Farout a lesson. The man was wrong. Besides, Tooter had an oncoming need to inflict pain. Finally he took a pistol plus his favorite whip and started slowly back toward their camp, planning to provoke one of their Negroes into a fuss. And then give him a good lashing. Farout would have to stand by and let him, because if he could fool the Negro into hitting him he would then have the right to have the black killed. Farout would not want to lose a valuable property and would have no option but to stand by and see a master at work. Since Virginia had caught Tooter red handed his need to inflict pain was becoming almost desperate, and whipping one of Farout's slaves to a bloody mess would do nicely.

As Tooter was moving softly toward their camp he heard the low growl of a dog pleading, "Please, let me loose."

A voice from the darkness proclaimed:

"Best you go no closer to my master's camp. This here dog been taught good."

Tooter stopped short and replied:

"I was just checking to make certain you were all safe."

George replied:

"We be just fine, Mr. Tooter. Mr. Farout he give the dog your smell and then we put his watchin collar on. So's if I turn him loose he come after you iffin I lets him. And I am agonna lets him if you gets much closter. You best go back to your wagon now."

Tooter did just that.

The dog was very disappointed.

The Farout party slept quite well.

Eventually Cooper Tooter got a ferry across the river but made slow time even though the weather had become much improved. He found a tavern to stay in most nights and that presented an unusual challenge; it was commonplace for men to share a bed in these country taverns. Due to his particular taste that was extremely tricky, as sleeping with another man for Cooper Tooter was akin to a normal man being bedded with a strange woman. Finally, after one very ugly incident, he decided if he could not rent a room to himself, he would simply eat at the tavern's table and retire to his wagon. Cooper Tooter took only enough money from the lining of his coat to pay for the day's needs. His bills were very large denominations from the Citizens Bank of Louisiana, the best known and strongest bank in the South. He had a problem getting the first large bill cashed and had to use some gold coin.

The chest containing his great coat and its fortune was chained and padlocked to the wagon, plus his special coat was also completely covered by his toys, which presumably would scare off just about anyone who might get a chance to peer in. He took one or the other of the toys out from time to time to play with, as he longed for an occasion when he might really have somebody's hand to set the thumbscrew to.

Cooper Tooter pulled to the side of the road and watched as the coffle of slaves came along, with the men chained into two long lines marching side by side. The women and children walked beside them if there was room, and scattered about if the road became too narrow. They were being either marched south or taken over to the river and put on a boat which would take them south to auction. It was a time of great southern migration of slaves from the northern slave areas. The cotton gin had revitalized the southern states' economy where cotton was the predominant crop, and now many more slaves were needed to provide the required cheap labor. In 1840 there were 2,487,000 slaves in America. In ten years the number had shot up to over 3,200,000 and by 1860 there would be at least 4,000,000.

There were many who thought the institution of slavery would fall of its own weight; however, with the cotton gin owning slaves down south became quite profitable once again. Cotton had been mostly a curiosity crop grown on some islands off the coast until the cotton gin made it feasible to process short stem cotton in quantity. Now, one person turning a crank could produce as much usable product as dozens used to by hand. Prior to the cotton gin most Americans generally had one set of clothes made of homespun wool or animal skins. Ordinary people were buried naked because clothing was so hard to come by. Wealthy folk might have two or three sets of clothes, and the nobility or very rich might have several garments of linen or silk. Whitney truly thought his cotton gin would help free the slaves, but instead it only strengthened their bondage. Perhaps it is poetic justice that the government canceled his patent, and he never made a dime from the device.

In any event, with the coming of the cotton gin, huge affordable quantities of cotton became available. Shirt makers, pant makers, and dress makers bought the cloth as fast as the factories could turn it out. Anyone could now have clean clothes and there was even fancy cotton woven into colorful patterns to give a sparkle to the fair young maid. A new industry was born, personal hygiene became a social requirement, sweet smelling soap profitable to make and the bath a moral issue. It was now your own fault if you stank.

Revitalization of the cotton plantations sent itinerant slave buyers prowling the northern areas buying slaves wherever they could find them, being guaranteed a profit at the auction down south. Any slave with strong negro features was generally the most desirable, for if they ran away people would be more apt to question their happenstance. The price followed life's cycle itself, with young females who were in their prime child bearing years bringing the most. At about age 22 the prices for a male or a female were about equal and as they grew a bit older the male price would become greater, peaking for him at about age 27. In 1850 when it cost about $10,000 to build a nice home and $20,000 would build a small mansion, the price of a prime male at the New Orleans slave auction was about $800. A well known Savannah slave dealer by the name of Joseph Bryan dispersed 460 slaves for a Pierce Butler who fell into serious financial arrears in 1859. This was a very similar holding to the slaves on Island View, and the records show that the Butlers netted $300,205 after commissions. The largest ticket at that sale was

$6,180 for a mother and her five grown or nearly grown children, and that same day a separate prime male of substantial size and strength brought $1,750. Skilled slaves brought a premium based on that skill; however, a light skinned pretty young female who was apt to become a white man's concubine was the highest priced of all. One of the most exceptional sales ever recorded was a 22 year old very light skinned tall female, with blue eyes and beautiful long curls. She is described as being of uncommon beauty, grace, intelligence, skill and manner, plus also possessing extraordinary musical abilities. Her description reads very similar to that of any recent Miss America. The sale ticket: $200,000 (currently 4 to 5 million dollars).

Most owners gave little if any concern toward keeping the slave family together, resulting in one of three being sold at least once before they turned 40. A similar ratio of one in three so called marriages of the slaves was also destroyed by selling the pair to separate masters. Slaves could no more be married than a pair of horses could be; however, the master would have some sort of bonding ceremony if nothing more than have them jump over a broom together. Louisiana's slave laws were often used as a model for others and was the only state to have a law that forbad the selling of a slave child away from its mother before age 10. There are no recorded instances of a master ever being charged with such a crime even though two out of five slaves were sold as children. Oddly enough, in 1855 in the state of Louisiana, approximately one in seven slaves was the registered property of a free black. The community saw free blacks as such a problem that laws were passed in 1857 to make it practically impossible for a master to free a slave. Almost the only grounds for doing so were if the slave saved the master's life, or at least one of the master's immediate family. Other than that, it was a precarious process, first of all requiring proof that the slave's conduct had been far above reproach for the last four years. Even then the freed slave was generally compelled to leave the state and could hold no claim to his or her family.

The practice of breaking up the family in the northernmost slave states became so common during this time that slaves normally kept their heads down and trembled with fear as the slave buyers prowled their master's place, terrified that they alone might be sold down the river. Being "sold down the river" has been a horrifying thought for a long time.

Copper Tooter caught up to the man obviously in charge of the coffle and struck up a conversation, inquiring mostly about the possibility of needing one of their charges disciplined. He was severely disappointed when advised his services were not needed.

Restless, disappointed, frustrated and angry he came into western Kentucky and inquired until he found people who knew where this place called Three Creeks was.

Eventually he found directions to where the Tuttoors lived, stayed at Dody's tavern, went across the road to buy a small present for his brother, caught sight of the fair Mrs. Purdy, and then set out to see his kin.

The brothers had not gotten along at all when they were younger, and Cooper Tooter knew his brother thought his taste in bed partners was quite extraordinary, having tried to engage even him in bed when they were younger. Both sons, however, had been good students of their father's peculiar skills, and his legacy to each had been a set of tools of his trade. They each called them their toys.

Brother Tuttoor was not particularly happy to see Brother Cooper Tooter, but after all he was blood. There were a great many reasons Tuttoor was not particularly glad to see his brother. Certainly the most predominant and important one was that he knew his real name, and there were those who still sought a certain Quinton Tooter for cause. Probably the most imminent reason was that brother Cooper Tooter knew that Quinton's wife was the issue of a black woman; therefore, both she and the boy should be considered slaves. Law on this issue varied from state to state and sometimes even year to year in any given locality. Heredity was determined by the mother and in some areas if the great-great-great-grandmother was a Negro, all of a given female's children were slaves, while yet at other junctures one only had to be one eighth black, and in some localities a fortunate few of those with that limited amount of negro blood in them were to be set free at age 31. The Latin tag for the law was *partus sequitur ventrem* which basically translates, "That which is brought forth follows the womb." A mother passed slavery to her offspring like a birth defect, especially from her daughter to her daughter to her daughter to her daughter in perpetuity. It made no difference if the father was a slave or a free man; therefore, the son of a slave women and a white father such as Junior, had it little if any better. Tuttoor had stolen Maud from a group of young females to be auctioned, and therefore she was not duly recorded to him at the parish; however, she had always assumed he would have no trouble with that particular detail. Maud was completely subservient to Tuttoor, for although everyone assumed she was white, she was well conditioned to be subservient. After all, she had started life as a slave and felt naturally compelled to quietly take his abuse. Besides, her only real joy in life was their son who Tuttoor also let pass for white.

Tuttoor realized at once that his brother's presence might well bring other complications, for if Cooper got mouthy it might well be that the Three Creeks community would scorn him even more. Especially if they thought he claimed an illegal marriage to a Negro woman, as opposed to living with his female slave and slave boy. Any such attempted mixed marriage was punishable by law, and what's more, in 1857 Kentucky had passed a law forbidding any new free blacks; therefore, brother could easily put him in a legal bind. Furthermore; even being thought of as being illegally married to Negro was a bit way much....even for the likes of Tuttoor. In any event, Maud was the mother of Junior whom he openly claimed as his son and whom he truly did not want to degrade to slave status.

Brother could certainly be a troublesome issue; however, Tuttoor was reasonably confident that both Maud and Junior would be considered whatever he said they were. It was very near impossible for a Negro to prove or disprove what a white man said.

Quinton Tooter was masquerading as Mr. Tuttoor because his story was not a pretty one. He had been run out of the deep South where he had worked at a prison in which slaves were held, many of them runaways who were caught in the process. For a fee, these slaves or any other which a master might bring in, would be punished and of course this was his job, which he dearly loved. He became overly aggressive and after having caused serious discount in the value of some number of slaves for resale, he was dismissed. He then got drunk and gained access to some unfortunate souls off the street and was punishing those who had committed no offense, nor whose masters had ordered such. After much debate, the local officials had demanded that he pay restitution to the owners, leave the state, and to be arrested if he set foot in the South again.

In debt to those he was to pay restitution to, out of work and desperately on the run with his stolen slave and their son, he had stumbled across this abandoned shack at Three Creeks and moved in. They now lived off her garden and what he could shoot and more often than not what he could appropriate from some unsuspecting neighbor. There was a ready market for various kinds of wild animal skins, but he was too shiftless to try that: hense, there was very little cash. He could seldom go to Dodys for store-bought whiskey, and was really quite tired of making do with the rot-gut brew he made; however, he stole some pretty good stuff from time to time.

The brothers tried to visit but after they got past wondering if their father was still alive, and whatever happened to their mother, they had little in common. Tuttoor (Quinton) ordered Maud to bring whatever there was to eat along with more whiskey as they continued their casual conversation. Tuttoor soon brought up the Junior incident and how enraged he was with Purdy, and how he must get even. He also spoke of how Purdy's wife was the most beautiful and desirable female he had ever seen. She was of little interest to Cooper, however, so he chose leaving her involvement in their scheme up to brother Quinton. Soon the brothers had an animated conversation going that lasted well into the night, and well into the whiskey jug. By morning they had a well-polished scheme to entertain themselves.

Henry had run the mill right up to midnight on Saturday, and was shutting down for a week to tend to some much needed repairs and also take the opportunity to get a few days off. Junior Tuttoor was now working at the mill a few hours each day and right off it seemed he had a natural talent for the mill's machinery plus he tried hard to please the customers. Tuttoor seldom frequented the settlement but he sent word that he would allow Junior to spend time at the mill for pay, so as long as Junior brought every dime home to him. Junior had asked Henry for half of his pay in money each week, but save half "on account" for some other time. Junior enjoyed being helpful at the mill but the real treat was to eat a meal up the hill with the Purdy boys. Besides Trisha and Mattie cooking lots of good stuff, their mom was fun, always cutting up and acting silly. He wished his mom knew how to laugh.

It had been a wonderful weekend at Three Creeks. The traveling preacher had married a young couple on Saturday and held Sunday church services over at the school-church too. Everyone had come, many of them on Saturday, spending the day over at the store "provisioning" or at the mill waiting for their grain. Between the picnicking, ball games, races, horseshoes, playing music and just plain visiting they waited for the bride and groom. Mattie played her fancy fiddle and neighbors from far and wide sat in awe as she played the wedding pieces, and then again later at the party when she joined in with the other musicians to add her citified flair to a few of their country favorites. The sky was clear and the moon was nearly full making night about as bright as day, so those who had somebody home to chore stayed till late Sunday knowing they could see well to get home. It was a great gathering, mostly a party with church thrown in by a fine young minister who spoke well, and who was not so much hell-fire and brimstone as he was a teacher. John's main employee, Mr. Morris, was turning out to be a real jewel, having just the right amount of take charge without becoming pushy. Between him, his well trained staff and John, they had nearly sold the shelves bare.

Monday was a day made in heaven; the Kentucky sky was so blue that it almost hurt the eye and good smells of Mother Earth permeated the air. Mid-afternoon Mattie started down to the garden spot below the hill to gather some fresh bounty and see what wild blooms the valley had left to offer. She loved to pick a bouquet from the 25 kinds or so of the ever changing variety of beautiful wild flowers and to dig in the fertile bottomland dirt. As she dawdled along the stream, she passed by the great mill wheel and marveled at how seldom it was quiet around there, for most generally there would be some wagons and drivers waiting about for their milled grain. She arrived at the garden and marveled once again at how nature decorated this lowland all summer long, then picked a wild rose and smelled it while passing through the garden gate to dig and pluck.

Johnson and Sledge, the evil-minded pair that had frightened Mattie, and that she always tried to avoid, certainly had not been wedding guests or over to Three Creeks for church, but they were passing through. The pair stopped at Dody's tavern for a spell until finally Dody's brother who was in charge for the day refused to sell them any more, so they wandered outside. And caught sight of Mattie.

It was truly unfortunate that Dody and his family were taking the day off after the big wedding. Not one of them was around and they all knew of the incident; any one of them would have watched the pair and have warned the Purdys. Instead Dody's brother paid little mind as Johnson and Sledge watched greedily for a while as Mattie went strolling along with her basket. She passed the quiet mill and splashed along the creek like a child, until she was way down by the garden where she picked a flower and held it to her face. She then continued on inside the gate, for John and the boys had built a sturdy fence around the garden to keep the critters from enjoying everything they grew.

Johnson and Sledge could barely contain themselves as they looked at each other knowingly. Leaving their mules a fair distance away, they crept down into the valley where they had Mattie Purdy trapped. Like a bunny in a box!

When Mattie realized the presence of others in the garden they were standing right over her.

Quite startled, she stood up and faced them.

"Well now, the fair Mrs. Purdy."

"May I help you somehow?"

"You bet you can!"

They both grabbed at her and Johnson succeeded in getting his hand inside the front of Mattie's clothes and tore them away. He was amused and a little baffled at the wrap she wore to support her breasts, for he had never seen a woman do that before. He tore it away as well, exposing her to the waist. While Johnson held her, Sledge took his razor sharp hunting knife and stuck it into Mattie's waistband, cutting her skirts and all else away. As they stood there looking at her magnificent body, Johnson remarked:

"Ah, a sure nough blonde"

"There is a overhang right over there. Let's take her over there cause somebody could come along here I reckon, but we can be out of sight over there for sure."

There was no point in Mattie's screaming for there was no one with in earshot to call out to.

"My husband will see you rot!"

"I don't see him right now. Too bad. On the other hand that would be good cause I would like to give the arrogant son of a bitch a taste of this knife!"

The muscular Sledge put his hand behind her neck with his hand on around to cover her mouth, and lifted her with his other arm through her bare bottom. Johnson grabbed on too and they carried her struggling and flailing out of the garden over to the small cave where they threw her on the ground. She immediately sprang to her feet and stood staring at them with fire in her eyes. Mattie had the beauty of a mature woman now; still buxom and shapely with her flat stomach, she looked softer and even more robustly feminine than she had as a teenage bride. Her breasts had some wear and tear from four boys; however, they still held their magnificent shape for she always supported them just as Mrs. Purvis had taught her. They now rose and fell as she stood heaving from her breathlessness. Both men continued to petrify poor Mattie with their knives, until Sledge finally put the point of his against her left breast hard enough to draw a bit of blood.

"Now you, if you behave and do me real good you might not get hurt cause I want you looking fine for the next time and the time after that.

I am always going to be out there waiting for you; you're just going to have to wonder where and when. You better be quiet and do me real good. If you don't wiggle like a fish I just might cut this part off."

"Gentlemen, please! I am the mother of—

Sledge put his hand over her mouth.

"I been wanting you ever since I first saw you. You are mine now, so shut up! All you are going to do is what you done a thousand times before. It ain't gonna hurt so get on the ground. Get ready. Get ready and do me now, or I'll make it so you cry every time you look in the mirror."

Sledge stuck the knife to her throat and once more drew a bit of blood as he forced her to the ground. Mattie desperately thought of her options, and would die if it were only she that she had to worry about. But four motherless boys?

Meanwhile Johnson nervously licked his lips. Even seconds here would be wonderful. Besides, he owed her one for the whack on his head with the hat blocking tool.

Mattie closed her eyes, prepared for the inevitable as she prayed out loud:

"Dear God, please rescue these poor creatures' souls from the dark places they are."

Then, a different sort of sound caused Mattie to open her eyes a bit, and she stared in wide-eyed amazement. A huge Negro man with a chest as big as a barrel and small hips set on top of legs built like oak trees had stepped from around the false back wall of the overhang. Johnson, who was eagerly waiting his pleasure, turned to follow her gaze and ducked just in time to avoid the full force of the walking stick; however, Bos knocked him sprawling to the ground anyway. Sledge was on his knees where he was preparing to assault Mattie, and as he began to regain his feet this huge Negro man hit him perfectly with a right uppercut. The blow lifted him completely off of the ground and sent him flying with a shattered jaw, minus some teeth, and with his nose crushed to one side. Bos then spun and knocked the recovering Johnson unconscious with one blow. Sledge regained himself somewhat and came up with his knife still in hand and threw it hard, burying it deep into Bos' inner thigh. He then took off running. Mattie was on her knees by now and grabbed Johnson's knife where it had fallen, and reached it to Bos. He tried to follow Sledge; however, the deeply buried knife had wounded his leg too severely for him to run. Mattie and Bos watched helplessly as Sledge disappeared into the trees.

The huge Negro limped back to where Mattie now stood in a state of wide-eyed amazement. He turned his face away as she spoke to him.

"Who wha wha where did you come from?"

Bos continued to look away.

"I just be in dere mam."

"How bad are you hurt?"

"It pretty bad mam."

Johnson stirred and was staggering as if to get up on all fours, so Mattie grabbed Bos walking stick and swung it hard at his head, just like she swung the bat when she played ball with her boys. Johnson fell senseless. The walking stick was the perfect weapon and she continued thumping as hard as she could with it, striking him first on his head, then in his face and next across his shoulders. She then jammed it repeatedly end first into his gut and crotch, and whatever else she could find to hit, she hit and hit and hit. Finally, after she was exhausted and sucking hard for air, she made her way back to Bos who was now sitting on a large rock. He had pulled the knife from deep in his leg and sat grasping both of his hands over the enormously angry looking wound. Still, he purposefully avoided looking at her. Gasping for air she collapsed to a sitting position on the rock next to him, where some sharp edges shocked her back to reality.

Except for her shoes, Mattie was stark naked!

As she raced back to the garden to get what was left of her clothes, Bos sat on the big rock and reflected miserably on how much trouble he was really in.

He could not keep running, in fact he could now barely stand, let alone walk.

He was a runaway slave.

He had hit not one, but two white men.

He had seen a white woman naked.

Where Bos came from, they could kill a black man for any one of these offenses.

It had taken several days, but by the end of the week Mattie was able to mostly force the wretched ordeal down at the garden to the back of her mind. Mattie was a strong person and now she had Bos to nurse and was back in the safe confines of her home. Meanwhile, John Purdy had spent hours talking to Simpson and continued to be puzzled as to his next course of action. John always valued the older man's counsel, and in particular this time, for there was much at stake in this mess.

Simpson granted indeed that this was a complicated muddle. First of all they agreed that John should have killed Johnson the moment he first saw him. That would have been a "hot-blooded" killing and the law went easy on men who killed their wife's assailant in hot blood. Johnson was now locked in a grain bin up at the mill and John had taken a few days to think on it, so if John went back to the grain bin and killed him now, it would be in plain cold blood. That was a completely different matter. A premeditated thoughtful cold blooded killing, even in this circumstance, was punishable by at least 20 years in prison if not by hanging.

The confounding issue of course was that there was a runaway slave in the formula. The punishments for harboring a runaway or even helping a slave escape were well spelled out in the Fugitive Slave Act of 1850. This law made it mandatory that anyone and everyone must help return a runaway slave to their owner and was especially severe with those who did not. This big black fellow had risked it all to keep Mattie from being raped and John absolutely insisted that turning him in was not an option, yet if the law became involved there was no way that Bos' presence could be explained.

John was adamant; Bos would be protected until he was able to travel.
This was not optional.
Period!

The big fellow had a very serious wound and there was no way he could possibly get back on the move for some time to come. From the appearance of the wound, that was going to be quite a spell, and in fact Mattie was very worried because by its current appearance infection was probable. Mothers just know about such things. Mattie was taking great pains in changing Bos' bandages when she and the boys delivered food down at the little cave by the garden spot. She asked him repeatedly if he would please move up to the house. He was fearful to do so and although he was being hidden, well fed and nursed, Bos desperately wanted to keep moving north.

Johnson was a mess, having some loose teeth where his jaw was broken and a severely crushed nose where Bos had hit him and that says nothing of the beating Mattie had given him with the walking stick. She had broken some of his facial bones, an arm, some ribs, and he was terribly sore where she had driven the stick straight into his gut. He was also especially sore in his crotch. Mattie never went near where he was locked in the grain bin over at the mill, although Henry had given him a corn shuck mattress and set buckets of water and some mush in the dark bin for him.

John really liked the way Teacher Brown seemed to reason things out and asked him to join Simpson and him in their conversations about Bos. Brown concurred. The only sure way to keep the Negro safe was to avoid having the law involved. This meant either killing Johnson or letting him go. Brown also thought too many people knew about the incident and they would never get away with killing Johnson days later. Plus, there was no telling where Sledge had run off to and he was also a wild card in the deal. Still, if Sledge reported the Negro, his own presence at the scene would have to be explained, making it unlikely but uncertain if he would ever do so. If the Negro's true owners or someone else who knew him showed up, there would undoubtedly be some tall explanations to make, but other than that, they could probably develop a cover story that the locals would want to believe.

The only solution Purdy, Simpson and Brown could come up with was to scare the hell out of Johnson and let him go. Simpson and Brown would show great support for Purdy and try to scare both Johnson and his partner, Sledge, enough they would never show their faces around Three Creeks again.

The other remaining wild card of course was if someone recognized the big black fellow for there were thousands of runaway slaves and slave catchers, and committees of owners were always out looking for runaways. The good news was that Three Creeks was still somewhat off the beaten path and only a few of them ever stopped by during their searches for runaways. John and his confidants finally concluded that either Johnson or Sledge might possibly go to the law, but with what they had been trying to pull off, that was doubtful. They also questioned that anyone would make it all the way here from the western riverbanks of Louisiana, searching for the huge Negro who called himself Bos.

The bad news was that these were all chances they simply must take.

Simpson stuck his neck way, way out:

"Everybody knows I have dozens of slaves and am always looking for a bargain. Never thought that big fellow I bought from that itinerate slave buyer would come in so handy on his very first day."

Purdy was fast on the uptake:

"Yeah I guess I better buy him from you; after all, my wife thinks he is pretty special."

"I'll take $100 more than I paid."

"I never owned a slave before, and you know I do not believe in it, but this one is a very, shall we say unusual case."

Purdy handed Simpson $100.

Simpson proceeded to write out a bill of sale for one large Negro man, about 25 years old who answers to the name Bos. Farther described as almost six and one half feet tall and having a large chest and with legs like trees.

"Owning a slave is no big deal. About one in five who already live in Kentucky are slaves. We own about 200,000 of em. Join the smart people. Here, better take this and have it recorded, in about 100 years."

Teacher Brown immediately became a co-conspirator:

"I remember seeing that coffle come by. Must have been well over a hundred or so and the fellow said he could not even remember where he bought them all. By the way, Simpson, it was very kind of you to give the school such a nice gift. $100 will buy a mighty fine new set of reference books and maps. I will write you out a receipt in the morning right after I order them."

Simpson smiled wryly and handed Brown Purdy's $100.

"You are too smart to be just a school teacher."

"Thanks. I have done a few other things in my lifetime."

Purdy marveled about friends willing to take such chances for him without even being asked to do so, and knew he would return the favor five fold if given the chance. They realized that too, and knew he was not a man to forget. People need friends like John Purdy.

The three of them went back to the mill where they took Johnson outside and set him leaning up against a post. His head was bandaged around his jaw, his arm was splinted and he had heavy wrap around his broken ribs. Simpson got right down in his face:

"Do you remember what you and your partner Sledge were trying to do?"

"Barly." Johnson managed to respond.

"What were you thinking?"

"Wus drnk."

"What?"

"Drunk."

"That is no damn excuse."

"Slorrey."

"We could have you hung."

"Yeth."

Brown came over, and for the first time ever, Simpson and John Purdy saw him armed. He was wearing a Colt six shot with a nine inch barrel in a well-worn holster now tied securely to his leg. It was an enormous piece weighing about five pounds!

Brown looked Johnson straight in the eye:

"Can you throw your hat in the air."

"Noth."

"Somebody throw his hat in the air."

Simpson obliged and took Johnson's hat and threw it about straight up over his head. Brown drew the big iron from his hip and fired six rounds perfectly to keep the hat floating in space. As the hat fell to the ground, Brown flipped out the cylinder and replaced it with another loaded one in less time than it takes to tell. He then dropped his aim and using his left hand to fan the hammer, in about four more seconds he fired six additional rounds into the post, very, very close to the top of Johnson's head. All 12 rounds had taken about 20 seconds.

"John Purdy is my friend, his wife is my friend, and his children are special to me. Do you understand what I say?"

The terrified splinter-covered Johnson could hardly get his breath, and a trembling "Yeth Slur" was all he could manage.

Brown continued his interrogation, as both he and Simpson were both now right in Johnson's face.

"If we let you go, will you stay out of Three Creeks?"

"Yeth, Oh, Yeth Slur!"

"Forever?"

"Yeth!"

"Will you keep that skunk Sledge out of Three Creeks?"

"Oh, Yeth!"

"Where is he now?"

"Don't know."

"Where do you think?"

"Running."

"To where?"

"Away."

"Will he find you again?"

"Probly."

"Where do you two live?"

"Shack ofar ta ingin country."

"Get gone, a long ways gone away."

"O tay!"

"Soon!"

"Will go nowth."

John stood with his hands on his hips:

"I will have my Indian friends stop by, so go get your stuff. Your shack is not safe for you any more. Do you understand?"

"Yeth!"

Brown stuck his finger in Johnson's face:

"I am here to tell you if you ever show that ugly face here again you will have me and everybody else within ten miles to reckon with. I for one would like nothing better than to gut shoot you and watch you die slow. I want you dead. Do you hear me? Do you understand what I say?"

"Oh, Yeth Thur, Yet Thur!"

"Apologize to Mrs. Purdy."

"Yeth thur. Whes slee be?"

"I am right here, Mr. Johnson."

"Plezz fodiv me."

"Probably take a long time Mr. Johnson. Right now all I want is to see you gone."

"Yeth Mam."

So, completely against all of their own wishes, they loaded Johnson on his mule and set him loose.

Afterwards John walked up to Teacher Brown;

"That was quite a show! You seem to have a lot of hidden talents. Since we are getting in so deep together, I like to call all of my dearest of friends something beside Mr. What name do you use other than Mr. Brown?"

Simpson was a bit wide-eyed himself;

"Yeah, me too."

Brown responded as he holstered his still smoking pistol and turned back towards the school house;

"Well, they used my initials H.W. on the wanted posters, but I would really prefer if you all just called me Brown."

A goodly distance away, Sledge rode out of the woods and up beside his partner. Johnson hardly recognized him. His nose had not been set properly and it was now pretty much to the side of his face, pointing more sideways yet. He was minus several teeth on the noseless side of his face.

"Been here watchin. Bout all I could do. I fell pretty hard getting out of there and my bad knee is givin me lots of trouble."

"I figured you'd be close. Damn! Sledge, that nigger did a job on your face!"

"Hard to get used to looking or eating like this. Anyway I figured they was a takin keer o you better than I could right now."

"Yeth. But I shore got tired setting in that grain bin."

"I got our stuff in a wagon I stole up here. We best get gone."

"Yeth. I need to lay down in the wagon, cause sittin astraddle this mule hurts."

"We need to get gone. Let's go up to Missouri for now. We can lay out and get more well."

"O tay."

Sledge peered at his partner more closely;

"From where I were it sounded like that fella Brown shure could handle a pistol. Looks like he did not hurt you none though."

"They soft hearted. Face sore as hell, crotch sore as hell were the woman hit me in the balls, ribs hurt the worst. Eat all I could."

As Sledge helped his partner get in the wagon he made a promise;

"Get you well, then we'll come back for another visit. I am going to shoot me a big nigger and then I'll serve you up some nice blond woman bottom." Sledge hitched their old mules to the wagon and then helped Johnson lay down in the back.

This time one of the passengers wished the mules would move even more slowly as they plodded away.

Away for now, anyway.

In the following days Mattie took care of Bos the best she knew how, even boiling the bandages as she had heard that helped. Still the wound on his leg became more angry with tell-tale long red lines appearing, causing both her and Brown to look at it with more concern each passing day. As he stood watching Mattie bandage the wound, Brown confirmed that he too was pretty certain blood poison was setting in. Finally the wound demanded drastic action and they decided it would surely have to be lanced to let the enormous amount of infection drain. What happened next completely amazed them, for as they carefully drained the wound it began bleeding profusely.

The bleeding got worse and worse.

Brown seemed to have several approaches to the crisis and he and Mattie tried everything they had ever heard about. The blood flow simply could not abated. In spite of an expert use of alum and a tourniquet Bos' life was spurting away.

Brown had a resolute expression on his face.

"Mattie, the only thing I ever saw work on such bleeding was to cauterize the wound."

"Where can we find a doctor to do such a thing?"

"No doctor I know of would come all the way over here to treat a Negro, or for that matter could get here in time anyway."

"What happens if we do not find somebody?"

"He will die, Mattie, or if we keep the tourniquet on he will at least lose the leg."

"Do you know anybody who might cauterize it. Anybody else at all?"

"I have done it."

"How many times have you done such a thing? Who was your worst patient?"

Brown raised his shirt and pointed to a huge scar with burn marks that ran clear across his gut.

"I was my toughest case."

Bos reluctantly allowed himself to be brought to the house. They fastened him down on a large table so that his threshing about would not create problems, and the bleeding leg was tied even more securely to a strong board. Bos was wide-eyed in sheer terror, very near panic, for he knew first hand about slaves and hot irons. He could not imagine someone using a red hot iron on you so something good could happen. Mattie looked down at the wretched creature and then sat on the table so she might squiggle in, until his head was on her lap. She held a large glass of whiskey to his lips and insisted he drink it, every drop. Then she cuddled the huge black man's head and sat with one arm wrapped around it, wiping his face with a cool cloth in the other hand.

Bos felt something on his face so he opened his eyes to look up. It was a tear. She was looking down at him, crying! A beautiful blonde headed white woman was crying over him. Him. A runaway slave that if Coopert ever caught, he would whip, burn all over with a white hot iron, roll around in the nail barrel, and then set the dogs on. As he lay there Bos made a mighty resolve. If he got well, anybody else who ever tried to harm this exquisite creature would definitely have to get past him first. And it would not be easy. He would die first.

After Bos finished the whiskey, Brown gave his patient a biting stick about three quarters of an inch in diameter to clench in his teeth. He then poured on more bacon grease, and holding the knife by its handle he stirred the pine knot fire until the knife was white hot. John continued to try and keep the blood flow down by managing the tourniquet and still wash the blood away as Brown spread the wound so he could see what he was doing. Mattie tried to sooth Bos as she and John both looked on, for neither could imagine anyone having the guts to do such a thing to another, Negro or not. When Brown started doing what he had to do, Bos simply could not suppress the low guttural sounds that escaped his throat. As the smell of seared human flesh first reached her nostrils, Mattie heard the biting stick snap.

Virginia told Mammy what was coming and Mammy in turn had assembled the entire Island View household staff, and laid down the ultimatum. Mammy might seem to others as just a happy go lucky plump senior household slave, complete with a big smile to show off her mouthful of pearly white teeth. Make no mistake about it. Everything that happened, or did not happen, inside the walls of the mansion was in her domain. If you pleased her, she was sweet as honey, but slack your duty and it was cotton pickin time! It was unfortunate that she held no dominion outside the walls, except for the kitchen building, for the grounds would certainly have been maintained differently. Virtually every spot in the huge mansion appeared as if company was coming any minute now, and refreshments were always at the ready for guests who never came anymore. Mammy would never have thought of herself as such, but she truly was an efficient executive. Today she was humming a happy little tune for it was a fine day and she felt up to about anything. She would need absolutely everything she had.

"Child this is a day I have prayed would come."

"Mammy, you know your part?"

"Yes, Ma'am."

"No matter what I say, you say no."

"Yes, Ma'am."

"Even if I threaten you with the whip?"

"Yes, Ma'am."

"And the others?"

"They know what you say do."

"Do you want me to talk to them?"

"No, Ma'am. Not less you just wants to."

Virginia said mostly to herself:

"I am so scared. I am scared to death, Mammy, really scared; it may not be so bad though. Still I hear it can be hard. Don't you give in, Mammy."

"No matter what, I get you down and set on you to get you away from the whiskey."

Then Mammy scurried away. Amanda, the slave in charge of all of Gotfield's caregivers, was instructed on how to conduct herself and was trying to prepare herself, but she was even wide-eyed fearful. Terrified.

Poor Amanda considered even thinking that she was to disobey Missus to be an unforgivable offense, and she felt particularly vulnerable. Most of the household staff could simply disappear because being invisible was part of a household servant's training from Mammy. The unfortunate Amanda had lots of regular daily contact with Virginia, and could not simply disappear with the others while all this was going on.

But still, Miz. Virginia had told them to.

Just on the whiskey issue.

But still, it was to disobey.

It could be a rough week.

And it was.

John Norman, along with his middle son Lance and an old and dear friend, the retired Dr. Kahn, arrived promptly as promised at 10:00 Monday morning. A pleasant tea was served while they sat about and chatted. At about noon Virginia started wanting a drink but was able to easily pass it off. About 2:00 she began to shake just a little bit and knew a drink would settle her down. It hit Virginia hard about dinnertime, with her shakes becoming impossible for anyone to ignore. It was about then she indeed began to desperately want and need a drink. About midnight, her flesh begin to crawl and when she got on her knees and tearfully begged Mammy so very pitifully for just one small drink of whiskey. Mammy wrapped her arms around Virginia and held her in loving embrace, but Mammy wasn't even tenative. Along towards morning Virginia was so desperate for a whiskey she was threatening to skin Mammy alive and was looking for a whip while she pillaged through all of the hiding places in her room that she had ever hid a bottle.

With the dawn came the bugs. Thousands and thousands of bugs. They were everywhere. Then the snakes. Her bed was covered with snakes and then there were snakes with the twins' heads on them, and then the snakes started eating the bugs. Virginia cowered in a corner shrieking for someone to kill the snakes, as Mammy tried to hold her and calm her down, but she was terrified, for the snakes were everywhere and there was no place to hide. She needed whiskey and there was no damn body that would help her. All these so-called friends were just there to laugh at her and Dr. Kahn was just a damn fake and why did he care what her heart rate and blood pressure were. If he really cared he would give her whiskey. Damn Lance Norman any way! How could he possibly know what she was going through because he had only seen imaginary snakes and these in her room were real and she, by God, needed whiskey.

Dr. Kahn gave her something and Virginia collapsed on her bed and slept for a while. When she woke she was alone. She jumped out of bed for she remembered there was always whiskey in the great library and so she slowly opened the door preparing to creep down there. Mammy, resting on a cot across the doorway, barred her way.

"You wants to go for a walk, honey?"

Virginia slammed the door in her face, went back into her room and decided she could make her way off the veranda and find whiskey. But this time Lance Norman joined her, offering his arm as though they might walk down the veranda stairway together. She grabbed him, sort of tussled with him and then threw up all over both of them.

"You cannot understand how I need whiskey." She sobbed.

He held her back as a friend would hold a friend away from the fire and looked her straight in the face.

"I am so sorry, but the truth is I do understand, Virginia. There is none. We threw it all away."

Virginia became hysterical:

"All of it? Surely to God not all of it!"

Dr. Kahn again offered some relief, but very little even when Virginia became violently ill. She sweat, she cried, she shook, she ran from the bugs, she tried to kill the snakes, she threw up, she soiled herself, she had chills, her heart raced and her blood pressure went high to low and back to high. All this while the good doctor could do little except keep a close watch both day and night. When Wednesday came, Virginia was completely exhausted and stank so one could smell her from clear across the room. Her breath was rancid from retching and retching, and she had strained so hard trying to puke that she had bled from her eyes, which were now sunken in their sockets. She had not kept any food down since Monday lunch, and had aged 20 years in those three days. Mammy had cleaned her up time after time, but still, Virginia stank and looked grotesque as she wept from under puffy eyelids covering deep sunken holes above her snotty red nose. She still desperately wanted whiskey but at least the snakes were gone. Most of the time anyway.

Mammy had her completely undressed and was attempting to clean her up yet one more time, when Virginia collapsed to the floor and started crawling about on all fours. The old black woman sat down and her mistress crawled over to her so the old slave might hold her head. Virginia collapsed face down in to Mammy's lap and retched again. Mammy could not reach a coverlet so she sat there and lovingly held her stinking, hiccupping, snotty, trembling, retching, naked mistress. One of the richest women in 1850s America was also the most pitiful one.

Virginia de Falco Dinkins lay naked, both body and soul.

Time stood still.

John Norman continued to drill Mammy; Mammy, are you sure you can keep her under continuous watch for the next few weeks?"

"She ain't gonna breath ifin I don't lets her."

"She can be mighty clever. Are you certain you got all of the whiskey?"

"I'm done throw it all away, and I look everywhere for more. Even if der be more she gona have to drink it whiles me or Amanda watch and I am here to tells ya that ain't gonna happen."

"I will be back out in a few days. Watch her like a hawk. Do not underestimate her. She may have a bottle in the icehouse, or the cook-house or even down in the quarters. She cannot be let out of sight."

"Yes sir, Mr. Norman, Mammy understands alright."

The old black woman was the happiest slave in the county, for after these horrible years, if she did her part right she was going to get her Missus back!

Finally, Virginia asked Mammy to have someone prepare a tub full of hot water so that she might take a bath. Mammy's mouth full of white teeth looked like the rising sun as she hummed and lovingly prepared the bath water herself. Later in the week when John Norman came back out he was impressed for he thought Virginia had done remarkably well. As a matter of fact his Lance had gone cold turkey many times that took much longer and were far more excruciating. He shared that with her, congratulated her and they had a nice visit about times gone past. He took his leave feeling pretty good about things:

"Virginia, you must really want to rid yourself of the demon. They say that sometimes happens when one has a new mission in life."

Up in Kentucky, the day after Brother Cooper arrived, John Purdy was out and about the neighborhood again promoting his business and keeping up with the neighbors far and wide. He took notes on what major purchases each family wanted to make and frequently took orders for goods he must bring into the store. John was a popular figure, for he carried candy to all the kids, and was a respected confidant with those he visited. Habitually he was seen riding like the wind on his magnificent stallion, Star, and as often as not he rode Indian style without saddle or bridle or neither.

John was always up for the racing challenges laid down by his Chickasaw friends, who would trail their ponies in behind wagons of grain they brought to have ground at the mill, or when they brought in their beeswax or furs to trade. Together they laid out challenging courses tracing out in the open and through the trees, with each participant required to grab flags of their particular color along the way. Star could outrun any one of them on a straight run; however, the more experienced Indian riders on their more nimble ponies would gain the advantage twisting through the turns. Everyone around stopped what they were doing to watch and cheer the riders, who always wound up collapsed and laughing at the end of the race which was normally at the store where the crowd congregated. John, admitting defeat, would give the braves their prizes of sweets and tobacco and remind them if he ever won they had to make Mattie some nice Indian ware. The Indians would spend their waiting hours teaching and showing John the finer techniques of handling his magnificent animal. With just knees, or hands, or shifting his weight, or his hold on the mane, or voice commands or all combined, they taught John and Star to thread a needle. John knew first hand there was absolutely no finer light cavalry in the world than these braves and their ponies.

One of John's normal routes took him out by the Tuttoors. The Tuttoor shack was not far from the road and it sat where one could easily peer out and see passers by, but it was difficult to see clearly as it sat in among the brush and trees. The old cabin shack stood about 15 feet by 18 feet with a fireplace on the back wall and a small front porch. Maud and Junior had chinked the logs against the wind and papered the inside walls with newspaper. She had also hung a curtain across one corner to separate the homemade bed frame and corn shuck mattress from the crude kitchen with its homemade table and chairs. Maud had done the very best she could, but the place really needed to be burned down. Junior had built for himself a lean-to as a room, using the outside wall of the fireplace as his back wall, then covered the open side with animal skins. Except in the most disagreeable weather, heat from the back of the fireplace made the lean-to tenable, and he much preferred being there, away from his stormy and unpredictable father. When Uncle Cooper Tooter arrived, he took the bed which left Tuttoor and Maud with a pallet on the floor. Cooper had also backed his wagon into the small three-walled pole shed out back which still left room for his fine mare and Tuttoor's horse. The mules had no shelter.

When Cooper Tooter had first seen the ramshackle place, he immediately reasoned he would soon move on, for he was particularly disgusted by such quarters and especially the smell of urine around the front door. Maud and Junior went back to the woods of course, but his brother found that too much trouble and simply eliminated standing on the small porch. As the head of family Cooper would soon move them all to a place more fitting to a person of his means, where these underlings could then serve him both hand and foot. Cooper Tooter also reasoned that in the unlikely event his plan to become lord and master failed, he would soon move on. Alone.

The brothers Tooter knew that John Purdy was frequently out by himself and they could pick the time and spot to fit their scheme. Sure enough, as if on cue, while they were anxiously wondering when they would get their chance at him he came thundering by that very next day. The clods flew up high behind as he sat the back of his charging white stallion as comfortably as most men sit their rocking chair. The brothers Tooter were elated. It had been a short wait. Tuttoor knew full well John would be headed home before dusk, and as John had not yet met Cooper Tooter, he could be the perfect diversion. Per their plan, as John came galloping home Cooper was lying on the ground, playing possum with his face away from John, and holding his leg as if he were in deep pain. Star slowed down and stopped on command, halting right in front of Cooper which pleased John such that the animal would get a special treat tonight. He dismounted as Cooper, still lying face down in the dirt, moaned and gasped:

"I think my leg is broke"

"Where is your horse?"

"It ran away."

As he squatted and reached out to the man, Tuttoor slipped from his hiding spot with a large club and hit John smartly on the temple. When he collapsed they quickly secured the bag they had brought for just this purpose over their victim's head and then dragged him into the nearby woods.

As John slowly regained consciousness, he began to realize his circumstance, of being bound to a large tree in a kneeling position with a hood over his head. His ankles were tied together and his arms were pulled tightly around the tree overlapping each other so as to stretch the skin on his back taunt. He was both barefooted and stripped to the waist.

"Well now, Mr. Purdy, I see you are finally awake. It seems as if you have been acting like a smarty as of late!"

John tried very hard but his foggy mind could not recognize the voice.

"My friend here tells me you had your boys gang up on that fine young Tuttoor boy and disrespected the whole family."

John immediately knew what this was about. His muffled voice came through the bag:

"Tuttoor, I will have your hide."

"Well now we will report your lack of respect to Mr. Tuttoor but he is not here and does not know anything about this. We are just friends of his, and as friends of his, we think you got way too big for your britches, Mr. Purdy. A man has to respect talents such as Mr. Tuttoor has, and such as we have. Here, let me demonstrate."

Twhack O Pop!

John felt the lash brush his head as it popped but a fraction from his ear and, momentarily at least, he was thankful for the hood covering his head. The pop was enough to damage an uncovered eardrum.

The unfamiliar think that it is the popper on the end of such a whip snapping in the air that makes the noise. And that is true, sort of. What really happens in a properly constructed whip is that the energy in the large end of the whip becomes more concentrated as the whip diameter becomes smaller and smaller out toward the end. The pop from a whip properly swung comes from all of that energy suddenly hitting the popper which then actually breaks the sound barrier. The popper breaking the sound barrier on a good whip properly swung is loud enough to steer or stop the lead team in a twenty-mule hitch or to change the direction of a stampede.

Someone or somebodies popped their whips time and again within a fraction of an inch of John's head, and each time the noise was louder than a shotgun blast right at his ear. Each pop made him react involuntarily, to jerk as far as his bindings would allow. As he listened to chuckle after chuckle in the background, and their laughing at his dance he could also hear low voices challenging each other to get even closer, placing bets on the next given lash.

"Mr. Purdy, we would like to take a message back to the boy's father, our dear friend. Would you please have us tell him you are a sorry lot and that he is by far the better man than you? You best have us tell him you are scared as hell of him and will respect him as the better man from now on."

This time the fiery end of the lash seared the soft tissue in the small of John's feet as it danced over the tenderness of that part.

"Purdy, speak up! We are waiting your answer."

"Hell no!"

Whack!!

The lash hit John a bruising blow across his bare back, from high left to lower right.

"Mr. Purdy, there is no need to cuss for it's not polite. One can hit with the whip to hurt or cut or both. Now let's hear you say that Mr. Tuttoor is a man to be feared, or I shall have to show you a cutting lash."

John remained silent.

Swish O Thwack!

The lash cut John's back a wicked gash from the top right to the bottom left, making a big X with the first mark which had only left a welt. Through the searing pain John felt blood running down his back. Although he was ashamed to admit it even to himself, for the first time he could remember John Purdy felt completely helpless. He was getting scared.

Cooper Tooter's face was a mixture of evil and ecstasy. Every since Virginia had exposed him, he had harbored a psychopathic need to hurt somebody and it had kept building until he was about to burst. Now, on his first day here, he was getting his share of this man. He relished the next hour.

Junior Tuttoor burst into the small clearing screaming, with tears of anguish on his face;

"No! No! No! No! Stop! Stop! Stop!!!"

"Shut up, you young fool, he doesn't even know who we are!"

Junior fell to his knees to put his arms around John, then grabbed on to the rope holding John to the tree and commenced shielding him as best he could.

"Get the boy out of here!"

"Get out! Get to the house and keep your mouth shut or you'll get plenty of this whip."

"Go ahead! Whip me! Mr. Purdy is my friend. Hit me. I dare you. Hit me instead! All you ever do is beat on me or Ma. Neither one of you have the guts for a fair fight. You too! Hit me, Uncle, I can't hurt you!"

"That whelp is crazy! You should have control of him. Now Purdy knows it is us and anyway that boy will tell if we let him go. We have to kill them both!"

"We are not going to kill my boy. I need time to think."

"Why not? I'll kill him. Your precious baby boy. Ha. Hell, we both know what he is! Now he's betrayed us. He thinks more of Purdy than he does you!"

"We are not going to shoot the boy! Get out of here!"

"Not on your life. This guy I never even met can send me to prison. That ain't about to happen! Besides that, the whelp's put in with Purdy, so he'll not be any good to you. If you have no stomach for it, I'll kill both of them."

Whack!

Junior felt the wrath of his dear uncle's whip! Again!

Whack!

As the whip bit through his clothes, Junior set his mind, yet more determined than ever to hold on as long as he could. He wrapped his arms more tightly around John's bare back and shoulders to cling his very best. He screamed at the top of his lungs:

"Is that the best you got!"

His father shouted:

"Get out of the way so I can shoot Purdy and not hit you!"

Cooper Tooter's psychopathic need to hurt somebody was now in complete control and he didn't care who it happened to be. The kid would do just fine! He swung his whip. Hard.

Whack!

The whip tore through Junior's shirt and bit like a chain.

Junior flinched but started mocking his uncle:

"Go on, you sissy! You she/he! That's what you are, a degenerate she/he bitch. Don't be afraid to swing, you prissy sissy bitch!"

By now, Cooper Tooter was strengthened by his fury and stood waving his pistol around:

"Out of my way! And stop hollering and screaming and making so much noise. Nobody pays attention to whips popping but hollering will get people wondering. We ain't that damn far from the road!"

Tuttoor grabbed on to Cooper's gun hand;

"Stop hittin him! If anybody gonna hit the kid it's me. And keep that gun pointed away cause we ain't shootin him neither!"

Cooper Tooter kept a grasp of the gun in one hand and his whip in the other, attempting to swing the whip as he thundered;

"Well it's plain to see that kid aint't scared of you and he's got no respect for you. You're scared and afraid to do what's got to be done. You're a miserable failure at being a man."

Cooper swung his whip indiscriminately.

Whack!

Tuttoor stood facing his brother waving one fist, and clawing at his gun hand with the other:

"Don't you ever say that to me, you degenerate son of a bitch!"

Three of John's Chickasaw friends were the first to burst onto the small clearing for they had silently trotted up in softskin moccasins and heard Junior shouting at his uncle. They surprised the pair and quickly wrestled the Tooter brothers to the ground before either realized they had company, or could get a weapon pointed. Mr. Dody, plus Brother Henry and schoolteacher Brown, were only a minute behind.

"What in the name of God?"

"Do not hurt the boy, do not hurt the boy! Do not hurt the boy!" Were the only muffled words John could get out.

As the others set John free and uncovered his head, Brown grabbed Tuttoor by both sides of his shirt:

"What in the name of all that is Holy were you up to?"

Tuttoor mumbled.

"Tell me what you thought you were doing! Explain yourselves!"

"Mumble, Mumble."

Brown was close enough for Tuttoor to feel his spit as he screamed into his face:

"By God, I said explain yourself!"

John finally found his voice.

"They did not show their faces, nor had I seen them with that sack over my head. They knew I would not be able to testify against them if I never really saw them. They are real cowards. Whipping me with a bag over my head all because we taught the boy a lesson in being normal instead of being bullies like they are. They knew I would figure it was him, and Tuttoor wants me to be scared to death of him."

By now the Chickasaws had the brothers securely bound with their own whips. The Indians looked at each other:

"We show them how to be afraid, Mr. John. As how did you say, 'Scared to death?' They will shake and quiver at mention of you. And we make sure anybody knows who they are with one look."

Brown growled;

"Horse whipping a white man in Kentucky without a court order will get you 20 years or a hanging. Do what you want: they won't go to the law. Don't kill em but make em wish to hell you had."

Leaving the Indians in charge of the perpetrators, the white men started managing John and Junior towards the house, getting them to the spring wagon that Dody had quickly borrowed from a couple of customers so he could come along for the fun. The large bloody gash across

John's back looked nasty; however, Junior had taken several more lashes than he, so John carefully put his arm around the boy as they held on to each other for the three-mile ride. Neither mentioned it, for they need not bother. They both realized that Junior Tuttoor could never go home again.

John asked Dody:

"How in Heaven's name did you know to come?"

"Simple. Star trotted by without you, but saddled up with the bridle hanging over the saddle horn. We figured you were playing Indian and had fallen off somewhere up this away where he come from. We were all planning on getting a good laugh at you walking home, and getting a drink out of you if you weren't hurt and needing help."

John shuddered to think at the probable outcome had he not been playing Indian, but had simply stopped and dropped the end of a rein on the ground. Star was a well-trained creature and when John set him loose and then disappeared, he would always head immediately for his stall at home. But Star was also rein broke to a fault, and had John simply dropped a rein on the ground, Star would have stood where he stopped all night long, waiting for his master to return and mount up. John could not help but wonder if that would have ever happened.

Anyway, the big stallion would get two apples tonight.

The Chickasaw had a reputation as friendly peaceful types, inviting strangers into their camps to share what they had, and often as not, their captives were taken into the home and made part of the family. Chickasaw captives were more apt to be made to sing and dance for entertainment as opposed to being run through a gauntlet such as the more brutal tribes required. They were not thought of as mean or brutal toward their enemies or those they captured; however, that did not mean the Chickasaw did not know how. The Tooter brothers were dumped by the shack after they had been given special treatment by the braves, mostly because they had been sadistic to their friend. The chief would heartily approve, for John was also a man who had the blood of a Chickasaw chief in his veins. At any rate, neither brother would ever hold a whip again as neither had a complete thumb, index or center finger on either hand. Their ears were notched and their nostrils were slit.

A hot coal had been touched to the tip of the tongue and another one still bound between the toes caused excruciating pain. They both of course had been emasculated.

When Maud Tuttoor responded to their cries, she demanded of them her boy's whereabouts, for he had raced to try and stop the foolishness after she had given him what details she had overheard. Tuttoor managed to point to the village and make her understand her son had gone with the others. Showing absolutely no emotion she dragged them into the shack one at a time and attempted to tend their wounds. Maud pondered as to who knew how to wreck such havoc on a body with so little loss of blood.

Must be a learned skill.

Down in Louisiana, Virginia sat out on a beautiful veranda, visiting with Mammy. The old Negro had been like her rock as she dried out, and Virginia was quick to realize that only one who truly loves the other can absorb such emotional abuse and strain. Virginia had loved the older woman as long as she could remember; however, if possible that love had become even stronger and mixed with a great deal of admiration and respect. Today Virginia was asking for a history lesson. Mammy never forgot much.

When Mammy was a child, during the time between 1817 and 1830, the city of New Orleans recorded over 41,000 deaths from yellow fever. Those 3,000 to 4,000 deaths each year were particularly devastating considering the small population. In spite of the twin scourges of yellow fever and cholera, by 1840 New Orleans' growing population of 102,000 made it the fourth largest city in America. Virginia knew it had recently been a particularly bad time, for history records 17,000 deaths during 1853, ˆ54, and '55 from yellow fever alone. Cholera was a completely different issue. On occasion neighborhoods, plantations and tributaries running into the Mississippi Delta were brutally hit by one scourge or the other. Mammy remembered the fever devastating Island View when Virginia was a little girl. During one such season much of the family and slaves worth several fortunes were buried. The suffering was incalculable.

"Mammy?"

"Yes, Miz. Virginia."

"How well did you know my Grandmother?"

"O' I knowed her pretty good. I was already a young woman when det old yellow fever kill her."

"What was she like?"

"She was a perfect lady. My momma and my grandmomma always help here at the big house. We all be out in the cookhouse getting ready for a party at the big house or something when your grandmomma comes in. I would get in the corner and be real still like my momma said, but your grandmomma always find something sweet and give to me. Seems I remember her most holdin out some cake or a cookie."

"What else do you remember?"

"She like you. Real smart in books and stuff. Never tried to let on but when I be turned down dey bed I hear her kind of telling your grandfather in her gentle kind of way what he need to do. He always seemed to say; Okay. he do it that way. I supposed he did."

"What else?"

"She always look after the slaves, made sure they ate good, why she even came to church once in a while down in quarters to hear what we was being learned. Probably caught that old fever looking out for somebody else."

"Do you remember the year of the fever?"

"Of course child, watched em bury my momma, my poppa and my grandmomma. Took your grandmomma and six more from the big house. Took all the white overseers. Took lots of slaves. Why there is way more than 150 graves out there in the cemetery all marked that year."

"Who taught you to count?"

"Your grandmomma. Started to teach me to read too, but Master was afraid to have a slave that could read so he put a stop to it."

"I remember Grandfather being scared to do a lot of things and he was so stormy."

"Yes he got that way. He needed the help from your grandmother's talk. He picks your father for husband to your momma because he thought he could help run the place. You know your papa; he was a lot older than your mama and had run someplace before. He marry your mama cause that for sure make him rich some day. She marry him cause your grandfather say so. After all that it turns out your grandfather would not listen to a thing he said, and finally your poppa just stop trying to tell him anything. It ain't my place to say so, but your momma should got to pick herself a nice young man."

"What about Aunt Marybeth?"

"Your grandfather pick her man cause his poppa was big shot of the bank. He thought having the banker's son in the family would get the bank to go easy on him. Marybeth and him never care for each other very much either, but he marry her on account of Island View, and she were also afraid to say no to her poppa. Marybeth would not move to town with him so they wound up here. Your Gotfield's papa got tired of

Marybeth being so cold. Missy's momma have an older sister, Gloria, that looked just like Missy does now, maybe even prettier. Your Gotfield's papa, he gets to liken her bed better than Marybeth's so he put Gloria in that house where all the meanness go on and then he spent more time there than he did here in the big house."

"Really?"

"Your grandpoppa, he raise old thunder with Marybeth's man about that. One night the two of em, Gloria and Mr. Gotfield's poppa, they just disappear together. My oh my what a rukus Marybeth and your grandpoppa have after that, got to screaming, shouting at each other just something awful. Her poppa tell Marybeth there ain't no worse disgrace for a southern lady than to lose her man to a slave. After they fight, Marybeth had us pack some stuff and stop a boat on the river. She gets on it and dat be the last we ever see of her."

"So Gotfield's father ran away and left him and his mother for a slave girl?"

"Yes honey, but not just any slave girl. Gloria was probably the prettiest slave girl ever was. She was young and smart and everbody knowed she really wanted him in her bed. Couldn't and didn't wait for night time they said. I think he really want her bad too, cause he gave up his son and a wife who was for sure gonna own half the biggest plantation in the country."

"Did Grandfather write Marybeth out of his will right away?"

"Child, I wouldn't know about such things as that."

"I bet he did."

"All I know is your grandpoppa got pretty sad after that and your momma say she gonna leave too unless he put some money in the bank for Sister Marybeth. I heard your grandpoppa tell Mr. Rawson not long for he die that sister Marybeth never take a dime."

"Did she ever write?"

"Not that I was ever told."

"So my cousin/husband lost both his mother and his father to a young slave girl. I never knew why his mother left or why his father disappeared for that matter and you know I was just a kid when my mother and father died. So that's really how come Grandfather wound up raising both his grandkids and no one to help?" It was more of a statement than a question.

"Your grandpoppa went through a terrible storm. Lost his wife and advice giver, lost his trusted white help, lost lots and lots of slaves. Some of them slaves were good friends and he loved em. He had more slaves die than most any other plantation ever have. I heard him say so. He almost had to sell a part of Island View, probably would have ifin it not be for Marybeth's man's family owning the bank. Your grandpoppa he had to be a good man at lots of stuff but he get pretty strange before he die. You know that."

Virginia sat musing, rolling all of this around in her head. Grandfather de Falco may have been good at some number of things, but choosing husbands for the women he controlled was not one of them. Maybe she thought, just maybe, I understand a little of it and why my grandfather would never allow his own two daughters' names ever to be spoken. It must have been guilt that caused him to make everyone pretend as though that generation had never existed. Virginia stood up and looked out towards the island, lost in thought, sorting down the facts, pondering again and again to herself. Her grandfather probably just did what he thought he had to do, and right now at least she was feeling a teeny bit of remorse about her feelings toward him. He had held the plantation together through what must have been an ungodly time and for certain his ever letting part of it fall into other hands would have been devastating in his mind's eye.

Virginia was brilliant when it came to sorting things out. She concluded that after all was said and done her mind had been in a prison all its own these past ten years and even after Grandfather had died and people could talk, she just never really cared enough to ask why it was like it had become. Now, at least she understood a little better how she got where she was. He would have felt that he must prevent losing a part of Island View for any reason, at any and all cost. He would have paid any price.

And that included her.

Up in Kentucky the brothers Tooter were bellowing again: they called Maud like she was a dog and treated her worst.

"Here, swoman here!"

"Det in here and empty this chlamber plot."

"Det me sometlhing to eat."

"I need new blandages."

"Clean sme up"

"Help me smove out to the plorch."

The bellowing just never stopped.

The brothers Tooter were truly ungrateful patients and bullies by nature. They both remained true to form, even in their diminished state. Their tongues were healing because the Indian's intent there was for lingering pain, not excessive permanent damage. Quite to the contrary, some of their toes were growing together so that their feet would always bear the effects of the hot coals. In a few days each of them could stand, but shifting weight to the front of a foot was impossible, and they crept slowly about moving their feet side to side somewhat like crabs. The two fingers and stubby thumbs that remained on each of their hands worked well enough; however, both the Quinton Tooter of days gone by and his brother Cooper were grotesque creatures to look at. Bedding together had always given Quinton the creeps, but they were both much too sore for either of them to sleep on the pallet. Quinton Tooter had always steadfastly refused to share any bed with his brother Cooper due to his strange tastes, but now there was no choice as there was but the one bed in the shack. Quinton Tooter and Brother Cooper Tooter made stranger bed partners indeed.

Interestingly enough Brown was quite correct: neither Tooter felt that they could possibly go to the law as it was an undeniable fact they were caught horsewhipping the leading citizen in the community. That could cost 20 years in prison, and besides that issue, Quinton knew he would undoubtedly spend more time in prison for failing to pay the owners of the slaves he had damaged. Cooper especially did not want to see a sheriff, for he still had a fortune in stolen cash.

Maud had her patients sitting outside in the fresh air looking at each other, in disgust, both realizing full well one was about the mirror image of the other. Slit nostrils and notched ears are hard to ignore. They were bemoaning their fate bitterly when Cooper changed the subject by demanding something "fit to eat" as opposed to the slop he claimed Maud had been serving.

She summed it up:

"There ain't no money to buy nothing: You get what I got."

Cooper managed to get up and crab walk into the shack behind the curtain where Maud overheard him rummaging about opening his trunk. Cooper's sore hands made it impossible to pick a gold coin out of one of the little individual pockets they were sewed into; however, he finally was able to grasp one of the bills. He crabbed back out and handed her a $100 bill on the Citizens Bank of Louisiana.

"Glet to Tlhree Cleeks and glet something flit for me to sleat and glet enough to slast for a swhile. And you bletter get at sleast $90 in gold for that bgill or I will slave your hideth!"

"Okay, I will get some stuff tomorrow. I want to see Junior anyway."

"No, you glo now!" Cooper demanded: "I said glet moving!"

He crabbed over and took his place.

Maud rode the mare to town and rushed into Purdys to see her boy. She was disappointed when she learned John had taken him out to the sawmill; however, they were due back in an hour or so. She presented the $100 bill to Mr. Morris who consulted his list of good money and gave Maud $95 in gold. She went across the street where Mrs. Dody informed her she was in luck; in about an hour she would be taking the day's baking out of the oven and there would be enough for her to have a whole basket full of fresh cake and bread. Maud accepted the piece of pie and coffee Mrs. Dody offered, and then sat quietly, for there were some awfully important types at a nearby table talking quite loudly

Two of the three men referred to the third one as Judge, and seemed to be presenting him with a dilemma.

"Judge, are you certain of that?"

"Absolutely. A slave never really owns anything. When the slave found the money it still belonged to whoever lost it, or if that person could not be found then it belonged to the slave's master. So it is very clear! This fellow Drake the slave gave the money to bought the slave from the master, with the master's own money."

One of the other chaps pondered;

"So Drake could neither buy him nor free him, because he actually had no right to either the money he used to buy him, or what he kept for his services? There was a lot left over and the slave gave it all to Drake, and apparently Drake has let it slip through his fingers. No wonder Drake's wife is mad as hell. She will kick his ass out of the house or want a divorce. Or both."

The other man:

"Hell yes! She will be heading out to the City of Kansas to dump his dumb ass. Me and my woman have lived together so long I tell her we must be common law married by now, but when she is mad she swears that is where she is heading."

The Judge smiled:

"Drake would be a lot better off if he would have claimed his wife found the money and he just wanted to free the neighbor's slave. Even if Drake's missus did get a divorce, he would get at least two thirds of her so called find. That would be worth a whole lot more to him than any slave him and his neighbor are fussing over. A slave is worth the price of a slave, but a rich ex-wife would be worth a lot of money. Especially if she found the money that made her rich while Drake was married to her. That goes for common law wives as well."

After Mrs. Dody gave Maud an enormous sack plus a large basket of the best of everything they had cooked for a $5 gold piece, Maud then found Junior and gave him a quick hug. After promising to be back soon, she trotted the mare back out to the shack. Maud rattled around in the cabin for a while, watching the pair out on the porch smashing their delicious meal into their mouths with what fingers they had left. Finally both of her patients dozed off. Quietly she slipped behind the curtain and opened the trunk and at first gazed in horror at Cooper's toys. Thumbscrew, branding iron, hand or leg cuffs, tongs made to separate finger and toe joints. She knew Quinton had some of this stuff too for he had threatened her with it in years gone by. God she hated these men.

Inspecting Cooper's greatcoat covering the trunk bottom and full well expecting it to hold a pocketful of cash she quietly lifted it and was amazed at how much it weighed. Putting her hand first into a pocket she found an open seam and was fishing about, when her eye caught a slit in the lining. Examining this more closely she reached her hand in and felt some of the bills. As she pulled out the first bill her eyes flew wide open for never had Maud seen bills of these denominations before. Big numbers. Maud knew her numbers to 100 but some of these bills had three zeros as opposed to the hundred dollar bill he had given her to go to Dody's.

As Maud continued to feel about she began to tremble. In addition to the paper money, there were dozens and dozens of gold coins sewed securely into little pockets in the lining. There was more and more and more. Maud had never set foot in a bank but there had to be as much money in this great coat as any bank might ever have.

As the plan begins to unfold in her mind, the first real smile in ever so long flickered across Maud's face.

She crept out and saddled Cooper's fine mare, then slipped back in and quickly gathered into a sack what few things she had that were worth keeping. She put on Cooper's greatcoat, then buckled his gun belt to the outside, for with the great coat bulking her up, the gun belt fit just right in the smallest notch. The weighted down coat and the heavy pistol felt good. She led the horses up to the front door, and stomped back up to the cabin:

"Well, I am a going now."

Both men were slow to rouse from their whiskey deepened slumber, so she allowed time for their appraisal of the situation.

"Tlake off my cloat!"

"Det black here swoman!"

"I'll tlake tle hidle off youth!"

"Your jlob is to tlake clare of us, youth blitch."

"Do not youth dare tlake my horthse!"

Maud smiled her sweetest smile.

"Taking a horse out of your own barn can't be stealing."

Coopert snarled:

"Dived me my cloat!"

Maud decided to empty the chamber pot as her one last bit of service. Smiling broadly she distributed its contents by giving each one an equal share poured over his head. Then, on the finest mare and saddle she had ever mounted, Maud led the other horse down to hit the road that went to Three Creeks.

The brothers Tooter sat and bellowed.

Maud never looked back.

Mr. Purdy, I am a asking you to look out for my boy, cause I can't take him with me."

"Why not? He could be a great help."

"You don't know bout me."

"What is there to know."

"Will you swear to not tell nobody."

"Of course."

Maud knew John Purdy's stand on slavery. Besides that she trusted him and was unafraid to tell him the truth:

"Mr. Purdy, I am really a slave. In fact my momma was for sure a registered piece of property. I don't know about me, but I am probably registered as a slave down in Louisiana somewhere too. Tuttoor claims he got the right and if I am not already, he could register me as one for sure cause he got me outa the auction when I was about 10 or 12. He went by his real name, Quinton Tooter, back then. He stole me, but nobody could prove that now."

"You must be wrong."

"No sir, Mr. Purdy. If my momma is alive she is a slave. Tuttoor he got the records on her and my grandma too, but I'm white lookin and so is my boy. In fact someday you got to tell him if ever he has babies that his wife not been bad if one be dark cause he got plenty black in him."

It didn't make a bit of sense to John, but Maud was correct, for slavery was like a birth defect passed down from mother to daughter. It was all based on the maternal bloodline and if her mother was a Negro slave then by law she was also a slave, and therefore Quinton Tooter actually owned her and Junior too. It all depended on Negro blood and Quinton Tooter probably did have the records, and if so it would be whatever he said it was. Maud had not simply stayed with Quinton Tooter all this time because he allowed her to pass as white. She assumed he owned her and certainly he or his brother could definitely report her now so she could soon be just another slave on the run. Although the brothers were not about to go to the law, there were hundreds of slave catchers out there who would be happy to oblige. Maud reasoned that she had to disappear, for without her presence Junior's slave status would be impossible to prove. Heartbreaking as it was, the boy would be much better off if she were nowhere to be found.

"When do you want me to tell him, Maud? Ever?"

"Maybe a few years will pass and change things. Folk forget. Tuttoor may die. Who knows, but don't tell him now. He might tell on himself trying to get me to stay."

"You want to say goodbye?"

"Lord no. I couldn't take it. You tell him I love him and always will. One more thing though."

"Yes."

"Is this here enough money to buy him what he need and get some good book learning?"

"Yes! My oh my, yes!"

"Tell him you got it from me and the two of you use it smart like. I got plenty more ifin that's not enough."

"I don't want money to take in your boy, Maud. He saved me from the whip."

"You keep that. Make a gentleman like you out of him."

"Where will you be?"

"I heard there be a place out west of here in a place called Kansas where they don't ask many questions and where you can get what they calls a territory divorce by simply swearing you want one."

"Maud, if you think you are a slave, how can you be married? Are you really married? Anyway, I hear you have to swear abandonment which means you have not seen your mate for at least one full year. Maybe you just ought to go north."

"Nope. A year will pass pretty fast if you just got yourself to look out for. Anyway we live so long together and everybody thought we was married. If he don't prove up that he owns me, then we must be married by law of some kind. I hear em talk about what they calls common law or something like that, and if he finds me all this money will be his if we was still married. If he proves me up as a slave then his brother can claim the money back, but if I was married to him and get divorced he can claim two thirds of it to be his cause a divorce will pretty much prove we was married. Don't you see? Either way Junior will be safe from being a slave Mr. Purdy. If Tuttoor can't find me he cannot prove nothing and if he does he will claim me as his wife to get the money."

Maud had to smile: "Would you believe that rascal of a brother of his pay me so good for nursing him?"

John smiled too. One thing for certain, the two whip masters would never hear from him where the money went. Maud looked so sad and yet happy, if indeed that is possible. She sat laughing and crying at the same time. She was anxiously looking forward to guaranteeing freedom for her boy and at the same time hating the prospects of not seeing him grow to manhood. Besides that, she would be free of Tuttoor and she hated his very guts. Maud sensed that John Purdy thought her decision was probably the only smart one to make, and after all he was the smartest man she knew. That was good enough for her.

"Work him hard, teach him good and tell him I loved him. Every day tell him I loved him. Please."

With that she dried her eyes, squared her shoulders and mounted up. Without a backward glance Maud flicked the reins and headed to this place called the City of Kansas.

Mammy's face was very, very stormy as she entered Virginia's room. "Miz. Virginia, yo better come down stars. There be a lady to see you."

Geneva Chouteau was about 40, quite obviously French by name and also by appearance. She was not especially pretty, but she was quite striking and extremely well dressed. She carried herself with quiet dignity.

"Good day and welcome to Island View. I am Virginia Dinkins."

"Yes. And I am Geneva Chouteau."

Virginia inquired:

"Please make your self comfortable. May I be of service?"

"This is very difficult at best, so I might as well say it out right. I have brought Gotfield's son and daughter to see their father. They miss him so."

"I, er, I, I ah beg your pardon Mrs. Chouteau!"

"Gotfield and I have a family. There are two children, a 15-year-old son and a 17-year-old daughter. He came to see us almost every day until his sickness. We miss him so and I know he would like to see his children."

Virginia's head felt light and she grabbed furniture to steady herself.

"Surely this is some tasteless joke."

"No. It is true. Gotfield and I have always loved each other and hoped we would become one, but then your grandfather demanded the two of you marry instead, so we had to settle with, with ah, second best, and only having each other part of the time. He is very precious to me and our children."

Virginia at first did not want to believe this, so naturally she had trouble comprehending how it could be true; however, as she ran it through her mind she quickly reckoned it could be. He went somewhere almost every day, not that she had cared. In fact she never really cared at all, and certainly for the last few years she was at least woozy if not completely drunk most afternoons when he left the house. Stiffening her back she rose and thought cunningly to herself, "Well there is one sure way to know if she is a fraud or not." She smiled a slightly wicked smile:

"Why of course, Geneva, bring the children."

The two of them emerged from the carriage as summoned and presented themselves, awkwardly but quite politely. They both displayed impeccable manners and showed a truly amazing amount of dignity for just youngsters in such an awkward scene. Janice was an attractive and proper young lady. Alfred was a nice but gawky-long-stretched-out young man who had yet to get use to the fact he stretched clear out to wherever. Taking them in tow, Virginia led the way to Gotfield's room and flung open the door. There was obviously no play acting in anyone's reaction, for one cannot be that good without lots of practice on the scene. Gotfield's chair was positioned such that he could gaze out the window and he currently was doing so. As the slave girl swung him about to face the four of them and his face lit up in recognition, he immediately stretched open his one usable arm and the three all tried to rush into it. Geneva, Janice and Alfred embraced him, slobbers and all, as only those who truly love one another do. Tears ran from Geneva and Janice's faces in spite of tremendous effort to smile and be brave. Alfred took his father's hand in his, he then dropped to one knee and almost whispered:

"We have missed you, Father."

Janice knelt on the floor and laid her head on Godfield's knee facing away so that he could not see her tears. Gotfield could only mumble:

" gaa da bumga yeeea da glocyyaa yaaa yaaa yaa yaa duh bumga duh."

Geneva managed to stay nearly composed but turned to Virginia and remarked in a wavering voice;

"He is such a gentle man. He sits by the hour and reads poetry to her, and he has never even been impatient with his son. He has taught him so much about life and they share a great love of books. He has given Alfred a priceless collection of the greatest books ever written. Gotfield is always asking him what certain passages really mean."

Virginia had to leave the room. She was in daze and right now she had a sudden desire to get drunk. Very drunk. She told Mammy, who was standing by with a very pensive look on her face, to let their guests out when they were ready to leave. Then she absented herself. Virginia went to her room and sat staring at the wall for a long time.

A very long time.

At first she cried bitter tears, but then Virginia began to laugh at herself. She had been so smart, thought she, catching that crook Cooper or whatever his real name was in only a few days of looking things over. Yet she had lived her complete married life with a husband who had shared life with his real love. For 18 years. He had given up nothing and had a rich life complete with family and all, in easy distance, of course, so he could go there almost every day. She on the other hand, had paid an incalculable price and nearly lost her very soul. Virginia's analytical mind could not help but examine her true emotions once more, and finally concluded she was mad as hell at being betrayed, however, "anything but" heartbroken. She truly had paid Gotfield scant attention for some number of years as she had never cared much for him at all. She had always considered him gutless although since becoming aware of "opening ceremonies" in the slave quarters she now considered him more of a predator. Every Negro girl there must remind him why he grew up with no mother or father. He must hate it here.

Then the realization hit her like a well swung 2 by 4! It was being here with her that he hated. Her prison was his prison too. What a terrible influence he had always been on their sons, urging them on in their debauchery, for his reality was: her boys reminded him that Island View was far and away more of a prison than if it had bars. She had foolishly spent much of her time in solitary, but he was by far the smarter of the two and managed a furlough almost every day. To just down the road. To the anxious arms of a warm-blooded woman. And to these lovely, well mannered children who were now crying over him and missing poetry recitations or discussing the classics together.

Virginia pulled her call rope. She did not have to wait but a moment, for since going cold turkey she was under 24 hour surveillance. The household servants were "tag teaming" her, and one always was a second shadow. With all that was going on today, Mammy had thoughtfully replaced whoever was on duty, so she would be the one close by.

"Yes, Miz. Virginia."

"Did you know about Mrs. Chouteau?"

"Well some of the other darkies tell me, but I never seen her up close before."

"Who told you?"

"Daniel. He drive Master's carriage there most days and he tell me bout it, but I don't want to hear, it so I tells him to be quiet."

She found Daniel polishing a harness and told him she needed a carriage very early in the morning, so have one ready. After a long and restless night, daybreak found Virginia dressed sitting on her bed waiting for Daniel and the carriage, which appeared ten minutes earlier than she had requested. Entering the carriage she instructed Daniel:

"Take me where you took Master most days!"

Daniel looked confused and then sheer terror filled his face.

"Oh, Miz. Virginia!"

"Yes, Daniel."

"Miz. Virginia, I can't not to do that."

"Daniel, take me where you took Master most every day. Now!"

"Please, Miz. Virginia! Please! Oh, please Mam!"

"Let's go there, Daniel!"

"Oh, please, Miz. Virginia!"

"Let's get started, Daniel."

"Oh Mam, but Master say ifin I ever take anybody else there sides him being along, he done have the meat whipped off my bones and sell me to a rice plantation as a field nigger."

This was indeed a horrifying prospect for poor Daniel! A rice plantation was a field slave's worst nightmare for they spent their day in mud and insect infested paddies. The insect bites were wretched and their feet had bleeding cracks and sores much of the time. It was as miserable an existence as a slave knew about, and a threat to be sent to the rice paddies was terrifying. Especially to a household slave.

"Daniel, you take me there! Mrs. Chouteau was here yesterday."

With all the diversions of Gotfield's stroke, the twins' incident, plus discovery and dismissal of Coopert, the harvest at Island View had virtually come to a standstill. Most of the cotton was still in the field. Virginia's experience in such matters came from when she had followed her grandfather around until she was about 14 years old. At 15 he saw her as a threat to conserving the estate for she would soon be grown. Then, just before she was 16, in what he considered a stroke of brilliance, he considered her woman enough for him to arrange for her marriage. And after all, a southern plantation woman's foremost job was to look after the household and be gracious. She hungered for the opportunity, but Grandfather never allowed her the same familiarity with the operation nor business input that he eagerly accepted from her grandmother. Some would have said that he was afraid of her brilliance and that she might well be hard to handle.

At any rate, Virginia now faced the challenge of managing this huge cotton harvest almost alone. The Negro slave driver "turncoats" were virtually useless as they really commanded little or no respect from the group; in fact, it was quite the contrary. The turncoats were universally hated, for they had managed almost exclusively by fear of being reported to Coopert. One of their more important job tasks had been to regularly have some slaves for him to inflict pain on, especially for the coming weekend. Fear of feeling the lash themselves had caused them to pick some of the others for the most minor of infractions.

Virginia visited extensively with Amos and Ramos who were rapidly recovering from their beatings, as only young bodies do, but each of them was still facing a long recovery. They were wise beyond their years, offered intimate knowledge of the plantation's slave community, and were smart. She determined these were fine young men with years in the field already, but had little else to offer except plain common sense.

Following her own intuition and the beat-up twins enthusiastic reaction to her plan, Virginia called a picnic assembly with every Negro on the plantation ordered to be there. She instructed that enough butchering be done for a feast, with plenty of leftovers for each family to take home as well. Most of the Island View slaves had rarely even seen a good cut of meat the last few years, let alone gotten to eat one. Now here there was plenty for everyone. Additionally each Negro woman was given the ingredients to prepare a huge portion of her very best dish and asked to bring it. Even though they had had little to work with for some time, many of them could cook wonderfully well. The feast was just that. There was every dish one might expect providing the finest eating the Island View slave community had any remembrance of, and Virginia felt compelled to walk among the crowd cautioning them not to eat themselves sick.

At the height of excitement and fellowship, Virginia called all heads of families together to give each family group their assignment. She explained they were either an Amos team family, who got red armbands, or a Ramos team family who received blue ones. The workers' capacity had been very deliberately divided, taking into consideration 8 to 14 year olds, older adults, and those in their prime. This selection process designated each as a "full hand" or "half hand" based on their capacity to pick, and excepted children under 8 who were to be watched by the old but able. As hard as it was for an Island View Negro to imagine, children under 8 were to stay out of the field and play!

The winning team families would be first to all get brand new shoes, plus there would be a huge butchering on the plantation with the winning team getting the hams. The second place team would get the shoulder meat. There would be no "losers." At another celebration party, the second place team would serve the winning team a feast, while second place ate fatback and beans. Miz. Virginia had taken the turncoat slave drivers' whips and held them, along with one that had belonged to Coopert, up for all to see. Then she hacked them into pieces. The winning team would have the honor of burying the whip parts in the slave cemetery. If harvest was accomplished by a given date there was a $2500 prize to be divided evenly among the family heads. The prize reduced to $1750 and then $500 if alternate dates were missed. The prize money created an incredible air of excitement, for no Island View slave could remember having ever owned four quarter dollars at the same time.

Virginia spent the entire day of the picnic getting to know her people and by late afternoon she could call all of her nearly 100 heads of family by name. Late in the day, after the feast and team assignments, she called everyone around. All of the woman were ordered to gather close by her, and then they marched as a group over to the place. The straw piled around the wretched building with the opening room was good and dry, plus there was a goodly amount of grease and oil strewn about. The men folk were given sacks if it became necessary to beat back the flames, and nearby water tanks were already filled if need be to control the fire. Gotfield was carried to the very front row.

Missy was given the honor of throwing the first torch on the place; however, every Negro woman who wanted one was given a torch to throw.

Most did.

Next morning, every half hand and full hand on the plantation, including the ex-slave drivers, were waiting at the end of a row for enough light to pick cotton. At dawn's first light Virginia stood in the family cemetery near the very head of Grandfather Enrique de Falco's II grave, watching the building where all of the debauchery had taken place, still smoldering in the distance. She knew her great great grandmother had been brought here after having been spirited out of Spain, to avoid her living life in shame or more probably, of having someone run her through with a sword. The very man who was charged with safeguarding her great great grandmother's soul had set her aside, to become a prince of the church. In spite of her having been so foolish, her loving father had found this far away sanctuary and had taken great pains to have her spirited away. Virginia pondered for a while at the current wretchedness of the place. And of the misery forced upon her and poor Gotfield.

Perhaps it was meant to be; the bastard child that her Spanish princess ancestor carried to America's shores died at birth. She bore many more children, but only one of them survived the fever that later killed both her and her Italian husband. She had named her first son Enrique, after her father, and Enrique lived to manhood and pressed on, loving his servants, and watching out for them, and caring for them. Her Grandfather, Enrique de Falco II, unfortunately did not inherit his fathers' brains or his compassion.

Enrique de Falco II didn't deserve the honor of carrying such men's names. Virginia looked down at his grave and figured about where his face would be, and carefully drew an X with her foot.

She squatted exactly there and relieved herself.

It was nearly incomprehensible to the Purdy family how their world had been so savagely turned upside down, and in such short order. Johnson and Sledge were boorish, crude people who leered at Mattie any time they caught a glimpse of her, obviously wanting to touch and feel. Unfortunately, even after the step ladder incident neither John nor Mattie had fully given them credit for such violent intentions against her. Tuttoor on the other hand was always an enigma, being blustery and seemingly on the very edge of violence most of the time. John had always considered him a yellow coward and knew damn well he would not, nor probably could not, have cooked up such a scheme on his own. His type simply was afraid of a fair fight and would have always wanted at minimum the two-to-one advantage that his long lost brother had conveniently provided. Junior shared with the Purdys that about all he really knew was that the other man, Cooper Tooter, was an uncle who had showed up from a south Louisiana Mississippi river plantation called Island View, and that he was known there as Mr. Coopert.

The human body's recuperative powers are often nothing short of magic. John Purdy's feet took longer to heal than his back; however, it would be his back which would bear a scar of remembrance forever. Mattie continued to gently rub salve over his scabbing back and kept insisting that John take it easy and soak his sore feet each day. His back and his feet pretty much incapacitated him for about a week, and he could not help but marvel at how this 120 pound woman shrugged off her own terrifying encounter to fuss over him and Junior, as well as the more slowly recuperating giant black. By necessity Brown had probed ever so deeply; however, Bos' wound was finally taking on a fresh healthy look of healing. John respected Brown's gutsy performance no end, for he doubted that he himself would have had the nerve to do that to another, Negro or not.

Junior on the other hand took his licks while still wearing his clothes, so he was by and large bruised mentally, rather than severely cut up by the lashes. He tried to make light of it, claiming that he had often received worse marks when Tuttoor had simply been drinking. Junior never even considered going back out to the shack, and in fact he assumed he was unwelcome there and no longer had a home. He was understandably very anxious about his mother, for such as it was, it had been her home too. Junior had heard of mothers giving up their infant babies because they loved them so much; however, he now considered himself practically a full grown man. As such he would like nothing better than to protect and to be with her to help, and therefore, Maud's leaving made no sense to him at all. John kept his promise and told Junior only that she had a bit of money and that in a year or so, maybe, just maybe, he would explain where she was and why she had to leave without him. He also told Junior that Maud was well, but not to plan on seeing her for a long, long time. John especially made it a point to tell the boy every day that Maud's last remark before she rode away was, "Tell him every day I love him." John did this because he said he would. And because he doubted very seriously that Junior would ever see his mother again.

The entire Three Creeks community was outraged to its core, with most wanting to go out to the Tuttoor shack and burn it with those two scallywags tied inside. Then they would form a posse and go lynch Johnson and Sledge, which would take care of all four of them, real proper like. John and Mattie intentionally said very little about the two attempted rapists, for they realized full well that if the law got involved there would be some tall explaining to do concerning the big black. Bos was starting to heal but nowhere near ready for John to haul him north, let alone ready to resume running. Brown and Simpson continually tried to turn most of the attention to the Tooter brothers, in order to gain recuperating time for the big man. Simpson was having difficulty with his conscience anyway, and thought John should assume full ownership responsibility, truly becoming Bos' master. They all realized they would have to take the continuing chance of someone showing up who might truly know where he came from. John was philosophically against slavery and becoming more so all of the time, so he now struggled mightily with the idea of his family or customers thinking of him as a slaveholder.

The third week after the whipping, the men of the area gathered out at the shack on a bright Sunday morning before church. Every man from the area, excepting the preacher, was there, and it had taken everything he had to convince them not to burn the place with the brothers inside. Brown was the spokesperson:

"We will all be back after church. Be gone!"

Quinton whined pitifully;

"Please, I have no whereth to go."

Cooper blustered;

"How dare slyou. Do you knowth who I lam!"

Brown stood with his hands on his hips:

"We do not give a crap who you think you are! Go, or stand by and watch. I for one hope you both stay right inside because I wanted to tie you up and leave the two of you in there to roast."

Brown turned to join the others with their task at hand. The neighbors cut brush and piled it up against the shack then poured some grease on it they had brought for the purpose.

"We light this and the shed too when we come back. You have about three hours. Suit yourselves."

Brown mounted his big Cayuse and headed back with the others to church where the preacher did not say one word about forgiveness in his sermon that day. He didn't want to and sensed he best not anyway.

"This is allt yourn damnt fault you slupid blastard!" bellowed Cooper.

Brother Quinton snarled back;

"Ist not. You wanted to hlurt slomebody blad. It didn't matter whot slo longa as you heardt lem slcream. I just wanted to plound him with his shirt on. But no, you wanted blood."

"Youth wanted to wlhip him ust as blad as I did. Anyway what we gonnsta do?"

"Blest we tlry to harmlness them old mules."

"They must be klidden. It's Slunday."

"Probably the preacher talking about Godth being mad."

"Can you movth any bletter?"

"Noth. Not mulch anyway."

"Well lets tlry to get some sluff out of here."

The duo crab walked about, finally getting a few things into the trunk and the two of them drug it outside. The old mules were so docile they got them mostly harnessed, but had an impossible time with the buckles on the mule bonnets, which caused old Mollie to kick at Quinton Tooter. One can pull a horse's ears through a bridle head strap, but you best respect even an old mule's ears and use a bonnet so as to buckle the strap behind those ears and not touch them. Those ears are the mules' pride, which was quite actually more than could be said for the brothers' right now. About mid-afternoon the crowd came back, finished harnessing the mules properly and threw the rest of the pile of junk on the wagon. The Tooter brothers sat a safe distance away from the crowd, looking pitifully incapable of taking care of themselves, let alone doing anybody else harm. The shack burned like tinder and, sure enough, in about twenty minutes, the neighborhood had one less shack. Quinton Tooter had no clue as to their next move, while the only conceivable thing Cooper Tooter could think of was to get back to Island View and to the gold he had buried there. He knew he was forbidden to go on to the Island View property, so his main concern now was how he would proceed once he got back close to the plantation. Compared to what he recently held, the gold was not a great amount, but now, excepting a few clothes, his toys, this wagon, and a pair of old slow mules, it was all he had left.

Cooper Tooter flicked the reins over old Mollie and Bigun, who eased into their slow ambling gait. By necessity their route took them right through the settlement, so as they passed through some of the people came along the road to hiss and boo, while virtually all of the youngsters came up close to try and spit on them. The miserable pair looked stolidly ahead but as they passed by the Purdy Mercantile Store, just out of the corner of his eye, Cooper saw a large Negro apparently scrambling to get out of sight. Cooper snapped his head in that direction so that he might get a better look and stared after this disappearing Negro giant. He had a chest the size of a barrel, and small hips set on legs like oak trees. No! Could it really be? He was almost certain. He in fact was certain. Few Negro men ever had such a build as Bos.

The old mules lumbered along at their own pace making painfully slow progress; meanwhile the brothers sitting on the springboard had little to say to each other. The two wretched looking brothers were facing their calamity in very different frames of mind, with their notched ears and slit nostrils constantly reminding one to the other full well what they looked like themselves. They could barely stand to glance at each other.

Quinton felt so very sorry for himself. His slave/wife had tended his every need and lately he had done nothing for himself, except to slip around and steal what he could. In his own way he had truly enjoyed having a son, although the whelp had turned against him, which was either regrettable or unforgivable. He was uncertain as to which. Certainly the Indians had seen to it he would never have another.

Cooper, on the other hand, was trying to think of some way to modify a whip handle so he could manage it with just his little finger, the one next to it and a stump of a thumb. Perhaps only two fingers would work if the handle had holes to put them through, and anyway, he was certain he could manage a hot iron and turn the screws. As he looked over at his brother who sat there with his chin quivering a good part of the time, Cooper Tooter was disgusted. Where were his brother's guts? He had never felt that sorry for himself. Ever! Even when their father became outraged when he found out about his peculiar taste in bed partners and punished him by selling him for the night to some drunken sailors.

As Cooper Tooter reviewed his last few weeks, he reminisced miserably of how his fortunes had changed since he was known as Mr. Coopert of the big house. Before his trip to town with Virginia, he had held a fortune, along with grandiose visions of becoming part of the landed gentry and southern upper-class. Even after that humiliation, when he rode into Three Creeks he was well mounted, fairly rich, not bad to look at, and sported some fine weapons. He was also an undisputed expert with his collection of some rather unconventional instruments which he must now learn how to manage all over again. Suddenly, except for change from the money he had sent Maud to buy food and groceries with, he had virtually nothing. Until he got to the gold, his fortune included exactly what there was on this wagon: a few clothes, his toys, the wagon itself, and a broken down old pair of mules. Not merely was the cupboard almost bare, he must now share and put up with a whiney brother whom he had never cared for anyway, and who had absolutely nothing left to offer in return.

That is a long, long, long way to fall.

As the old mules made their way a few miles south on Bluff Road they came to the riverbed and stopped right in the middle to drink and cool themselves. This wide area with its slow running shallow water was a perfect place to put in the road crossing, although it stretched about a hundred feet to either shore from out in the middle where they stopped.

Quinton did not like it;

"This mlakes me nervalous as hell. I doth not swilm a lickth and theres aplot of that water."

"Aw it tain't a floot deepth"

"I know but it's slcary as hellth to me."

"Relaxth."

Old Mollie and Bigun decided to go on across and started the long pull to gain the top where Bluff Road then ran in and out along the river bluffs for most of the next mile. The old mules stopped to heave for a while every now and then, but finally made it to the flats up on top of the long gradual hill. The views from the bluff were spectacular, both far into the distance, or straight down into the roaring river way below. The river was very narrow along here, tumbling through the narrows which made it both fast and deep before it widened out to the shallows they had just forded a couple of miles or more back. As old Mollie and Bigun stood heaving, Cooper got out of the wagon:

"Youth bletter get outh and strletch, we goth a slong day."

Quinton got out to crab walk over to look over the edge and stood gazing at the scene below, wondering what the future might hold for one such as he.

He did not have to wonder long.

Cooper ran from behind to push with all he had, and was elated as he watched the screaming cowardly bastard flailing about as he bounced off the bluff face to then fall into the currents well over 100 feet below. Cooper had an absolutely elated look on his face for now at least he would not have to listen to brother whine and could spend what little he had left on only himself. Cooper's feet hurt terribly from not having been careful in the way he walked, and he watched the blood seep through his toe bandages. It was low enough price to pay.

As he sat there with his feet throbbing he vowed to himself that he indeed was the pain master, and those who caused him pain must pay quite dearly. His mind settled on Purdy and a most cruel smile came over his face. The Indians were merely Purdy's pawns and it was obviously with Purdy where there was a score to settle. Well, Purdy's blonde woman could be a good pawn too. Yes, indeed. He would leave the law completely out of this, for this was a personal issue. He and the Purdy clan had unfinished business.

As he jostled along, Cooper Tooter racked his brain but simply could not come up with a foolproof plan to get back onto Island View. He knew he was less than unwelcome, yet somehow he must get to the cemetery and dig up the gold, for that gold now constituted his entire fortune. Cooper Tooter flicked the reins on Old Mollie and Bigun who somehow sensed they were going home. They quickened their pace, ever so slightly.

On this attempt to retrieve the gold, Cooper Tooter floated down to the island in a stolen boat, sneaked up the bank, crawled to the cemetery and poked frantically about in the dark. It was pitch black and the new double marker for the boys was exactly in the wrong place. Unfortunately he had memorized the precise location of his buried hoard by taking exact measurements from the fence posts in front of the old bastard's head stone. Never in a million years did he anticipate there would be a new fence plus twin markers plus two individual markers plus another decorative separate fence put here. In the dark of night he could never reconstruct or make sense of his memorized map and probed for hours with no results. Fighting panic, at dawn, he crab walked and crawled back to the river. Empty handed. Again.

A few weeks after Gotfield's stroke, Geneva had apparently taken it upon herself to locate a nurse who claimed great success in treating stroke victims. After consulting with their regular physician, Virginia found no objection to the exercise routine or herbs and special medications she brought with her. The incantations were a bit much; however, Nurse Katherine's treatments seemed to at least make Geneva feel better. It certainly all appeared to be harmless enough, and somehow or another it seemed to help Geneva communicate with Gotfield better than anyone else could. Nurse Katherine gave Amanda, his charge person a great deal of help and stayed over night from time to time just down the hall in a room so assigned.

Since Geneva and Gotfield's other family had shown up, Virginia allowed them free access to both his room and a nice visiting area that was originally the sitting room portion of the master bedroom suite. The master bedroom suite and its surroundings were a marvel into themselves, with Master's bedroom set on the upstairs corner, having Missus' bedroom accessible through large pocket-style sliding doors which completely disappeared into the paneled dividing wall. When the doors were opened the two rooms became quite intimate. At a time when the two of them were being particularly abrasive with each other, Gotfield had caused a large piece of furniture to be set on his side of the door opening. Not to be outdone, Virginia had ordered in a couple of boudoir chairs to sit on her side and then to go him one better, she also ordered up finished boards to match the woodwork and to be fit at the bottom of each sliding door. The boards matched their surroundings quite nicely, being all but an invisible part of the trim work as they held the doors firmly closed.

The visiting room, which was now accessible only to Gotfield's side, opened completely to a screened veranda with a magnificent view to the river. It made for a delightful place to relax or to have one's breakfast served. Or to keep an invalid. An outside screened walkway or promenade led from the visiting room past the missus room and several smaller two room suites, then continued past several simpler bedrooms to a sitting area for the others. At any rate Gotfield's surprise family now spent a good deal of time in his sitting room as it was easy access for his wheel chair. The children's visits seemed particularly good for him.

Virginia finished her cold tea. It really wasn't bad, but she missed the sting of bourbon. Her ever-present shadow of a household slave watched, from a respectful distance of course, as Virginia stepped down off the front veranda stairway and selected some flowers to take up to the boys' graves. It was not totally their fault that they had fallen through the very cracks of civilized behavior, for they truly had been terribly misguided. They were her sons and somehow through the pain she must accept they had undoubtedly brought it all on themselves. In her heart she knew they deserved what they got. Still, there is no other pain that compares to a mother's loss of a child, and she had lost them both. Certainly it was they who had ignored her, but she was the adult and should never have let that happen, insisting instead that she, not Gotfield, be in charge of their upbringing. Fredrick and Godfrey were flesh of her flesh and blood of her blood, and they really had needed special attention. As their mother, she could not deny she had failed them. Unmitigating guilt combined with deep sorrow frequently tore at her guts, and Virginia knew full well these were burdens she would take to her grave.

Virginia enjoyed wandering across the yard, which was now a great display of the new grounds-keeping effort, then came to the cemetery and placed the flowers on the boys' graves. She pulled the few weeds that were just popping up and quietly surveyed the plantation, for there was a great view of the mansion and its surroundings from here. As Virginia stood there reflecting on recent events, a small flat bottom boat floated down river toward the island, with the person on board rowing about sort of in a circle. Dawdling about. Virginia stepped behind the big tree at the corner of the cemetery and affixed the picture in her mind. There was no fishing gear; however, it had always been quite common for people to just float by and gawk at arguably the greatest showplace of the South. The captain of the little rowboat held up a spyglass, surveying the grounds in great detail as his little boat slowly floated by.

After turning her attention back to the cemetery, something caused her to glance again at her grandfather's grave. It first appeared that someone had been digging not far from the very spot she had relieved herself. Dropping down to her knees, she could still tell nothing, except there were marks everywhere. Dozens and dozens of them. Someone appeared to have been poking around all over with an iron bar or a long knife or such. She was anything but superstitious but what in Heaven's name—. She appreciated and enjoyed the slaves grooming up the place, with everybody taking yard duty from time to time and maybe, just maybe, they were starting some weird project fixing up the cemetery. Probably not. That was the one place most of them preferred to stay clear of. And the person in the rowboat? Just the idle curious no doubt.

Back at the mansion Virginia pondered a bit more and then cleared all of it from her mind. There was a new baby down at quarters and she was going to take down her standard baby package that contained some number of things one should have for a new baby. Under Coopert's regime far too many infants had died, for he had quickly forced new mothers back to the fields. Part of the rules now were that new mothers were to be fussed over, and given time off to simply enjoy their new babies with others even being assigned to do their washing and cooking. As Virginia walked down the mansion steps with her arms loaded, Mammy stood with her hands on her hips and shook her head:

"Yo gonna be mistaken for a man if you don't start a dressing right. Yo momma done roll over in her grave she sees you dressed up in dem boy clothes."

As she hung the sack over the saddle and mounted up she giggled and then smiled her wicked little smile. Maybe Grandpa was having trouble getting used to her riding astride her mare, and those marks were where he was boiling over.

The young slave girl was breathless for she had raced like the wind:

"Miz. Virginia, Miz. Virginia, come quick. Somebody be driven old Mollie and Bigun up de road!"

Daniel had sent the girl, for he had recognized the old mules wandering gait from as far away as he could see them, although they seemed to be hurrying. For them.

Virginia handed the new baby back to its mother, mounted up and trotted back to the mansion. Climbing down from her mare Virginia handed the reins off to Daniel and stood watching as old Mollie and Bigun slowly ambled closer and closer. When Virginia could see more clearly she reckoned she was looking at what must be the ugliest man ever. The creature got down off the wagon and sort of crab walked up close enough that she could tell he bore hideous marks made by something or somebody.

It bowed.

"Miz. Virginia."

She stood transfixed. When she finally recognized him she was unable to hide her further amazement.

"Miz. Virginia?"

"Yes Mr. Coopert, or actually it is Mr. Tooter, is it not?"

"Miz. Virginia I bleg you. Please, please don't runth me off I gled help oh so very bladly."

"What in heavens name?"

"Miz. Virginia, I was cloming black to return all of your money when I got caught by the slavages. They tookth my horse, and almost every tlhing else including the money. They clut me up for no reason at all, except I was simply just splort for them. I have been such a blad man, Oh, such a blad man. You see the plice I am plaling for being such a blad, blad man"

He fell to his knees:

"Please, Oh please, let me stlay hereth, I have no whereth else to glo."

Virginia was flabbergasted. She believed little if anything the poor creature said, except for one point. There she totally agreed. He had definitely been a "blad, blad man."

"Please. Please. Oh please."

By any name he might have chosen, Cooper Tooter had heard enough poor souls beg for mercy he could pick from the very best pleas. He hoped against hope she would not ignore such pleas, as he always had.

"Mr. Tooter I see you as nothing more than a common thief."

"Please Oth please. I will clause you no troubth."

"Probably not, Mr. Tooter."

He fell chest to the ground, his face almost on her feet, still on his knees and his rump in the air. Apparently the next step would be to lick her boots.

"I have no whereth else to glo, I have nothing. I am slo slore. I am hungry. I needth more tlime to get wellth. Oh please oh please oh please." He sniffed.

She weighed the probable outcomes. It would be a plus for the slaves to see this hated son of a bitch groveling down in the quarters. He always made himself even more indispensable by being the only one he let fix those infernal wire teeth in the gins. He could teach somebody to do it correctly. He knew the reasoning of why sometimes in the past they sold on New Years day along with all the other plantations, and some times they held out waiting until later. There were all of those other pestering questions for which there was absolutely no one else to ask.

"Just until you are as well as you are going to get Mr. Tooter. No longer. You may sleep in one of those shacks down in quarters we plan on tearing down. I will have some of the women save their leftovers for you from time to time. Mr. Tooter, you have the lowest rank of anybody on this plantation and if I hear of you being even impolite to one the slaves I swear by Heaven to have Sheriff Davis haul you to jail. By the way, Mr. Tooter, you will take over the cleaning of the outhouses to earn your keep."

He gagged at the thought, but figured he would be here but a very short time. In daylight he could inspect the cemetery and set a marker where to dig, retrieve the gold by night, and get gone.

Later that evening Virginia sat relaxing in her room. Some day this had been. There was a rustling about next door in Gotfield's room, and she supposed it was simply changing time again; however, it sounded more like someone was moving furniture. She glanced out into the hallway and smiled as she already knew whoever was on alcohol watch apparently got potty a break when she went to bed, and would disappear for a bit right then. As she blew out her lamp to retire for the evening Virginia continued to hear noise at the connecting door. Whatever the noise was, it should not concern her. She thought about the little boat with the extra curious captain. There was also the interesting coincidence of Tooter's return.

As she tried to drift off to sleep she let her mind wonder about on the subject.

Oh well. Nobody wanted to do her harm.

That was a fascinating and interesting thought though.

Suddenly Virginia sat straight up, clutching the bedclothes to her chest in sheer terror. Afraid to leave her room she bolted out of her bed and pulled her call rope. It had been severed and came free in her hand. Quickly she grabbed a chair and tilted it in front of the hallway door under the knob, and then scrambled over to lock the windows. Fighting the oncoming panic in her gut she rolled up the covers on her bed so it that it would appear she was still in it, and then clamored in behind the boudoir chairs.

How stupid can you be? Stupid! Stupid! Stupid!!

It was a wonder she was still alive!

It became a nightmare.

The trim boards held the sliding pocket doors firmly closed. Shortly someone shoved against her hallway door, but it was locked, of course. A key slipped into the lock and quietly turned, but even after considerable pushing and shoving, the chair under the doorknob held.

Virginia took measured breaths, tried to stay calm and waited.

Soon a shadow appeared at her balcony windows so she darted to the door only to find it now solidly fastened shut from the outside. With the exception of alcohol watch who had taken their potty break the minute she blew out the light, all others were instructed to keep their distance and respond to the maid's bell. Mammy insisted everyone always keep a respectful distance from her bedroom, especially when the door was closed. Now there was absolutely no way she would be heard through the heavy closed door. In horror she watched as the shadow tried to slide one and then another of her jib style bedroom windows open. Such windows have small double doors at floor level to allow one to walk out the opening. To secure such windows each had a latch plus these also had two metal pins in the sashes that slid into small pieces of pipe buried in the woodwork. Finding them all double locked, her prospective assailant quietly started working the locking pins loose in one of the windows. With just the right tools held in well-practiced hands, the window soon came free.

Virginia did not pray often, but tonight it was heartfelt:

"Dear Mother of God."

The plan was quite well conceived. The mastermind in the scheme, a traveling man, referred to himself as Dr. Darkness. He had received very specific instructions. First of all, Nurse Katherine must be able to swear that Gotfield was alive at the time. Secondly, Virginia's death must definitely appear either to be an accident, or to be from natural causes. Third, although he knew who it was, he would never have that confirmed, or meet with his employer. He had, of course, received half of the fee up front; the other half was due when the deal was done.

This was an easy one for Dr. Darkness. He simply had to slip into the house at the time of his choosing, and of course Nurse Katherine would see to that. She would change the invalid fellow afterwards so as to have fresh soiled clothing to strengthen her testimony. After Dr. Darkness quietly did what he did best, he could be on his way to his next assignment. There was some chap in Boston that had a business partner he apparently did not care for, so he had sent for the good doctor. His vials of "medicine" were the best chemistry had to offer, plus this time he also carried a prop, a not-quite-empty personal size barrel of whiskey made by the popular Booze company. Miz. Virginia was really going to get Boozed up tonight, and it would appear the poor dear had drunk nearly the whole thing. Imitating alcoholic poisoning for a drunkard was almost an insult to his level of skill. But it paid well.

He smiled to think Nurse Katherine really imagined she would become his full-time partner after this. He had lured her from a whorehouse in the city, with promises of being a continuing part of his enterprise. She would at least be a more respectful member of the community when she entered the big sleep. Nurse Katherine would have to be available to testify if need be, but after things settled down she would also sleep the deep sleep. As did anyone who could link him to anything remotely dishonest. When others had served their purpose they all slept. Permanently.

Dr. Darkness was only mildly irritated by the blocked door. Nurse Katherine had missed seeing the trim boards holding the connecting doors shut; therefore, he had to regroup. As far as the hallway door was concerned, it being blocked did not alarm him at all, for women who slept alone in a big house often did that. Minor inconveniences. He was like a cat and found himself on the veranda that ran past her bedroom. First window secure, second window secure but there was the third window in the bay window set. He had just the right tools to soundlessly work the locking pins loose.

He would gain access.

Dr. Darkness always did.

Along with the small barrel of Booze, just to make absolutely certain these days, he now carried two vials of his sleepy time medicine. It was a secret formula of his very own, and once on assignment to take care of that fellow over in South Carolina he had mixed up a batch that did not work very well, which caused things to become awkward. Now he always carried a spare vial, one each from two different batches. Just like the royal family he thought, they always wanted an heir and a spare to the throne. Alas, he was so far down the list to inherit he simply had to go into business for himself. Came to the "Colonies" on a special assignment for a member of the royal family and liked it so much he stayed. Even in the rooten tooten ways of men who carried five pounds of iron on their hip, there seemed always to be a good market for his skills.

After she had realized the wretched conditions on the plantation and what had been going on, Virginia experienced times when guilt concerning her boys nearly overpowered her. She had repeatedly looked with disgust at the whips, eagle claws, push daggers, knives, swords, brass knuckles and pistols they had carried about in their garish effort to simulate real manhood. Their collections, particularly the gold inlayed Toledo tigerclaw daggers, thoroughly dismayed her. Finally she had the whole pile brought up to her room and placed in a bureau drawer. Frequently, when she was having trouble sleeping, she would just sit and look at this ghastly array of misplaced bravado. Staring at it reminded her of what her boys had really become, and somehow gazing at these things brought a bit of peace to her troubled soul. Now, thanking the heavens they were there, she reached into the bureau drawer and with both trembling hands grabbed the first pistol she came to. Steadying the weapon by laying its barrel in a v-shaped notch in the back of the boudoir chair, she waited. The first window held fast, the second one too, but ah ha! He slid the third one open.

A percussion cap Colt .44 with a full load of powder makes an incredibly big flash and creates lots of smoke when it goes off. In a closed room the sound is deafening. Dr. Darkness saw the flash but didn't hear a thing, for at that split second the slug was passing through one of his ears, headed toward the other.

The household sprang to life in an instant and before Virginia could compose herself either Amos or Ramos literally destroyed the door as he walked through it into her bedroom. He saw her cowering behind the boudoir chairs, and holding the light in one hand, he picked her up with the other as she was struggled to her feet, still clinging to the smoking gun. It was only after her faithful surrounded her she dropped the gun and allowed herself the luxury of anger.

By damn!
Virginia could barely contain her fury.
She knew who!
And she knew why!

At dawn they examined the intruder. Smaller well-dressed fellow. The little personal sized barrel of whiskey still had a bit in it and Mammy immediately took charge of that. The intruder had a vial sticking in his pocket, and another had been placed carefully on the window trim. With the exception that a chunk of one side of his head was gone and he was bloody in spots, he actually looked quite immaculate. Dr. Darkness always took a bath and put on fresh clothes beforehand, as this was his way of honoring the soon to be dead. He always took a bath afterwards as it was his way of trying to feel clean. This time someone else would have to give him his bath.

Sheriff Davis arrived late afternoon and pronounced Virginia one of the smartest and also one of the luckiest women he ever knew. He had brought lawyer Rawson along as requested:

"Virginia, I am more than a little concerned at having to come back to Island View. Do you have any idea what any of this could be about?"

"Sheriff, I am scared to death!"

"We will look high and low for this so called Nurse Katherine. Do you have other thoughts?"

"No."

Virginia had plenty of other thoughts, just not on Nurse Katherine right now. The Sheriff looked at the Booze keg, and took the body and the vial for evidence. The other vial lay out of sight, unnoticed under the window trim where Virginia had pushed it with her foot.

"Mr. Rawson, may I have a few words."

"Certainly, Mrs. Virginia."

As he rejoined the sheriff, Rawson cast a parting remark:

"Mrs. Virginia, I have no idea. It would be whatever the court said and that might well depend on how the magistrate was feeling that day. I will start researching when I get back to town, but I do not expect to be able to give you a solid answer. An answer that I could defend anyhow. On the other matter of your name, I suppose you can call yourself what ever you want, so long as you sign documents with your legal name."

"Thank you, Mr. Rawson. Do what you can."

Later that evening Virginia excused Amanda and the other young slave woman who was helping with Gotfield today, with promise she would now care for him. Closing the door firmly behind her as she entered his room, she walked over and stood directly in front of him with her arms crossed. Virginia gazed into his eyes in absolute cold fury:

"You're in this aren't you, you lying, conniving, cheating immoral son of a bitch!"

Gotfield, slouched and slobbered. He waived his one good arm around and mumbled incoherently, but the look in his eyes told her he understood every word she said.

"You wanted me out of the way so your bastard family would have first claim to the whole damn place didn't you? If I am dead the whole place passes to you, no matter what shape you might be in. With our boys gone the only claim to your estate would be your bastards. Right? What a brilliant idea! How very lovely. How thoughtful of you. What a concept! Island View, the bastard kingdom."

She got down really, really close, where he would feel her breath as she hissed in his face:

"All I had to do was die."

Amanda was very upset as she came running down to the breakfast table where Virginia sat finishing up her second coffee.

"Miz. Virginia, it's Mister Gotfield. We got him up okay and we clean him okay but when I give him his medicine he just gasped and fell over. Now he ain't okay. I think he, he, he—. Miz. Virginia, I think maybe he dead," she sobbed.

Virginia got up and put her arm around the terrified slave.

"Don't be frightened dear, it's no surprise. We all knew it was just a matter of time. I will go with you to have a look but if you are right we may have to get him laid out."

Turning to Mammy she continued:

"This time let's make absolutely certain that every one in this part of the state knows. For heavens sake, now the poor unfortunate mistress of Island View has to bury her beloved husband."

Virginia was quite uncertain the threat was over yet. It was a mighty strange coincidence that Cooper Tooter had shown up this very day, and she needed time to think. Anyway, that fellow with the vial sure knew his stuff and if he made the substance himself he certainly made a good batch this time. It smelled somewhat like castor beans.

"Daniel, what do you know about firearms, pistols in particular?"

"Not much about shootin, Miz. Virginia, and everything about cleaning em up. All about loading except for puttin in dey caps. Dey boys always made me clean um up and load em most of the way. Kept dey caps to demselves. Never pulled the trigger on one."

"Amos, and you too, Ramos, will you have Daniel show you what he knows about the guns. I want one of you three close all of the time. There still may be those who wish me great harm. Watch very carefully at the funeral and stay close to me, but take care not to let anyone see that you are you armed unless you absolutely must. I will have the ladies make you nice new suits with plenty of room to hide your pistols."

She went to her room and returned with some of the boys' collection and started passing them out.

"Miz. Virginia, I feel more equals to holden a pitchfork or a club."

"Then you must practice and practice. You must know what it feels like and you must know where it is apt to hit. Daniel knows how to load the pistols."

Then Virginia smiled her wicked little smile;

"Go down to quarters and get Mr. Tooter to show you. Don't let him have a loaded pistol. He probably could not hold on to it anyway, but he can certainly show and tell you how to hold and shoot. Do not be surprised if you three make him very nervous."

"Yes Mam. It sure be strange calling him Mr. Tooter instead of Mr. Coopert."

Island View plantation sounded like a battle ground for the two days leading up to Gotfield's funeral.

"Miz. Virginia."

"Yes, Amos."

"Don't you be worrying none about seeing shadows and stuff out side. Some of em is standing about out there at night now."

Virginia supervised funeral preparations and tried to relax while the most able of the field hands cleaned up and dressed their very best, waiting for their turn up at the big house. They had all come through the darkest of valleys together, but now she stood on the hilltop, like an angel spreading her protective wings. As she held the light way high so they might find her, Sam Houston himself could have not penetrated the line of watchful Negroes vying for the honor of guarding their Miz. Virginia.

As Christmas time approached things had pretty well returned to normal at Three Creeks. Every child far and near was welcome to choose a little trinket from under the tree at Purdy's store, so every child far and near had to come by, of course. This made for unusually brisk traffic and business. Mattie's father was coming for a Christmas visit and Grandfather Grasher and John had organized a huge surprise. Christmas was still weeks away and the family could hardly wait: however, it was Mattie Purdy, wife and mother of four, who was the most impatient kid of all. Junior had put his bully days far behind, and Mr. Brown now had no trouble maintaining order at school, as every boy there was in awe and pressed him to see his fast draw. To their everlasting disappointment, he kept his gun put away. Hiram, who had witnessed the entire affair with Johnson leaning up against the post, continued to repeat the story and Brown kept getting faster and faster and closer and closer to Johnson's head.

As summer had turned into fall and fall had turned into winter, Brown spent time coaching Junior, and especially Bos, how to speak properly. Trisha had fewer and fewer of her melancholy spells and was teaching Junior and Bos manners. They reported she was "taking no prisoners." John continued to coach the young men on personal hygiene. Bos limped around making himself generally useful the best he could, with everyone expecting him to recover fully. Meanwhile, Junior was a natural with both the machinery and the customers over at the mill, for he was big, strong, and becoming quite personable. The new Junior made up his mind to be indispensable.

He continued to wonder desperately how anyone could love you so much they must run away. His mind dwelled upon his mother sometime every day, generally at night so no one could see his tears.. Junior began to accept Trisha as his surrogate mother, although he truly missed Maud. Trisha needed someone of her own to mother, and he needed someone's gentle touch, so as the weeks went by they began to fill in admirably for each other. John was out and about the neighborhood riding Star like the wind and actually won a race with his Indian friends, but he gave them tobacco and candy anyway.

The Purdy kids continued to be pure boys, and full of "spizerintcium" as Mattie would say. John and Mattie tied very hard not to play favorites but little Harvey sort of begged the question. He didn't like it when people said so, but Harvey was a beautiful child with the bluest eyes and golden curls. One thing for certain, he was the peacemaker and the politician of the bunch. By six years of age he seemed to understand people better than most adults ever would. For example, one time when Harvey was charging through the house he found his mother crying. Mattie had just read a letter from her father telling her that Mrs. Purvis had passed. Harvey called his personal stampede to a halt:

" What's the matter, Momma?"

"Mrs. Purvis has died."

"She must have been bad sick?"

"No, not really. Ory found her just sitting at the kitchen table, waiting for him to pick her up at her daughter's house. She had packed up some sardines and spinach that she was taking to a lady friend, and she just sat down and died, I guess."

Harvey made an awful face at the prospect of eating such stuff. Then he spoke gently to his mother, who was smiling through her tears at the face he had made.

"Blackfeather says that is what an Indian wants, to just not be sick."

"Well, I guess so, but she was as dear to me as my own mother."

"Did you want her to be real sick so you would know it was time?"

"Of course not, but I really wanted to see her again sometime, and now she is gone."

"Well it is okay for you to be sad, even if she's not."

Mattie was sitting on the sofa, so little Harvey crawled up beside his mother and stood on his knees facing her so he might put his arms around her neck. They were embracing each other when Trisha happened by. Little Harvey summed up the situation for Trisha as though he were a wizened old sage:

"I'm helping mother be sad."

For years some number of youngsters, including the Dody girls, came over each week for Mattie to teach them to read music and to play the violin, instead of the fiddle. It was often screechy as the dickens; however, Mattie would always play before and after to demonstrate the lesson which made it all worthwhile for anyone close at hand. Harvey loved his violin lessons and would frequently steal in and sit quietly through someone else's just to hear his mother play. It was winter now, but in summer it could be warm in the house, so frequently they went outside to escape the heat.

On one such occasion Mattie's hair came loose so she shook it completely out and, as her dress gently fluffed in the breeze, she continued playing with her beautiful golden hair brushing down over the instrument. One of her standard teaching pieces was Brahm's lullaby, and she always finished the lesson by playing a very elaborate rendition of it to demonstrate how one could play a piece, either very plainly, or very complex and fancy if one practiced enough. After she finished, Harvey came and stood behind Mattie with his arms clasped around his mother's waist for ever so long, pressing the side of his little blond head up against her back:

"That is my very favorite one ever, Mom. You are so pretty with your hair like that."

Mattie treasured such incidents and had concluded long ago that such times were why mothers kept coming back for more.

As Christmas approached Mattie was now her frisky self and everyone had their favorite Mattieism:

"Going to church does not make you a Christian any more than standing in the barn makes you a horse."

"How come a sharp tongue and a dull mind are found so often in the same head?"

"Man with one chopstick gets pretty hungry."

"If you are too open minded your brains may fall out!"

"Age is a mighty high price to pay for maturity."

"No husband has ever been shot while fixing up around the house."

She would wonder out loud for all to hear:

"Is the coff—ee the person a cough—er coughs on?"

"How can there be a silent scream"?

Or, "a small crowd?"

"How can anything be almost exactly?"

Or "found missing"?

"Can you be alone together?"

Mattie's take on money:

"Money will buy you a house, but not a home.

"It will buy you medicine, but not health.

"It will buy a clock, but buy you no more time.

"It will build a church, but not introduce you to God."

Mattie's take on intelligence:

"One is intelligent if they know that a tomato is a fruit."

"One is wise if they know not to put a tomato in the fruit salad."

Bos was beginning to feel unthreatened most of the time now, and his new "master" Mr. John treated him so kindly the likes of which were still hard for him to imagine. He ate better than he ever had, sometimes even taking breakfast or lunch at the white table. Bos not only had clothes to wear, he had clothes to change into and he took a bath very often so as to not be offensive to Miss Mattie, or Trisha either, for that matter. He liked Miss Trisha well enough but he, like Junior, considered Mattie not as a woman, but as an angel. Bos and Junior Tuttoor shared a small cabin that had also been hastily thrown up at the same time as a big house raising for another family that had moved to Three Creeks.

Mr. Deay was the local blacksmith, and after one look at Bos he immediately propositioned John to apprentice his new slave.

"With a build like that and especially with those arms, I can make him the best smithy there is in the country."

John and Bos had talked long and hard about John taking him north. They discussed endlessly what he would do up north, how he would live, how he would support himself, and the probability of being caught "up there," as well as down here. If he went up there he probably needed to go all of the way to Canada, for the American Slave Recovery act of 1850 was very specific and pretty severe on those who did not return slaves to their owners, even from the free states. For reasons such as this, some states no longer allowed newly free blacks at all. Bos could not imagine it being any better for him anywhere in the world than at Three Creeks, Kentucky, with John Purdy as his master. Besides, with his angel right here, having some one from Island View discover his whereabouts was a chance he was most willing to take, and he pleaded to stay. So they agreed.

John heartily approved of him working with Mr. Deay and kept a tally of the stipend he received for his slave. Bos would never have imagined that he was saving up to have a bit of money on hand when his master thought the time seemed right to set him free. Mr. Simpson and John remained the best of friends, but had sharply different views on the issue of slavery, each getting even more convinced in their own position as time passed. John simply did not believe it was moral; in fact, he believed it was immoral to own another person, but even so, he kept Simpson's bill of sale on Bos in a very safe place. There was also the paper Maud had given him on Junior because Tuttoor used to continuously threaten Maud with filing his claim on her and then selling her boy. Tuttoor had this paper he waived around, and insisted whoever's name he put on this particular paper would own Maud's boy and could take him away. She was still terrified that it might be true so, as her "fall back position," before she fled Maud had begged John to put his name on "that line right there."

"If he files on me and they catch me, any slave catcher come for him, he'll already be your slave."

It was a blank bill of sale on Junior and certainly of questionable legality to John's way of thinking, but to ease the poor woman's mind he had complied. John reckoned if push came to shove, much to his chagrin, he might really own two slaves.

Both Maud and John had reasoned there might be more questions than John would want to answer if he walked into a bank with her, so when Maud left she had listened very carefully and done exactly as he suggested. Because she was carrying so much cash, John felt the need for a friendly crowd, so as promptly as possible Maud was to find a respectable looking family on the road to St. Louis. When Maud rode out of Three Creeks she timed it so as to quickly catch up with the MacDonald party that had just stopped at the Purdy's store, where they had impressed John as very decent people. They were going to join yet more family and cross the Mississippi at St. Louis, then head west to be early at homesteading in the Kansas Territory. The two brothers and their families welcomed an extra companion having no idea they were actually the security department for a walking bank. When she and the McDonalds arrived In St. Louis, she begged her leave, and took the letter John had prepared straightaway to John's contact at the biggest bank in town. The clerk whom she ask for, Mr. Jefferies, as John had specifically instructed her to do, could not imagine what this large plain looking, road weary woman could possibly want with his big boss. Mr. Jefferies finally appeared, looking somewhat askance:

"Yes ma'am; may I be of service?"

She handed him the letter that John had prepared.

As he read it his face brightened into the broadest of smiles:

"And how is my friend John and his beautiful wife and their family?"

The clerk was amazed when Mr. Jefferies invited Maud back to his private office. When the door closed, Maud started unloading her coat by handing Jefferies two thirds of her fortune. John had fastened the paper money in bundles, sealed each bundle with wax and then initialed each one while the wax was hot. It was obvious the bundles had not been tampered with; however, Jefferies obviously counted the money anyway. He signed the receipt John had prepared and then gave her a very official looking bank document. The numbers looked exactly the same.

"These bank notes are on the Citizens Bank of Louisiana, one of the strongest banks in the country and certainly the strongest bank in the South. We take very few banks' money at face value, but these are good anywhere. You are a smart woman, for there will only be a very small discounted amount when we settle."

"What does that mean?"

"There will be a fee for taking these bills back where they came from."

"Mr. John said you would charge me some, but you would be fair. Is that what a fee means?"

"Yes. That's what a fee means."

"Okay"

"What name do we use on your account?"

"Maud."

"Okay Maud. But we need at least a first and last name."

Maud hesitated. She never wanted to hear the names Tuttoor or Tooter or anything close to them again.

" Sir, I just got one name."

"How about we add Purdy."

"Purdy Maud?"

Jefferies smiled.

"Well, ah, yes. Why not?"

"Okay Mr. Jefferies. I'll be Purdy Maud."

"Sign here, Purdy Maud."

"I don't write none."

"Do you know your numbers?"

"Up to 100."

"Can you think of a number you would never forget?"

"Yes."

"Put it on here twice and make a mark."

9999X was one of the more important accounts the bank now had.

As she was still carrying a small fortune, Purdy Maud was pleasantly relieved to be able to rejoin her companions who had now found yet more family and who were all still waiting their turn at the Mississippi ferry boat. (There were times the wait lasted six weeks!) More comfortable now that most of her paper money was in a safe place, Maud continued to keep the gold lined coat always in view and was extremely careful with her official looking letter and personal note. Mr. Jefferies had sent a letter of introduction to his son at his new bank, in this place called the City of Kansas.

It would have now been far easier for Maud to take a boat up the Missouri, but she was in no hurry. After all, she had a year to kill. The McDonald clan invited Purdy Maud to join their family and continue west to a place they knew about out near the new Ft. Riley military post. There they would join the advance members of their family who had sent word that they had found a river valley just like the Garden of Eden, and they were comfortably surrounded by free-staters and close to military protection. The entire McDonald clan truly enjoyed this helpful hard-working woman, and all of them admired her fine bay mare.

"You folks has been good to me and I'd like to go on with you'ens so maybe we can meet up again out there. When you all get settled, maybe I can try and find you out towards the Ft. Riley place some day. Right now I got some business here in the City of Kansas."

Purdy Maud went straight away to Jefferies son's bank:

"Mr. Jefferies, your papa said you could be trusted completely."

"Well, thank you. I like to think so."

"You don't tell nobody, never, ever for no reason that I came here, Is that a deal?"

"No one! For no reason at all? Ever?"

Maud was very insistent:

"No. No one! Ever, ever, never! Never atall."

"For good news or bad?"

"Nope. Never ever!"

"There might be a reason that was good for you."

"Somebody out there might try and trick us, so when I say never I mean never!"

"As you say, Ma'am."

After swearing him to absolute and total secrecy, she introduced herself, made her deposit, and then started looking for a place for her and the horses to live. Wondering about and pondering her future, Purdy Maud was completely taken aback by the feverish activity of the town. In 1853 it had been but a few shacks thrown up on a bluff with a makeshift wharf on the river. Then in 1854 Congress passed the Kansas-Nebraska act and coincidentally a Mr. McCoy chopped a trail from the bluffs four miles south to his development of Westport. After that, a flood washed away the fine Independence, Missouri, wharf with its iron strap railroad which then made it quite difficult to get to the town's center. When, by accidental necessity, boats started stopping a bit farther west at the river bluffs, in 1855, 56 and 57 the City of Kansas literally exploded. Independence, Missouri, soon lost its status as the final outpost to the frontier, for the starting point of the trip had moved a huge 18 miles and two or three days farther west past the unpredictable Blue River.

At this time St. Joseph was a much larger town, and Atchison and Ft. Leavenworth were thriving, which kept Americans who lived east of mid-Missouri mostly still thinking of the City of Kansas as nothing more than a frontier outpost. It took quite some time for easterners to realize that in just three years the four-mile strip between the City of Kansas docks and the town of Westport had burst into what well may have been one of the busiest business centers ever in the land. As she rode that strip in the fall of 1859, Purdy Maud was no less than flabbergasted.

There were Indians, Negroes, Mexicans, Frenchmen, Germans, Irish and every other kind of white man all racing about in hundreds of wagons, on horseback or simply on foot. There were 450 businesses, including 40 manufacturers, five sawmills, 16 hotels, 26 saloons and an untold number of gambling houses and brothels! Whiskey ran altogether too freely in a town where it seemed nearly everyone was carrying a gun if not two. Purdy Maud soon found out the town was so rough, particularly down around the docks at night, that even outlaws with any brains at all avoided the place.

Over 700 freighters had docked at the newly emerging river wharf in 1859, and one or more of the 60 passenger boats plying the Missouri River now made scheduled stops almost every day. Land promoters met the westbound passenger boats with bands and buggies offering to take anyone who would go the opportunity to see their plots, with spectacularly inflated prices. In three years in an America of only 27,000,000 white people, some 4,000,000 of them would "light out for the territories" with a significant percentage of them passing through the City of Kansas. From this unglamorous point, and taking everything they owned with them; man, woman and child commenced their incredible journeys. Some headed out the Santa Fe, others out the California, but most of them headed out the Oregon Trail.

Purdy Maud watched in wide-eyed amazement as the greatest migration parade in the history of America was stampeding by. It was no wonder that many of the pioneers wanted to promptly get on out the trail, for locally there had been an incredible amount of violence. It originally all had to do with the pro-slavery folk arguing and fussing with the abolitionists. Although violence was still prevalent down in southeast Kansas, the worst of it in the City of Kansas part of the territory had occurred a couple of years back. Maud would soon watch meanness and violence between these two factions flaring up just about everywhere again, although now the violence by one side or the other was mostly thievery or sometimes just meanness for meanness sake.

The stories Maud had heard about getting a territory divorce were true. Kind of, anyway. From the passage of the Kansas-Nebraska act until Kansas became a state, there were three separate governments that claimed full governing authority, and over time the first such government to claim such authority actually became known as the Bogus Government. In this instance several thousand pro-slave Missouri men went over into Kansas, formed a government and adopted the entire Missouri set of laws. Then for good measure they added some very tough penalties for anyone who even objected to slavery. Before they came home they reestablished the capital at a convenient spot for themselves, right on the Missouri-Kansas border. Shortly thereafter, two more governments were formed, one by Kansas pro-slave residents (mostly) at a town called Lecompton. Then another by the abolitionists who made Topeka the state capital. After all of this there was still no system of courts in place; therefore, anyone seeking a divorce had only one option. They must appeal to the Territorial governing body for a bill granting their divorce, which is presuming of course they could figure out where it was.

At any rate, cause for divorce was about the same in all of the states:

- Impotence at the time of marriage
- Another spouse living at the date of marriage
- Adultery
- Becoming addicted to drunkenness after marriage
- Desertion, which is to mean absence without good cause for one year

The big, big difference in the Kansas Territory became a Judge named Pettit who presided over divorce requests to the Bogus Legislature. Neither Judge Pettit nor those who reported to him ever refused a request, even if the complaint were cold feet or long toenails!

At any rate, judges armed with commissions from the Bogus territorial government immediately set up shop and successfully wrested the divorce business away from the state of Indiana, where Judge Pettit had previously built it into an industry. The Bogus judges made it as convenient for the woman as they possibly could, sometimes actually setting up shop at the closest available point to the general eastern public, right at the bend in the river where the muddy Missouri first touched the Kansas territory. If one swore they had not seen their spouse for a year, and presuming said spouse could not prove otherwise, these Kansas Territory divorces were considered valid and could actually be offered as proof of a previous marriage. Pettit's influence spawned a grand enterprise. One simply had to go over the river to the Kansas Territory and see the judges, who in fair weather would accommodate all by having a table set up right on the riverbank. They arranged for some enterprising fellows with flat bottom boats to bring over as many as six women at a time, three up front and three in the back. The boat would be landed front first and the judge would recite his little piece, requiring each woman to respond appropriately when asked. The boatman would then turn the boat around and put the back end against the riverbank so the judge could repeat the process. The judges figured that a lady sitting with her end on a boat seat and that end of the boat touching Kansas Territory was good enough.

After all had given their names, sworn they had not seen their spouse (by name) for one whole year, and paid their legal fees (of course,) the judge handed them a document and declared they were legally divorced, based on the grounds of abandonment. It became the grandest divorce mill ever, with hundreds of women and an occasional man flocking to the banks of the Kaw. Most often the women would return within the hour to the steamboat they had come in on, to head back down river free from their troublesome mate. Hundreds of others, however, had barely scraped up the $30 or $40 to travel to the Kansas shore and pay the modest fees. When these unfortunate women returned to the Missouri side they were happy to be free, sad to be broke, and with no place to call home. Residents of The City of Kansas included hundreds of women who had come to get a territory divorce and then were forced into the world's oldest profession in order to eat. Presuming she could beat out all of the other applicants, a shop girl could earn about $4 or $5 a week. Room and board in modest accommodations ran $6 or $7 a week. When Purdy Maud arrived, a host of inexperienced prostitutes lined the streets, looking for any man with $2. By the end of the Civil War, these City of Kansas women would be known throughout America as "The Fallen Angels."

Back on the Missouri side of the Kaw there were opportunists who recognized a business opportunity with an unlimited supply of talent, and continuously recruited among the beautiful and more desirable. Aside from sheer physical beauty, some of these chosen ladies could speak several languages, play musical instruments with great skill, and were gifted conversationalists with impeccable manners. They could be taught the finer points on how to pleasure a lonely man of which there seemed to be a goodly supply with the right qualifications, that being $2 or $3. Many of these women whored only long enough to save enough money to leave, which in turn made room for the continuous supply of fresh new faces on the street.

Purdy Maud was appalled at what she saw in some of these women, and as she looked at the fear, confusion and heartbreak, Maud remembered full well the gut-wrenching existence of being powerless and abused. After her third week in town, Purdy Maud set about buying a big house, fitting it with as many beds as it would hold, buying foodstuff in huge quantities, and giving what support she could to those fortunate enough to pass her muster. Her deal was simple. Go earn what you could in an honorable fashion and put half of it in the house's general fund. Keep the other half for yourself. Your bed might be head to toe with another woman out in the hall, and a day in the kitchen was long and hard, but at least you didn't have to be a whore.

Purdy Maud was soon making daily rounds begging businesses for support for her house. A Mr. Shoemaker, who owned a big wagon shop, summed it up quite well:

"It is a simple deal. She's got more nerve than an abscessed tooth and she'll ask anybody for help she can get cornered. She will take your last nickel or last sack of flour for them women. Don't matter which."

He was absolutely right.

Soon, among others, she even knew the operators of the best brothels in town. It became well known that some of the sporting houses, in addition to being her best donors, often referred women to her they thought were unsuitable to enter the trade. Every week Maud rode her spirited mare four miles out on State Line Road south of Westport, to where Alexander Majors was building his fine new home. Majors was the operating genius behind the enormous transportation company that controlled the freight traffic on the Santa Fe Trail. Russell, Majors and Waddell had combined their three firms and now had 1700 drovers, 500 wagons and 7500 head of oxen out on nearby pasture land which they measured by the square mile. Russell had his office in Leavenworth where he kept in close contact with the Army of the West and where he was also an activist in town and territorial politics. Waddell had offices over in Lexington and concerned himself mostly with administration while Majors, the operational genius, insisted on keeping his office over at the trail's head.

Majors was a pious man and sought to hire men of good character who were forbidden to drink, swear or stop overnight within commuting distance of a known brothel. A typical Majors trail unit consisted of 26 wagons under command of a wagon master and his assistant. Each wagon, which could weigh as much as 5000 pounds, was pulled by 12 oxen driven by a bullwhacker and his blacksnake whip. A herder brought 40 or 50 extra oxen along at the rear as spares. The unit was expected to make 15 miles each day with each trip being highly planned, including an ironclad rule to observe the Sabbath. Majors paid one dollar a day six days a week, insisting that absolutely no travel, and only what work was necessary to the success or security of the unit was to be planned for Sunday. If a drover brought records from the wagon master showing he was at church on Sunday, he received the full $7 for his week. Their regular church attendance made his drivers well known and considered to be of good character and trustworthy the entire length of the trail. Majors was a great contact and confidant for Maud, and after making his acquaintance, she seldom ever had to pay any shortfall herself.

Purdy Maud had an uncanny talent for talking with a woman and seeing inside. She generally picked up on honesty, integrity, high moral standards and a helpful heart, all in a single interview. Maud did not care if they were homely as a fence post or pretty as a queen, she wanted the good women. She was seldom wrong.

There were also thousands of stories among the men passing through the City of Kansas, as they headed out to virtually every destination west of the Mississippi. Soon, a stop by Maud's place was a planned part for some on this trip, especially for single men who claimed or could prove to be of good character. Many other visitors were men who had lost their good wife on the trail, and needed a mother for their children. Maud had the same uncanny knack of identifying good character in men and sent dozens on their way; however, with her express approval, some number of "her girls" headed west for a whole new life, married up with a man of very recent acquaintance. It was pretty intimidating for any man to have a woman step forward to accept him, agree to marry up with him, and then have the other 30 or 40 women stand up with the bride. At any rate, dozens and dozens of thankful woman would one day bless the moment they caught Purdy Maud's eye. After learning how to read she would sit by the hour reading letters from "her girls" sprinkled from Mexico to Canada and from Missouri to the Pacific. She could remember each and every face until the day she died.

Time passed quickly and soon Christmas time was at hand. Being without Junior at the season caused Maud to miss her boy even more desperately. She absolutely knew in her heart that her presence would be poison to his future and took what comfort she could knowing that he was in good hands. Maud frequently wondered if she could possibly be legally married to that rascal Quinton Tooter, who had sneakily changed his name to Tuttoor, and if so, could he still seize two thirds of the money if he found her even after she got her divorce. At any rate she was going to wait her year and divorce him all legal like. Besides, she had no where else to be. What she did know for absolute certain was that he was the boy's father, and it made no difference that his father was white, if Tooter "proved up" on her then her blood would absolutely destroy her boy's future. She prayed that if she could stay hid from him for a year then if he found her his greed would make him claim her as his ex-wife, as opposed to his run-away slave. She hoped that the rest of a year would pass quickly and tried to focus on the others who so desperately needed her help. Taking comfort in the fact that for the first time in her life she was in a position to do so, she decided to make Christmas the best she possibly could for the others. With that in mind Maud went down to the bank:

"Mr. Jefferies."

"Yes, Purdy Maud?"

"With that last money you give me from your father paying me to use my St. Louis money, I got about what I started with except for buying the house. Right?"

"Yes. You have about what you had when you first come in, if you do not count the money you paid for the house."

"Best give me about $600."

"Certainly. That is a lot of money, Maud."

" I know, but I need that much."

One of Maud's unspoken rules was that unless they were out on a hired assignment the women must be back at the house at early evening. Tonight she gathered them all about her.

"Which one of you girls would go back home if you had the money?"

About half of them held up their hands while the other half murmured among themselves about how there was nothing to go back there for. She handed each of her girls $10 and to those who wanted to go home she gave an open ticket, good for about any port on the Mississippi or on up the Ohio. With a happy heart that still ached for her boy, Maud fought back the tears and swallowed the big lump in her throat. Finally she was able to croak it out:

"Merry Christmas."

The majority of Island View's slaves could not remember the Master ever helping them to celebrate Christmas, and for years it had been an all but a forgotten, joyless occasion. This year, however, as Christmas approached there was an air of excitement and much to look forward to. There were already some new bigger cabins and Miz. Virginia had designated the order in which the most dilapidated slave quarters would be torn down or repaired, and the process was well underway. Serviceable plain furniture had been mass produced with everyone having a good bed now. Everyone was also now wearing their new gray clothes plus a touch of color for the women from the boxes full of colorful bandana kerchiefs. Sewing lessons continued and all of the women were encouraged to participate with a couple of the more capable women still in charge. Slaves with special skills now wore a stripe of green, and everyone was trying to figure out what they could do to get one.

Each slave family had now staked out their own garden spot for the coming spring.

Requests were noted for additional hens for those who wanted them. The slaves finally got the concept that any family could sell their extra eggs or chickens and keep the money.

Virginia arranged to buy a good many Hampshire hogs from up in Tennessee, for the breed produced huge long and lean animals highly favored for wonderful bacon and fatback. Every family now had at least one sow and many were attempting to make them into pets.

A fertile plot of land was designated for next year's cornfield. The corncrib was refilled for winter. There was no lock.

Two small grinding mills were delivered to be shared by the families so they might make better cornmeal.

The hog trough the smaller children had been forced to eat at was set aside. They were now to eat at the table and chairs with their family. There were even highchairs.

Shoulder meat, fat back, sweet potatoes, dried fruit, molasses, honey and salt were supplied in fair but controlled amounts and would continue to be. There were sacks and sacks of beans.

The older men were given some fishing boats so they would have more bounty to share.

Slaves now only had to ask permission to leave the plantation; however, most had been virtually in prison for so long that few had anywhere they wanted to go. Plus it was also a very long walk to all but one other plantation.

New mothers would be waited on by the others a bit for the first three months and would be assigned light duty so as to enjoy their babies, or learn how to take care of a first born if that be the case.

The Amos and Ramos harvest teams remained virtually unchanged. Island View was going into next season with no overseer or head drivers. Just Miz. Virginia. She had no whip!

The work week was to stay at five and one half days a week unless they fell way behind, and so long as work was reasonably on schedule they would quit with two hours of daylight still in the day to tend their gardens, or chickens, or pigs. Or just visit.

Each slave was classified as a full hand or a half hand and told exactly what was expected of them the coming year. Any full hand would be expected to pick no less than 325 pounds per day. Those who did not would lose privileges but would not be whipped. (They could not imagine.) Virginia revised the reward system up just a bit. Four hundred pounds of clean picked cotton in a day would gain a small reward, increasing up to a full whole dollar for anyone who got as much as 525 pounds in a day. The slave from over "ta Mr. Gilbeert's place" who could pick as much as 600 pounds a day had demonstrated how she did it. Several of Virginia's people made up their minds they could do that too, and started practicing on becoming human windmills!

The stronger men would now be assigned alternately to carry the hampers to the wagon, so a picker would lift no heavy weights during the entire picking day.

The old slaves were assigned to keep fresh drinking water at the ready or watch the little ones. Anyone, including the oldsters, who met or beat their expectation next season would be given a reward. A large fenced in playground complete with shelter house and picnic tables was to be built down in a shady spot on the riverbank. It was to be complete with swings, teeter totters and the like, plus it was to be enclosed by a nicely decorated fence so the oldsters did not have to chase the kids or fear the close-by river. Last but not least, reading and numbers would continue to be taught and she now required the adults to study until they could read most of the New Testament and count to 100.

A white minister was hired to occasionally hold church and there would be a Christmas special church. After church each youngster would pick a wrapped present from Miz. Virginia's big pile, and then there would be a feast.

On this fine Christmas morning, the slave children who were old enough came to where she stood by her carriage loaded with presents. Even though they were all dressed in their very best, most of them were quite nervous, for they must introduce themselves. As their mothers held the smaller ones up close for her, Virginia surveyed the throng and could not help but privately wonder which among them were her grandchildren with the "precious" de Falco blood in their veins? For most, it was their first really close encounter with the woman who owned them body and soul. She laid her hand on each child, looked directly into their faces and smiled.

"Merry Christmas."

Christmas time in Kentucky came at last, and Grandfather Grasher showed up riding ahead of a heavily-loaded wagon pulled by four splendid but exhausted horses. He had made quite a journey. When he departed Pennsylvania he had boarded the boat and supervised the loading of several huge crates. At Louisville he disembarked having made prior arrangements for Purdy Mercantile at Paducah to receive the crates. From Louisville, after a visit with John's family, he went by train to Chicago where he cemented his relationship with a huge new account. And where he found the merchandise he was searching for. His next train was to St. Louis, where he stopped by the Holshers for a visit.

Mattie's grandfather Emit Grasher had immigrated to Pennsylvania from Germany with Gerald Holsher, they being the best of 22 year old friends, even though Holsher was Catholic, and Grasher was not. Both were redemptiors, whereas the Captain of the vessel held contract on their labor and could sell their services to whomever for whatever, for however long it took to redeem their passage fee. In Pennsylvania that meant perhaps five years; however, some of the Germans coming in through New Orleans were bound for 14 to16 years. Young Grasher had a gift of language and, at the age of 22, could both read and write most of the European languages. At the time Holsher had mostly a strong back to offer. Grasher was immediately redeemed and bound to a gentleman in the import business for three years. Holsher was finally selected by an agent who represented a chap over in St. Louis who needed muscle power, which he was bound to supply for the next five years.

Within weeks Grasher uncovered an ongoing scheme used by some dishonest employees to dupe his new master, implemented by using language and documents he did not understand. His appreciative master straight away made Grasher an employee by adding a nice monthly salary to the sizeable bonus he presented him. Grasher immediately sent his bonus to Holsher so that he might redeem himself, and furthermore arranged with his boss to have Holsher's sweetheart brought over. Her passage was an incentive bonus from a ship owner for using a given boat for a huge shipment. For their very first Christmas in America, Emit Grasher gave his friend, Gerald Holsher, five years of his life back, plus his sweetheart to share it with.

Grasher's parents were much too frail for such a journey at the time, and by now the rest of the Grasher family had pretty much scattered to South America. Therefore, when Holsher had saved enough money to repay his debt, Grasher insisted Holsher instead use the money to bring his parents. Then it was his youngest brother. Then his sister and her husband. Grasher continued to help with his shipping contacts and with plain hard cash money until Holsher's entire extended family had made it to St. Louis. In 1840 there were about 5,000 German immigrants in St. Louis; however, by the Civil War the number of new arrivals equaled that each year. Now in 1859 there was a two-block square of early arrival Catholics in the German Town of St. Louis, where Mathew, Mark, Luke and John shared equal billing. Then it was the Pope. Next up the ladder was Mattie's grandfather, Emit Grasher.

Gerald Holsher arranged meetings for Mattie's father with the biggest prospects St. Louis had to offer, and they were flattered that the most prominent businessman in the city had asked for a bit of time to meet a friend of his. Holsher also held two family receptions at his palatial estate in Grandfather Grasher's honor, as Holsher damn well insisted that the current generation know what a dear relationship there was between the families. That seemed apparent enough, for there were such a large number of men named Emit as to be confusing.

After their visit, Holsher had dispatched one of Holsher Brewing Company's boats down the Mississippi river along with a driver, this huge freight wagon and four of their magnificent draft animals. Plus a fine buggy and team complete with its own driver, for Grandfather Grasher's personal comfort. The Holsher boat doubled back up the Ohio to Paducah, where the Pennsylvania crates were waiting to be loaded into big the wagon along with the merchandise Grandfather had found in Chicago. They then headed to Three Creeks with wagon and buggy traveling overland together, the big wagon crammed with huge boxes and crates, which had been secured against the weather, their markings now all carefully painted over. All other available space in the wagon was loaded with several barrels of premium beer.

Mattie was more anxious than any child on the place, but John and Father Grasher insisted they must wait for Christmas Eve and she could hardly stand it, especially after she eavesdropped on her father:

"I found every single item on our list, John, but it sure was a tussle. I found the most important piece in Chicago."

After unloading the wagon in the barn they sent the drivers and teams home after they had helped cover the entire pile with a huge canvas.

Finally the time came, and Mattie was completely bemused.

First there were some big baked clay pipes. Then came the iron pipe followed by the Chicago crate that held what John happily announced was a ram pump:

"The Egyptians used these thousands of years ago. There would never have been a city of Jerusalem had they not known how to build these."

Mattie cocked her head:

"What on earth does it do?"

"It will pump water out of a moving stream to up way high and for a long ways. You do not have to touch it. If the creek water stops running, you can work it by hand but the water never stops here at the main creek, and running water is what makes it work."

Next there was a tank, and yet another tank with what looked like a cook stove firebox built in. When the water closet came out of its crate, Mattie started smiling broadly for now she knew! The Purdys were going to have indoor plumbing! Mattie had been raised in a fine home with a gas line, water line and sewer running to every house in the neighborhood. She had never complained once about the more primitive conditions John had brought her to, but she always missed that luxury most of all. Junior looked at the plans and understood them at once. The magic pump would pump water from the creek to the tank mounted up on its stand. Water would be warmed by the sun or run down to the other tank and be heated by its firebox on the way to the tub. Cold water from the main tank's other pipe could also go to the tub or flush the water closet, and the tile would carry the effuse away. Pure genius.

The huge final crate was then uncovered and when the side came off of it, Mattie shrieked. Then she began to cry. She jumped up and down and between twisting first her hair and then her skirt like a little girl. She clasped her hands together over and over again. She could not believe what she saw. It was her mother's piano! Fine pianos were rare in rural Kentucky, and Mattie had but few opportunities to sit at one since coming to Three Creeks. She was an accomplished violinist but only a fair piano player and the piano was woefully out of tune from its travels. Nonetheless, after the hammers were released, Mattie held up th entire process as she sat softly stroking the keys while distant memories of her mother at this fine instrument came flooding back.

Indoor plumbing would be very nice.

This was a gift for all time.

The piano tuner had spent the night before at Dody's tavern and after they got the piano into the house, he soon was plinking away. By nightfall the piano was in great form.

Mr. Brown came over and listened to Mattie for a while.

"May I?"

"Of course"

He sat at the piano and played some of the best piano one might ever hear. The style became known as Boogie Woogie

John sat in pure wonderment of this man, Brown, and could not help but wonder why a man such as him was teaching school in a place like Three Creeks. He seemed happy enough with whatever they could afford to pay a few months out of the year and to just hang around being generally useful the rest of the time. He willingly conducted free math and reading lessons in people's homes and at a time when many thought such learning was wasted on the women, he specifically insisted the women be included if he were to come.

He was nice looking.

He seemed to have plenty of money.

He was obviously quite well educated.

He played good music.

He was a fast draw artist and an incredible shot.

He had a fine horse and great weapons.

He went out of his way to avoid confrontation.

He had nerves of steel.

He was better than most doctors.

He had an incredible scar across his gut.

He had once referred to wanted posters with him on them.

He insisted every one simply call him Brown.

He had proven himself a friend without reservation.

The lively Christmas day feast included Mattie's father, John's parents, Henry and Ruth, Brown, Mr. Morris, his wife and children, Bos and Junior, plus the boys of course, who were so excited they were just barely under control. Trisha had outdone herself cooking for a week ahead of time, leaving Mattie in charge of desserts. John cooked the meat over an open pit and prepared venison, beef and turkey in abundance and the Holsher beer was simply splendid.

It was a wonderful again to be in Three Creeks.

"Merry Christmas."

Finally it was the cusp of spring, 1860, with some of the braver Kentucky plants and trees already forcing their buds. Mattie had pretty well put both of the incidents behind her, and John was of the opinion that if you dwelled on such things as the attempted kidnap-rape, and his horse whipping, you could let it "eat you up." The Tooters had been dealt with and paid a heavy price for their mischief while Johnson and Sledge apparently had fled the country permanently, for neither had been back to their shack. John forced his attention to other things. After all, the store was now loaded with inventory as *'the'* time of year was at hand.

Grandmother Ella would soon follow the servant she sent down the Ohio from Louisville to open up her Paducah home. Besides spending time with her son's family, she loved springtime in the beautiful valley where the Tennessee River flows into the Ohio.

Down in Louisiana, planting time at Island View was coming up fast and Miz. Virginia was gently trying to dial her slaves back. There was far more acreage than they could possibly deal with, but they were all wanting to plant just a few acres more to show her what they could do. It was a delicate balance to not curb their enthusiasm and still be realistic in letting them do their very best.

Over at the Kaw's confluence with the Missouri, springtime boats into the City of Kansas were once more dropping off women by the dozens who went looking for the divorce judge. All the while Maud was working the docks looking for the precious few she could help. She gave as good as she got from the friendly hassling she received from the large group of Irishmen that seemed to control the extra curricular activities down by the river, and they were generous to her cause to a fault. It came a cool snap over the entire country and the fire still felt extra good in Kentucky on the evening of the 15th of March, 1860.

Virginia de Falco, Purdy Maud and the Purdy household settled into their beds looking optimistically for what tomorrow might bring.

It was about midnight when Hiram Purdy came staggering out of the boys' sleeping porch dragging brother Harold and screaming wildly for help!

"Dad! Mom! Dad! Help! Help!!"

John tumbled out of the master bedroom into the pitch dark, with Mattie following immediately behind with a lamp. One didn't need a light to smell and feel the smoke in the air. Heavy green acid smelling smoke was lying all across the floor, billowing and tumbling from the sleeping porch door where Henry had come struggling out to then drop to all fours puking up and gagging.

"Ring the bell, Go ring the bell!" Mattie screamed!

"The water kettles are full! Go throw water!"

John quickly counted heads and rushed into the sleeping quarters looking for Harvey. The sleeping porch was ingeniously designed with six-foot high dividers between each boy's space, with all rooms then having one corner open to the center for heat from the cast iron stove. It was sort of a square four leaf clover with the stove at the center and with the stem leading out to the living room. Entry to each section was down the "stem" hallway to the stove and then into each of the four spaces from its open corner. The smoke was the very worst in little Harvey's section right at his empty bed. John searched frantically about the area until he simply had to come out for air.

Hiram was ringing the school, or "call-to-worship-bell" with all of his might. This was the neighborhood signal to assemble for school through the week, for worship on Sunday, or the "I need help" call any other time. Back into the bedroom with a wet rag over his face, John felt desperately about, his lungs burning with the terrible smoke as he kept frantically crawling and lunging about, gasping and touching and feeling and searching as only a father would, or perhaps could, do. Flames broke through right about Harvey's bed, and flickered across his small form huddled in a corner behind and under it. Singeing the hair off his arms and his eyebrows, John shoved the bed aside, grabbed his son and staggered out into the fresh air. In an amazingly short time the entire Three Creeks adult neighborhood was assembling. The new water tanks were full, plus two big iron kettles of water were being prepared for an early start on washday tomorrow. With the creek also close at hand the fire was contained in fairly short order, and with the exception of the smell from smoke, damage was mostly confined to Harvey's corner of the boys' sleeping porch.

Harvey never moved.

Brown stretched him out on the floor and worked over him, pinching Harvey's nose and blowing his own breath into the lad's lungs and then forcing the air out, over and over and over and over. Brown was like a man possessed. He absolutely refused to give up, until, after ever so long, John softly laid his hand on his friend's shoulder:

"I think it's time to quit."

Mattie, had fearfully stood close at hand, watching. She collapsed to the floor and pulled the head of her last born into her lap, clutching his smoky little head to her bosom. As she sat on the floor she started rocking back and forth at her waist, and a haunting cry of anguish started from deep within her very soul. It tumbled over her lips again and again and again.

Those who have experienced much of what life has to offer most generally agree there is no pain to the heart like that of a mother who has just lost her child. John came and sat on the floor with his arms around them both as she held their baby. They wept together.

Daybreak found a solemn neighborhood gathered to support one of their own.

Junior was simply inconsolable.

His little buddy was gone.

The first to make him feel he could be normal was gone.

The first to make him feel welcome was gone.

No more shadow jumping or riding around on his shoulders as the Roman soldier. His Roman soldier was gone.

Trisha led Junior away, knowing from first hand experience what Mattie and John had to do in order to work their way past these first few hours.

Brown pulled John aside:

"John, you better come and look at this."

"What are you looking at?"

"Come see."

It was obvious the fire had been set.

The more distant neighbors began pouring into the settlement to be of help where they could. All parents in that day lived in constant fear and concern of everything from snakebite to appendicitis or dysentery. Many, if not most, of these woman had lost at least one of their own. As the neighborhood woman started to prepare the little fellow, they were horrified that someone had done this thing on purpose, and both their anger and sympathy were genuinely heartfelt. What made it even more heartbreaking was that Harvey looked as though he should jump up any minute and shout "surprise." Mattie insisted on doing most of it herself. She bathed him and washed his face. Washed and combed his hair. Cleaned under his fingernails and dressed him nicely.

And kissed him time after time.

Little Harvey Purdy's funeral was by far the largest gathering to date in Three Creeks, Kentucky, and the Purdys were nearly overwhelmed by the show of respect and support. John and Mattie tried to show appreciation to every one who came and to assist ever so many who traveled overnight in order to be there. The most notable guest was 80-year-old Gerald Holsher. Although his friend Grasher had done well right off, it had taken Holsher time to get organized; nevertheless, he had done very, very well. The older man insisted on paying his respects in person, both to the family and to the great grandson of the man who had given him his freedom, his sweetheart, and his family back. His five brothers, his sister, and all of their extended families owed this man's memory a debt they would never forget, but could never fully repay. Gerald Holsher and three of his sons had traveled both day and night to get there. They brought their "coach and four" downriver as close as possible on one of their brewing company's steamboats and then hired a local who was familiar with the roads to press ahead through the night with a guiding lantern. The Holsher delegation arrived barely in time for the service, their fine teams still in lock step although even in the cool weather they were completely lathered up, and the color of road dust. It was an absolutely Herculean effort for a young man, let alone an 80 year old with a shock of snow white hair now covered with the same color dust.

They laid little Harvey on his inseparable "blankee" that Trish had pieced together and stitched for him from hundreds of pieces when he was just a baby. Then, they put in some of his other favorite things. Last of all, as they closed the coffin, Mattie added fresh hot cookies and bent over her baby to give him a long, long smurzle:

"That has to last me a very long time."

This was the very moment that brought John's grandmother Ella Purdy to tears. Up to then she had managed to keep composed and be the comforter, but that was the very moment that finally got to her. The 70-something, 107-pound, gray-headed fireball turned to John,

"We got to find the son of a bitch and kill him, John. I'll go with you. I can still ride like the wind and I won't slow you down. I promise. I need to look down a gun barrel at this one! Can I go too?"

Junior and Bos helped Harvey's three older brothers carry him over to the graveside. Simpson's carpenter slaves who had built the beautiful small red cedar wood casket stood gathered with the rest of the Negroes a distance away until Mattie asked Bos to bring every one of the slaves up close. The casket's finishing touch was a pair of beautifully detailed hands carved from the white of cedar, fastened to its lid by a woman who sold her carved walking sticks to the Purdys. The white wood carvings of a child's hand reaching into an adult's showed beautifully against the smooth, varnished red cedar.

The Chickasaw had their own ceremony complete with muted drums on a nearby hilltop.

The minister gave what comfort he could and few if any were surprised at how he finished his remarks:

"This is not the will of God; this is the work of a very evil person. The God I serve does not take little boys from their families by setting fire to their house in the middle of the night."

For the very last part of the service Mattie took her violin from its case, removed her bonnet, shook out her beautiful mane of honey blond hair and walked over to stand at the head of the unfilled grave.

The sun was brilliant.

The Kentucky sky was so blue it almost hurt one's eye.

The breeze was brisk and smelled of spring and new life.

Her hair brushed softly over the instrument.

The breeze fluffed her long black dress.

For a long moment she stood like a statue.

She composed herself.

Then gently drew her bow.

In a place far, far away St. Peter had to smile as one of his newest little angels managed to hold on to a couple of cookies he had just snitched. All the while he was chasing the notes of a magnificently complex version of Brahm's lullaby about Heaven's gates.

The location they picked for little Harvey, and therefore the Purdy graveyard for generations to come, was a grassy knoll about halfway between the house and the garden. It was a beautiful spot surrounded by maple and cedar trees with a profusion of wild roses, plus some 20 kinds of wildflowers for their appropriate time of the year. From this spot one could see over to the rock-climbing part of the creek, see the great mill wheel, and watch people come and go; both there, and along the road as well as along the garden path. It was a peaceful place but one would not get lonesome there.

After most had said their goodbyes and headed for home that afternoon, John and Mattie returned and stood holding hands at the fresh little grave. It was now covered with some of Kentucky's bravest springtime blooms that had been placed there.

"Promise me something John."

"Okay."

His Mattie looked so sad. He turned to her and the red in her eyes and the pain lines on her face broke his heart. Again. He had seen her so very sad only one other time, that day she learned that Mrs. Purvis had passed. That was inevitable and she accepted it as such. Now, this woman he had loved with all his being from the very moment he laid eyes on her was absolutely destroyed. When he gathered her to him, her uncontrollable trembling forced the "grit" in his blood to boil to the top. Adrenaline and anger buried John Purdy like snow pouring down a mountainside avalanche.

"I promise you, Mattie. What am I promising?"

When you know for sure."

"Yes?"

"Do not let them die easy."

Still facing her, John dropped to his knees on the fresh little grave, crushing some of the blossoms with his knees. Taking Mattie around her hips he pulled her to him so he might bury his face in her abdomen. Then he looked up into her face:

"Mattie Purdy, I swear it on the grave of our lastborn son. This day I swear to you by all by that I am, or all I ever will be. I swear to you, I swear to Harvey, I swear to God, and I swear to all else that is Holy. This is my covenant. He or she or they will not die easy."

John Purdy swore so to his Mattie that day.

Perhaps even more significantly, he swore so to himself.

After such a tragedy, time is the only healing balm. In the weeks that followed Harvey's death, John and Mattie were so inseparable that one was rarely seen without the other. Their inner circle and family all "closed ranks," and gathered around to grieve together. Grandfather Grasher could not possibly make it in time for the funeral; however, he came back and stayed for three weeks. Grandpas are not supposed to have favorites but he had always showed a bit of favoritism to the youngest grandson as each came along. He was terribly saddened by the chain of events, but being a man of faith and a wise man who had lived much of life, he was a beacon guiding them back toward normalcy. For several weeks someone from John's side of the family was in and out almost every day. The neighbors were fantastic in their support, but they too had lives to live and drifted back to their own day to day.

Simpson's carpenter slaves came over and had the house repaired in short order such that it showed little if any trace of the tragedy, except the ever-present faint smell of smoke. A smell that haunted everyone, especially so John and Mattie, for it constantly served to remind of a little boy gone. And the dastardly deed. Finally, lives truly begin to return to normal. A different normalcy to be sure, but as normal as it would be for a long, long while. The summer flowers finally brought with them the new normal for the Purdy household.

John bought a well-trained watch dog from a trainer up toward St. Louis, who had a reputation for producing the very best. The dog was friendly enough until strangers showed up at night time. Duke the dog was mostly boxer it seemed, but really just a big mixed breed that Mattie fed so he would follow her commands best of anyone's. Bos, his favorite playmate, cleaned up after him and now, for the first time in his life, the sound of a dog's bark no longer scared Bos half out of his wits. The pain in Mattie's eyes broke Bos' heart and there were a few times ever that a huge black man wanted so desperately to get his hands on somebody and break them in to pieces. He simply needed to know who. And find him.

The box from Colt came. There were four beautiful nickel-plated .44 caliber six shot models made especially for the Dragoons, men who were trained to fight both on horseback or hand-to-hand on foot. These guns were so incredibly accurate that in tests they were as effective as a common rifle, making them far superior to a musket for up to two hundred yards. With the shorter seven and one-half inch barrels and only two and three-sixteenth inch cylinders, they were intended to be worn on the hip. His new gun belt was a hand-tooled work of art and John already had a nice saddlebag holster and a larger colt "horse pistol" for heavy work.

He took one of the new smaller ones over to Brown and made him a proposition.

"Teach me how to really shoot one of these things and pick one for yourself."

John realized very quickly he would never be as fast on the draw as his friend, but soon he was quite pleased with his own accuracy.

Brown agreed these pistols were truly masterpieces:

"Finest piece of iron I ever held on to. Mercy! John, in my opinion the draw is really the small half of it. Until you learn to kind of throw the shot where you want it to go, having the guts to take an extra split second for careful aim while you're looking down the wrong end of a gun barrel is damn well the big half. I doubt you will ever get to a quick draw face off with the characters you are looking for. My experience says those kind won't face a man, but you sure need to watch your back. Anyway, I hope target practice is all you ever get to use this for."

At first Mattie hated shooting one of the infernal things but she did. Over and over and over again, until it no longer scared her. While John was gone, she would sleep with one close at hand and Hiram would sleep with another, for the Purdy household was now an armed camp. Mattie was a woman of strong faith, and after a while she seemed to have come to grips with how things were, and how they were going to be. She started becoming somewhat her old self.

They really hadn't talked much about it, for they did not have to.

One early summer day John started packing a bedroll, so she helped him get his stuff organized as she had when he took off on some business trips before. He wanted to travel light this time and chided her as he kept taking out as much as she put in:

"I can get by without that."

"Where are you going first, John?"

"South. I have talked to everyone, and no one, including any of the Indians, has seen Johnson or Sledge and apparently their shack has not been used in months. We know the Tooters went south but only one of them showed up. That seems pretty strange. A fellow who looked like that would be hard to miss, but our so-called Tuttoor seems to have disappeared, which makes me wonder if and why they split up. For Junior's sake I hope it was not his dad, but I think it has to be the Tooter brothers or Johnson and Sledge. Bos told me where to find Island View so I'll start there first. A Sheriff Davis down there confirmed Cooper Tooter is back there and maybe if I talk to his brother just maybe I can pick up Juniors' Dads' trail. Both of them were in pretty tough shape and would need quite a while to get completely well. Anyway, I'll feel like at least I am doing something.

Mattie sat on the edge of the bed:

"It is a shame the arm of the law does not seem to be long enough to find these people. Your father and mine have both offered to hire Pinkerton men to go find these characters. Are you certain you don't want somebody to at least go with you, or hire someone to hunt for them and report back?"

John Purdy never swore an oath lightly in his life, and besides that, Grandmother Purdy's words still rang in his ears.

"Mattie, we have waited on others long enough. I know where to find one of the Tooters and can start from there. Besides, about all we know about Johnson and Sledge is that they still trap over in Missouri and on out west. They will show up somewhere sooner or later. The store is in goods hands, and you have lots of loving people around you. I must do this for our boy."

"I am glad you feel that way, John. I do too. I miss him so. How long do you imagine you might be gone this time?"

"I have no idea. There is a one of those new telegraph wires in Paducah. I will send word to my father from time to time when I get a chance."

They lingered in the bedroom for a while. He had held her last night as well, but it could be a long time until next time. Later she wore a brave little smile as John checked his saddle, saddlebags and the waterproof bedroll. As he mounted up, she flashed all of the smile she could muster:

"Remember. Don't ride Star any faster than your guardian angel can fly."

Later that day, John and Star reached the Mississippi where he caught a south-bound ice freighter taking on firewood. It was hauling ice packed in sawdust from Minnesota all the way to New Orleans where $5 a ton Minnesota ice brought $150 a ton in the summer of 1860. The captain welcomed both him and Star aboard.

"My name is John Purdy."

"People just call me Captain Mac."

"Thanks for making room for my horse."

"I'll probably charge more for him than you. Do you need to cover up the critter's head?"

"No. He will not frighten. He is well mannered."

"He is a dandy."

"Thanks."

"Big un"

"Fun to ride."

"Pretty fancy iron you are carrying there, young fellow."

"Thanks again. I like it."

When they came to Memphis, the boat had a stop to make and John was amazed that there were already over 500 other boats berthed, with plenty more looking for a place to tie up. After securing the Marybeth 2 Captain Mac found John as they were walking down the stage headed for shore.

"No use waitin round here, we gonna to be just a little while. The mate can handle all this. Come on. I know where we can have a fine old time, if you know what I mean."

"Thanks, but no thanks, Captain."

"Ain't a ugly one in the place!"

John had his own list of right and wrong. Besides, with Mattie waiting at home, no other woman stood a chance. Ever.

"Go ahead, I need to exercise the horse."

John and Star wandered the fascinating riverfront, then he had a beer at one of the more respectable looking places and watched as others admired his mount. Captain Mac returned as planned, mostly sober, and as another boat wanted their slot they must cast off right on time.

"I know right where you need to go, young Mr. John boy. Hug the west bank for bout a mile and this @#$% island sticks right up in your face back in a little bend in the river. Great place cause it never floods on that side of the river and it is nice and deep on the river side of the island but too shallow for most anything tween the !@#$%^ island and shore. They got another big landing on down bout a mile where they load their cotton. Fella used to own his own^%$#@! boat."

A few days later Captain Mac, while still marveling at the fine knife with the letter P on it that John had just traded him for a ball of fuzz out of his pocket, gave explicit orders to ready the ^%$#@ stage (gangplank.) The old man was a master at his craft and gently held the heavily loaded boat against the current at the island's deep-side landing. They both took a minute to admire the view up to the magnificent mansion.

"Iffin you ready to head back up river, you tie two white flags on that tree right ovta yonder and watch for me. I will tell some of the others who also got room for your horse to watch for em if I go by fore your ready. I'll be back in eight days. Tomorrow is day one. I know every man jack on this river and a few rivers side thisin. I am goon kinda spread the word to keep a lookout some them fellas you been talking bout. Sounds like the sons of bitches alls need be shot. I enjoyed your company, John boy, and hope I get to haul you back upta Kentucky. Good luck, son."

Someone was obviously paying close attention, because a slave came down and started winching the skiff over, so John and Star might come ashore and kept their feet dry.

"Welcome to Island View, sir."

"Thank you. My name is John Purdy."

"Yes sir, my name be Daniel."

Daniel looked apprehensively at the big stallion. John handed Daniel a lump of sugar.

"Give him this."

Soon Star and Daniel were the best of friends, and the three of them walked up the glistening chipped marble lane toward the mansion through yards where every bush or tree was trimmed to perfection. All the wood sashes and doors on the mansion glistened with fresh paint or varnish against the timeless stone structure with its tile roof. Daniel held Star's bridle, as John took off his hat and mounted the steps to the massive front doors.

"Want's that I should rub him down, Mr. Purdy?"

"Let's wait a bit. I certainly hope there'll be time for you to."

"Me too, Mr. Purdy. Be an honor to take care of a horse like this."

The door swung open before he could knock, and a sort of lanky tall lady with long legs even for one of her height appeared. Her huge mane of salt and pepper grey made her appear even taller yet. The lady of the house wasn't exactly beautiful, but she was pretty enough and she certainly was striking. She held out her hand:

"Good morning, sir. Welcome to Island View; I am Virginia de Falco."

After about half of an hour Virginia and John were chatting away like old friends. Yes, Cooper Tooter was still here. He was definitely an unwelcome guest, but he was also serving a purpose.

"Mr. Purdy, we, er I had a pretty frightening experience and I have allowed the scoundrel to stay on for one reason and one reason only. I want, no actually I need, to make certain he was not involved with a threat on my life. The local sheriff has come to the conclusion that he was not, but I am still not so certain. I am certain of one thing though. I am certain that I am sick and tired of seeing him around. You may have come in the nick of time for I was about to have him escorted him off Island View for the second time. He stole a lot from me and mine, Mr.

Purdy. He stole a good deal of money but more importantly he stole our dignity and he almost stole our souls, our very right to call ourself human."

John was really wondering how far he should confide in this woman, for she seemed quite unpretentious and was being downright candid. He had not established it as fact yet, but in all probability Maud's fortune had really been stolen from her. He did know one thing for a fact. Bos belonged to her. Poor Bos. He had tried not to show it when he found out John was headed to Island View, but the huge black man was scared absolutely witless.

"I need to talk to Tooter."

"Oh, there's no hurry Mr. Purdy. He is not going anywhere. Please, would you care to freshen up? It's time for lunch. Will you be staying overnight? You may have your choice of rooms, for it's only me and the household staff in this entire place."

"That would be very kind of you."

She turned to Amanda:

"Please have Daniel come in."

"Yes ma'am."

"Daniel, did you do as I asked?"

"Which time, ma'am?"

"Oh, you know, down at Tooter's shack."

"Oh, yes ma'am. I did it. And I did it real good."

"I am counting on it."

"You got no worry, Miz. Virginia."

"Stake your life on it?"

"Yes ma'am."

"And mine?"

"Yes ma'am."

"Thank you, Daniel. And by the way, if Mr. Purdy would like, please groom that beautiful beast of his. I never saw such a magnificent animal. Take him down and show the others. A horse like that is a show all by itself."

"Me and dat Star horse, we be the best friends. He like old Daniel combing out his mane. I go sho de others."

"Mr. Purdy, I would offer some wine with lunch, but I am an alcoholic and there is no such thing to be found at Island View. My loving staff is very efficient."

She was so disarming that John had to further discipline himself against sharing too much just yet. He looked out past the beautiful nook where their lunch was spread and saw a young Negro who looked an awful lot like Bos, working in the flowers. He looked over and the same one was at the other corner. His gaze shifted back and forth.

"How in the world do you know which of those young men is which?"

"I don't."

She added sort of a pointed afterthought:

"But they are both mighty handy to have around."

Lunch was delicious and unhurried. Afterwards she announced she was changing clothes and instructed that John be given opportunity to try on and wear some other boots.

"Those handsome boots are far too nice to walk where we may wind up, and I don't think you will need your gun."

When she returned she was dressed much simpler and John noticed the skirt split like a pair of pants, so it mostly looked like a skirt that stopped at her shoe tops. (Mammy was making some headway here and there at least.) There were several pairs of boots to choose from, and John found a pair that fit pretty well, all the while wondering what dead man's boots he was wearing. He assumed she meant she did not want a gun down in the quarters so he took off his gun belt and hung it over a chair back.

John and Virginia took the lengthy walk back towards the slave quarters although she had offered to get a carriage. He needed a walk and with her long legs she easily kept up.

"Would you mind carrying this, Mr. Purdy?"

As they walked briskly along she handed him a small box to carry, which he thought it quite heavy for its size.

He sat with a filthy towel across his lap, looking out the door of the slave cabin. Seething. Swearing. Infuriated. At how things were then; and how they turned out; and especially about the latest turn of events. A few weeks ago when he was known as Mr. Coopert, the Island View

Negros shrank from his presence as he strutted about, and they were especially terrified when summoned to his presence. Now, as Cooper Tooter they mocked his looks and the men saved up to come urinate at his door.

Cooper Tooter was expecting guests soon, for he had seen Daniel parading about with Star. There were simply no two such horses. As he waited for John Purdy, Tooter trembled with rage for he knew full well how humiliating it would be for Purdy to see him in this dilapidated old slave cabin, set right next to a hog pen. In fact, the back wall of his cabin was a part of the fence along with three other such old cabins that made the corners of this particular pig pen. Hogs now lived in the other three and the bitch Virginia allowed the other "pig" to live in the forth. He seethed with rage not knowing which of his approaching visitors he hated the more.

"Mr. Tooter, there is a gentleman here who would like to talk with you. He would like to know about your brother."

John knew that Cooper Tooter was not his man. Virginia assured him that he had been under careful watch since the day he showed back up. He may well have arranged for something before his return; however, every minute could be accounted for since then. Even his sneaking up and prodding around the cemetery at night was duly reported by watchful eyes. John wanted to know specifically Tooter's brother Quinton's whereabouts, plus anything else of general interest.

'So, the victorious Mr. Purdy and Miz. Virginia."

"Mr. Tooter, I think Mr. Purdy might be holding something you have been looking for. Show him what you have in your hand, John."

It was the final straw for the once powerful and cruel master who enjoyed nothing more than the shrieks of his victims. He had always found watching his victim writhe in pain most erotic. Now, reduced to living with the pigs and face to face with the two whose guts he hated the worst, Tooter's rage overwhelmed him. Immediately recognizing the container John was holding and unable to control himself he went on what one might call "overload." Seeing John Purdy in possession of the very last dollars of his ill-gotten fortune was more than his mind could take.

"How did you get my gold!? That is my gold! My gold! Give me my gold!"

Virginia seized the package from John and waived it in Tooter's face.

" I think not, Mr. Tooter. I think it is mine!"

He was now so angry he was weeping. Tooter's face turned purple, his grotesque features becoming a horrific caricature as he pulled the pistol he had concealed under the old towel on his lap:

"Give me my gold! If my brother had had any guts, Purdy, you and that worthless slave boy he called a son would be dead! Well he is dead and I am not! Give that to me or I'll kill you both just like I killed the gutless weasel! You should have seen the coward flapping about and heard him scream! Will you scream like a coward, Purdy? Let me hear you scream! Go on, Purdy! Beg me not to blow out your brains. On your knees. Beg, damn you! Beg!"

Virginia remained undaunted and continued waiving the box of gold in Tooter's face:

"You swine! It's a disgrace to the other pigs to have to live with you!"

Tooter twisted, and holding the gun in both hands he pointed it straight at her nose. John desperately made a move to get between the two: however, Virginia cut him off with her body. She thundered:

"Tooter you are the most worthless crazy degenerate son of a bitch the world ever had. You and Geneva Chouteau tried to kill me didn't you?"

"Geneva Chouteau treated me like dirt. She would not even talk to me. She was afraid I would contaminate that candy-assed boy of hers. I don't know nothing about her trying to kill you, but I wish by God she had. I will. I will kill you both right now. I don't care if I do hang!"

Virginia was at point-blank range when the pistol's hammer dropped harmlessly on a cap that had been water soaked at least five times.

When John boxed as a young man he was pretty good, mostly because as a kid his grandfather Purdy had taught him how to get his full weight behind his fists. He hit Tooter with every ounce of his 220 pounds. John hit him again and again until Tooter collapsed back into the wall, doubled over sucking for air after John knocked the breath out him with a fist buried deep into his gut. The next punch was John's best punch, straight to the chin, and sent Tooter tumbling through the greased paper window. He landed right on top of some three-day-old pigs.

Any farm boy will tell you that a sow hog can be dangerous. A hog cannot turn its head sideways nor lift it to get a good bite; however, to a creature on the ground where it can get at it, a mad or frightened hog can be a killing machine. Especially so a sow who just had pigs. Especially so some enraged three-hundred-and-fifty pound Hampshire sows that charge to the rescue but can't tell whose squealing little piggy is being squished.

The first one shredded an arm.

The second one spilled his guts on the ground.

The third one took Tooter's ugly face mostly off.

Then the three sows grabbed pieces and shook them, just like they always do when a hog kills a snake.

The only other time John Purdy ever felt this weak in the knees was the first time Mattie kissed him. If ever there were a horrific way to die, being eaten by the hogs must be it. The sows were only doing what Mother Nature had hardwired into them as they protected their young, but what happened was grisly. Cooper Tooter was as evil as any human ever born, yet to hear even the likes of him screaming and flailing away in muddy hog manure with 1000 pounds of Hampshire sow tearing away, was mind shattering.

Virginia was stoic.

Charlie, one of the ex-turncoats, had the bad luck to be close at hand, and was just walking by when he witnessed the entire thing. Charlie stood transfixed, as pale as a black man can get.

Virginia spotted him:

"Charlie."

"Yes a yesss a mmmam'am!"

"Charlie, put some corn in the trough up the other side of the fence gate and when the sows are all up there, close the gate."

"Yaa yaa sess ma'am."

"Mark those sows. I have read where any hog that has ever attacked a human should be considered quite dangerous. After we wean their pigs, we better butcher those three. I do not want the children around them. Tell whoever they belong to that they each can have another. It's a shame. They had nice litters."

"Ya yayaess ma ma mam ma'am."

"After you get the sows pinned up, have someone help you take what is left of Mr. Tooter and put him in a hamper or bag or something. Bury him up along the other hog lot, but don't bury him to deep. The sheriff may want to see what is left of him. I doubt it though."

"Yayayaess mam mam'amaham."

Virginia turned her attention to John:

"Thank you for trying to get between me and Tooter. You are a brave man. He had a pretty good two handed grip on that pistol for only two fingers on each hand, and the way he pulled the hammer back was ingenious. I would guess he practiced that a lot."

"Virginia, you knew that gun would not go off didn't you?"

"Let's say I was planning on it. Big time."

"Why in all of the name that is holy did you not tell me? I could have had a heart attack!"

"Oh come now, John, you are young and the picture of health. If you would had of looked any less riled up and not tried so hard to protect me, he may well have caught on."

"That was some act."

"When Tooter came back I demanded that he lay out all of his things. He only got to keep what I said he could keep and I confiscated all of his ghastly things. I think he told the truth about killing his brother because he had two sets of some of those horrid instruments. Crushers and shackles and branding irons. They are awful. At any rate, he always had any of Island View's slaves he though might give him trouble either watch him polish and shine his so called tools, or have them do it themselves before he abused them. Some of the second set are rusty, and the way he loved his, well I just know they can't be his. I bet they belonged to his brother."

"The gun. Where in God's name did he get a gun?"

"I had Amos and Ramos, the twins, have him be their coach and show them how to shoot and reload. I had a gunsmith put in a stop block and I also had Daniel soak the pistol caps in water several times. Then the twins just happened to forget and leave it at his shack. It looked in fine shape. I needed the very real truth out of that scalawag and I figured if I got him mad enough the truth would come roaring out. You just happened to be here. Do you believe what he said?"

"Yes. I certainly do. How did you know it was the right gun?"

"Well, life is full of chances and you have to take one once in a while."

"That is pretty gutsy. One other thing, Virginia. The gold?"

"Tooter was obsessed with the family graveyard, sneaking up there in the middle of practically every night. I had some of my people start skinning off the sod and digging about and then replacing it. I was going to have the place sifted but we found the gold almost before we got started. Over $3,000 worth. He was in such bad shape he must have not been able to dig very well for it was only a foot or so deep and right in my grandfather's face. Anyway, if you believe his ranting as I do, then we neither have to wonder about the brothers Tooter. You got your answers and I got mine. Knocking him out into the furrowing pen was just a bit of good fortune, wouldn't you say?"

"Well ahh, I guess that's one way to put it."

"Mr. Purdy, I may be a bit late for dinner. Do you mind a rather late table?"

"No. No that would be fine. In fact I doubt I can eat much."

"Mammy can find you a drink, I am sure. There is a bit left in a small keg from the Booze Company, probably enough for a good stiff one."

John truly hoped their might be enough for more than one.

"Have Amos or Ramos show you around. It really is a grand old place. Or feel free to wonder around by yourself."

"Thanks."

As they reentered the mansion John noticed his boots by the door, where you could now see your face in their fresh shine.

Mammy appeared as if by magic.

"Mammy, see if you can't find Mr. Purdy something to drink stronger than tea. He could use one right now."

"Yes Ma'am, there may be a spot or two."

Virginia de Falco excused herself, then walked up to her room closed the door and leaned back against it. She put her hand over her mouth and retched as she collapsed against the door, slowly sliding down it until she was leaning against it in a sitting position on the floor. She sat with her eyes closed. Had Virginia not focused her mind on Tooter's instruments of torture she might well have cracked right then. Tomorrow maybe, or after she talked to the sheriff, she would have Amos or Ramos dump all of them into the river. Right now the iron lady needed to sit and compose herself.

Then, she had Geneva Chouteau to deal with.

John took his drink down to the stables where Daniel not surprisingly had Star looking ready for show. He sort of blushed as he walked by the washhouse and recognized the linens a young slave girl was holding up for inspection as his own. The pretty young woman was waving them around like a flag, looking for more stains. She had them white as snow. The slave quarters were in a major state of renewal and repair. The slaves that were not still in the field working, mostly some older women and smaller children, were all gathered about in little groups talking about events of the day. His mind must be playing tricks on him. It seemed as if every other child made him think of Bos. Ah yes, Bos. How was he going to handle that one? John Purdy might be a lot of things, but one thing for certain, he was honest. He was honest with himself and he was honest with others. He had to tell her. He just simply had to.

Virginia and John were sharing a late dinner table that same evening, and as she was drinking tea John finishing the bourbon.

"Virginia, I am pretty sure I know where your money that Tooter took is, or at least who has it."

"Really?"

"Yes. Cooper Tooter's brother Quinton had a wife, or a slave he passed off as his wife. They had a son. After the Indians worked them both over she came by and asked me to watch out for the boy. She also gave me enough cash to educate him and asked me to count the rest of a fortune.

"About $30,000?"

"Yes. About a third of it in gold. A bit more. The rest was bank notes on a bank down here, the Citizens Bank of Louisiana."

"Well Sheriff Davis figured that one out pretty close. I never believed Cooper Tooter's story about bringing back the cash he had stolen for a minute. Where is this woman now?"

"I am not really certain but she was headed to Kansas. The City of Kansas to be exact."

"Wherever is that?"

"Clear across west and up towards the north side of the state of Missouri."

"That is a long, long ways from here."

"You can get there by boat easy enough if you have the time. Anyway I advised her not to carry it all, and to put $20,000 in a bank my father and I use over in St. Louis when she passed through there. She was going to carry the gold with her. I full well expect she did what I suggested, for she was scared and is not a very sophisticated person."

"I need to think about what you have just told me."

"One more thing. I have a slave of yours called Bos."

"I already was pretty certain of that. The fact is I knew he was there and I was wondering if you were going to tell me."

"How did you know?"

"Tooter wanted to make up to me by going back to Kentucky after this Bos. He wanted to become a Mr. Coopert all over again and be a gentleman slave catcher and asked for me to finance the dogs and offered to catch Bos for free. He claimed a certain John Purdy stole him and planned to keep him, for he was a greedy storekeeper who was nothing more than a common thief. After what Tooter had done to my family, can you imagine his humiliation at having to come back here or asking me for anything? He lived his last days as a pretty miserable and desperate man."

"We prefer to think we nursed Bos back to health rather than stole him. He saved my wife from being raped and got himself horribly cut doing it, very badly wounded in fact. He was well equipped to run, and I am pretty certain he would have made it."

"Oh really!"

"Yes. He is now very special to Mattie and me."

"I am pretty sure I would not recognize him if I saw him, although I understand he is a big one. He took off about the same time everything else started happening and we never even got around to mounting a search with all that was going on."

John grimaced to himself. All that fear and worry for naught.

"Virginia, I want to buy him. I will pay you way more than what he is worth."

"He must be special!"

"He is just that. He is very special, especially to Mattie."

"I will sell him, John, but I want to see this black man who risked his life and a pretty good chance to be free for a white woman. You must bring him back here so I may see him. Then I will sell him to you."

"It is a pretty far piece down here. How about $2,500?"

"We'll see."

"$3,000?"

"I want to see him. Bring him to me, and then we will cut some kind of deal."

John figured her to be a woman of her word, so he best quit while he had a promise. To further set his mind at ease, Virginia then scribbled a contract on Bos services from the time he left until a year from today.

"You owe me one dollar so you won't be a crooked thief any more and you must bring him back so I may see him before this contract expires. I like having you around."

There was that wicked little smile again.

Next morning, the carriage moved along at a nice clip as John and Virginia went into town. He would have much preferred to have been riding Star, who trailed along behind, but the carriage ride was pleasant enough. First stop for John was the telegraph office. He wanted those back at Three Creeks to know what he knew, so he wired his father who would send a carrier to tell Mattie. John had just one more stop in the South, to go see an old Negro slave woman who belonged to a man named Farout. Then with any luck he hoped to catch Captain Mac on his way up river. He liked the old cuss.

They spent the night at Liggets and this time Virginia did not ask for someone to accompany her and her friend. She hoped the town would start talking, for this tall handsome man with his athletic build and different kind of drawl would make any women who knew her turn green with envy. Alas, he was a perfect gentleman.

Mr. Cox knew just about where Farout's place was. John could start asking for better directions when he got closer.

"There is a tavern up at Gaines corner that's a good place to stay all night. It's about 35 miles up there and Farout's place is fairly close."

"If it is no farther than that, tell Mammy I will be back to Island View for another late table."

Virginia smiled. She would wait. She really enjoyed sharing her table with this tall Kentucky gentleman. He was well educated, mentally alert, spoke of playing music, was a gifted conversationalist and had fine chiseled features including a strong chin. He made her feel like a teenager for he was, as they say, a heartthrob.

At the edge of town, John took Star's bridle off and hung it on the saddle horn. It was time to clear his mind so the miles flew by as Star did what he liked to do best. The Gaines tavern set him a nice morning snack as Star rested and the proprietor gave John directions as he knew exactly were the Farout place was. John had started at daybreak, so by mid-morning he was again making Star take it easy as they turned up Farouts' lane to their place, which was noticeably better kept than any of the other small farms in the area. The fences were in good repair with real gates, as opposed to just some wire strung across the openings, and the house and slave cabins glistened from this distance. He dismounted to more fully walk Star down as they continued up the lane.

As luck would have it the first person he came to was a large old Negro woman working in the garden. She was bent over with her back to him. John had to smile. It was quite obvious from this position that she was very well fed.

"Good morning."

She sort of jumped, stood and turned around:

"Good morning, sir. I didn't hear you. My what a pretty horse."

"Thank you. Is your name Bessie by any chance?"

The smile disappeared from the old black woman's face.

"Why yes, my name be Bessie."

"My name is John." He reached into his saddlebag and then handed her a small package.

"Your friend said thanks for letting him borrow this. It really worked well."

She unwrapped the small magnet and needle with its two little pieces of light wood.

"He said you would know what to do with it."

They both knew full well if she admitted to knowing anything, let alone actually helping a runaway slave, Bessie's life could very well get complicated.

"Well now, how be my friend?"

"He is well and safe. He has a nice place to call home."

"My, my. Well now me and de Lord can talk bout other stuff. Be my time to go for too long you know."

He smiled at the healthy looking old woman and replied:

"Your friend sent his love."

Bessie choked up just a bit, and as she turned back to her gardening she sniffed:

"Dey dogs dey won't hurt you none, they just make noise till dey put der collars on at night. Dey missus she be up der in de house."

He took his cue and led Star on up to the house.

John took off his hat and knocked on the door, but as he had been pre-announced by the frisky dogs Steven Farout walked around the corner where he had come in from the field. They shook hands and started what was to become a lifelong friendship, for as Scots-Irish they had much in common. They visited until John simply had to go, and he departed the Farouts with just enough estimated daylight to reach Island View before dark. He had traveled the last number of miles before and although it was three days before the very dark of the moon, certainly twilight would not confuse them in familiar territory. Star was chomping at the bit after his rest and would have much preferred leaving the bridle out; however, John held him in check. The Indians had taught him much about taking care of his mount and he was very attentive to this animal he loved.

As they moved briskly along John spotted some mules in a field and mused to himself; a mule will stop or slow down before he hurts himself, in fact he will generally stop or slow down, then look around at you as if to say, "This is it, partner." A mule's eyes are set differently on their head than a horse such that they can see all four of their feet. This in turn makes them very sure-footed and great for climbing canyon rims and such. These great eyes also lend towards good night vision, so a mule will most often stop in their tracks either day or night before jumping off a cliff. Not so a spirited animal like Star. A horse will run until he hurts himself or even drops dead, and it is up to the rider to watch out for cliffs.

Tired but not exhausted after a 75 mile day in the saddle, John dismounted and started cooling Star down by walking him along the plantation's chipped marble drive. In the twilight his thoughts turned to Mattie and the boys and he prayed aloud they were all safe. He desperately missed being with her. Her companionship. Her humor. Her smile. Her touch. His mind returned to Louisiana as Daniel stepped out to take Star's reins.

"He has had a long day, Daniel, take special care tonight."

"Yes sir, Mr. John. I take good care o him."

John walked up the steps and went inside.

Virginia had waited dinner and looked simply elegant tonight with her hair pulled back in chignon, the perfect look to complement her exquisite new dress. High styled women wore their bodice cut way low anyway, but this was truly something else. The top was of transparent silk and it was way more than quite obvious there was nothing under what there was of it, except skin. She stood unnecessarily close and crushed her large skirt and petticoats into him just to take his hat. He was really quite surprised at how attractive she was when she put her mind to it. John could help but wonder where one got such a revealing ensemble. As she hovered closer, her expensive perfume was delicious.

"Would you care for a drink while you freshen up for dinner?"

"Why yes, that would be nice."

As she handed him the bourbon she again stood unnecessarily close.

"I brought some nice wine for you. Do you prefer white or red with your meal?"

"What are we having?"

"Beefsteak, roast pork, baked chicken and fried fish."

"My word! That sounds like a lot."

"Oh, the others will clean it up. Amos and Ramos can eat a lot and the others enjoy their own cooking as well. Red or white?"

"Either will be fine."

"You may have both. Surely you must be tired of wearing your traveling clothes. There are some fresh things in your room."

There was that wicked little smile again.

She murmured,

"I think I have you sized up about right."

Taking the glass of excellent ten-year-old bourbon, John went to his room to freshen up, entering just as one of the twins was leaving from having warmed up a tub for his bath. She must have spent a fortune to get this done in only one day, for sure enough there was a fine new outfit laid out on the bed. The jacket and the shirt both fit as if he had measured at least twice with a master tailor, and this certainly had been put together by a good one. The tailor was indeed a professional for Virginia had ordered the pants tightly fitted, and the chap had left extra room in the top of one leg. Good tailors always inquire as to where well-endowed gentlemen keep certain appendages in tightly fitting breeches, either left or right pant leg. Obviously she had noticed he "dressed left." As he donned his new finery, a cross between a smile and a grimace occupied his face. He wondered if he were a horse or a mule; however, there was one thing he knew for certain.

There was a cliff coming up.

Back in Kentucky a similar drama was about to unfold. Bos was truly enjoying his stay out at Simpson's place, for the slaves here had it about as good as the Negro ever did. Simpson's father and his grandfather before him had sincerely believed that it was the white man's duty to own and care for the black, for they were like children and it was not right to leave them on their own. First of all, blacks had a soul, and when they reached the age of accountability, their soul must be saved, and secondly they must be cared for physically. They must earn that care. The Simpson slaves lived in well kept cabins, far nicer than some of the white folk around, and they were also well clothed, including nice Sunday wear. There were herds and flocks and gardens at their disposal. They worked hard. Very hard.

Simpson had a diversified operation with whiskey being his main cash crop. When preacher Elijah Craig's barn caught fire in 1789, the fire charred the barrels he had prepared to store his whiskey. He used them anyway. Quite by accident Elijah discovered that aging whiskey in an oak-fired barrel gave it a whole new taste and smoothness. With his discovery the bourbon business became a long term process for evermore, with the more patient brewers making the finest stuff. No one for miles and miles around came even close to Simpson's quality and taste; therefore, he could sell three times as much of his six-year-old product as he could produce, and at very premium prices. His ten-year-old was unmatched.

Simpson kept one crew busy almost the year around clearing more land, while producing lumber, barrel staves and firewood all at the same time. The family held a huge acreage of timber and was methodically harvesting the trees and turning the most favorable into crop land. There was always the grueling work of stumps to dig out and Simpson's most severe punishment was to put a slave on the stump crew for an extended period of time. That was also true for any one of his three sons that might be in disfavor at the moment, for even though there were dozens of mules to do the heavy pulling, stump crew was tough duty. The three sons were an industrious lot and the entire family including Mr. and Mrs. took turns spoiling little sister Betty Jo "till she stunk." Mrs. Simpson always said Betty Jo was a surprise, not a mistake mind you, but a sure enough surprise, for she could have well been a granddaughter. With three adult brothers and older parents plus a house full of slaves always around, Betty Jo could never lift a finger to take care of herself. Even if she had wanted to.

It was now more profitable for Simpson to buy a great many things from Purdy Mercantile than to produce them on the farm; however, the operation with its various craftsmen could be very self sufficient. Andy was Simpson's old blacksmith and very good at his trade but "old" was the operative word. His understudy had broken an arm causing old Andy to fall way behind with his tasks, so Simpson arranged with Mr. Deay for Bos to spend time with Andy. For a couple of reasons. First of all, Bos could keep up a conversation and lift with one hand more than Andy could by straining with all his might. Deay readily agreed to hire him out, for he figured there was a lot Bos could learn from the old man, for Andy was indeed a master of their craft. Simpson's second reason was Sarah. Sarah was a lovely black slave woman and should be married and having babies by now, but she had found no one she favored. Furthermore, all of his Negro men were intimidated by her for not only was she pretty, Sarah was quick of wit, well proportioned, large boned, and stood a bit over six foot tall. Neither Simpson nor his wife would ever insist on marrying off their slaves to each other unless they both found it agreeable, that is until a female was 19 coming 20. Before age 20, the Simpsons would pick the female a husband, for they felt it was their duty to keep her from being tempted by having the woman living in her own home and raising her own babies. They also wanted their men married young as well, for a man with a bed partner was far less apt to give trouble or attempt to run away. That was even though their lot was about as good as it got for blacks, and few if any of Simpson's slaves ever even contemplated escape.

There was also the continual issue of too much intermarriage of their slave families; therefore, Simpson continuously sought fresh bloodlines. Besides, he reasoned, Purdy did not like owning slaves anyway.

While at the Simpsons, Bos took his meals with Sarah's family and he found himself stammering and feeling awkward as Sarah hovered over him and sat much closer than need be. This giant of a man was more concerned with cleanliness than any man she had ever known, and Sarah liked that. Bos, who had been with a great many of the women on Island View, now found himself with a funny feeling in the pit of his stomach. This beautiful tall woman who was apparently unafraid of his size, kept flashing her smile at him, and chose to be close and touch him when the opportunity presented its self. After supper her family found other things they simply had to do and left them alone. It was two days before the very dark of the moon and cloudy, yet Sarah blew out the light so they might better see the stars.

"I am kind of scared when it's this dark."

She huddled up very close.

Very, very close.

Finally, a man big enough to fit.

Sarah had never been with a man.

She decided it was time.

Old Randy once had been in great demand in every direction from Island View. He was by far the best fiddle player anyone knew and once did innumerable weddings, parties and dances. Coopert had put a stop to his being loaned out for such events, for he did not want Old Randy telling the others how slaves elsewhere lived. Miz. Virginia had him playing for her again, and tonight he was playing softly in the anteroom next to where dinner was being served. Of all the things Mammy did well, supervising a fine meal was close to the top of the list. Tonight the meats were tender, the gravies superb, three kinds of hot bread with a lavish assortment of vegetables and spreads graced the table. Virginia drank fruit juice and tea but kept both John's red and white wine glasses full throughout the entire meal right up to the fresh fruit and superb desert brandy. Having dined at the finest hotels in New England, John now knew those poor eastern souls really had it second best.

He sort of rolled his shoulders and stretched his neck.

"My, I am not used to a full day in the saddle."

Virginia walked around behind him and began to massage his neck and shoulders. John knew he must get Mattie some of that awesome perfume. The soft romantic sounds of the fiddle made him think of Mattie and her violin and how he missed her.

Longed for her.

Needed her.

"Here, maybe I can loosen you up a bit." Virginia purred.

John knew full well Virginia and he could be cavorting about the dining room stark naked and he could take her right on the table, yet any slave who caught a glimpse would never ever breathe a word. Not one. Not ever. Virginia's body was fully prepared to take a man. She kept licking her lips which were now full and soft. Her eyes were at about half or two thirds mast and her breasts looked as though they were equipped with cutting tools, about to punch through the silk.

John spoke huskily as he abruptly stood up. One glance confirmed he too was ready to engage:

"Best we go check on Star. He had a long day too."

Virginia stammered for something to say but quickly recovered her poise.

"You can relax, Mr. Purdy. You passed the test."

"Test, what test?"

"I only knew two men I thought were completely trustworthy. Now I know three. You just joined a pretty elite club."

They walked out to the stables to find Daniel watching over Star like an only child. John pretended to accept Virginia's excuse.

But come now. A handsome, tall, athlete, engaging, well to do, educated, and smart man like John Purdy knows a thing or two.

He particularly knows a woman on the make when he sees one.

Up in Kentucky things were turning out differently for Bos. Unlike John, Bos had never been around a willing and anxious woman. Certainly there had been a few of the younger Island View slave women who thought it was okay or even kind of fun. Mostly there had only been terrified younger girls or other men's wives and women even old enough to be his mama. And always there was Coopert watching to get himself roused to the point Bos never knew for sure what would happen next. This was different. Very different. This lovely creature wanted him, held him and caressed him as though he were something very special. Mattie's touch had also been loving, but in such a very different sort of gracious way. Certainly Sarah's family had cleared the way, but no one except maybe Bessie's God knew what they were really doing. His thoughts turned momentarily to Bessie. Sarah's touch was sweet, kind of like a young Bessie's touch would be but still, way different than that had been too.

It was dark. Very dark.

Bos was as gentle as a man can be when he took Sarah for his very own.

Island View was an enormous piece of land measuring approximately 5 miles along the Mississippi River and going back about 11 miles, thus consisting of some 35,000 acres. The original Spanish land grant was to a Mr. de Falco, who's father was a very rich ship owner and well connected at the Spanish court. De Falco senior had saved some important sorts' necks and also loaned large sums to other powerful figures. The plantation was in payment to his young son for graciously volunteering, at a time when a certain princess of the highest order was in a family way. It was really all quite awkward. The baby-to-be's real father was a highly placed member of the clergy, just promoted and soon to be on his way to high office in Rome. In compensation for the couple's abrupt departure for the new world, and to insure continuing discretion, the clergyman himself also arranged for significant contributions. The mother-to-be and her unborn baby, as well as this new husband whom she hardly knew, were admirably taken care of.

At any rate, early southern planters "ate up" the land in a matter of years and left it lying wasted, churned up and dying. They then simply "picked up sticks" and moved on to a seemingly unlimited supply of fresh land. Virginia's ancestors had recognized this circumstance early on, and simply asked for additional grants totaling up far more land than they could possibly ever use. There was of course some of this immense acreage unsuited to cropping, but the vast majority of the holding was pristine and could be most highly productive. Never was there a significant percentage of the land grant under cultivation at one time, for the full property presented far too immense of a challenge for one operator to possibly manage.

Early American land titles were ridiculously vague, for it was not until Jefferson's time that the orderly measurement of land using Gunter's chain became widespread. Then pins were driven into the ground and a standard chain was used to measure from one known point to the next. Ten square chains became an acre with 640 acres to the square mile, and six square miles became a township. Not so with Island View. As opposed to listing exact metes and bounds and townships which the land covered, the multiple Spanish land grants were confusing, jumbled and vague. To wit:

"Beginning at the creek and running to the clump of trees at the gully then running twenty poles to the north," and so forth, and so on. There was one thing however that was exceedingly clear to Geneva Chouteau that fine morning. The Sheriff and Mr. Rawson had explained it perfectly well.

The house that Gotfield had titled to her did indeed sit on one of the Island View land grants; however, he had provided her a quit claim to the property as opposed to a warranty title. In plain English this meant Geneva owned only exactly what interest Gotfield had personally owned. Virginia owned the other half. Furthermore, as confusing as the land descriptions were, it could be argued that the improvements sat at the juncture of two separate grants. If this were the case, she owned only one half each of the slave quarters, a garden spot and a really nice grove of trees and just maybe one half of the house itself, but not half of the land it sat on. Furthermore, all of the slaves now recorded in Geneva's name had been fetched over from the plantation; therefore, titles to them could be just as effectively argued. Rawson was gratified in a way, for Gotfield had quietly used another attorney to handle this affair and the fellow had really botched it up.

At any rate, the only way it appeared that Geneva could hold unblemished title to anything was to pay Virginia one half of its value. That presumed, of course, that Virginia would agree to accept her offering.

Geneva was dumbfounded.

Gotfield could communicate considerably better than he had let on to Virginia, or Amanda and the other staff for that matter. He actually could write quite legibly with his one good hand. Geneva's entire involvement in the attempt on Virginia's life had been to secretly mail a letter for him and then to unwittingly introduce Nurse Katherine into the household. Recently, since it had fully dawned on her what had been going on, Geneva was spending hours on her knees asking God to forgive her for having ever mailing the letter. She miserably regretted even touching it, once she presumed its content. Geneva had also somehow felt in her heart that nurse Katherine was a part of some kind of plot, yet she had taken her into Virginia's home. She assumed that alone probably made her a culpable accessory to the fact.

Getting Dr. Darkness was all Gotfield's idea, and at a very late date he had hinted at the wretched letter's contents. Geneva had still felt very subservient to Gotfield, who after all was still head of their household, yet she pondered over and over how he had even come to know contact information on such a man. To her everlasting regret, instead of alerting all concerned, she had become paralyzed by the idea and allowed the scheme to unfold. Geneva loved her children fiercely and wanted them well provided for, so Gotfield's hinting at the possibility of Alfred and Janice possessing all of Island View presented far too big of a temptation for her to resist. He had continually insisted and assured her that he had things under control and, to her everlasting regret, Geneva had kept her suspicions to herself.

Now she was a suspected felon, held only questionable title to her home and slaves, plus she also knew that the investments Gotfield had settled upon her would be in question as well. Before the incident, she was quite well off, but now all that she could really call her own was a bit of gold she had accumulated, a modest account at the bank, and a small inheritance she received from her mother years ago. Her appalling realization was that were it not for the attempt on Virginia's life, no one would have ever bothered to look these things up. She and the children would have continued to be well off, with perhaps even Virginia as a benefactor and friend. Now she was financially ruined.

More importantly, Geneva Chouteau was so full of remorse she could barely function.

Damn Island View!

John was down watching the river after having tied the signal flags exactly where Captain Mac had told him to. It had been an unbelievable week, and he could still close his eyes and see those 350 pound Hampshire sows tearing at Cooper. He needed some down time and was anxious to get back on the boat and head up river to his Mattie and their boys. And to tell Bos it was going to be all right. The Marybeth II was a pretty fast boat for a freighter and the river current was slow to normal which meant they could make as much as 10 miles an hour upstream. It would be the very dark of the moon the day he expected the boat; therefore, they would have to take it easy a good part of the next few nights. Captain Mac had told him he used 25 cords of firewood a day. Not really. John smiled as he remembered the crusty old cuss' picturesque speech. What he had really said was he used 25 @#$% cords of firewood a day but he would have a %$#@ light load compared to the ice he had been hauling on the way down and he would be able to carry three or four days at a times worth of wood going back @#$% north! Anyway it should be a pleasant trip.

He found himself as homesick as a schoolboy. John wondered if anything unusual was going on at home. He missed Mattie so. He watched absent mindedly as the carriage stopped up at the house and from the landing where John stood it looked like some young people got out and stood at the door for a spell, even after someone opened it. John stayed down at the river for a while, eventually going up to the house and letting himself in. He could not help but to overhear their conversation.

"Mrs. Virginia, I don't know what to do. She left these sealed letters for you and this note for us to come over here."

The girl was close to hysterical.

The young man was trying to act brave.

"What else can you tell me?" Demanded Virginia.

"She left this bundle for you. I am so scared!"

"Let's sort it all out. Mammy would you please have someone bring strong tea? Some very strong tea."

From previous conversations with Virginia, John knew who they must be, and decided he best leave them some privacy.

One of Island View's fine mares had come in season and Daniel had asked if Star could do the honors, as he would relish a colt from his fine animal. It was now later in the day, about the time they were going to put the two horses together so John wandered about for a bit and then went down to the stables. After a while Virginia came down and for ever so long she watched him leaning on the fence. John first realized she was there when she slipped her arm under his and held one hand on his wrist, the other on his biceps. As they watched Star do what nature had intended she leaned her breasts into him:

"This 'one mare' policy for humans gets in the way sometimes doesn't it?"

"Sometimes." was all he could think of to say.

He turned and looked her in the face for a moment. She was so open. So ready.

She held on to him as they started back towards the mansion. Damn, he wished she did not smell so of lilac today.

"Were those Gotfield's other children?"

"Yes, and I need you to hear this. I certainly can't think this one through by myself."

"Okay"

"Geneva is gone. The children are afraid she may do herself in."

"Kill herself?"

"Yes. They say she has been very melancholy since just before Gotfield died."

"Before he died?"

"Yes. Before he died. Here read this."

"She handed him a very neatly lettered message, plus three scraps of paper.

He read the long one first.

Dear Virginia,

I have asked God's forgiveness a thousand times and now I ask yours. Yet I cannot find it in me to forgive myself, so why should either you or God?

I had no intent ever to do you harm; however, after I suspected Gotfield was putting the plan into motion I stood by and failed to bring it to light. I will never forgive myself for being so weak. I have signed any interests I might have including the house, the slaves and my accounts, over to the children with you as their guardian. They are pure and good. I am not. They will only know what you tell them about the dastardly thing that was planned. Do as you see fit. I knew it was wrong then, I know it was wrong now. It was a horrible thing, yet I did nothing. One so weak deserves not to live. Certainly I am an unfit mother.

With remorse and humility.
Geneva.

The scraps of paper were in a shaky but quite legible hand.

The first read:

The letter you mailed put plan in motion to gain all of Island View for our children. G.'

The second note in the same hand read:

Damn it. Quit asking questions. This thing must happen for our children. Quit being so soft.

The third read:

Damn it, woman. Get yourself together.

Virginia de Falco and John Purdy talked all night long:

"Virginia, do you recognize this as Gotfield's hand?"

"No."

"Geneva could have written all of these."

"Yes she could have, but she has forsaken her children. I think she is hurting very badly."

"It could be, but how are you to know. She is probably broke, so maybe she needs a free home for them. Maybe she thinks she may go to jail."

"They are wonderful young people and I have so much. I can never spend a fraction of it."

"How are you going to feel waking up every morning being responsible for your husband's bastard children?"

"Oh, John! That sounds so cold."

"Well it's true. That's what they are. Will they remind you every day of how things were? Virginia, you need a new life and you can have a new life. Any kind of a new life you can want or imagine. You are young, very attractive and very rich, so you need to thinking of how things are going to be, not how they were."

"Yes I do, but right now the only man I ever met that I want touching me and sharing my morning coffee is already taken. I think her name is Mattie."

John flushed. There was no mistaking her point.

Virginia continued:

"John, I spent nearly half my life in a prison with my cousin/husband. For the last five or six of those years I chose to kill the pain with whiskey, but he instead had chosen from the very beginning to live the life he always intended. I gave him far too little credit. He worked his way around our grandfather getting so weird and demanding from the very start. Gotfield was the smart one after all. Anyway, those youngsters may be bastards but they have de Falco blood in them."

Her eyebrows knotted:

"Come to think of it that may not be such a good thing."

John probed:

"He hired a professional to kill you!"

"Yes but I got his man, and I got,—-ah -He ahh didn't get it done."

"You were lucky."

"I need someone around me except servants. I don't see me running this whole thing by myself very long. It's a three or four people job to do it right"

"Hire somebody."

"Who?"

"That man Farout was the brightest man I have met in a long time."

"He has his own farm."

"Give him a business proposition he would be a fool to pass up."

"These young people seem too good to be true. My own boys were er, ah unique. Hell, they were slime balls."

"Maybe they are."

"What?"

"Too good to be true."

"What would be wrong with bringing in these youngsters to share, both the responsibility and the wealth?"

"Nothing if you can let go of the past."

"John, I have secrets buried so deep in my soul that putting these children's background in there with them would be simple. Anyway it is not their fault they are who they are and I have to forget that along with a lot of other stuff. I'll go crazy if I dwell on the past. They are sure going to have a lot to forget too; maybe they can help me look forward."

John kept probing:

"Maybe Geneva is just trying to stay out of jail."

"Could be. But wait, that does not make sense at all! There was absolutely no proof she knew anything until she wrote this letter. Sheriff Davis said he had no evidence or proof of any kind since Nurse

Katherine has disappeared. This letter is her confession. Now they have her."

"Maybe the nurse showed up. Maybe she wants money from Geneva that Geneva doesn't have."

"Could be, but if Nurse Katherine is smart she hasn't stopped running yet. She slipped out the door while we were all trying to figure out what was going on and disappeared like the morning fog."

By morning's twilight Virginia had made up her mind to bring the young people under her roof to see if they could all build a new life together. Maybe she still had it in her to give loving advice and point youngsters toward productive and satisfying lives. This time she would be inexorable instead of relinquishing input on the rules, for she knew first hand what happened when there was no continuing effort to build character and responsibility. She could also teach a class on the older generations putting money and position ahead of their youngsters long-term happiness.

Virginia did not want the night to end, but at dawn they broke up their conversation and she reluctantly went to her room and lay across her huge bed. Virginia found just spending time with John very stimulating, and as they had sat visiting so intently she truly saw him as her very soulmate. Sitting on the edge of her bed she tried to reason with herself. She had known him but for a week! How could anyone feel this way after knowing a man a week? How could a woman actually want a man she had known for only a week to completely possess her? Still, this was no schoolgirl crush, for she was a full grown woman and he was an adult. She got up, stripped naked, and freshened herself. And stood with her hand firmly on the bedroom door handle. For a long time.

In those moments Virginia de Falco would have given her very place in Heaven to go down the hall and lie with John Purdy for an hour. And to then turn this whole cursed plantation and everything it stood for over to him.

Instead, she lay down and buried her face in the pillow.

So no one might hear her sobbing.

And cursing.

"Damn Island View."

Later that same afternoon Virginia asked John to accompany her as Daniel drove them both to Geneva's house, or at least to the house she and the children had lived in. Virginia, Janice and Alfred talked for a long time, turning to John for advice or comment on a regular basis. Finally, Virginia suggested and invited the young people to come and live with her at the mansion:

"It will take a while for us to get used to each other and you may not like it there, but we can give it a try. It will be a bit much getting used to both such a big place and me all at the same time. One thing for certain, we can find plenty of places to hide from each other if we get on each other's nerves."

Alfred was pensive:

"I had hoped to go to the academy next year. May I still do so?"

"Of course."

Alfred continued, talking pretty much to himself:

"That would leave Janice all alone though, and I will not do that if it seems to hurt."

Janice was steadfast:

"We still cannot imagine why Mother left; it is so hard to try and understand. When father died she must have just fallen apart. She must not be all right. If Mother comes back and we have moved away she will be devastated, so let's us wait just a while longer. Then if she does not return I would be very grateful not to have to live here without her. That's presuming of course you would even let us stay in the house. It's yours anyway I guess."

Virginia put her hand on Janice's arm:

"You are almost too old to need one, but your mother did ask me to be your guardian. Besides it's probably all our house, not just my house. Who knows? Anyway I doubt very much that your mother will be coming back. Not for a long time at least."

John's advice was sought and he gave it:

"If she ever is coming back I would think it will in the next two or three weeks. If not then, never."

"That's it then! If Mother is not back in two or three weeks we will move to Island View if you still want us."

Virginia stood up:

"Since I am supposed to be the guardian, I better check with the slaves and see if there is everything you need to get by for a while, so where are they, and who is the most responsible of the bunch?"

Later as the carriage made its way back, John pondered:

"I can see why you or anyone else would like those young people. They seem exceptional."

"Gotfield and I certainly made a mess of it, but maybe he gave me something to live for after all. Who knows? Our try at it was a first-rate disaster even if we didn't have much to work with. But those two, they would make any mother proud. Anyway, I won't even run into them unless I am looking for them. Look at the size of this place."

Daniel had now stopped on the drive, right up front of the enormous mansion surrounded by its impeccably manicured grounds. Walking up the steps, the door opened for them at just the right moment, and as John stepped aside for Virginia to enter, he stood on the front steps, still pondering for a second or two. As she had said "the place was something else," but that was incidental. John Purdy was much more in awe of the woman than the house she lived in.

There were two more days to fill before Captain Mac and his freighter were due back, so they took most of one day showing John the four corners of the plantation. Virginia took particular note of some cropping going on at a far corner which came as quite a surprise, and which also meant more law business for Mr. Rawson. Before sundown she gave John a tour of the libraries and galleries. Walking into one room which had strong security measures, she handed John a pair of gloves.

"Put these on or my grandfather will come back and spank."

They looked at priceless treasure after priceless treasure, including some statues that were hundreds of years old plus some ancient weapons and knife collections out of Spain that were truly amazing. There was also a sketch done by Michelangelo's own hand of work he had been commissioned to do on the ceiling of the Sistine Chapel. Another piece was what they called a "cartoon" of the painting he was to do of the Last Supper.

There were some note pages in Galileo Galilei's own hand of details he would include in his book, *Dialogue Concerning the Two Chief World*

Systems. He was deemed a heretic because that book suggested the earth spun and the heavens stood still. His book enraged the Roman Catholic Church such that they kept Galileo under house arrest from 1642 until he died in 1652. Naturally these notes should not be kept in Rome

John asked permission to look at another piece up close. As he examined the hand written Latin document he determined it was of a religious nature. He was spellbound:

"Del Video. It has been a long time since I took Latin and did my Latin chants. I recognize Del as 'the' and 'Video' as middle. The middle of what? What does Del Video Anglican mean?"

"You are a protestant, right John?"

"Yes."

"I am catholic, and that document is a copy of Queen Elizabeth's instructions on how we are to get a long with each other from back around 1600. It kept us from killing one another for at least two centuries. It means to compromise. I give some and you give some, by order of the Queen no less. I am to forgive your protestant wrongness and you will forgive my catholic wrongness and we will press on together."

"Why is this copy so special?"

"She was thought to have secretly made a mark on a few of the copies to signify she had examined them, and they were truly as she intended. Additional copies were to be made only from these. This one is her hand marked copy that she sent to the Pope. Look right here."

John would like to have spent weeks browsing these wonderful treasures, wondering aloud if there were any other such priceless collection in private hands.

The next day they divided their time between galleries and Gotfield's old office where she asked John a thousand questions. Although he did not have a clue about raising cotton, his business sense was keen. As an outsider he asked a lot of questions which a cotton grower would have assumed everyone already knew the answer for. By the end of the day Virginia had pages of notes and a dozen ideas on how to run a better business, including a fresh approach to cost accounting and record keeping in general.

The night before Captain Mac was due back, John stood down at the riverbank in the dark moonless night, impatient as a child waiting for Christmas. Next morning Mammy packed a basket of the plantation's finest treats for him, and Daniel prepared a sack of mixed grain for Star as John said his goodbyes and anxiously waited. Virginia on the other hand was noticeably quite sad and determined to turn her attention towards moving in her new charges as a way to keep her mind off John Purdy. Already she knew. She would soon be in for a lonesome time.

After waiting till afternoon of the day when it became the very dark of the moon, Johnson and Sledge headed down the trail towards Three Creeks to finalize their plans. A hideous drama was planned for the Purdys' home tonight. A couple of miles out of the settlement they met up with a third man, and the three sat and pow wowed for a while. They interrogated the stranger thoroughly:

"Sure glad we found out Purdy was gone. We owe old Sadie for spilling the beans when she came across the river. Anyway, you get the dog?"

'Yeah, Duke the dog ain't coming home tonight."

"Give you any trouble?"

"Hell no! You're talking to a man who's handled a bear and a pack of wolves by his self let alone a bobcat. Ain't no dog gonna give me no trouble."

"What about that big Nigger?"

"He is out helping at somebody's named Simpson all week."

"Damn. I wanted that big boy to be a beggin when I pulled the trigger. I'm pretty messed up from him a hitten me."

"Oh, you look pretty with all them teeth gone and your nose all over to the side of your face. Real pretty."

"Shut your mouth up. Anyway did you see the other big kid?"

"There."

"Teacher Brown?"

"He's there. But if we'd be quiet he'd never know. He lives clear across the road."

"That other woman."

"There too."

"The guy that runs the store?"

"Same as Brown. Across the road."

"Okay then, you get first at the other woman if you want. You get your pick out of the store. Anything you want. They got some good stuff."

The stranger shifted the stick he was chewing to the other corner of his mouth:

"That Dody place is a good place to stay. They feed good. Told em I had to rest my mule for the day and just needed to hang around. I went over to the store and messed around some too. Got a good look at everything. What I want is in the store. I already know where it's at so I can be in and out in half a minute. You two can have both the women."

"I just want the Purdy woman. If you two don't want the othern we can be quicker. Don't take heavy stuff from the store; we got to move fast."

"Yeah, we'll just get the Purdy woman, then promise not to hurt her unless anybody shows up looking for her. Sure hope she can set a mule good cause we're gotta move on out fast."

"It's gonna be about as dark as it ever gets around here. Them clouds make it even darker. We better plan on lighting the lantern and turn it real low up where we tie the mules. We just might get in and out with out ever waken anybody up we don't intend to, but it's too dark to find them mules quick if we wind up with there being a light in the house, and then come out in the dark."

"Them boys going to wake up."

"Yeah, I hope not. I still hate it that little fellow got it. We let that fire get away."

"Well they was supposed to rush out to put it out so's we could grab her."

"Yeah I know, but still, he was just a little kid."

When they first heard the steamboat's whistle, John though it was a mighty extravagant five-note whistle for a freighter, then watched in wide-eyed amazement at the boat that actually pulled up to dock on the deep water side of the island. The Marybeth 5 was well over 300 ft long, and 50 foot wide with huge paddle wheels on either side. It was likely the most extraordinary passenger steamer to ever grace the Mississippi. Captain Mac, dressed in a fine looking captain's uniform, waved broadly from the deck as he expertly supervised securing the enormous vessel.

"Ahoy!"

The 400 or so passengers were now gathered at the rail, straining to get a good look at the magnificent Island View mansion and its grounds. Amos (or Ramos) winched the skiff over to the island and Captain Mac sprang down the stage holding out his hand.

"Hope you don't mind me bringing the other boat. I saved you a nice room and we got a swell place for the animal to bed down."

John was incredulous:

"Merciful Heavens, Captain! Are we sure I can afford this?"

"I have to put you on a freighter when we get to Vicksburg. He'll be there by the time we are. It's gonna be a slow trip cause there's a little more current than sometimes and we got some big stuff floating. As dark as it is at night time right now, it will be slow going after dark too, but at least you're gonna start your trip in style. This is the second shakedown cruise for this rig. First time out she was a @#$%^& disaster so some of the folk who put her machinery together are on board and they may make some changes on the go so I #$%^&* decided I better do this one cause when you own part of the !@#$% business there are some things you just need to do for yourself. The rest of these folk are just out for a party and helping me make sure the !@#$%^&* boat will stick together and her crew is all up to snuff."

He lowered his voice:

"They sure paid a plenty, cause we are only out for a few days. She'll take her first real trip up river in about two weeks. This time we're just meandering around making a bunch of changes to some of the machinery on the go and that's agona slow us way down, but we really ain't going nowheres anyway. Besides checking machinery I'm picking lead cooks, stewards, checking out dealers and seeing if this is the @#$%^ crew I want to keep. These fancy-assed folk are all just out having fun for a few days, and I can party at night with em cause we won't be moving along much at all in the #$%^&* dark."

John could simply not imagine this was the same plainly dressed fellow who so vigorously colored the air with his picturesque speech on the trip down. Virginia, on the other hand, was listening with great interest as Captain Mac stared at her.

"@#$% you look like a woman I know." He slipped.

"Captain, do you have any room left?"

"Why yes, ma'am, we are hardly two-thirds full."

"On your way back could you put me off close, so that someone might fetch me home?"

"How about right back here. We are just out fooling around and need some practice stops to make."

"I could be ready in just a few minutes"

"How about we have everybody get off and I'll have the crew bring some more tables and we'll serve refreshments right here on the Island."

"Would you think a look at the big house would be of interest?'

"Ma'am, we got half the New Orleans social register on board and these kinds of people would kill to get a close up look at a place like that. Damnation, if you don't look like a woman I know."

For the next hour and a half the boat passengers took turns riding the skiff over, then walking up the beautifully kept lawn to step just inside the enormous mansion. Mammy was posted there to point out a few things and then Amanda showed them out the double doors in the ballroom's three-story-high glass wall.

Most could hardly wait to tell "the others" that they of course had been invited to the showplace of the South. Captain Mac could just hear them at their next affair as he fluttered his eyelashes and giggled in a prissy voice:

"And whyyyyy, my deeeeaaarrra, the baaall room is just so, so, so unbelievable, I could hardly believe my very own eyes, awwll that priceless art and such. The place is just so enormous and I truly doooah hope yoooalll can be invited there tooo sometimes dear."

In well under an hour Virginia had handed Captain Mac a rather fat envelope and fairly well skipped up the gangplank, simply overjoyed with the prospect of a few more days with John Purdy. As they were shown to their first class "owners' suite" which was actually two bedrooms either side of a nice sitting area, John could help but wonder how he was going to avoid falling off the cliff this time.

Virginia's had paid scant attention to her wardrobe as of late and therefore it was quite limited. She had but the one stylish new dress that she had worn when John returned from Farouts'. With the thoughtful matching under-shift that was part of the ensemble, the thin silk top was beautiful and actually quiet modest. Oh well, these people all knew she was a cotton farmer anyway so no use putting trying to put on airs. As for John, he could care less that he had only the dinner ensemble she had bought for him to go along with his small traveling wardrobe. The rest of the passengers, who had enough clothes with them to change three times a day, would just have to get used to them looking the same much of the time. Truth be told, Virginia could have been wearing field clothes, for having seen her home, and with the handsome John Purdy at her side, the striking Virginia de Falco was the envy of every woman on the boat.

In the main, the rest of the passengers were very well heeled and quite friendly. Most were men with their wives, although there were quite a few older chaps accompanying their "daughters." There were also a number of lone men who had come mostly to gamble at the high stake table games that had been widely advertised. And gamble they did. The boat had no more than gathered full speed when the table games started, which fascinated John no end. He had played cards all of his life and there was poker, faro, roulette and blackjack plus a craps table. Virginia had once played all kinds of cards with her grandfather and then her boys, so she enjoyed watching as John played a few hands. They then moved on to inspect the vessel. Here again one can only think of one word to describe the Marybeth 5: opulent. Marble floors, beautiful woods, fine furniture, and wonder of all wonders, they each had a private water closet! Their suite of rooms also had its own private butler on call. They sat at Captain Mac's table for dinner where Virginia obviously felt compelled to decline the excellent wine; however, when mealtime came it was simply extraordinaire.

John deserved his reputation as a business visionary, for that first night at the Captain's table he met a chap who was promoting a different kind of photography using a new process called the Collodian system. Using a glass "negative" plus a few chemicals, almost anyone could now make an excellent picture at a cost far less than a Daquerreo, which was the only other type commonly available. John saw at once that this new system could make excellent family photographs available at a price the average family could afford. He ordered a system on the spot and began thinking about the young employee he had in mind to put in charge, and where the studio would be. The math looked very good, and besides, such a service would be an excellent reason for people from far and wide to come by Purdy Mercantile. As he pondered their business empire his mind returned to Three Creeks. He yearned for Mattie and the boys and truly hoped all was boringly quiet on the home front.

Johnson and Sledge plus their co-conspirator led the fourth mule behind them and then stopped a goodly ways away, waiting until they were certain the Purdy household had settled down for the night, and everyone was sound asleep.

As they dismounted the stranger whispered:

"I can't see a damn thing. Four mules make too much noise to get any closer, or we'll wake up folk we don't want woke up. As dark as it is, somebody better stay with the mules."

"Yeah. We could get in and get out and still be in trouble if we can't find the mules."

"Instead of you coming to the house, why don't you keep a gun ready and a lantern to signal us just when to go in and again when we get back outside. The two of us can get the Purdy woman. You're the best shot and still pretty much crippled up with that bad knee to move very fast anyway. You stay with the mules."

With the last minute change in plans, Sledge found himself reluctantly agreeing to stay behind with the mules, while the other two took to their assignments. The stranger crept up onto the connecting walkway between the store and the darkened doorway of the house, while Johnson waited at the bedroom windows with Mattie's light-tight indoor shutters. Sledge held the mules at the edge of the timber, licking his lips in anticipation as he waved the lantern to put their dastardly plan into motion.

When the bedroom shutters and the front door both burst open, mirrored lamps burned holes deep into the darkness. Brown never missed at this range, especially so a silhouette against a mirrored light making such a perfect target. Hiram crouched inside behind a table with another .44 but neither he nor Henry got a round off before the stranger fell lifeless, with one hole through his head and another through his heart. Chickasaws still preferred the bow and arrow of their ancestors to the white man's pistol for close-in night time combat. Mostly because a sentinel cannot tell where arrows are coming from, while a pistol gives off a tell-tale flash. A first rate Chickasaw warrior could keep eight arrows in the air at once and even one who was a bit out of practice could keep six in flight. An accomplished warrior attached the feathers on his arrow such that it spun in flight like rifling spins a bullet. This refinement allowed him to hang over the side of his galloping pony and shoot with amazing accuracy. Standing against a tree while shooting at a startled and surprised man in the full light of a mirrored lamp was merely target practice for a boy. The first arrow hit Johnson in the neck piercing from side to side but missing the jugular. The second pinned his hand firmly to the window, the third tacked his arm to his side and the forth buried itself right between the shoulder blades.

Blackfeather had ordered Mattie and the younger boys to stay down out of any light, while Dody and Morris had sprung the trap. After Brown dropped the stranger at the front door, he stayed low as he turned and emptied his revolver in the direction of the lantern. Brown knew it would be foolish to chase after whoever it was in the pitch black, for he had been in enough of these situations to realize that the light to his back would make him the perfect target. He was wise to assume that whoever had the lantern also had a rifle, and was still out there.

Johnson lay in agony with arrows sticking out everywhere, with one still firmly pinning his hand to the wall.

The stranger lay dead where he fell.

Morris and Dody blew out the lights.

Mattie, Hiram and Henry held the Colt .44s and a rifle ready.

The Purdys and Trisha sat in the dark, in a circle facing outward.

Brown reloaded, and Blackfeather readied more arrows as they waited in the pitch black.

It seemed the dawn would never come.

Brown, Dody and Henry finished patrolling the area at first light and determined that Sledge, along with two of the four mules, had apparently disappeared.

Before heading south, John had asked everyone, especially his Indian friends, to watch his family. The Indians had spotted the trio when they first crossed back to the east side of the Mississippi, and had kept them under constant surveillance. Blackfeather had even crept close enough to their planning session to overhear last evening's entire conversation. Dody had become quite suspicious of the third man who was simply too curious, and then when Duke the dog disappeared the local men went on full alert. Purdy's friends wanted to catch Sledge and his partners red handed and to get this over with once and for all. No more clever trap was ever sprung.

Except there was a last minute change in plan.

Except Sledge was still out there.

"Mrs. Purdy."

"Yes, Blackfeather."

"You know I heard them talking?"

"Yes I do, Blackfeather!"

"I haven't told you yet. They set the fire."

"Well, after all this, that's not a big surprise. Are you certain?"

"Yes. They killed your boy."

Blackfeather and Brown were determined to find out from Johnson what they could before he died. Later Blackfeather took both his and the stranger's scalps over to the creek where he washed and dried them off, and then presented them to Mattie.

She handed the reddish one back:

"You keep that one, I just want Johnson's."

She then asked quite pointedly:

"Don't I have to pickle this or salt it down if I want to keep it for a long while?"

That same night, after a phenomenal dinner, John had wandered down to the lower deck to check on Star and when he returned Virginia was holding court with two or three of the single gentlemen. He was delighted. Maybe this cliff had a nice stairway down. The ship's orchestra was small but outstanding and featured a great singer. After dinner the dancing, drinking and gambling held everyone in pleasant embrace while the great boat very slowly churned its way up the moonless Mississippi. John found an empty seat at the Blackjack table and Virginia immediately came close to stand behind him and watch. He was by far the lightest bettor in the game and surprisingly the only one who won more than an occasional hand. He was enjoying his good fortune as Virginia leaned over and whispered:

"Excuse yourself for just a bit. Have them save your seat."

He did so and as she pulled him aside she asked:

"Where is your gun?"

"In my room, of course."

"Go get it."

"Why?"

"Cause you are going to need it."

"Why?"

"Please go get it."

When John returned with his .44 tucked under his jacket they gave him back his seat and the game continued. As the next few hands were played Virginia engaged the dealer as he was reshuffling the deck.

"Did you know that the kings in a deck of card each represent a famous one?"

"Yes but I can never remember them all. Spades was King David and clubs was Alexander the Great but who are the other two?"

"Hearts was Charlemagne and diamonds was Julius Caesar."

"Yeah, that's it."

She rambled idly on:

"Did you know that if you take all the letters it takes to spell ace, king, queen and all of the other cards in the deck you have 52 letters just like there are 52 cards in the deck?"

"Why no, I did not know ..."

Virginia struck like a cobra, surprising the dealer sufficiently as he was finishing his shuffle, that she was able to wrest the deck from his hand.

"There is no nine of clubs or jack of spades in this deck." She announced calmly:

The dealer jumped up and would have gone for his gun except for the look in John's eye. And the nickel-plated colt .44 aimed at his guts.

Captain Mac swooped over to the table at once. Virginia spoke calmly:

"He has a booster under his shirt!"

"A what?"

"He has a spare pocket right at his belly button on the inside of his shirt! See how the shirt is a little bit soiled and has just a little more room between those two buttons?"

Captain Mac demanded of the dealer:

"Unbutton!"

"How dare you! No!"

Captain Mac literally tore the dealer's shirt front off.

There was the booster, with both the nine and the jack tucked safely inside, each in their own little pocket.

Captain Mac went in to what might best described as "a state of high piss!"

"You@#$!!!@#$%^%$#@@#$%^&cheating %^&*()@#$$$#@ bastard. Here we are trying to put the finest ship in the South on the !@#$%^&*river and draw the best clientele and you sit there and cheat like a common @#$%^&*!@#$%^& gutter thief which you !@@$% are!!"

Dealers such as this one commonly banked their own game and paid the boat a percentage of the take for the right to deal. Played by the rules, blackjack pays the house about one percent if the players are all experts and all know what they are doing. Much more if the players are amateurs. One percent does not sound like much, but even if everyone is an expert player, for every $1000 that crosses the table, the dealer will make an honest $10. In an hour of high action, that can be very substantial. Taking out a few high-count cards doubles or triples the dealer's advantage. Add to that an ability to pull the card they need from where they know it is, and the dealer makes a fortune.

There was an uncommon amount of money on the table because a dealer in a game such as this needed to be prepared for several of these high rollers to casually wager the yearly income for a working man on the turn of one card—all at the same time. The dealer was allowing John to win his modest bets; however, not only was he boosting cards, he was also double dealing plus dealing from the bottom of the deck on the big wagers. The big-time dealer was a very good practicing card mechanic; however, he had the misfortune to run across one Virginia de Falco. Captain Mac booted the crook off his boat, "close enough to shore he should make it" and then after each bettor pulled his bet back, he divided up the dealer's bank six ways. One share apiece for the players at the table, plus a share for Virginia who all the others thought should get double at least. She would not take double, so they divided about $37,000 six ways and the merriment started all over again.

John could not get close to Virginia for the other men hanging around, as she explained over and over again how her boys had used to "play" at being card mechanics. They knew if they got by her they were getting good, so their favorite game became trying to fool Mother. Virginia fibbed just a bit for she explained her sons' cheating as "childish play" where she had learned all their tricks as they tried them, time after time after time. The part about them trying time after time after time was true enough. She explained to her little crowd of admirers yet once again:

"First I spotted the moves, the special square cut little finger nail and the wide spaced buttons. The first clue to start watching him was his continuing to let John win the smallest bet at the table while no one with a big bet ever seemed to win. Anyway, I simply counted down the deck a few times and knew..."

John melted away and went down to the lower deck As he rubbed Star's magnificent white coat and watched the dark starlit water churn out under the lanterns at the back of the boat he smiled. "She simply counted down the deck a few times and knew....." John was absolutely certain he had married the most feminine woman he had ever met, but there was no question that Virginia de Falco was by far the smartest one. There was absolutely no doubt about that. Maybe, just maybe, if he stayed out late enough tonight she would get what she had so obviously been wanting.

Star was lying in some nice fresh straw, holding his head up with his feet stuck out to starboard so John sat down and leaned with his back against Star's, to stick his feet out to port. As he sat there dozing Virginia came looking and found him. She sat down in the straw and leaned up against Star, beside him.

"Come on, John, you don't have to sleep with your horse."

"I am surprised to see you down here, and even more surprised to see you by yourself."

"Oh, they are a nice bunch alright. Some of them are very nice, but I am afraid the bar has been set pretty high."

"Really?"

"Yes. He must be well over six feet tall, look like an athlete and have strong handsome features, particularly his chin."

"Oh."

"He must be well educated, like art, and music, and furthermore he must also be a gifted conversationalist."

John asked quite pointedly:

"Does he absolutely have to dress left?"

Virginia was glad he could not see her face flush as she stood and held out her hand to help him up:

"Come on, John, I promise to behave myself."

"Promise?"

"I Promise. For now anyway."

Mattie sat way back from the window looking tired and drawn. John had been gone about three weeks and she was so very lonely for him. And now she was trying exceptionally hard not to be so scared. "Chief," cousin of Piomingo, had taken charge of security and moved eight braves plus the married ones' wives into a camp just up stream from the house, and store. There was always one of them walking "perimeter guard duty" keeping a watch on anybody and everybody that came close. He had instructed Mattie to stay out of the store, preferably in the house, and to always keep a gun close at hand. She hated the gun part the worst. Night time found at least two people on "interior guard duty" with either Bos, Junior, Henry, Brown, Morris, Dody, or Deay in addition to Trisha, the boys, and at least two Indians close by. Chief had promised to watch out for Mattie and by damn he was a man of his word.

Blackfeather had helped Brown interrogate Johnson "quite thoroughly" before taking his scalp. Johnson had been pretty certain Sledge would hang around trying to get to Mattie because "having" her was all he ever talked about in recent months. That seemed always to be his main topic of conversation even well before the first kidnapping attempt, and Johnson truly thought Sledge might try to kill Mattie if he could not kidnap her and have her for his very own. Sledge was an excellent shot with his big bench rifle and probably out there just waiting his chance at one solution or the other.

And that was exactly the case.

Sledge had worked his way up plenty close to the house and store to be within his range; however, he could never get a shot at her or anybody else that mattered, except the big black. At first he was overjoyed that the big black was out in the open but thought it strange the way he was sort of parading himself about. As Sledge was carefully drawing a bead with the big rifle his brain kicked into gear! That was exactly what the big nigger wanted! He was wearing a bright red shirt and using himself as bait so whoever else was watching could spot him if he fired the big gun.

As Sledge let the hammer down, he wondered how stupid can a nigger be? The word brave had never been in Sledge's vocabulary.

The front counter at the store became guard central and every man in the neighborhood looked through their barns and sheds and any other hiding place they could think of, and reported back. Simpson also had his slaves walk every creek and river within miles looking for any clue, but there was simply no trace of Sledge or two of the four mules Johnson had established that they had brought with them.

During their interrogation of Johnson, Brown, and Blackfeather had confirmed the duo still trapped up in Missouri, habitually going up the Mississippi to St. Louis each season. They then followed the Missouri River up to near Jefferson City and from that point they worked up along the Osage River valley where Johnson also had some family. Their most productive trapping routes still ran along the Osage River upstream to Osceola, Missouri, near the Kansas border. Another of their good runs was up an Osage tributary called the Grand River which ended about a hard day's ride from the City of Kansas. The two of them ran their traps and wintered in their hunter's shack located on some of the very highest bluffs overlooking the Osage River. The Osage River started about a hundred and fifty five miles up the Missouri from St. Louis near the state Capitol at Jefferson City. Their hunter's shack was sort of central to their hunting grounds and not far from a small French settlement called Versailles. Each season they brought pelts back to the St. Louis fur market and then floated back down to Kentucky, "cause good whiskey was cheaper and they knew some river women who took care of their needs better down there."

One of these river women was a casual observer when preparing to paddle her "John" boat over to their new cabin across the Mississippi. Sadie had quite unwittingly reported to them she saw Purdy board a boat with his magnificent white horse as she sat chatting away, waiting for them to regain themselves so she might be of service yet one more time. Johnson had also insisted that the third man was a casual acquaintance and pretty much a loner who owed them money for a mule and some gambling. His original deal was time with the other women and his choice of goods out of the store, plus his gambling debt would be considered paid. He had agreed mostly because he was in their debt and he was a trapper too. There was, after all, this unwritten code, which had now cost him his life. Sledge was going to share Mattie just a bit with Johnson because he was his partner and for 25 years they always shared everything, but long term Mattie was to be exclusively his.

Mattie was pondering all of this as she set staring blankly at the wall. Simpson's carpenters had hurriedly built some solid screens to set in front of the windows, and she was hiding behind them, a prisoner in her own home. Suddenly she cocked her head, then jumped out of her chair and raced out the door with a surprised Indian in close pursuit. She had immediately recognized the faint but distinct sound of Star's thundering gallop, and running for all she was worth she met John 100 yards up the road. He slid from the saddle as Star reared to a stop and Mattie nearly bowled him over racing into his arms. Mattie Purdy's only sin was that she was the most beautiful of woman. So very, very beautiful that a crude and bizarre man had become obsessed. As terrified as she was, she had been brave beyond what anyone could ever expect. Now her John was home.

"Oh, John, we know who killed Harvey and it's, it's, it's been so awful, so very awful, so very, very awful. Oh, John, it's been so bad. It's terrible and they have to guard me and there's somebody outside the house all the time and sleeping in the living room and I have to stay away from the windows and I try hard not to be scared but I can't sleep and there are so many guns around and I can't go anywhere or do anything and they came cause you were gone so Trisha sleeps in our room with me and a gun and I have been so lonesome and they killed two of them and I have his scalp but one got away and there may be more and most of them think he will be back to get me and they killed Harvey and I have missed you so desperately just hold me please hold me please—hold me."

John Purdy didn't have a clue what had happened; however, there would be plenty of time to find that out. He did know one thing for certain. He would not leave his Mattie again. His place was at her side until this thing was over. She collapsed against John, and as he lifted her into his arms like a child she put her arms around his neck, snuggling her head onto his neck at his shoulder.

He carried Mattie home.

Later as John came out from the bedroom where he had helped Mattie strip and then tucked her into bed, Trisha was standing close by. She had been sleeping with Mattie in their room while someone else always slept in a bed that had been placed right out front of the bedroom door. A couple of Indians had been spending the nights right outside, one on either side of the bedroom wing.

"She has not eaten much or slept any for days, John. She is scared out of her mind. So am I. We all are. I cannot imagine how she has taken it, most people would have cracked by now."

"Thanks, Trisha."

John went back into their bedroom and from habit he too stripped naked before lying down by Mattie as she lay thrashing about in a fitful sleep. He moved close pressing her back to his chest and held her, which seemed to calm her a great deal. Soon she slept more soundly. John was afraid to move for he might awaken her as they lay on their right sides with her buttocks against his hips, his hand over her left breast. John held Mattie close and pulled his knees in behind hers, forming a protective half circle around her. Lying there with the woman who meant more to him than life itself, John felt their hearts begin beating together. As one.

Sometime in the middle of the night she awoke. Unlike the sweet and delicious moments he dreamed of while he was gone, she came to him furiously, almost desperately. At her moment she threw her head back and forth, crying and moaning and gasping for air. She dug her fingernails into his back, and clutched her arms and legs around him like a drowning person clutching at a lifeboat that was slipping away. Mattie promptly fell back asleep, having said nothing at all.

John lay staring into the darkness.

Blackfeather was very smart to have kept Mattie out of the light that first night, and completely out of sight the days that followed. Mattie was smart to continue to be scared as hell. Even though Brown had winged him, Sledge stuck around all night waiting for a shot at someone and hoping against hope to rescue Johnson. He could have cared less about the other guy. As he watched, pitch black immediately enveloped the entire scene again, and he heard Johnson's screaming and moaning, but there had been no sound or gun flashes at the bedroom windows so he knew this must be the work of Indians. Sledge had both heard the gun and seen its flashes at the front door, and that guy was good. Damn good. After shooting the stranger, when Brown quickly turned to empty his revolver at the lantern, had Sledge not been holding it out to his side, Brown would have drilled him too. As it was Sledge only had flesh wounds in his right forearm, some from broken lantern glass and one where a bullet had burned a deep slash. The bullet wound stung furiously making it difficult, but not impossible, to hold his big bench rifle. Such a piece got its name from the fact it was so heavy one normally laid it across a bench or some such to steady it. Doing so, an expert marksman such as he could hit a horse at three miles.

Sledge was both a master woodsman and an expert hunter who had spent his entire life hiding from large game that was always much better than a person when it came to discovering your whereabouts. In a stroke of brilliance he hid the saddles and other gear, then turned the two best mules into one of Simpson's more remote pastures where they could simply disappear into the mule herd. As they were searching that very same pasture area, the extra tall Negro girl with the older man had no idea how nearly they came to getting a taste of his pistol. The two were fortunate that he chose not to give himself away, for they came very close to where he was hiding under leaves covered with mule dung, to hide his smell in case there were dogs. The next day he patiently worked his way close enough to the house twice, but it sat in among so many trees that he never saw Mattie, nor could he get a clear shot at any one else that mattered. His sore arm kept hurting and getting stiffer, making it more difficult but not impossible to handle the big rifle. Then, when Chief and the other Indians formed up their camp, Sledge decided there would always be another day and reluctantly decided for right now at least, it was time to move on. He never saw Johnson again and damn, after 25 years together, he was going to miss him. Sledge became aware that John was home and so he cunningly recollected his two mules and headed out, all the while swearing to himself that someday he would get the woman for himself and get even with the others on Johnson's behalf. Never mind that it was he who had started the whole affair.

The morning after his return John slipped quietly out of their bedroom into the hall, where he could see that Trisha had taken the guard bed in the great room for the night. He didn't wonder long if they had waked her up in their midnight frenzy, for her knowing little smile told him they had. When John arrived at guard central it seemed everyone he knew was already gathered over at the store, and as they filled him in he was completely humbled.

"A man can ask no more than to have friends such as you have been to me."

Bos set him straight:

"She is our Mattie too."

Chief spoke softly:

"There are two young braves with me up on that hill whose families knew well the pang of hunger. Some may have died had it not been for John Purdy. We are proud to be your eyes and ears. The Chickasaw never forget."

John Purdy knew he too, would not, nor could not. Ever.

The group decided that after John had time to think, they would meet with him again to decide what was to happen next. Back at the house he checked on Mattie and found her still sleeping so he quietly slipped over to sit down in his big chair by the bed. As he sat gazing, just watching her breathe, a million thoughts went racing through his mind.

Of the joy of just being around her.

Of her zest for life.

Of her humor.

Of the four fine boys she had presented him.

As she slept Mattie had thrown the covers completely off and, after 18 years, it still took his breath away to look at her. She lay with her mane of honey blond hair billowing around her face, and for the first time ever he noticed a few gray or white ones. There were now little wrinkles at her eyes where she had used everything from hunks of ice to gooseberry juice mixed in clabber milk to try and make them disappear. Her lips, which were thin and drawn last night, were full and had their little turned up corners again. He gazed at her breasts, remembering how she had cried when she had told him Sledge had threaten to cut off her nipples if she did not perform well when he had her cornered down at the garden. After four boys they showed some wear and tear but they still had their fine shape, for Mattie had always used Mrs. Purvis' magic exercises to get and keep her womanly parts in shape. Particularly after she delivered. Her flat little stomach would always carry a few faint stretch marks, but in typical Mattie fashion she had each of them named after her sons, and wore them proudly. Her legs were long and straight connecting to that flat little stomach at the golden tuft.

As John sat just looking and thinking, Mattie stirred, opened her eyes and stretched luxuriously full out on the bed. She was his woman so, to her, his looking at her like this was like his looking at a part of himself. She was never embarrassed for him to see her so, and just lay there and yawned, repeating a Bible verse to herself that Mrs. Purvis had made her memorize:

Therefore a man shall leave his father and mother and cling to his wife, and they shall become as one flesh. And the man and his wife were both naked and were not ashamed.

She flashed her sweetest, most dazzling smile:

"Looking at what you are stuck with?"

"Mattie, you know I love everything about you. You are smart and a wonderful wife and mother. Now don't let this go to your head but I also just happen to think you are beautiful. Incredibly beautiful."

"John, need to come back to bed?" It was a question.

"No, but we do need to talk. Chief says they can stay a while more."

"John needs to come back to bed." It was a statement.

"Brown thinks Sledge is long gone."

"John needs to come back to bed now." It was a softly worded, reaching out, open armed invitation.

Mattie I—

"John, please come back to bed." It was a personal request.

Oh, what the heck.

Mattie was well rested and felt somewhat secure once again, so at midmorning breakfast she seemed to some extent to be returning to her usual frisky self. She was not there yet but the boys thought her change in demeanor was nothing short of miraculous.

She kissed John on the top of his head as she hovered behind him at the breakfast table, with her arms down around his neck:

"You may be only one person to the world, Mr. John, but you may be the world to one person."

John seemed quite serious so she sat down and settled into the conversation.

"I am planning on offering a reward, in fact a substantial reward, for Sledge. We will redouble our search for the creep, but I doubt he is even close to here anymore. There are simply too many eyes watching for him, and surely someone would have seen something by now. If he is still close it is you he wants, Mattie, but he might take me or one of the boys out of frustration."

"We can't take a chance on that. Maybe I should be out and about."

"No you don't, Mom!" Came back the chorus.

"Your mother's idea is not a bad one. Not if we control where she is and how vulnerable she might be."

"I could work over in the store."

John smiled. The old-timers used to come in and wind up buying more woodworking equipment than they could possibly ever use, for that was Mattie's specialty. They loved it when she smiled and offered such cautions as:

"Now Mr. So and So, remember when you are out in the cold that before you use this fine axe you want to warm it by the fire. A cold axe can sometimes break if you hit it hard on ironwood or persimmon."

These hardy souls would hang on her every word like it was the first they ever heard of such a thing, even if they already had a box of "broke cold" axes at home. It was an honest chance to go one on one with Mr. John's stunning wife.

"That is a good idea. If he sees you going in and out he might get brave and we could get him. You could sell axes again. We could keep a watch on both you and the store." John teased.

Mattie colored up just a little:

"Well I do know a lot about woodworking tools."

Bos, who anymore was pretty much treated as a part of the family, appeared in the doorway.

"Mr. John, sir."

"Yes, Bos."

"Well, ah."

"Go ahead."

"Sir, you told me I could stop worrying, but Mr. John I can't stop wondering."

"Hey, everybody, I met Miz. Virginia who owns Bos. She signed a hire out agreement on Bos that goes back to the day he left. He is no longer a runaway!"

Bos smiled until it looked like the top of his head might fall off.

"She promised if I would bring him back where she could see him she would sell him to us. Bos, she wouldn't know you if she saw you. She wants to meet this big black man who risked it all for a white woman."

Bos' smile went away. Willingly go back to Island View? Not likely.

"Bos, you would not believe what she is doing, she is being very good to your old family and friends. She wanted me to be sure and tell you that Amos and Ramos were well and are house slaves now. She threw away the whips and the place looks wonderful. She got everybody new clothes and is building some new cabins out where every family can have a nice garden and there are plenty of good eats with lots of chickens to lay eggs and lots of hogs. A whole lot of hogs."

"Mr. John, I don't want to go back there much at all."

"I believe her, Bos, and while we are there I will take you back to see Bessie."

Bos wanted badly to see Bessie again and to believe Miz. Virginia was telling John true. But he knew she drank a lot.

"Don't be scared, Bos, we'll go back before the contract is over and if she does not sell you to us, I will take you north myself."

Bos smiled again. When John Purdy was being serious, Bos believed every word he ever said.

"Yo tell him, Miz. Mattie?"

"Not yet, Bos, but I will"

"Tell me what?"

"Bos has a new friend but we'll talk about that later. Promise."

John would not insult the Indians by offering them money for what they had done, but he might offer to hire some of them as guards in the future. He had an enormous quantity of food delivered up to their camp, much of it nicely preserved stuff that they could take home when they went. He gave the woman who had kept the camp some jewelry and the men each a fine woodsman's hatchet in a leather holster. He tried his dead level best to tell Brown how he appreciated him, but Brown just sort of dismissed him:

"Hell, I let the bastard get away when they changed their plan. I'm better than that."

In a couple more days the community pretty well determined that Sledge had cleared the area. John made a special effort to thank everyone who had taken part in looking out for his family and found every neighbor still keeping his rifle close by, hoping they would be the one to get this guy Sledge. There was a rumor there was to be a reward, but that was not really the point as most of them just wanted this guy for John and Mattie's sake. The Purdys were both liked and respected. Besides that, they were quite essential to a great many people. The store had been added to three times and was overflowing again.

Three Creeks now had its own harness and leather shop right next to the blacksmith shop not far from a wagon shop where they also sold plows. There were also some excellent seamstresses who sewed in a dress shop over in its very own store corner and a handicraft area that was nothing short of wonderful. There would soon be a photography studio right next to where the barber cut hair. Purdys had financed each of these new ventures except the blacksmith shop, taking their profit when a service was preformed or when the finished goods were sold at their store. John had continued to spawn little cottage industries such as the toothbrushes and tooth powder and Mr. Morris now spent much of his time buying handcrafts from the locals. He also had a trusted staff member who bought their sorghum molasses, honey, beeswax, grain, butter, chickens, furs and such. Purdy's was by far the most successful store of its kind in the countryside, being the forerunner of what would one day become known as a shopping center. Purdys either bought, or arranged to have someone buy, whatever merchantable goods the locals had to sell. They sold virtually everything the locals could possibly want, except whiskey. They obviously did sell fired barrels for those who wanted to age their own.

John encouraged Simpson to give Dody preferential treatment and for Dody to retail Simpson's limited supply of ten-year-old bourbon, which by now was truly famous. Simpson had perfected a system to filter the whiskey through charcoal, prior to aging, which made it truly a coveted drink. The ten-year-old bourbon along with their superb hospitality was making Dody's Tavern known as a destination in itself. A goodly number of guests were coming these days just for the Dody hospitality, to buy a sparse gallon and to shop across the road among the handicrafts and see the saddle makers or seamstresses at Purdys.

The grain mill kept busy around the clock plus John and Simpson had also invested in a steam-power sawmill. They located it far enough out of town toward Simpson's to keep the mess and noise from being a problem and where Simpson's work alone kept it busy a good part of the time. The Simpson-Purdy lumber yard was a popular place to buy sawed lumber or bring your own logs to have them sawed. Junior was in his element when he went out there to maintain the equipment and had a particular gift for saw sharpening. Both he and Hiram were going to read for admission to Transylvanian College in the fall and Brown had them close to ready. Morris had a substantial sized staff to help in the store but they still needed more room, plus more help. The place was making so much money it was almost an embarrassment.

In the middle of all this, John Purdy kept in close contact with the law and his mind sharply focused, spending much of his time planning for one thing. John had never hurt anyone in his life, although he was a pretty fair boxer as a youngster when they had boxed with padded gloves for fun. He roughhoused and gave one of his boys a playful Dutch rub from time to time. That was about it. When he went south, it was on a mission of discovery, but now he knew who the enemy was. He knew who killed his boy, terrorized his family and wanted to brutalize his wife.

Every time John watched Mattie's face when she came across some of Harvey's things, or he just happen to catch her standing in Harvey's corner of the sleeping porch, his guts knotted up. Especially and particularly so after they came back from stopping by the grave. They had found Duke the dog all sliced up and buried him at the edge of the new cemetery as well. Mattie had placed him a marker there that she made by burning a verse into a fine piece of oak with a hot wire. John knew full well Sledge would put him or another of his boys there too, if that was what it took to get at Mattie. At the very first John may have been a bit more businesslike than emotional when it came to finding Sledge, but the smoldering deep in John Purdy's soul soon burst into a raging fire. Brown had taught him something about how to handle a gun but he needed practice, for he did not yet consider himself nearly good enough.

He fully understood his life's mission.

He had a man to find.

And kill.

Less than a month after John's return, a messenger rode into Three Creeks looking for Mr. John Purdy. The letter read:

Dear John boy,

A buddy of mine, Captain Baldwin, on his boat the River Rose, is sure he took that Sledge fellow and his two mules up past St. Louis and let him off the Missouri River at the Osage. Traded one of the mules for the ride. Thinks he was hedded into Missouri or even Kansas. Missing teeth, busted up nose, right size. Right color hair. Had a grety big rifle. Been shot in the arm. Wish we had a one of them new picture things they was showing on the boat. Miz. Virginia made lots of friend after you got on the freighter to go on home. Found an honest dealer. Thanks on that othern. Found a good Captain too so going back to the freighter to haul ice and leaving the party busines to some one else. Come take another ride and bring your horse. Thanks again for the knife, carry it every day.

Capt Mac

John thought of little else now and completely focused on the mission. Mattie continued practicing every day with her Colt .44 too, and she was now actually quicker on the draw than John. He, on the other hand, was getting deadly accurate. John Purdy was determined that while Sledge was still out there he would not leave Mattie in the care of others again, with but one possible exception. He would be comfortable if she wanted to go back east to her father's. Hiram was old enough to stay home and look out for himself but they would definitely send the two younger boys to their Grandfather Grashers for now and prepared them to get on their way. John asked Mattie if she wanted to go too.

John Purdy was ready.

He gently turned Grandmother Ella down but asked Mattie to make her own choice: Go to Pennsylvania, or come with him.

She chose to be with him.

John needed a picture for the wanted poster. Bos' friend Sarah was also known as "Sarah of the good eyes," and was quite artistic, having made drawings of Simpson and his family which were excellent enough to be hung prominently in the Simpsons' fine home. Brown was an incredible amount of help for was an expert interrogator, as though he had a well-rehearsed list of questions for a dying man. He was also an expert observer for he knew that Sledge had a four inch long scar on the back of his left leg, and a round scar from a childhood burn on the back his right hand. Sledge's most distinguishing characteristic, save the busted up face and nose, was the big hairy mole on his left shoulder. Mattie of course remembered ever pore and wrinkle and Bos' memory picture was also vivid. After just a few attempts Sarah had it perfectly. John now had his picture. He added the notices above and below it.

The team was impressive, well financed and well equipped. John supplied each of them with plenty of gold coin plus the best and newest, which included breech loading rifles and all of the rim fire cartridges they chose to carry. Additionally Brown carried his sixteen-inch gaucho knife, its scabbard tucked at an angle inside his gun belt across the small of his back. Blackfeather also carried his finest bow and a variety of arrows. They were to stay at country taverns along the way; however, each carried enough gear to spend the night comfortably wherever their part of the mission found them.

By day Mattie was seldom out of John's sight and they rode continuously for her to get in shape for hours in the saddle if need be. The Purdys refused to blame anyone that Sledge got away and were absolutely thrilled when Brown announced, before even being asked to go, that he felt strongly he had a job to finish:

"That's wonderful, H.W."

"John, my name is Horatius Woden Brown. That is a combination of Latin and antient Greek for 'Brown's brilliant child born of a Wednesday.' I hate it! So would you please! All of you do me a favor. Just call me Brown. Anyway, you were after a couple of cripples when you went south. This guy is cunning, resourceful, a woodsman, one hell of a shot and I think about half crazy. I should have been ready for a change in plans and had more people out there. I'm better than that! Anyway, I have a little experience in this stuff and school is out this time of year so I need something to do. I don't want the wrong people getting hurt and I am going with you and that is that."

And that was that. And that.

Along with Brown there was Bos who would jump off a cliff for Mattie, but first point out there was a higher one over there and want to make certain she did not really want him to jump off the higher one first. Mr. Deay readily agreed this was more important than blacksmithing for awhile, for he too realized that a man Bos' size would stop most trouble before it even got started.

Joining this impressive pair was Blackfeather, who respected John Purdy more than any other white man he ever had even heard about. Most of the Chickasaw considered John Purdy a brother who deserved full credit for easing much of their suffering once upon a time. Besides that, Blackfeather was a warrior and had lived his entire life for such an opportunity as this.

John Purdy was considered by most who knew him as a business visionary. As a Special Forces commander he was nothing short of brilliant.

Sheriff Ike Adams, who had authorized offering the reward, wished he could go too, but his other duties kept him in the state and the law was spread way too thin anyway. Furthermore, they had no idea where the quest would lead, nor how long the team would be gone, as it would first move to St. Louis and then divide to assume two separate parts of the mission. Brown and Blackfeather would immediately take a boat up to the Osage River, then ride up the valley inquiring along the way as they went to check on Sledge's cabin near the village of Versailles, Missouri. If no luck, they would then move on up through the old Osage tribal country all the way to Osceola, Missouri, for Brown had found scraps of an Osceola newspaper in the stranger's mule pack. If no sign of Sledge yet, then they would double back and go up the Grand River toward the City of Kansas. They had a list of specifics John had asked them to take particular note of, and there was never a better pair to scout an area.

The Chickasaw and Osage Indians had been unfriendly with each other for generations; however, a matter such as this would be different. With the prospects of a huge reward for a white man the Osage already hated, Blackfeather was certain he could enlist help among the few, who were still scattered along the river, all the way over to their main area in the Kansas Territory. Brown planned on the two being in the City of Kansas in a couple or three weeks, hoping to have Sledge in tow. John, Mattie and Bos would overnight with the Holshers and make arrangements for someone in St. Louis to pass out posters all over town and to all wagons headed west.

When the St. Louis part of the trip came, Bos was especially anxious to get on, for by now there were 30 active slave broker-dealers in the city and it seemed to him one of them was examining this curiously huge black man at all times. To Bos it seemed forever, but finally they boarded their boat to the City of Kansas. Each half of the team carried letters from the law at home to encourage the support of what local law enforcement they might encounter. John would soon turn his attention east from the City of Kansas until the rest of the team showed up, then they would all press on westward if the search need continue. Under different circumstances it would have been a grand adventure.

The trio caused a bit of a stir among the other steamboat passengers, for the beautiful young matron and her husband were both armed. The huge well-built black man's eyes never stopped moving as he watched over her even more intently than her husband did. No one dared give any lip when Bos joined them at their first class table for his meals. Besides they had paid $16.00 a piece for first class tickets from St. Louis, plus extra for their horses.

The City of Kansas was as much of a surprise to them as it had been to Maud. The boat captain strongly advised:

"Don't keep them guns so up front looking. This is a tough town, Mr. Purdy. Somebody would want to try her out for sure."

John stuck a smaller pistol in the back of his belt and Mattie put her .44 away, until they got the lay of the land so to speak. Bos, except for his size, was not particularly noticeable among the diverse throng that milled about the dock, as one out of four or five already there were black. Mattie was fascinated by the numerous Indians, Mexicans and the especially large number of German and Irish immigrants. The trio first stopped down at the docks at the American Hotel and encountered pure bedlam. The hotel was now at the point of ringing a bell when there was any food available, and the ballroom currently served for men to sleep on the floor using their own bedrolls.

The clerk looked at them somewhat askance:

"Sorry, folks, this hotel has served 27,000 guests in the past two years. I reckon we really could have accommodated maybe 4,000 quite nicely."

The town geography was also astonishing, for the riverfront landing was at the bottom of some bluffs, about 130 feet tall. Men had cut numerous gullies up from the river to the hilltops and by now these same gullies had earned the place the nickname of "Gully Town." It seemed that buildings were simply hung to the side of the hills with one house having the street dug away from its front, so as to make the street more level yet once again. And so the owner, yet once again, was adding a street-level floor making it a three-story house, built from the top down. The river-front landing was piled high with merchandise that included everything a settler could possibly want or need, just waiting for someone to haul it up through the gullies to the over crowded warehouses. Bars, gambling places and brothels too numerous to count lined the wharf and its streets.

Fresh looking inexperienced prostitutes looking confused but determined were everywhere. Two in particular caught Mattie's attention. One of them was a very pretty black head and the other a young skinny freckled face, with emerald colored eyes and beautiful red hair. She overheard the younger one, who was little more than a scared witless kid, trying her sales pitch in a definitely Irish brogue:

"It would be real nice for ya now t'wood. I ain't ever been, you know been, ah done it, you know, and the other girls they say I should get double."

"How much is double?"

Her prospect looked tired and was old enough to be her father. He had failure and disappointment written all over his face; now that his dream had gone sour he was headed home to try once again to pick up where he had left off. Someone else had found all of the gold.

She started high figuring she would have to come down:

"Aye, it twood be eight dollars it twood."

He reached into his pocket and came up with seven dollars total. He studied it for a while, then handed her three of his precious dollars.

"Ain't you gonna pay me more extra cause it's the first time and all?"

"Honey, I don't know where you go when you are not here, but go there. Please, just for me. Go be a little girl for one more day."

He hugged her and walked away.

The incident left Mattie speechless, with tears.

They were thoroughly entertained by the area's exploding population plus the thousands of others who were just passing through. Whiskey flowed all together too freely. (The same year the City of Kansas boasted 1500 full time residents, whiskey sales for the area reached 540,000 gallons. A lot of it went west in the wagons, but a lot of it also immediately went down somebody's gullet. A whole lot.) It seemed everyone was armed looking for an excuse, and gunshots were heard frequently. The prostitutes seemed to be everywhere, and a couple of brothel operators took one look at Mattie and begin to question her circumstance, for they could but imagine what one who looked like her could do for business. Even though she was immaculate and quite well dressed, the very moment she seemed to be alone each operator in turn was insistent, annoying and insinuating. They both backed off when Bos appeared as if by magic, literally forming a wall between Mattie and them. Men raced about cussing their teams, moving material up from the river docks, looking for other people, chasing an Indian or just rushing somewhere. For the first mile stretching from the river up through the gullies out to the flats, it was pure bedlam.

Proceeding south by hired hack three or four miles past the bedlam, they arrived in Westport, which boasted three hotels at the time. They found the 30 room Harris House, where they established themselves. The hotel maintained an excellent stable for its guests and was all together a remarkably civil and upscale hotel for where it was. Even if, Yellow Woman, the indian wife of a multi-millionaire by the name of William Bent did live in a tepee out on the front lawn of their close-by mansion.

For a few dollars some boys were anxious to pass out flyers with instructions to put one into every business, plus get one to every wagon-train master and to each boat passing through. In short order they found messengers to take posters east to Liberty, Independence, and all other public places even way out toward the Summit fork in the road. Posters soon covered Lone Jack and every other tavern or public place. The Purdys and Bos then settled down to wait for Brown and Blackfeather and see what might develop next. John continued to ask about for Maud Tooter or Maud Tuttoor but no one had heard the name.

The City of Kansas-Westport axis was a merchant's dream. In 1854 by government treaty for their lands, all Indians were to receive $100 per year and Westport was the closest place for them to spend their cumulative $300,000 annual stipend. Then, after the floods washed out the Independence dock with its strap iron rail line to the city square, once again, by necessity, boats began unloading at the deep water natural landing at the bluffs. It was but just a few more miles up river; however, soon the advantage was obvious. The loaded wagons did not have to cross the unpredictable Blue River, and they could start a huge 18 miles, and two or three days closer to their destination. The center for outfitting westward bound wagon trains moved pell mell from Independence to the City of Kansas and quite coincidently, the migration swelled to immense proportions. In 1860 fortunes were being made if one could just get the goods that pioneers, settlers and Indians needed and wanted. For a moment or two John Purdy actually forgot why he was here, as he imagined a store such as his at about mile number two of the Westport Road. His mind snapped back to attention like a drill sergeant after a raw recruit. There was no time to wool gather. He had a job to do.

John was looking for a copy of the *Enterprise*, the local newspaper, when she walked in the hotel, shrieked and rushed over and hugged the breath right out of him. He was caught quite by surprise, suspecting but not really knowing who she was.

"Mr. John, Oh it's you, Mr. John! Oh, Mr. John!"

As he tried hard not to be rude, he held Maud back where he might see her face a moment, and then he too hugged tightly.

"How is my baby, tell me about my baby, my baby?"

"He is well, Maud. He is fine. I have sent two wires for you on the new telegraph wire. Even the bank couldn't seem to help, and the telegraph people could not find you. You can come home. Tuttoor and his brother both are dead."

The hotel manager, whom she had come to beg scraps from for "her girls" produced a chair where Maud immediately collapsed and sat laughing and crying.

"Tuttoor. He's really dead?"

"Both of them."

"Too good to be true."

"It's true, Maud. Brother Cooper killed Tuttoor and then I happened to watch Cooper Tooter be killed by some hogs."

"Too good for the both of them. My boy, tell me about my boy."

"He is ready to read for Transylvania, Maud. Mr. Brown thinks he will get it."

"What is a Transylvania?"

"It's college, Maud. Where you go to get much more book learning."

"My word. My word. Oh, my word! Me with a gentleman like you in the family. My word. Oh, my word."

John was remembering Maud as the only one he ever met who could laugh and cry so well at the same time when Mattie showed up, and came and sat beside Maud and held her hands. Maud sat speechless and tried to smile through her tears. Finally she kind of pulled herself together:

"I never got the wires. But that ain't no surprise cause nobody knows my real name here and the bank man was not to ever tell nobody bout me no matter what. I thought maybe Tuttoor might try and trick me.

Anyways at least I fer sure know I can trust Mr. Jefferies at the bank. Fact is I stole your name, Miss Mattie."

"So we call you Mattie now? I like that."

"Well not exactly. I am called Purdy. Purdy Maud."

"Well Purdy Maud, you are welcome to use the Purdy name. I got it from my John, and I have always been proud of it."

"My boy. I have got to see my boy. He was the only sunshine I ever had till I got my girls. I got to see my boy. Oh, Mr. John, wouldn't it be safe for me to see him now?"

"You can go home, Maud. It's all okay."

"What will happen to my girls? I've got to think of my girls, but Lord I want to see my boy!"

"I did not know you had girls, Maud, did you, John?"

"Oh, Miss Mattie, they ain't really mine but I keep 30 or 40 all the time. Got 37 right now. The poor creatures come here to get a divorce like I did and wind up having to whore to get enough money to eat. I just try to help some of the good ones get caught back up with life. But if I go now they ain't nobody gonna look out for em. I was in here beggin for the leftovers from yesterday cause they throw away a lot of good food here and we need stuff like that. What can I do with my girls if I go home? Damn it all, I am home, I got more reason to be here than in Kentucky ceptin for my boy. But I got to see him and tell him I love him. What can I do, Mr. John? What can I do? Tell me what to do."

"Well for one thing, Maud, we can all relax for just a bit. Then together we can figure out what happens next."

John also had some thinking to do to of his own. There was this certain tall lady named Virginia who would most definitely like to know Maud's whereabouts.

"I don't think I can stand up right now, I am a shaking so. You are a gift from God. My word! My word."

"Let's go home with Maud, John. We can see her safely home and meet some of her girls. Come along too, Bos."

It was a fair walk out the road towards Independence, but not far enough to saddle up the horses and there was no carriage to hire that was apparent. The place was big, but no bigger than Maud wished it were. Beds were everywhere with sheets serving as room dividers in bedrooms intended for one bed which now held four; however, there was complete order and the place was spotless. Maud had a very small room to herself and there was a dining area where they sometimes ate in shifts because of their number. There were also some small sitting areas crammed in here and there plus one large room where, by crowding in, all of the residents of the moment could gather. Often as not for a wedding. From time to time, one of them would bring in a woman that Maud simply could not refuse, so the new girl and the one who found her would sleep in shifts. Everybody seemed to work at being kind to each other and there were no complaints or criticism. An overcrowded room with a pallet on the floor at Maud's suited the ones she hand picked far better than the biggest, fanciest private room at the highest price house in town.

Here they did not have to whore.

The group was quite upbeat when they gathered around to see who and what Maud had brought and as they entered one chipper little brown head smiled and looked back and forth at Maud, then at Bos:

"OOOEEE, Maud!"

She pointed at Bos.

"Go find one like that built in white."

Maud was justifiably proud of her place. Out back in what used to be a carriage house were "industries." Here were several ironing boards, washtubs and sewing tables. There was also a place to list domestic or childcare requests and another for sick care.

Maud explained the lack of activity:

"They is always more hands to do 'It' than we got 'It' to do."

Back at Maud's little room, Bos stood outside as John and Mattie crowded in. Maud had a bed, plus a few clothes and a small table, currently piled with scores of letters.

"I am a learning to read. These are from my girls. Here read this."

'Dear Maud,

Mr. Klotz was as you thought he would be. He is kind and considerate, not even once ever acting mad at me. There is plenty enough to eat and sometimes he brings me wild flowers. He never onece tried to sleep in my bed till I asked him if he wanted to. His little girls are taking a liking to me. They still miss their mother and I see him and them all standing by her grave from time to time. It is best they not forget her. I feed them, brush their hair, read to them and tend their hurts best I can. It will take time. The wind blows every day and rain seems precious. It is a hard, but good life here. If not for you I would be on my way straight to hell. I will never forget that. You are always in my heart.

Love Marie

The next read;

Dear Maud,

Mr. Fowler is a good man. It is a wonder somebody else had not got him before he showed up. He does not drink at all but he sure was anxious to wife me. That's alright. He got himself clean and was a gentleman about it. In Kansas we saw Indians in the high country. We pulled the wagons in a circle several nights and stood heavy guard but turns out they were just older ones and hungry. We started the trip with 50# flour, 50# bacon, 20 # sugar and 10# coffee for each. Our hunters had good luck with the buffalo. We traded them some of all of it and I now have my own Indian dress and Mr. Fowler has a extra fancy tomahawk I got you some nice beads if we ever meet again. It was a long hard trip and the little girl in the wagon behind ours got sick and died. Appendicitis we think. Another got run over by a wagon. Some adults died too but we made it fine. This looks to be a wonderful place to live, cool and fertile. We got a good piece of it. It is so wonderful not to get beat if you don't feel like given pleasure right that minute or when the gravy is too thick or the soup gets cold. If it is a girl, in about four or five months our first born will be named Maud.

Love Wilma

Mattie could help but get teary eyed.

Maud held up two or three other letters:

"These is the ones that make me cry. They all don't work out so good. I'd like to go get these ones back."

A few weeks earlier on his way up river to Missouri from Kentucky, Sledge had sat on the River Rose in complete disbelief. Twice they had tried to get the blond Purdy woman for him and twice they had paid a price. This time a very heavy price. As he sat brooding, he eavesdropped on the only other paying passengers on this awful junky freighter headed upriver for another load of mules. The women were on the River Rose because the Captain was a pretty nice man, and when he spotted the bunch huddled on the Memphis dock, he charitably agreed to take them all clear over to the City of Kansas for $50. This was virtually every cent they had, save what they needed for the judge; however, the captain was quite pleased with his deal. They were pleasant company.

No. 1 "What you going to do after getting your divorce?"

No. 2 "Got no idea. Don't want another man though."

No. 3 "I am going to try to get back home to my kin over in Ohio."

No. 4 "Home to my folks. Aye. Thatid be the last place I want to go. My daddy make me marry that old geyser any way, now he did. That old preacherman was nearly 50 years older than me, he was. Couldn't do nothing if you know what I mean. Speaken of mean that not being able to do, ya know the bedroom stuff, made him mean. Aye. Real mean. He paid my daddy a lot for me though, plus a whole barrel of whiskey to boot. Daddy and him said it was the Lord's will. I ran away once and Daddy caught me and took me back. I got a good licking over that, I did. Old man said he would kill me ifn I tied this again."

No. 5 "That's awful. Have you got anywhere to go at all?"

No. 4 "Nope. But working in one of them houses would be better than the way life was a lining up for me, so it twood. They say it ain't so bad if you close your eyes and play like it is somebody you like or something."

No. 6 "You got to watch out I hear. Sometimes they bite I hear."

No. 4 "Well the woman I talked to said that when you're young and fresh they will pay you two dollars or sometimes even three. She saved up enough to leave in six or seven months. The ones that stay longer gets old quick."

No 6. "That would be a long six months."

No. 3 " Better than 40 years of what I was a putting up with."
No. 1 "I guess I am the lucky one. My man just took off. Said there was gold and silver both in them mountains out west and he was tired of looking at me anyway. Left me with nothing cept a bill at the store. Sounds like some of us, we may be in the same business before long."
No. 2 "Well I guess me too. I recon."

Sledge looked at them more closely. No. 3 was black headed and very, very pretty. No. 4 would weigh about 85 pounds and was red headed with freckles. She might be 15 years old.

"I need to go back down to the river, John."

"Mattie, that is no place for a lady after the sun goes down."

"I need to go back to the river, please."

"Mattie, a beautiful woman like you. You will get insulted and I am sure it is not safe."

"I need to go back to the river, please, John."

Bos and John followed reluctantly as Mattie looked about through all the goings on, which could only be described as seamy. Finally Mattie spotted the one she was looking for. She was currently backed up against a wall with two cowboy looking types each holding one arm up against the building on either side of her. They were sort of holding her in a trap, kind of like animals toying with their prey.

"Well I don't think that would be normal and all, and I don't want to."

"We'll give you $10."

"Aye!"

"Here take it."

She held the money in her hand.

Mattie reached out and put her hand on the little redhead's arm.

"Give the money back."

"Wh Who are ya now I say?"

"Give the cowboys their money back."

One of the cowboys started to move threateningly at Mattie.

"Mind your own business. What do you want, a fresh face for your own place?"

Bos stepped in between them, and the cowboy quickly backed down.

"Oh, Ma'am, I just can't give the money back. Norma, she has been feeding me every since we got here and lets me sleep on the floor in her room. She has had to do it all, now she has, and she has shared, aye. She wants to save money to get back to her kin and she has spent a bunch of her dollars just on me."

Pretty black-headed Norma had been watching closely, and disengaged from her prospect to step over closer to now view the trio with suspicion.

"What do you want with Maureen?"

"I want to take her away from this."

"Are you going to take her where they are mean to the likes of her?"

"I want to take her where she is safe."

"What is she to you?"

"She is a little girl, trying to, to, to be all grown up."

Maureen spoke up:

"Nope. I got to do my share and pay Norma back. I ain't done nothing yet and it's time I helped out. She is a trying to save up to get back to her kin."

"Where are you trying to save up to get back to?"

"As if it were your concern. I'm trying to get anywhere over along western Ohio. I can walk from there."

Mattie searched her purse and found a $20 gold piece which she then handed to Norma:

"You better go get your things ready, Norma. I hear the first boat out normally leaves at daybreak."

They hustled little Maureen into the hack, and Mattie kept an arm around her all the way back to Westport where she led the bewildered girl into Maud's:

"Purdy Maud, I have one we simply have to find room for."

"O my, Miz. Mattie. Well, we'll find somepla ... Why Mattie, she is just a child. Come here, little lady. Come here with me. We got a nice place where you can take a bath and get some of that rouge and dirt off. Make sure and wash that beautiful red hair and one of the girls will fix it up pretty for you. We got some clothes from a fellow said he lost his girl and they are nice and clean. There is one gown that will sure go mighty good with those green eyes. We got some soup. You want your bath or something to eat first?"

Later that night Maureen lay on her floor pallet in the meeting room.

She looked very pretty the way the ladies had fixed her red hair.

She figured that she was way too big for dolls, but she hugged the one they had found for her up to her chest anyway.

She laughed remembering how Norma hightailed it out of there.

She wiped happy tears from her freckles

She was full. She was clean. She felt safe.

She slept the heavy, deep sleep of the innocent.

Geneva set staring dully out the window of the Louisiana mansion that she used to call her own, now completely overcome with remorse. She had resolved to kill herself. She had prepared the note yesterday, giving her blessing for Virginia to tell the children anything she chose to tell them. Still there was no doubt in Geneva's mind that no matter how discreet Virginia was, sooner or later they would find out she was implicated in the murder scheme. Geneva could but imagine how her children might react over their father's actions, maybe in a bizarre sort of way they might even consider it manly. But their mother? One can't keep such a thing secret for long, and she could never face Janice or Alfred once they knew their mother had allowed such an event to even take shape. Besides. The real issue burning in her guts was that *she* knew.

Virginia had been so decent and allowed both her and the children free access to Gotfield and their home, without conditions or acrimony. Geneva agonized that while Virginia slept in a cold and lonely bed, she, who had kept the love of their shared man, had also participated in the only act that could possibly be more dastardly than living in sin. She could stomach having broken the one commandment because she was Gotfield's first and true choice. But to break yet another? She could think of only one option. Geneva tried time and again to make peace for her troubled soul, but could get neither feedback nor permission from God. She knew it was a terrible sin to kill oneself but at least it was a way out and, after continuous hours on her knees, she could think of no other.

Geneva and Gotfield had a social circle over in New Orleans and had enjoyed life there when they could slip away; however, due to their peculiar arrangement they had kept very close to themselves near home. Although she lived in the fine home tucked away down on the corner, Geneva was virtually invisible to the close-by community. Here the children were her whole life and now she knew that soon she could not even face them. There was no close-by confidante, and since Gotfield had died she was so lonesome. So very lonesome. And so ashamed. The world was closing in, crushing her. There was no other choice.

It was time now.

Geneva bathed and put on a lovely dress, carried the small bottle into her room and lay on the bed, but then it occurred to her:

It would be horrible for the children if they had to live in the house where they found her. She wouldn't do that to them, particularly to Janice. For their sake she got up and walked out to a nearby work shed. She lay on a worktable and pillowed her head with the pillow she brought along with the note pinned to it, then straightened out her clothes.

She had practiced her final prayer:

Holy Father.

Forgive my sins. Forgive me my weakness. Forgive me for what I am about to do. Forgive me these nearly twenty years I lived in sin. I spent lonely, lonely times for his sake. But always, I loved him. I thought when I miscarried our first you had exacted your penance from me. Why was my baby not enough? His grandfather's greed for Island View ruined my life. And his. But you already know that. The only man I ever loved married his young cousin for Island View. I said nothing when the man we shared planned to break your commandment not to kill her, for Island View.

For Island View. All for Island View.

Take pity on my soul.

Damn Island View.

The little slave girl who had seen her enter the shed came running up, screaming and pounded on the door:

"It's hurting me. It's biting me!"

Geneva had firmly closed the heavy door which was way too much for the little one to handle, so she rolled off the table and stepped outside. The four-year-old darted behind her for protection from the huge Leghorn rooster, which was leaving bleeding spur slices along with his angry looking peck marks.

Geneva spotted a small weed scythe leaning against the wall and swung it at the big rooster like a field hand after some cockleburs, where by pure coincidence she cut its head off clean. Surprisingly there was also a bucket of water plus soap and a towel, all being quite out of place. Just there. As the headless rooster flopped about as they are wont to do, Geneva washed the child's hurts and wiped away her tears as they sat together and watched him. She wrapped her arms around the child on her lap and together they watched the rooster flop its last flop. Little Josie took great comfort in being held by Miz. Geneva for she needed protection and felt really safe now, cause that big old mean rooster had been flogging her but good. Josie stopped crying, cuddled up close and held on to Geneva tightly, even after her mother came over to the shed.

"I just went back ofta there for a minute. Gone longer than I should a ben I recon. I sure am glad you kill that old flogging rooster, he been such a aggravation. Come on, honey, we let Miz. Geneva go back to a doing what she was a doing. What you be doin anyway with all that water and stuff? You sure dressed up nice to be messin with cleaning sompun. Shouldn't one o us be a doing that? You need me to bring you some more water? My that be a big old bucket. Don't member no such a bucket round here. Josie sure grateful you be here, ma'am. She such a little girl and dat be such a big old rooster. Look at that smile."

Geneva wiped the remaining tears from Josie's smiling face with the corner of her lovely skirt:

"No, No I er ah it's all right. Just take care of her. I am, ah, glad that ... Glad ... She is going to be all right now? I mean it could have, if I were not here, the scythe where ... ?"

This had to be a sign. God was not through with her yet. He had need of her. He would even make certain she had the "wherewithall."

The day Virginia and John spent sharing business concepts, George was hustling about down at the docks, nearly ready to head back home. He was eternally grateful that he had a master like Mr. Farout who trusted him and would even send him all the way down to the river by himself. Few colored had it any better than he did, and George knew it; however, it was a long way home and George wanted to get started before dark. He kept his overnight pass from Master pinned securely inside his clothes because there were those who would challenge a black man out after dark. He spotted Geneva struggling to manage things all by herself and there seemed to be no one else down at the dock available to help. Before he mounted the spring seat, he checked one more rope holding the new gin on the wagon and then turned about and took off his hat as he always did when he addressed a white woman:

"Ma'am, can I help you with that?"

"Why, yes. Yes. That would be nice."

"Which boat ma'am?"

"That one, the one going to the City of Kansas."

"Where is that ma'am?"

"A long, long, long ways away."

Geneva had lots of practice planning and slipping about, so it had been easy to get the children out of the way and to get to the riverboats. She was fairly certain Virginia would be reasonable to her children, but had left a letter for the lawyers. Just in case. She was very pleasantly surprised to find how her personal funds had grown. Gotfield had always loved her and had always taken care of her, having never let her spend a dime of her own money. Since she had been quite young when she took up with him, the amount settled on her at her mother's death had now become fairly substantial.

Part of His plan?

She looked again at the correspondence from her cousin down in New Orleans. It read in part:

> *Our cousin Bernice takes in more orphans every day. She writes that the City of Kansas has black, white and Indian abandoned children and since she had so many of her own she is used to having youngsters around. Reverend Johnson keeps bringing her more and even though she has a very big house there is never room for them all. She has had over 75 baptized by now. Our widowed kinsman must be a Saint.*

Why had she received this at just the right moment?

Part of His plan?

She must change her name. She had never met Cousin Bernice Chouteau, but would not trade on her good name. Besides they would find out where she was before she was ready. If she did good works and lived a sacrificial life maybe, just maybe, someday she would be worthy of forgiveness. What would she call herself in the meantime? She had used a scythe, plus the soap and water, to clean up after the rooster. Why not Scythia S. Warooster. Scythia S. Warooster smiled. The lady was getting her sense of humor back.

Part of His plan?

Divine intervention or happenstance?

Rev. Johnson just happened to be down at the docks the day she arrived and someone pointed him out. For some time to come there was many a child who blessed the day that Sythia S. Warooster got off the boat in the City of Kansas. They would insist:

Part of His plan.

The will to live has long been recognized as the strongest identifiable human need. The Donner party would never have been heard of had it not been for their remarkable and sometimes gruesome attempts to stay alive. Those who take their own life are notable and newsworthy, while there are legions of known and unknown who have done remarkable things in order to stay alive. Maybe Geneva was just looking for a way out.

In any event, old Andy wondered who had moved all his stuff about. He simply went back to his cabin for a long sleeved shirt before he commenced to scythe down those vines behind the shed again. Every time he did he broke out and itched, so this time he brought that big bucket he found when he was river fishing and had it full of water. He was going to soap up and wash off right on the spot.

Curious.

It looked like somebody else had already washed themselves clean.

The River Rose had let Sedge off at the Osage River, which was quite familiar territory for him all the way up through the old Missouri land of the Osage. The Indians had signed a government treaty on this land in 1808 and officially moved on; however, there were still several Osage around. Sledge knew this land intimately plus some of the Indians as well; however, they mistrusted him completely due to past dealings. Sledge had been born to this country and hunted it for the 33 years since he was 12 years old, and he was a brilliant woodsman. Even though the craze for American furs in Europe was well past its peak, one could still make a living harvesting wild animal pelts. Particularly if one did not pay any attention to whose land they trampled.

The Missouri state capitol of Jefferson City was only about seven miles on up the Missouri from where Sledge got off the River Rose at its tributary, the Osage. There were several other smaller settlements along the Osage River up towards the magnificent high bluffs where their isolated old cabin sat. From about there, for the next 100 miles up the Osage River valley on west past several other sets of spectacular bluffs, 1860 Missouri was extremely remote. Along the river between or among any of these bluffs was a perfect place to disappear if that is what one had in mind. Sledge stayed in the cabin collecting himself for a while, and then headed up the sparsely inhabited river valley to tend to some business.

Per plan, Brown and Blackfeather got off their steamboat and inquired at every point of civilization up the Osage River. In due course they found themselves at the bluff top cabin that Johnson had described. The cabin had been used recently. This was made obvious by some scraps of food not yet moldy, along with fairly new ashes in the pit. There was also a freshly dug hole out back where someone had dug a small something up.

A natural phenomenon often causes ponds to form at or near the tops of these hills and bluffs, so Blackfeather was intently studying the mule tracks in nearby mud:

"You can tell the difference in any animal that walks on land. Only birds, fish and things that crawl are hard to tell one from the other. If you put your footprint here by mine, you can tell one from the other. I know his mule's print from those in front of John Purdy's house. Look at this right here. Sledge's mule made this print not long ago."

Brown considered himself a pretty fair tracker, but he had never encountered anyone nearly so skilled at it as his Indian friend. Blackfeather followed the tracks on up river while Brown hid out to watch and finish his map of the area; however, Blackfeather lost the trail at another main stream called the Gravois. He doubled back and rejoined Brown and they waited, watched and reconnoitered for one more day. They then moved on up the Osage. The duo continued inquiring at every point of civilization along the way to the Kansas territory, where the river name changed to the Marais des Cygnes. At the river town of Osceola, Missouri, they found a chap who knew for certain Sledge had just been there for Sledge had demanded some money owed of him. According to this chap, Sledge was for sure heading north, so they in turn headed due north and subsequently found themselves headed toward the village of Lone Jack.

About noon that same day, Sledge walked into the Tavern at Lone Jack, planning on having some food and plenty of whiskey and then slipping quietly away without paying his bill. Because of his intent to cheat the owner, he kept his hat down to cover as much of his face as possible, for he was easily recognizable with his squished over nose and missing teeth. He had dug up his and Johnson's silver hoard of about $88, and also collected $45 the man in Osceola owed him, but could see no real point in spending good money for what he might steal. Sledge intended to see first hand what those boat ladies were talking about and $133 would buy some mighty good times in the City of Kansas, sounds like. As he walked into the tavern, there were some rowdies gathered around a table looking at something. After they put the poster down he wandered over to get a look and heard them talking about what they would do with $10,000 if they had it. He casually picked up their poster and then sharply caught his breath.

It had his childhood scars along with the hairy mole, all properly positioned and well pointed out. As he stared in wide-eyed amazement, he saw himself with missing teeth and squished over nose, staring right back.

Sledge never waited for the proprietor to ask what he wanted, and once outside the tavern he immediately rode up the road aways. He then stopped and just sat on his mule, confused as to what to do next. Purdy, the rich son of a bitch, had put a price on his head. Wondering how in the world a poster of him ever got to a remote spot such as this, Sledge decided it was probably just by odd chance that the poster had shown up here. But still, he would need to watch close. Real close. He headed on west with his hat pulled down low whenever he met someone on the trail, which became more and more frequent the closer he came to the Summit Junction.

Near dark that same day, Blackfeather and Brown dismounted and walked up to the Lone Jack tavern. They were tired, for they had spent as much time in the saddle as their animals could take and they were riding tough horses. Brown was riding his big Cayuse and Blackfeather had another almost as large. Now both the critters and their riders were exhausted. The same rowdies that Sledge had seen earlier stood about outside, glaring at the pair as they approached. The apparent leader pointed at Blackfeather:

"We don't serve his kind in here."

"Well, you are 'out' here now so it won't make any difference 'in' here, will it?"

The tough, who was a couple of inches shorter than the six-foot two Brown, was quite emboldened by his whiskey and his well-armed friends. He grabbed roughly at Brown's arm:

"I said ..."

Brown swung around with his shoulders at right angles to the other man's, and coming from out of nowhere he hit with the open heel of his right hand, an unusual kind of a grasping blow which took the stranger's lower jaw completely out of its sockets. Using his left hand Brown grabbed the smart ass by the hair and pulled his head down to about waist high. Then, with a smashing trip-hammer blow with his knee, he drove the fellow's nose right into his face. As he let the chap fall to the ground Brown already had the Colt .44 in his right hand:

"Keep em put away, boys. We just want something to eat."

They walked on in and closed the door. Brown motioned Blackfeather to one side and he took the other and they stood motionless with their backs to the wall on either side of the door. In a few seconds the door burst open and the other three rowdies charged in, guns in hand. Brown's shot got the lead man's shooting elbow, and Blackfeather's knife sliced the pistol right out of the second one's fingers. They then stood with a pistol to each side of the third tough guy's head.

Brown spoke in exaggerated crisp English:

"Please, if you don't mind, old chap, I say would you mind to place your gun down more under his throat where you might aim a bit higher. I am fearful you might spatter brains all over my good hat, *partner.*"

After gathering up the group's knives and guns, the pair supervised as the "sick and wounded" mounted up, for the toughs were now a sorry looking lot indeed. Brown slapped the lead man's horse on the rump causing it to bolt away and shouted after them:

"Show up again and you're dead men. Please come back for more! I need the practice!"

Brown and Blackfeather then turned their attention to an open-mouthed tavern keeper, who was still stammering and trying to find his voice:

"They were here all day just looking for trouble. They run everybody else off. I sent my wife and kids next door and had to get my brother to set over there in the corner with a shotgun close by. You guys are quick; he didn't even get turned in your direction. Food is on me, men."

"Well I guess they got what they were looking for. Go ahead and keep those guns and stuff, because you sure got a mess to clean up. Say, you got any kind of pie?"

The tavern keeper looked at the poster Brown showed him for a long time:

"You know I don't think so, but still he seems kind of ... No. I guess not. I haven't seen him."

Meanwhile, Sledge also looked at the poster he had swiped; for a long time. He collected another one off a post at some cross trails and yet another off a tavern wall nearer the Summit fork. Sledge was not stupid; crazy perhaps, but not stupid. He knew things had changed.

He was no longer the Hunter.

He was the Hunted.

After having spent the night with a grateful host who would not accept a dime, Brown and Blackfeather enjoyed their breakfast and continued east, coming to the Summit Trail divide. The trail by now was a well traveled road which split into a V at this point with one leg heading due west some 14 miles to the first real stop on the Santa Fe Trail, a town called Olathe. The other part of the V went northwest leading straight in to the Westport-City of Kansas axis, passing through Westport about that same distance away. Olathe, Westport and where they stood were almost a perfect triangle. Their mounts had been pushed hard for ten days and were slowly wearing down and truly needed an easy day. The large pastureland right at the fork was the perfect place for a midmorning rest and both riders now sat in the shade watching their mounts graze among a couple of hundred oxen.

Brown wondered aloud;

"Blackfeather, why do you care so much for the Purdys? This is a hard and sometimes dangerous trail. Your wife has passed and your children are still kind of young to be without you. Not to be insulting but you are a country Indian. We are now a day's ride from a pretty good sized town where I understand that down by the docks it is as rough and tough as it ever gets anywhere. I hear sometimes it is way too scary for even the toughest outlaws. They stay away, but you are willingly going there. It could be a different kind of dangerous than you have ever known."

"I come because John Purdy is a brother to all Chickasaw. I come because of my sister's smile. Mostly I come because he is my faithful friend, and he needs me, for I am a warrior."

"Your sister's smile?"

"Yes. When I was a younger brave my sister had small children. They brought her great joy and she always had a smile. But then it came the bad year. We grew little food. Fishing was very bad. Hunting was bad. Many braves were sick and could not hunt or fish. My sister's man died. It is the custom of my people that a man must feed his own wife and family first, and give what is left to others. There was not nearly enough food for others to give her family, and so my sister must decide each day who would eat, for she herself must live to take care of any of her children who might also live. When one is so very hungry and has such hungry babies, the smile goes away. John Purdy brought food. Her children all lived. My sister got back her smile again. I hunt his enemy because her smile came home.

Blackfeather looked directly into the face of his traveling companion:

"Now I must ask you, my friend Brown, the same question. Why do you travel this trail we agree can be so hard?"

Brown got a far away look in his eyes and sat quietly for a long time.

Finally he answered:

"John and his wife are my good friends as well, Blackfeather. I do this for them but also I hunt this man because of my wife. She made me truly hate all men who prey on women. Her name was Bo Lee."

"Bo Lee?"

"Yes. Bo Lee."

"That is a name I have never heard."

"She was from a faraway land called China. My father was a brilliant physician and surgeon, and I helped him during my younger years. It always tore me up when we had to tell mothers and fathers or husbands and wives their loved ones were going to die, or were already dead. Mostly it bothered me when we had to cut and there was no way to kill the pain. After my mother died my father begin experimenting with painkilling medicines until he could not leave them alone. He killed himself with them. I had a fine education and accepted a wonderful job which was to take me to the land way out west by the big waters for a while. I met her there. Her family was among the first Chinese to bring their women. She was beautiful. In her own way she was as beautiful as Mattie Purdy. Maybe even more so. I called her 'My China Doll.' We loved each other and we loved the land of the setting sun and great water.

We had a wonderful year, then men stole her from me like Sledge now tries to steal Mattie. I most often took her everywhere with me when I went to see the things I was responsible for. This time I went away for only three days so she chose to visit her family. The men came while I was gone. They called themselves 'recruiters' and came into her village and kidnapped her along with some other young Chinese women. The recruiters made them all work as 'Joy Woman' in their pleasure houses down in Mexico, or they would cut their throats. The men made them watch as they cut the throat of a woman they had already used up, just to prove they meant what they said. After my Bo Lee got a bad disease from someone, they threw her into the street to die, but I found her just then. A few weeks after I found her, she left me a letter and a lock of her hair in this picture case, and disappeared. She knew she could never lay with me again so she just went down and walked into the ocean. Can you believe that, Blackfeather?"

Brown took a moment, then continued, pretty much talking to himself:

"I could have lived with that, but she couldn't—she couldn't,—she couldn't—she just couldn't—."

He turned his attention back to his Indian friend.

"They pulled her from the ocean, Blackfeather! Because she couldn't live with the shame. My Bo Lee left me a letter and a lock of her hair and just went down and walked into the ocean."

Blackfeather could gauge men's faces very well, but this time he read an entire kaleidoscope: anger, sorrow, resentment, bitterness, but somehow it was combined with softness and love. Brown pulled what appeared to be a gold pocket watch from his shirt; however, when he snapped open the lid it held the picture of a beautiful Chinese girl. He held it for Blackfeather to see.

"She couldn't stand the shame, Blackfeather. She just couldn't stand the shame."

Blackfeather could find no words in the English to express himself.

Brown continued:

"Her people and others taught me how to fight as the ancient Chinese did, and I went after those who took her from me. It took me five years, Blackfeather. Five long years, but I hunted until I caught every damn name she gave me, and some others too. I took much of their gold, and along the way I freed many of the women and burned their finest joy palaces. After that, the recruiters offered a big reward for me and sent 50 men to hunt. I lay in salt water and breathed through a reed sometimes for hours. I ran and kept one eye covered in the snowy mountains so I would only go snow blind in one eye at a time, and I killed my horse and drank his blood to stay alive in the desert."

Brown sort of absent-mindedly pulled the 16-inch gaucho knife from its scabbard that was securely fastened at the traditional angle across his back:

"Then, they sent 100 men after me, so I hid a long time way south in the land of the gauchos. Still my hate was hotter than this knife when I burned the bleeding from my guts. They all thought I was dead up in the rocks, but hate kept me alive. Did you know hate would keep you alive, my friend? It will! I came back. I lived on hate. I hated every waking minute and I dreamed hate when I slept. I ate hate and I drank hate and I kept hating and I kept coming back. And I never gave up and I never stopped hating. I kept hating and chasing and I kept coming back and coming back and I caught them, Blackfeather. Every damn one of them. I caught the boss man last when he was running so scared among the cactus that he crapped all over himself."

Brown absent mindedly fingered the big knife's razor sharp blade:

"His three main underlings begged on their knees as I showed them all how it was to get your throat cut by a surgeon. But him, well he was special. I sat and listened to him scream all night long as he tasted rattlesnake on rawhide."

Brown's extradionary tale explained to Blackfeather the discolored straw-blue appearance of the blade, for it had obviously been heated extremely hot. Blackfeather always considered Brown as gutsy as any man he ever knew, even now as he watched him despair. The big Indian gazed at his companion with a whole new level of respect, for Brown's tale of burning his own bleeding guts with a red hot knife was awe inspiring.

But, it was the rawhide that put him in a whole different league.

One can take a given type of rawhide, cut into very thin strips, a bit larger than the hair from a horse's tail, and braid them in an exacting fashion with a comparatively larger fat strip of a separate kind. The larger one is woven back and forth crossways. The two types of rawhide make the so-called warp and woot strands into a very strong braid, just a bit larger than the diameter of the lead in a common pencil. When such a dry braid about five feet long is soaked in water, it shrinks to approximately two feet long, and becomes almost as large around as the pencil its self. As the cord dries out it regains its length. One use for such a wetted line is to tie poisonous snakes away from a victim's face or genitals, then as the line dries it allows the snake to get closer and closer. When tied at their genital area, men frequently lose their mind waiting for the snake to get close enough to strike.

Or, as such a line is slowly wetted, it shrinks with incredible force. Another use for such a rawhide braid is to securely fasten it around the victim's throat, and then drip water on it, or dangle one end in a container of water. A variation of that is to support a large rock or log in such a fashion as to draw a second line tighter and tighter as the wetted rawhide dries out. A human can be heard gasping for air from a hundred yards away, as the combination of water and line can take hours to strangle the life out. At any rate all of the above are hideous ways to die.

Few white men ever knew how to cut the required rawhide strips. Or weave such a strand. Or had the guts to use it.

"Show me how you track animals so well, Blackfeather."

Brown obviously wanted to change the subject and Blackfeather was quick to acknowledge the pain still boiling in his friend's red eyes.

"All animals that walk the earth are easy to tell one from the other. If you have two dogs from the same litter you can tell one from the other. If you have 20 horses you will know each one. You cannot tell the birds that fly or the fish that swim one from the other, but animals are all different, like people."

Brown understood exactly what Blackfeather said, for he once spent time on a South American sheep ranch where the shepherd had dozens of sheep, yet he called each one by name.

"If we both stick our feet in the mud there by where the ox drink, your foot will look different than mine. All we must do is study each print. Come look. See this good print of a mule looks different than that one, see here on the print at this very spot. This print looks — this print—-is! This print!"

Blackfeather whirled around.

Sledge, or at least Sledge's mule, had been here in the last two to four hours.

Blackfeather and Brown both looked long and hard, but could find no other clear print on either fork of the heavily traveled trail. Finally they must decide which way to go. Brown insisted they stay together:

"Blackfeather, I want to be there to cover your back, wherever there is."

"Blackfeather is unafraid."

"This is not like back on the Osage. You had the advantage there because that was your kind of a fight. This is town fighting and I have done town fighting before. Maybe I am the one who is scared."

"Man who gives rattlesnake on rawhide is pretty hard to scare."

"That was different. Anyway, the rule is we stick."

"Okay! Which way, Mr. Brown?"

"I can think of no reason Sledge would go to Olathe; he has to be headed to the City of Kansas. The man at the tavern said all you could really get in Olathe was good water and good boots. Sledge would want women and whiskey, so he has to be headed for the river."

Blackfeather wavered:

"I think we could split up, one go each way."

"No! Besides Purdy would not want us to take such a chance now that we are coming into town."

"Okay, my friend, we head for your way."

They mounted up and pushed their slightly refreshed mounts toward Westport.

Sledge picked up another poster or two as he made for Olathe and wondered if his old mule could possibly make Santa Fe, New Mexico.

He looked about nervously as he rode into Olathe, for he had never had this feeling before, and was simply unable to tell if he were either mad, worried or scared. Being by himself did make him sad. He hated being by himself and missed Johnson very badly as he lay night after night and fantasized. One day, he swore, one day he would get the blonde woman for himself and kill those who got his old partner, but for now anyway he better clear out. Had he any clue that Brown and Blackfeather were as near to him as they were at the Summit fork, it would be hard to say if he would have panicked or lain in wait with his bench rifle. The irony was that as they each in turn had passed this fork in the road, they were within its range.

One uses a horse for speed but a mule for endurance, so while Brown and Blackfeather rested their horses, Sledge and his mule plodded on toward Olathe.

He soon asked the Russell, Majors and Waddell freight line wagon master, a Mr. Williams, for a job, but the trail boss explained he already had put his crew together back in Westport. Williams left off the fact that a chap who was as rough looking as Sledge never stood a chance with Mr. Majors' outfit.

"Can I stick along with you folk anyway?"

"We don't own the trail, Mister. If you are riding with us you ride back with the herder and the extra teams. Bring your own grub."

Sledge decided to stick with these 20-some-odd wagons for security as he had no idea what they might encounter on the way to Santa Fe. The very thought of unfamiliar and perhaps hostile Indians was unsettling. His old mule could easily keep up with the slow moving oxen for their 12 to 15 miles each day so he decided they would just follow along at the rear. His $133 was about five or six months wages for most working men and should last for quite a while, so he used some to buy a bit of grain for the mule and more for some whiskey and basic trail grub for himself.

Mostly he ate dust. And more dust.

Sledge learned much about the Kansas Territory as he sat listening to the other men at night. The prairie Indians were in the main not to be frightened of, but the Apache and Comanche high plains tribes some 200 or 300 miles on out west were fierce and warlike. The long and lanky Kaw were always wearing a red blanket, but the Delaware were short and stocky and always wore buckskin with moccasins to match. For the first part of the trip they would encounter mostly the familiar Osage and the Kansa who were friendly and quite curious. Here in the eastern Kansas Territory there appeared to be more to fear for the residents from the pro-slavers or abolitionists than from the all the Indians combined. Sledge got confused trying to follow all the events that had happened the last two or three years, and it seemed that the appointed governors of the territory could not keep up either. No official lasted long and the Kansas Territory was now known in federal political circles as the "Graveyard for Governors."

There was a pro-slaver convention and the Wakarusa war with anti-slavers then raiding Cass, Bates and Vernon Counties over in Missouri. An anti-slave guy named Lane even had an army, and a fanatic anti-slaver named John Brown had caused a lot of bloodshed but was run off by a pro-slaver named Atchison, who also had his own army. A place down south called Ft. Scott was kind of truce territory, where they all went from time to time but agreed to leave each other alone when they were in the town. The pro-slaver captain down there was a real crook named Hamilton, who would do anything for money, but the abolitionist main local chap was a man named Montgomery who was a "straight arrow." At a place up north, the Lane fellow even had a trail named for him and groups of anti-slave people were coming across Iowa, then down through the Nebraska part and had formed up towns like Lawrence and Topeka. The slavers had their towns and a government too, and the Russell who owned part of the freight company was very active and a big pro-slave supporter who lived in pro-slave Leavenworth. The recent anti-slave legislature that had formed now also claimed full territorial governmental authority as well.

Then there was the divorce deal. This politician named Lane had previously tried to divorce his wife; however, the first attempt at forming a government (which became known as the Bogus legislature) and which claimed absolute Territorial power at that exact point in time, could not seem to get around to granting him one. When the abolitionists formed a government of their own the frustrated Lane joined their cause, and was now a man to be reckoned with in Kansas political circles. History would record that Lane, one of the most powerful and violent abolitionists ever, actually joined their movement mostly because he was trying to engineer a favorable divorce for himself. Interestingly enough, Lane's wife took three of their four children back to Indiana where a Judge Pettit was from, and where she sued and was promptly granted a divorce. Indiana had been the easiest place in the country to get a "desertion divorce" for quite some time, and she went back home to get one. Shortly thereafter, and with Pettit's influence, the Kansas Territory became the easiest place ever in America to get such a decree. As the word spread, hundreds of women headed to the City of Kansas with scores of them just hanging around with nowhere to go once they were divorced. Some of these women, like the black headed one on the River Rose, were just beautiful. Damn it, he was going to miss that part.

There was plenty of talk about gold in the western mountainous part of Kansas; in fact they even named a town there Aurora (current Denver area) or something like that. The town's name was supposedly the Latin name for gold. Then just north of Aurora some guy named Gregory had made a real strike at a place which quickly became known as Gregory's Gulch. "They say it is the richest square mile in the world." Wagon master Williams was quite concerned for he was losing some of his best bullwhackers, who were leaving the firm when they made Santa Fe, to try their luck at the Gulch.

Anyway, when the freight wagons came to the tall grass country, he understood full well where that name came from. On this stretch some of the grass would hide a full-grown man on the back of a tall horse! The "tall grass" was like no other grass in the world, for it was just as nutritious brown and dry, even in winter, as it was when lush and green in an ordinary summer. Horses and mules required carrying along some grain for them to eat but the oxen simply grazed their way to Santa Fe, often among thousands upon thousands of buffalo. There were few trees and, often as not, one could see for miles with the sky making up about two-thirds of the view.

The Kansas summer of 1859 was the driest ever recoded. No measurable rain fell from early June through November and the drought lingered through 1860. A good part of the time about the only thing in view was land, sky and dust from a wagon train coming or going. And more dust. Wagon master Williams shared the records a fellow by the name of Hays had given him of the summer's records of trail traffic. Despite the drought, in the past 17 days, 289 wagons, 56 horses, 744 mules and 2,251 oxen had passed his Council Grove store.

There were an amazing number of spots on the trail marked with a name where someone claimed they planned to build a town. (After the Civil war over 6000 such spots in the Kansas Territory simply disappeared from the map.)

Sledge ate dust and more dust. Except for the dust he was really kind of enjoying himself until just past Council Grove, some 80 miles out of Olathe. It was just out of Council Grove he heard the wagon master tell the crew that Mr. Majors wanted him passing out posters for his friend from Kentucky, and he would need to go back and put some out:

"This Purdy fellow is looking for this guy hard. Set fire to his house and cost him a boy. Tried twice to get to Purdy's wife who Mr. Majors said is the most beautiful woman he ever saw. The guy's name is Sledge. Must be a real bastard."

And it was just out of Council Grove that the bullwhackers realized they had let $10,000 slip through their fingers, for come next morning Sledge was as far away as an old mule can go in one night. Daybreak found him hiding down among the buffalo and tall grass and the bullwhackers spent the day damning their luck and wondering where their tag-along had disappeared to.

This time Sledge was really shaken, for if this wagon master way out in the wilderness had posters, they all had posters. His face would soon show up at every crossroad and every trading post for the next 700 miles. Sledge was smart enough to know that he needed to quickly be somewhere other than the Santa Fe Trail. He had understood the others to say there were but few white men in Comanche country, which stretched some 400 miles north by west, so north by west it would be. In what he supposed to be somewhat over 100 miles as he approached the beginning of the so-called high plains country, Sledge came to a small spot of civilization.

A. M. Campbell's revered Scotch bride, Mrs. Cristina, was the first and almost only white woman here in Salina. She saw to it that there was no whiskey sold at their store on Sunday. The local Indians were still of gentle nature, and they would send a rider and ask of her:

"Big Father's day?"

If she said yes, that was okay. They would wait.

Sledge got to Salina on a Sunday and wanted whiskey so badly he became confrontational, almost to the point of pulling a gun on her, but decided best he bide his time. He bought more grain and trail grub, and asked for advice on crossing the high-plains country. The next morning he bought two jugs of whiskey and tied them on his poor overloaded mule before heading out. Mrs. Cristina advised him on how to avoid the hostile Indians by going on north to the Leavenworth & Pike's Peak Parallel Road and then west, which he did. Sledge was wonderfully happy when he "found" a great horse along the way, so much so that he left the unsuspecting chap his tired old mule. He was also greatly pleased that he found no posters along the way here.

It was greener up north and a good time of year to travel, so by using the considerable skills he had mastered from living mostly in the outdoors, Sledge managed himself completely around the Comanche countryside. To the richest square mile in the world. To a spot in the Kansas mountains, which could hardly be called a town, now known to the world as Gregory's Gulch. July of 1859 had brought some 10,000 people. August brought an amazing 30,000 more. By summer's end 60,000 more new miners would crowd into an area from North Clear Creek to Eureka Creek to Nevada and Spring Creeks. Winter of 1859/1860 forced many of the miners down to lower elevation or to give up and go home, however, with the spring thaw the more determined ones headed back to the gulch to join the equally aggressive 1860 swarm. This entire area had less than 500 souls before Gregory's find; however, in less than two years the number swelled to about 100,000 more or less permanent residents. In due course there would be a real town with real buildings and some semblance of law, but now, in these early days, people were simply swarming in.

These thousands upon thousands storming into "the richest square mile in the world" paid scant attention to anything, other than finding silver or gold. When Sledge arrived, people were living in tents, wagons, log cabins, dugouts, or maybe just a pile of brush they had pulled together. Every one of them had exactly the same dream. Right now it might well be called Sledge's dream, for he figured this was a good place to learn to prospect.

And try his luck.

And disappear into the crowd.

And that is exactly what he did.

Back in the City of Kansas, John Purdy sat downstairs in the Harris House. He was staring absently at an old edition of the *Enterprise*, trying to figure out what in the world he had done wrong. He had never seen Mattie in such a frame of mind. She was P Oed with a capitol P! He had spent the entire day going to Leavenworth for he had wanted to visit with this certain Colonel Albin up on post. Albin had the reputation of being "some soldier" so John wanted to pick his brain and took an early morning boat up the 20-mile river ride and galloped back. Albin had asked if they could continue their discussion over at a tailor shop where he had to go be measured up. These tailor shops were reputed to be "the best in the West," and among the best in the entire country so John decided to have himself measured up as well. Since Brown and he were almost exactly the same size, he ordered a suit for him too; however, Bos was over six foot five inches tall and weighed about 275 so he would have to measure for himself. Blackfeather would scoff at the idea of wearing such gear.

While at the tailor shop one thing led to another and Colonel Albin invited John and Mattie to a huge party coming up in a few days that a ranking officer was throwing to celebrate his marriage to a young widow. John was reluctant at first and told the colonel that he might be having other men join him by then, and the colonel immediately asked that he bring them as well:

"There will be plenty of men there without women."

John then suggested he knew where there were some ladies who, given proper accommodations, might enjoy such an affair. The colonel was delighted and invited all who would come. John came back to the hotel very excited about all of this and told Mattie, who had spent her entire day over at Maud's. Mattie had come back from taking her evening meal there so distracted she hardly noticed that the hotel had moved them into their most spacious accommodations. John found her in their new sitting room, took little note of her frame of mine at the minute, and was bubbling over.

"The party of the year, Mattie, and as many of Maud's girls as want to go are invited to keep the soldiers company."

"Men!" Mattie snorted.

"Ah wha ..." John was completely taken back by Mattie's reaction.

"Your biggest problem is you are one."

"A what?"

"A man."

"Well I don't remember ever trying to keep that a secret."

"That's all you ever think about."

"What's all I ...?"

"Company. All men want is some female company to use for a while and then you throw us away used."

"Who away?"

"Us women."

"Mattie, it will be a nice ..."

"All those women thought it would be nice to have a man who promised to take care of them and they just used them and threw them away."

"Mattie, this is a party not a a ..."

"All those men on the docks think it's a party, while all the women think it's it's ... uh ... uh .... How can a man think like that, like it's no big deal?"

"A lot of men are very caring and protect their woman. I try to look out for you."

"Ha. Just go down there and look."

"Mattie, there are hundreds, no there are thousands, of men passing through here who have no women or are away from their women for a long time. Put that together with all those women who are streaming in here to get divorced with nowhere else to go and no money and you get this. Mattie, this is not normal."

"We agree on one thing. What those cowboys were wanting Maureen to do was sure not normal. How can men be so- so- so casual and impersonal about such a thing?"

"Mattie, you may find this hard to believe but a lot of women would rather send their husband down there than to take a chance."

"A chance on what?"

"You know, a chance on having another baby."

"Preposterous!"

"It's true."

John was as right. The only effective form of birth control was abstinence, and some well-bred ladies willingly looked the other way as their husbands made use of certain available services. Mattie could not even comprehend such a thing. She had always looked with eagerness to her marriage bed.

"Nonsense!"

"Men and women think differently, Mattie."

"Well no kidding, Mr. Purdy. You may step to the head of the class!"

"Mattie, men, well, men sort of have a thirst for women that gets pretty strong."

"Thirst, huh?"

"Mattie, do you remember the year of the drought when Hiram was little?"

"Yes."

"Do you remember when we went to Paducah and were fooling around in the buggy and we kicked the water jug out and broke it.'

"You kicked the water jug out, Mr. Purdy!"

"Well anyway, how long did it take us to get thirsty?"

"I don't know. It seemed before long a drink was all we could think about."

"Remember the creeks were dry and the first place we stopped the farmer said he though his water would make us sick."

"Yes."

"And how the old man blew back the scum and offered us a drink anyway."

"Yes"

"Remember how hard it was not to drink the stuff?"

"Yes."

"Well that is kind of how sex is for a man. The want gets to be so strong that after a while sex is about all we can think about. There is one big difference. If a man goes without water long enough he dies. I don't know of any man who ever died for lack of a woman, but sometimes it sure seems like he might. Some of these guys are blowing back the scum and drinking anyway."

Mattie crossed her arms and practically stamped her foot.

"So they are all scum are they? They were not scum when they came here!"

"It doesn't take long for water to scum up."

"So I am a drink of water?"

"It's not always water, Mattie. Sometimes it's a strong short hot drink that burns, but other times it's warm and sweet like hot chocolate on a cold night, and sometimes, well sometimes it's like a long cool refreshing drink of sweet water."

"Humph."

"Mattie, sweetheart—"

"Don't you sweetheart me you, you, you man you!!"

Mattie sniffed, flipped her head, then turned away and looked out the window. The mood in here was far darker than it was out there.

"I think there were some newspapers downstairs that I have not read, Mattie. I'll be back later."

She never even flinched as he firmly closed the door behind him.

So, John Purdy now sat looking at a paper, but not seeing a thing. It was by far the biggest fight they had ever had.

When it was apparent the hotel was keeping the public area open late because he was there, John walked back up to their room and let himself in. Mattie was sitting in a chair in about the same spot he had left her only she had now changed into her gown and let her hair down. Even in the faint glow of the whale oil lamp he could see by her puffy red eyes that she had been crying.

"Hi." She was quite pensive.

"You okay, Mattie?"

"I think so. I kind of got caught up in it, didn't I?" She stood up and approached cautiously.

"That's okay, must have been some day."

"John, it's so unreal. The stories they tell. Maud told me not to get started asking, but I did. She said it would get me upset. Sometimes she says, sometimes she just wants to go kill somebody. Do you know some of those girls who wind up on the docks have a piece of oil cloth across the bottom of the bed so their customer does not even have to take off his boots. In twenty minutes she will be out on the docks looking for her next partner. If they are lucky the high priced ones work where there is clean linen once in a while and maybe even a fresh towel from time to time. Almost all of them that stay very long wind up on alcohol, or maybe even morphine or opium.

"Too bad. I bet most of them were once very nice."

"They all thought they were going to be like you and me once upon a time."

"Mattie, weird or not, I am glad I found you. I have always been glad."

He held out his arms and she grabbed him and buried her head in his chest.

"John, are you thirsty?"

"No, Mattie, they had some .... ."

"Are you sure you can't drink something?"

"Well, ah, maybe. What are we having?"

"There is a full menu."

"Mattie, it would be very nice, if you are in the humor to serve something. I really do need something to drink, come to think of it."

"Let's start with something with fire and a bite to it, and then later if you could get thirsty again I would get you a nice long slow drink of sweet water. Okay?"

Her gown lay piled on the floor.

The Leavenworth party was quite a "do," with the guest list including many of the leading citizens from St Joseph, Atchison, the City of Kansas and Westport. Plus, of course, the 16 of Maud's girls who had scrambled about putting something together to wear. Maud's ladies who had chosen to come were given the best quarters for the evening the post had to offer, quite properly chaperoned, and treated like royalty. They were also danced until they were exhausted with blisters on sore feet.

Bos looked splendid in his new outfit, and the few colored "buffalo soldiers" on post entertained him thoroughly with tales of the western frontier. The food, music, company and atmosphere were splendid, causing John to be especially sorry his other team members were not there to enjoy. It was an extraordinary good time, particularly for those unfamiliar with the military.

High style for the ladies was a very full skirt made of about 25 yards of material held out either by hoops or by all of the petticoats they could get under it. Three or maybe four of the more fashionable ladies with their skirts were about a normal sized room full. The skirt waistbands fit over corsets so tightly laced that a lady could scarcely get her breath. All this was topped by a skintight top with a good many "Dolly Madison" bodices cut so very, very, very low they created a peep show that left little from the waist up to anyone's imagination. Mattie's skirt by comparison was quite moderate in size and, as opposed to the other obviously well-to-do women, she could sit down quite comfortably. She also wore a very thoughtfully sewed four inch wide covering of lace as a ruffle at her bodice. Mattie's cleavage started way high on her chest and it disappeared quickly into the ruffles; nonetheless, when she moved, her full rounded breasts jiggled just a bit. They pointed straight ahead as they perched high above her naturally small waist, and although they were quite modestly covered, she was nothing short of sensational. With her radiant white smile, brilliant blue eyes, strawberry colored lips, and honey-colored curls piled up way high, as usual, the statuesque Mattie was the fairest maid of all. Mattie Purdy absolutely dazzled everyone she came in contact with and although she stood eye to eye with most of the men, sometimes, when John became preoccupied by others, Bos felt that he should stand beside her just to make his presence known. Quite naturally the story of these Kentucky people was shortly buzzing through the crowd.

Soon, every soldier on post, many of the area's leading citizens, plus all of those who worked for them wanted to be involved. They and all of their other acquaintances up and down the river were keeping their eyes open, watching for this guy. Before the party was over John had requests for about 500 more posters, and Alexander Majors asked for yet another hundred to scatter in the many other places he had contacts, besides the Santa Fe Trail. Later the "girls" helped Maud write every one of her past residents a painstakingly written personal note and included a poster for each of them.

By the time Brown and Blackfeather found the trio at the Harris House, plans were in motion for hundreds and hundreds of pairs of eyes to be watching. In addition to those on the steamboats running the Mississippi and Missouri rivers, there were now soldiers, miners, merchants, Indians, Irishmen, Germans, cowboys, bullwhackers, innkeepers, pioneers, whores and grateful second chance ladies scattered all over. These eyes covered every square mile of the Kansas territory, on down the Santa Fe, and out the Oregon and California Trails to the shores of the Pacific.

Waiting.

Watching.

Looking.

For the face of this man on the run.

All they needed now was time.

This fine morning John was grilling Bos thoroughly.

"Are you absolutely certain, Bos?"

"Yes Sir, Mr. John, I am. Absolutely! Absolutely certain!"

"There can be no mistake about it."

"Mr. John, when you done bent your back moving everything a woman has in her great big house, move it again, watch her stand an study it there, then move it again, done watch her look and look at it, then moves it all back where you started, you remember what she look like. Master took me there to lift, and lift I did. I done lifted and I lifted for that woman. When we was there Daniel told me he bring Master there most every day."

John was too engrossed to correct Bos' grammar as he and Mattie were gently doing these days.

Mattie joined them:

"Tell us again please, Bos. I came in the middle of this."

"Yes ma'am. Miz. Maud asked me to help a woman who was moving some stuff into a house not a far walk from her place. I went over to help. This man name of Johnson they said was a preacher was there too, and had brought some furniture and stuff. He had his slave there too and we moved a lot of things. The woman who was pretty much in charge was a woman who used to live right next to Island View. She took one look at me and turned away and went to the other part of the house and stayed there. She just hollered through the door to put things where we wanted to but I got a good look. She never wanted me to see her face but I did. She got herself all busy so as to stay away from me cleaning up after them children's diarrhea and wipen snotty noses. Told us to put stuff where we thought it ought to go and that ain't like her."

"Bos, don't use the word ain't."

"Mattie, for heavens sake! Bos, did you hear her name?"

"Yes sir, Mr. John, the preacher call her Miss Scythia but she go by a different name down there. Her name was Miz. Geneva then."

"Bos, do you remember what her house looked like?"

"Yes, sir."

Bos described Geneva Chouteau's fine southern home exactly as John remembered it from having been there one time. Right down to the work shed out back.

John had already wired his father to contact Three Creeks and get Junior started to the City of Kansas, with instructions to make all haste. Junior was also to bring an envelope that Mr. Morris would entrust him with. Maud was counting the minutes until her son got off a boat and was now delightfully happy that she could stay here and take care of her girls. John and Maud had concluded that after a nice long visit, Junior would go back, and presuming Transylvania admitted him, he could get some more book learning and then join her here. Or perhaps they could find a college closer by.

Time was creeping so very slooooowly for Maud as she waited for her baby:

"How many days more, Mr. John? How many days more?"

"Maud, if everything worked out just right, my father would have received the wire the next day, then he would have sent the messenger to Three Creeks that same day or maybe the next. Give Junior two days to get to the Mississippi and catch a boat, three or four more days up river, then eight to ten days more from St. Louis to here. It would be over two weeks, Maud. The party up on post was the ninth day, so I figure at least six or eight more days from now, so it will still probably be over a week longer. The boat Avery is the most dependable as far as schedule is concerned and I told Dad to have him try and catch it, and I bet he does."

"I can't hardly wait, Mr. John. I can't hardly wait."

" I know, Maud. Mattie and I are so glad for you, but Maud, we still need to talk about the money. You cannot keep putting me off on that."

"I know. When my boy gets here we will talk and then decide when he gets here. It ain't for me, Mr. John, but if I sell the house and give it all back, what will my girls do? And I want my boy to get some more book learning so bad."

John Purdy had been around the moneyed set his entire life and detested those who had money and who were flippant about it toward those who did not. He had no intention of letting Maud's place fold nor for Junior not to get his education. Still, he wanted her to feel like she was the solution, and it was she that made it happen. He was not about to give her the $20,000 cushion she had in the St. Louis bank, but Virginia had won him enough at the crooked gambling table to mostly pay for the house and get Junior started on an education. He and Mattie could well afford it, and she would be even more willing than he.

"Maud, why not let's wire and tell Virginia de Falco everything? She struck me as a very generous person, and a very fair person. Maybe she would be satisfied getting just part of her money back. Without you, she would not have a chance at getting any of it. I need to tell her about a different matter I have come across, so we could write her together. In fact my deal is important enough I will pay for a wire. Then we will write a long letter and explain everything down to the smallest detail. Let's start with a wire."

"Before my boy gets here?"

"Yes. I think the quicker she knows the better."

"Okay, Mr. John. I am a trusting your mind on this."

Five hundred miles to the south, Virginia de Falco sat quietly with her hands in her lap while lawyer Rawson looked down at his papers, afraid to look up. He was certain that she would see by his face that he thought she had lost her mind. Steven Farout stood looking out the window and his wife Bonnie sat bemused with sort of a far away look in her eye, smiling softly at her husband.

Virginia broke the silence:

"Mr. Farout, I do not know what else I can offer. I need a man such as you to take charge of Island View. Mr. Purdy said you have more business sense than any high-toned businessman he ever met back East. The local merchants agree on that. You are smart and tough but also generous and kind. Your morals are above reproach and that I truly admire. I have had you checked out and rechecked out and I probably know more about you than you know about yourself. Mr. Farout, you are my choice. What must I do. What else could you want?"

"Mrs. de Falco, your offer is more generous than any man could ever expect, for himself or for his wife and family. I am still astonished."

Rawson could help but nod his head in agreement.

"Mr. Farout, you're wife could be any kind of lady she chooses to be. The amount of money and business you will control in this responsibility is immense. Few people would dare not to be kind, or to invite the managing executive of Island View and his wife to every social function within miles. She may sit and be looked after, or get on a horse and ride with you each day if she chooses. The servants I offer her are excellent when it comes to caring for their mistress, her children and the grounds. Island View will pay for the best education your children can absorb. Every son of the landed gentry would seek you daughter's hand and your sons would be respected, although a bit feared I suspect.

The home I offer is very nicely done although if you choose, after we have a couple of good seasons together, you may build it to an even grander scale. I offer a fine salary and a bonus based on results. My dream for Island View is on these pages, Mr. Farout. I need help. It is all in writing and there will be no surprises. Mr. Rawson is an excellent lawyer and I have paid him to be quite detailed. I have also paid to have any other lawyer you chose to look at the employment portion of the contracts. Still I sense there is something amiss. Please, Mr. Farout. What else is there?"

Farout looked her straight in the face:

"Land, Mrs. de Falco. Land."

"Land?"

"Bonnie's people, nor my people, ever had land of their own. We have our own land. For as far back as we can go, no one in our lines ever owned their own land. My father and his father before him were thrown off the land because the owners were mad or dissatisfied. My grandfather's landlord burned his home. Bonnie's father took a gun and went after his landlord and then spent the rest of his life on the run. When we step out the door each morning, we know that cannot happen to us. When Bonnie and I come in at night all dirty, sometimes we chase each other about and laugh as we rub it all over each other. We love that dirt because it is our dirt. Our dirt from our land, Mrs. de Falco. Without land a man is nothing. What if you marry again and your husband has different views? What if he sees your plan as foolish? I know you say no whips, but what if he might be different. What if you think I get too smart for my own good or we simply have an honest disagreement on how things are to be done?"

Virginia looked back and forth between Bonnie and Steven and became still more disarmingly frank:

"Completely changing the way Island View operates and getting it into full production is a major undertaking, and more than I choose to keep track of, or frankly more than I can probably handle. You must always remember that I am a drunk. Never, ever forget that! Oh, when you have money they call you an alcoholic, but it is nothing more than being a drunk. I have not had a drink since shortly after my late husband's death, Mr. Farout, nor do I intend to, but those who seem to know about such things say I am but one drink away from being in trouble all over again. I have only my late husband's illegitimate children to share anything with, and we are doing okay, but it is quite an adjustment for all of us. The girl will marry soon no doubt, and the boy will be away at military school. I need someone to share this dream with. I also need someone with the guts to tell me to get my sorry ass out of the way because there is a plantation to run."

Bonnie looked at the floor, and Rawson actually blushed a bit as Virginia continued:

"You may sell no slave unless I specifically agree to each and every sale. You will manage as you do now, with no whips. You may sell no land nor place a mortgage on one single acre of Island View. You may sell nothing from any of the collections, or any of the art or even one rare book. Other than that, you execute the plan as you see fit. It is an extraordinary plan Mr. Farout. I will be your counsel to help with the bigger issues."

She concentrated on Bonnie:

"I expect to play the merry widow for quite a while. I never had a social life or courted when I was young. My grandfather took care of that by marrying me off so young, but I am enjoying it now and expect to look around quite a bit. Besides, the only man I ever dream about having in my bed is already taken. He has a beautiful wife with a family of boys and they live hundreds of miles away.

Turning her attention back to Steven Farout she continued:

I know you have had sufficient time to study these papers, but please reread page 4, the bottom half of 8 and the first third or so of page 9, plus the second paragraph on page 12. I had hoped that would all put your mind at ease."

Steven Farout looked at Virginia as she sat mentally thumbing through the contract. The woman was simply amazing. He switched his gaze to his Bonnie, who got up and stood holding her husband's hand:

"It's up to you, Steven, I told you when I married you I would follow wherever you lead."

Steven was not sold yet.

If anything, when they were sober, Virginia's boys had been good, maybe even excellent, at gambling. She always took pleasure winning those games, and today the stakes were enormous. She calculated that she held the queen and the ace of trumps while Farout held the king. Her ace had an enormous cost that went with it so she led with the queen and saved the ace for her last line of offense. It was a gutsy play because the game might well end before she could play her ace.

"Mr. Farout, the small farm right next to your farm to the east can be bought. He wants a little more than it is worth, but I have already paid him a fair amount for the exclusive right to buy it by the end of the year. We will add that to your holdings. Together that land and what you just bought, along with that you have always owned, would make a very nice place. You come help me for three years and after that, when and if you ever chose to leave Island View, all of that land will be yours. Your severance package so to speak. Surely, Mr. Farout, surely in the meantime you can find someone to farm your land. I am making a lifetime commitment and hope you are too but if ever you choose to return there, you will have a very nice place and plenty of money to provide your family a lovely home. In the meantime your slaves can do some sharecropping on your behalf on the corner of Island View over by where your house will be, or I will pay you a fair wage for their services.

Rawson got just a bit pale.

Virginia directed her attention to Bonnie:

"The house is quite secluded; however, it is large and quite nicely done. There is a nice library and some beautiful art although you will need to get some more things that suit your taste. There are a few empty spaces from where I returned some of the more rare pieces to the main house. When my ancestors came here, the first was a young man whose father had pressed him into service to marry a pregnant princess of the highest order of the court. The real father was a highly placed member of the clergy, and to show appreciation for getting him off the hook, and to guarantee their continued discretion, the clergyman had a lot of churches make 'donations.' For nearly 25 years many congregations continued to search for things to send along with their very best pieces to this 'mission' in the new world. The library and art now at Island View should really be on display for the public, as some of it is absolutely priceless.

Your house was built for my late husband's mistress and their two children who lived there for about the last six or seven years. There is a room each for your children and more, plus adequate quarters for house servants and cabins out back for your slaves. I must quickly say the ones who live in them now do a masterful job keeping the place up. The gardens are especially beautiful. We'll need to build something for Bessie unless you want her to live in the big house."

Bonnie was getting more impressed by the minute. This woman had definitely done her homework. The room grew quiet and Steven sat down. Bonnie stood to one side behind him and put her hand on his shoulder as he sat gazing at the floor. Rawson returned to studying the papers in front of him.

One minute.

Two minutes.

Three minutes.

The only sound was a fly buzzing somewhere.

And the ticking of a clock.

Virginia sat quietly.

Her hands folded in her lap.

Her mouth shut.

Steven Farout finally looked up:

"Mrs. de Falco, I think if we moved my slaves right into the middle of the rest, they would be very good examples for the others. All of them are smart enough to be a great deal of help."

Later, as their handsome carriage headed out so they might inspect their new home, Bonnie and Steven sat holding hands. She remarked as much to herself as to Steven:

"I really, really like her."

Then turning to her husband:

"Steven, you have just moved us up more rungs on the social scale than I can count. If our parents could only see us now."

Steven was pleased with the deal he had just made. It made him feel extremely successful. He was being a very good provider. They passed several nice homes along the riverway but as the carriage turned in the winding drive where they could see their new home behind the tree line, Bonnie's hand flew to her mouth:

"Oh, my heavens!"

As they mounted the steps the front doors swung open:

"Good afternoon masser and missus. You be here at almost exactly when Miz. Virginia said you be here. Yes sir, why dat be right to de minute almost."

Back in Rawson's office he watched as Virginia stood at the fireplace burning her so called ace of trumps:

"If you're grandfather knew I had even prepared an unsigned deed to that house and acreage over on the corner of Island View, he would roll over in his grave."

Virginia smiled her wicked little smile:

"He's going to roll over anyway. In fact if they have nicknames wherever he is, three years from now he'll be known as "Spinner de Falco."

Leaving Rawson's office, Virginia stopped by to see Mr. Norman:

"Virginia! You must be a genius! You got a full penny a pound more by waiting to sell. That is enormous. Everybody else was getting 14 or 14 1/2 cents back in January. You got 15 1/2 cents. It was good looking in the bale, but my word, you did better than anyone else I even heard about."

"Well, Mr. Norman, I wish I could take all the credit but I can't. You met my friend John Purdy. We would up riding up the river on a boat and he kept saying if he had a store down here he would be really careful with credit this year. He had ridden around a lot and we looked from the boat quite a bit too. He said even though Island View had a good start on a crop, it looked to him there was really only going to be about half of a crop of cotton this year and prices would go up."

"Smart fellow, sounds like."

Damned handsome too thought Virginia, as her heart skipped a beat just at the thought of him.

The messenger who found her in Norman's office remarked that it was about the longest wire they had received yet at the new telegraph office. Norman gave the chap a two bit tip and Virginia sat back to read.

> Am in City of Kansas with search team Stop Found Maud who got your Tuttoor money Stop Keeps women who are in desperate straits off street Stop Still has most but not all Stop Geneva Chouteau here also Stop Works with kids who have nowhere else right now Stop Am after man who set fire Stop and came back after Mattie while I was there Stop Will be here 3 or 4 weeks sure. Stop Wire me at Harris House Westport Stop John Purdy Stop

She handed the wire to John Norman:

"That, sir, is about as much news as you can get on one little piece of paper, wouldn't you say?"

Out in the Kansas mines on the eastern slopes of the Rockies, Sledge was finally at the right place at the right time doing the right thing. Although Jim, the next miner upstream, found virtually nothing, and while Jess the next miner down stream found only enough to keep hope alive, Sledge suddenly became a thousandaire, next a ten thousandaire and then he could not even keep track. A nugget is officially a chunk of gold that will not pass through a number 10 screen and while Sledge was collecting handfuls of them, most other miners could only talk of pinches of dust. Soon he was buying every pleasure in excess that could be bought, and in short order Sledge had debauchery refined to an art form. He called them bodyguards or claim watchers, but the two thugs that hung with him were nothing more than hired friends, for as a moneyed man he was most difficult to like.

Jeannie had never been sorry she stepped forward at Maud's that day. Jess had promised after one year at the mines if they had not made it rich, he would take her back east where he had family and a bit of land. Maud had him figured just about perfectly, and had advised Jeannie:

"He once had a good woman and knows what it's like. He's lonesome and he will take care of you cause he never wants to be lonesome again. It's hard on a man to lose his wife and especially hard with her trying to have his baby, and then lose the baby too. He will take care of you and in time he will love you good."

Other than the party girls, there were so few women in Central City that men would take a bath and then come by just to talk and to look at Jeannie, where she and Jess lived in their wagon with a tent stretched out back. Some of the few miners' wives who were at the camp took in laundry or did other "womanly chores" but Jess would not hear to Jeannie bending her back and busting her knuckles. Jeannie was good with a needle, so she would look through the clean laundry and patch, stitch, or sew on buttons and made almost as much doing that as the claim produced. While most were forced to cook over an open fire, Jess had gone to great pains to get her a cast iron stove and, if she could get the fixings, she enjoyed preparing nice meals from time to time. At such occasions they invited those who were befriending them the most to join. Still, it was a tough life and conditions were rudimentary to say the least as some 100,000 people jammed tightly into these mountain streams.

Every one of them praying to get lucky like this guy with the busted up face.

Jeannie read every word of Maud's letter three times before she opened the poster. She nearly fainted, then pulled herself together and scrambled to find Jess.

It was the man on the very next claim!

"Jess, how are we going to handle this? There are gunfights, knife fights, fistfights and drunks everywhere. There is no jail, no marshal and no law of any kind and he has those thugs with him most of the time."

"I don't know, Jeannie, I simply do not know."

They went out into the woods where they were more certain no one could hear before continuing their conversation.

"We can't let on, Jeannie. Someone with that much money can get lots of things done. It is not worth even a $10,000 reward to get shot in the head. I think the best would be to try and get word to Maud that he is here and simply keep an eye on him. It would be suicide to confront him. If her friend Purdy knows where he is maybe they can bring the law and come get him. With the luck he is having on his claim, he is not about to leave."

They could think of no better plan, so the issue became one of getting word to Maud as promptly as possible. There were not that many who gave up quickly, but there were those few who promised that if unsuccessful after a short try they would come back home. Jeannie had the right contact, for Ike had promised Hannah he would come back home to Illinois in 120 days, and now if he rode hard he could keep his promise. Jeannie had been nice to him and he owed her for the best food he had on his short fling at being a miner. He shook Jess' hand, gave Jennie a hug as he took the sack of foodstuff she now offered, and looked her square in the eye:

"I promise. I'll hand it to her myself."

Over at the Harris House in the City of Kansas, Mattie got up from where she sat reading to answer the knock on their room's door.

"Why, Mr. Majors, what a special and pleasant surprise!"

"Good day Mrs. Purdy, this is Mr. Charles Gilstrap. Charles, this is Mrs. Mattie Purdy."

"Please come in."

"John, meet Charles Gilstrap. Charles, this is John Purdy and this is their man, Bos. I want you all to hear what Mr. Gilstrap has to say. Mr. Gilstrap is one of our most valued wagon masters and brought back a message from our Mr. Williams, another of our wagon masters who was headed south. They passed on the trail."

Gilstrap stood with his hat in his hands:

Majors looked unhappy:

"Go on."

"Mr. Purdy, well I met one of our trains on the way headed south and well, Mr. Williams, the wagon master he sent word."

"Yes?"

"This fellow you are looking for, this Sledge guy, well he traveled along behind them for quite a ways before they figured out who he was. Some of em even seen that big hairy mole when they was swimming and washing off the dust. He took off when they got out the posters and some of em looked most of the next day. They found some stuff he threw away so to lighten up on his old mule, but that is all they ever saw. He seemed to have headed northwest out from Council Groves.

Majors added; "I am sorry, John, our man Williams is a good man, but he forgot the posters! They get awfully busy till the train sort of forms up and gets into a routine, and I guess he just forgot. I will speak to him."

"Don't be too tough. He has a lot to do besides pass out posters for some guy he never met."

Majors smacked one fist into his other hand:

"He doesn't have any more important things to do than follow instructions from the man who pays him!"

John smiled wryly:

"It has already cost him $10,000. I expect he will remember next time."

"Yeah, I guess I won't have to say too much. Not much at all, come to think of it."

Majors was obviously still very upset that Williams had Sledge in his grasp and let him get away, so Mattie stood up and smiled brightly:

"Gentlemen, please join us. They generally save the big table for us anymore, and the food is marvelously good. Bos, would you please get the others?"

Majors turned to Gilstrap; "Come on, you deserve a good meal after riding all night." He then offered Mattie his arm and the entire group went down to dine, where Harriet Harris and some of her seven daughters set them a fine table, and where Blackfeather was the only one who wished there was something more simple to eat.

John was lost in thought about this new turn of events; however, the rest of the group had a lively mealtime discussion about the Santa Fe Trail being such a busy two-way road. John mentally rejoined the group when he heard Majors proclaiming:

"The Arkansas river is far too difficult for the railroads to bridge. Sometimes we cross where it is a half-mile wide and double or triple team up because the banks are so soft. I am confident the railroads will never be a challenge for us there."

John started to respond, for he disagreed completely, but instead he chose not to, for it was not nice to argue with guests. He was somewhat concerned about his new friend anyway, for Majors had seemed quite thrown off balance as of the last few days. Sec. of the Army, John B. Floyd, had once again refused to pay the monies owed the firm, or to allow them out of their army contract. Majors had previously told John that 1857 had been a business nightmare. The firm had sent 700 teamsters along with 7,740 oxen pulling 645 wagons carrying 3,800,000 pounds of supplies west for the military. This business was totally outside the signed government contracts. All of this extra was created when President James Buchanan decided to move against the Mormons who were setting up their own independent society, which was seen as a threat to continuous settlement of the west. The military officials had insisted there was no other company who could possibly take on such a freighting task, and demanded they proceed. Majors' firm was to simply trust the government's written promise.

Then, in addition to almost 100 men, 70 some-odd wagons with several hundred oxen and a fortune in materials simply disappeared. Two years later they were still uncertain if it was due to Indians or the Mormon Militia; however, Majors still grieved for the men. To make matters even worse, and although they had the written government promise to the contrary, it now appeared the firm would have to stand good for the lost material as well as their own equipment. The war department currently owed the firm an undisputed $642,000 which they steadfastly refused to pay, even though Major's group had been required to borrow substantially to finance the government's huge extra shipment. All of this combined was now forcing the firm to stretch its credit to the limit just to stay in operation. No wonder he was distracted.

After their noontime meal, Majors and Gilstrap excused themselves and since no one needed to be on "Mattie guard," Brown took Blackfeather and Bos out to explore Westport while John and Mattie went back up to their room.

"John, do you like Maud?"

"What is not to like about Maud? She is a plain unselfish woman who had a hard life and is now trying to make life a bit easier for some unfortunate souls. Her girls would be lost without her. She thinks of herself last."

"I don't mean Maud, the woman. I mean Maud, the name."

"Oh. Well kind of, but it's not one of my favorites."

"How about Maureen?"

"Perfect for a redheaded Irish woman with freckles and some shape to her. Our Maureen looks like she is about ten instead of nearly sixteen. That girl's hips are not as big as one of Bos thighs. In fact she doesn't have any hips at all; she is shaped like a stick. She sure is slow to woman out."

"What woman's name do you like."

"Mattie!"

"Very smooth! You are certainly thinking fast today, Mr. Purdy. Thank you very much, sir, but what other name."

"I always associate a name with a person or people I know who have it. Outside of family names, I would say the most impressive woman I ever met was Virginia de Falco. The name Virginia gives me good thoughts."

"That would be a nice name."

"Why all the interest in names?

"Well, there is a 50-50 chance we'll need to pick a girl's name, Mr. John."

"Say what?"

"You're homecoming from down south was quite successful. I just know it will be our girl."

John wrapped her in his arms. She was 35, looked 25, and was the picture of health. It had been a few years but why not? Hiram was 17, Henry was 14, Harold was 11 and if sensitive little Harvey were alive, he would be coming up 8. Mattie had presented him with four fine blue-eyed sons who all appeared to have the build and personality of their father. If this one were a girl and she were very, very lucky, she would be and look like her mother.

Mattie decided to take a little beauty rest and John realized Sledge was not close by for the time being, so they could relax a bit now. After seeing Mattie to the room, he went down to saddle up Star and go clear his mind. He had a lot of thinking to do. Wow. Double Wow. His wife was pregnant. Sledge was on the run. The woman who was involved in trying to murder Virginia was right down the street. He saw another woman nearly every day who had about $30,000 of her money, and he still had to get Bos bought.

John Purdy never forgot for a minute why he was in the City of Kansas, but he was also a man of high principle and simply could not leave all of these loose ends. Mattie was especially anxious to get home now, partially to be better able to take care of herself and partially because she wanted to be working on Simpson to get Sarah of the good eyes bought for Bos. At least he could burn the papers on Junior when he got here. He smiled ironically to himself. Come to think of it, destroying his ownership of Junior would not be smart at all. He checked all of his personal slavery issues off in his mind; Junior probably did belong to him. Mattie was determined to buy Sarah, and he intended to do his best to make Virginia keep her promise to sell him Bos. For a man who was totally against slavery he was going in pretty deep.

On top of all of that he had not breathed a word to anyone about wanting to open a store here. As he led Star past some appreciative bystanders, he kept looking about. Among everything else they were short of, there were no shovels to buy and the merchants made no promises there would be any soon. Imagine no shovels. There had not been a shovel to buy for weeks and yet every wagon wanted and needed at least two when they headed west. There were 20 kinds of shovels and not one to buy today in the City of Kansas, or Westport. Mattie's father could come up with hundreds, or even a thousand, and ship them tomorrow.

People kept moving the West. First the West was anywhere west of the east coast, then West was west of the Appalachians, then it was west of the Mississippi. Now the West was becoming the ocean where the sun went down and the men who helped move the West would be rich. There would be railroads and there would be bridges and there would be even more fabulously wealthy men made here on this frontier. Yes Indeed! There was another Purdy fortune to be made right here, helping to move the West. On West.

John Purdy snapped back to reality. West was where Sledge was. His job was to lead the team west.

And find Sledge. And kill him.

The crop looked outstanding; however, it wasn't picking time yet at Island View. Farout needed time to wrap up his affairs but was already spending most of his time getting oriented with the gigantic operation and looking for two assistants. Meanwhile, Bonnie was indispensable. Virginia was packing for her trip, while Mammy was mostly lecturing.

"A white woman traveling with two young black men. What in the world are you a thinking. Fact is you ain't a thinking. That simply ain't done, yo be the missus or not, that simply ain't done! No sireee!"

"I can't take Janice, Amanda is starting her family, and any of the other girls who help with my room and such would be overwhelmed. I think Amos and Ramos would be fine. You claim you're too old too go."

"Well I just got younged up."

"Well good. Get to packing."

"You needs you some young slave women to look after you and help you dress and take baths and all. A personal servant or two. All the other plantation owners' wives that I ever met have some so's they don't have to do nothing but set and look pretty."

"Ha. Set and look helpless is what you mean. A healthy full grown woman who can't drag a washrag through her own butt is more to be pitied than admired."

" My Lord, woman, how you talk!"

"We may take Amos and Ramos too. I am just more comfortable with them around. They watch over me like I was their pot of gold."

"You is there pot of gold but they almost still just kids. But you spend all that money on boat tickets and then you won't have so much gold."

"They have more presence and are more aware of what is going on around them than anybody else I know, including most any white man. Anyway, if we want more gold maybe we will just sell a painting. A very rich man in Spain wants that ugly thing that hangs in Gotfield's old room. Says the model was his great grandmother or some such and he wants it badly. The artist who painted it got very famous, so now any of his paintings that come on the market bring a fortune. His agent took two years to find it and now won't take no for an answer."

The painting was hard for most to like, done in mostly yellows and greens with some dark brown and brick red thrown in. The subject was a young woman sitting on the ground and leaning against a church with one knee pulled up to her chest exposing either her undergarments, or her behind, depending on one's interpretation. Small wonder the Church had donated it way back when.

"Miz. Virginia, I think Mr. Gotfield just like that picture cause it show some of her underwear."

"Well, Mammy, I think it was because he wanted to look at somebody's bottom and I wouldn't let him see mine. Now go get to packing!"

The older woman walked away mumbling to herself:

"Lordy, lordy, how that woman talks."

It was common for rich southerners to travel with a maid or servant so Virginia and Mammy were a common pair as the "finest boat afloat" made its way up the Mississippi. There was very good light of the moon, so the captain could continue moving briskly and only need tie up at night one time. The current was moderate to low and the crew was simply brilliant in knowing where to find the slow deep water to move against, and thus, they made excellent time to St. Louis.

On their next boat, on up the Missouri to the City of Kansas, there were a few prissy self-important types who were also up on its extra fine cabin deck. Other than these few, Virginia and Mammy could have been stripped naked and ridden on the backs of ostriches and no one else would have paid any mind. The lower deck had several families minus their fathers, some of whom had gone ahead to find just the place for them. Other fathers were bringing wagons across, having sent the mother and children ahead for a much easier start to their great adventurer to the territories. Yet other complete families on board were going to provision once they got to the City of Kansas or St. Joseph. These families would all stay in Kansas or Nebraska, for it was far too late in the season to head way west on the Oregon Trail.

There were also about a dozen women headed for the Kaw River shores and they quickly formed into divorce groups and hung together, the largest group being pretty much at ease and planning on a quick turnaround. Many were enjoying their trip up on the cabin deck with a couple of them traveling with their replacement husband and a couple more with some kin or another. Then there were the others on the lower deck, wondering what would happen next and trying to not to be scared to death. Mostly this time of year, save the relatively few pioneers on board who were the stragglers, the lower deck was jam packed with men from every walk of life headed west to the famous Gregory's Gulch.

John was anxious to see Virginia.

Mattie wanted to meet her.

Maud was scared to death.

Geneva had no idea Virginia was on the way.

Bos was worried to distraction.

Bos had run away from this woman, and even if she did not recognize him, she owned every pound of him. Jackson County, Missouri, was highly in favor of slavery, with even the preacher owning some, and the locals took a mighty dim view of runaways. Even free blacks generally had it tough here. Bos took some comfort in the fact that he was now assigned to escort Mattie home. Mostly he was counting heavily on John to get him bought from Miz. Virginia before they started back to Kentucky. Mattie had promised him that when they got home she would turn her smile up to "full dazzle" and immediately talk to Simpson about buying Sarah. For the third or fourth or fifth time.

John's father had sent a messenger to Three Creeks the day he received the wire in Paducah, and Junior started yet that night. He made the Mississippi river firewood stop the middle of the next day, and immediately caught the first boat to stop there. He then jumped from the first boat to the Avery with less than an hour to spare and arrived in the City of Kansas in an astonishing 12 days. The reunion on the dock made even the hard core cynical tough guys stop and watch, as this woman and her son laughed, wept, and went squealing around on the dock as they hung on to each other for dear life.

Later that day the little group crowded into Maud's room:

"Now I can tell you, son, now I can tell you!"

"Please. It hurt so. I could never understand."

"I know, but it had to be."

"Why, Momma, why did you go away? I am almost grown and I cried like a baby."

"Did you give Mr. John the letter you was to get from Mr. Morris?"

"Yes."

John handed them the still sealed envelope that Morris had instructed Junior to guard with his life. Maud held her boy's hand:

"Let's read it together, son. You read it to me."

> 'Be it known that I, Quinton Tooter, do hereby own one female negro slave who answers to the name of Maud. She is branded with the letter T in two places: On her left buttock and smaller on her right breast. Her bloodline is as follows: Maud's grandmother Lisa was a full-blood Negro arriving here on the slave ship Hare from Sierra Leone, West Africa, in 1756 and such female was sold legally at auction with the sale duly recorded in the ship's log. Among children born of Lisa was a slave named Pearl, born 1791, who is a properly registered slave in the state of Louisiana, Madison Parrish, shown most recently as the property of Robert Eads in the 1850 census, page 44, book 166. Listed there among her children, Pearl had a girl slave named Maud, born 1819, who became my property. On or about Sept. 18, 1843, this slave woman Maud, daughter of Pearl, bore a male child. This Negro male child is called by the name Junior. I hereby swear he is the issue of the Negro woman Maud, and hereby sell and give full chattel and title to this slave (in accordance with the Madison Parish records in the state of Louisiana and such laws as may apply) to the name listed below. Signed Quinton Tooter
>
> The line below read:
>
> John Purdy

Junior was incredulous:

"Can this be true, Mamma? You don't look black. I don't look black. Could he really sell me?"

She revealed her breast where the letter T was deeply seared.

"Its true, honey. I got enough black blood to make us both slaves."

Finally Junior understood. He was quick to comprehend most things, but today was the first time any of this ever made any sense. He now understood. You truly can love someone enough to run away for their sake. He held his mother as they sobbed quietly.

Mattie was the first to break in:

"Hey! This is a celebration. John, do you have the other paper?"

"Youbetcha."

John handed Junior his emancipation papers freeing him from any slavery bond. Maud chimed in. "I wanted to burn that other old paper, but Mr. John said we best not. Mr. John says you best keep them hid somewhere." John explained his reasoning:

"Play like that paper never existed, but if ever there is question, at least you can prove you are free. Obviously no one can ever breathe a word of this, for Missouri is a slave state with strong feelings, especially so around here. They tell me of the 4,000 negroes up in this corner of Missouri, only 70 or so are free blacks and they mostly have it pretty hard. Here, even a free black's children are taken from them when they are 12 years old and apprenticed out, and the parents have no say in the matter. Maud, your status will change completely if any of the locals find out you are Negro, so is there anyone else we need to be concerned about?"

"I don't think of no one, nobody from back when he stole me would even know me now I don't think. I was young and skinny then. You might even say pretty. Just a girl."

"Okay this goes to our graves, but I must remind you both. Tuttoor was almost illiterate and could barely sign his name over at the store. This paper does not prove he owned you, but your blood lines are there and it was well written in a fine hand within the last few years."

John retrieved the paper from Maud and held it up to their faces:

"Even if Junior does have his emancipation papers, whoever wrote this knows what we know and they, or anyone else who comes across those records, could cause you both an incredible amount of trouble."

The cabin deck of The Marybeth 8 offered better service, food and amenities than the finest of hotels, and its passengers especially featured themselves as ladies and gentlemen. The cabins surrounded the boat-length dining room with each having a door facing out to the promenade deck and another facing in toward the dining room. The big inner-hall became a bar, lounge, dance hall and casino after the evening meal. The front two cabins were referred to as the owner's suite and connected through a private sitting room which stretched the suite to the entire front width of the cabin deck. Virginia booked the owner's suite for the Mississippi River part of the trip, and although Mammy would not be allowed to mix with the other cabin class passengers, she could relax and also take her meals in their deluxe private quarters.

Virginia still had pleasant dreams where John came to her and was her very own in the most intimate of ways, and now on the second leg of their journey as they approached the City of Kansas, she begin to mentally take inventory. She considered herself just a bit lean and also a bit hippy; however, she had those very long legs for even one of her five-foot ten-inch stature. Even after six years of hard drinking she still had a very nice complexion, plus a mane of salt and pepper hair set off by brilliant dark eyes over high cheek bones, and pretty even teeth. It was truly a Spanish aristocratic look. She also considered the fact that she was enormously rich a pretty good plus.

John and Mattie met Virginia's party and after laying eyes on the real Mattie and visiting just a bit, she laughed at herself. Virginia was a brilliant tactician but she was no fool. Narry a woman she had ever met would take a man away from this woman; that is if she chose to keep him. Virginia decided to try and become Mattie's friend instead of Mattie's competitor, providing of course that she could help herself. She had very strong feelings for John and now become truly concerned about making a fool of herself. The group soon found themselves in Westport where the Harris House had made suitable accommodation. As soon as the luggage was arranged for, Virginia was anxious to go see Geneva:

"She may get word that I am here and take off, so I want to go surprise her right now."

"She is not going anywhere. There are never less than six children in her house and although a couple of Maud's girls go over every day, Geneva is still the chief caregiver. Most of the children have to get well before she can consider finding them a home, and half of them are not old enough to walk yet."

"I want to go see her now!"

"Okay."

Geneva had been telling herself that someone had bought Bos and brought him here and that she actually was in a secret place. Deep in her heart she knew better. Completely absorbed in the care of the children, she only let her mind wander back to Island View as she lay exhausted in her bed late at night. Geneva had decided to face discovery when and if it came about, and thus was able to remain calm and unemotional when she answered Virginia's knock at the door.

"May I come in, Geneva?"

"Why, yes, I guess. We have some sick children here. Why don' I come out."

Virginia pushed her way in:

"I have wiped snotty noses and cleaned up babies' butts before. I want to come in. You are a long way from home, Geneva."

"Well, I did not think I had a home anymore."

"I of all people understand that. Your children miss you."

Geneva betrayed her own nervousness by talking way too fast:

"What do they know? Are they well? Do they hate me? Do you hate me? Are they okay? Virginia, I beg your forgiveness. God forgave me. Can you find it in your heart to for give me too? I was weak and the power and wealth of Island View for my children clouded my thinking. Money does strange things. I really never wished you harm. Can you find it in your heart to understand it was never personal, and forgive me? It was never personal."

"Come now, Geneva. It was pretty dammed personal when you stood by and let Gotfield plan to have me killed! You will never be one of my favorite people, nor do I know if I can ever really forgive that of you. I do not want you back on Island View, ever! And I mean ever! But if you love your children enough to stand by and let Gotfield have me killed, then surely you love them enough to share your life with them. There is enough love on their part to get over this thing. Write them and tell them you are alive. Let them come see you. They live with me now, but you owe them that. I grew up with no mother and I am not going to stand quietly by and let you do that that to them."

Virginia was standing with her feet wide apart and moved her hands from her hips to gesture with her hands, palm up. Geneva had full well realized what she had done some time ago, and now as she faced the intended victim, she could no longer maintain her stiff upper lip. Geneva collapsed to her knees and reached out to grab Virginia's hands. As she knelt weeping uncontrollably into Virginia's upturned palms, between sobs she managed to gasp out:

"I am so sorry. I am so sorry. Oh God, I am so sorry!"

Virginia actually felt a bit of compassion for the woman as she knelt before her and wept. Still, Virginia would never forget, nor completely forgive, what Geneva had allowed to almost happen. Geneva finally regained herself, stood up, and wiped her eyes and nose with her dress sleeve like a four year old.

"Virginia, please forgive me. God forgave me and sent me here. I'm doing the work he sent me here to do. These poor children have nowhere or anybody or anything. I think surely some would die so I must stay here to help, but I will write my children and they may come if they want to see me."

Before turning to go, Virginia's face softened a bit as she handed Geneva the incriminating letter.

"You better burn this. If the sheriff ever got hold of it your children would need to come see you in prison, instead of this edge of civilization."

Virginia then smiled her wicked little smile, and turned for the door:

"By the way, Geneva. Did God get you a cabin class ticket, or does he use deck?"

After Virginia concluded her visit to Geneva's she asked to be driven by Maud's. It was still early evening although dinner was apparently just over, and from peeking through the window there seemed to be a crowd still hanging about. Directly someone started singing and soon the chorus was strong. Maud had one luxury in the whole place, an old piano which someone was simply making dance. The women were enthusiastic to say the very least; however, the piano playing was exceptional. Directly there were vespers including a couple of church hymns, then the place quieted down and people wandered away. Most would sleep well, but Maud would not shut an eye tonight, for she expected Virginia de Falco tomorrow.

Maud's place could well be a thing of the past.

Mrs. Harriet Harris, hostess extraordinaire, spread her best feast for the Purdy party that evening, and the good Colonial Harris regaled them all with war stories until the hour was late. Virginia was amazed that white man, black man, Indian and chief were all so amiable, feasting at this frontier outpost at what she truly presumed was the very edge of civilization. There were hard men dressed in buck skin and soft pink men dressed in fine suits and although most of them were carrying guns, it seemed the gracious surroundings made gentlemen of them all.

Next morning Virginia, dressed in the very plain dress she had brought for the occasion, stuffed her hair back into a sugar shell bonnet and hiked the fair distance to Maud's, arriving at an early breakfast hour. A brown-headed woman who looked as though she had led a pretty hard life answered her knock and asked her to step inside. As Virginia waited for Maud, she quickly took in the whole scene of organized pandemonium. The ones on cook duty were fixing biscuits and eggs by the dozen while table setters were stepping over the chairs to be able to reach where someone else could be fit in. There were beds head to toe in the only hallway that she could see, but they were already made for the day. A very slight young redheaded girl with freckles brought her a chair; however, before she could sit down this large plain looking woman showed up.

Virginia stuck out her hand:

"Good morning. I am Virginia de Falco."

Maud felt a bit faint and was exceedingly nervous. She had planned heavily on John Purdy to be her spokesperson, or at least be there to help. Now she would have to go one-on-one with this woman and she felt mighty inadequate.

"Wee, Oh, ah, er, good morning. I am Maud."

Maud was expecting this woman to show up about midday with at least two slaves and a coach pulled by no less than four horses. She also expected her to be wearing at least a $200 dress and was now very surprised at her appearance. She was clean and fresh all right but Maud had taken in women who looked every bit as well dressed as this. She began to calm down a bit. But just a bit. Virginia pulled off her bonnet.

"I understand you have done a lot of good and befriended a great number of ladies."

"Some of em need help so bad."

"Can I meet a few?"

"Why, why yes. Nancy could you please come over here and meet Mrs. de Falco?"

"Call me Virginia. Where are you from, Nancy?"

After six or seven interviews, Virginia began to see the genius in this Maud woman.

"Maud, I understand you met my Mr. Coopert, or Mr. Tooter or what ever his name really was."

" Oh, yes, ma'am. He was, well he was sort of different, he was."

"Sort of a jack ass, wouldn't you say?"

"Well, yes! Yes, I would."

"Was he mean to you?"

"Yes, but I was used to it. I was ah livin with his brother who I was marri ... was just like him."

"Mr. Purdy tell you what happened?"

"Yes. Probably got what he had a coming."

"It was really too good for him. He was mean to me too."

Maud was liking this woman. She wasn't scary at all.

"Miz. Virginia, I guess you own about everything you see here. I took the money and run. But now I know it was all your money."

"And I already know that too, Maud. It looks like you spent wisely."

"I got most of it left."

"How much?"

"They is $20,000 over in St. Louis and about $4,000 in a bank here. I spent the rest on this house and stuff."

"Maud, the way I see it, I would never have gotten a dime back if it hadn't been for you. Why don't you keep this over here, and I'll take what is in St. Louis. That would leave you enough to run the place and quite a bit to have ready for hard times if they come."

Maud could scarcely believe her ears; however, being the student of people that she was, she quickly pulled Virginia into the game.

"Maybe you'd let me do something else. What do you think about we call the place Maud and Virginia's?"

"Great idea, Maud! That would truly make me very proud. Say, do you suppose *we* have any eggs left?"

Maud walked back with Virginia to the Harris House for she had a request to make:

"Miss Mattie, would you come over to *Maud and Virginia's* and listen to Maureen sing?"

Mattie was quick on the up-take so she looked at the pair with a bit of surprise:

"Why of course, Maud, and, er, ah, Virginia, I would be delighted."

"You and Mary Ellen are the only ones I know who was taught about music and such, but Maureen sure sounds good to me. Mighty good."

The little redhead had saved all her size for a remarkably big voice. It was an enormous raw talent, for obviously she was untrained; nevertheless, the big sounds out of her mouth were sweet and pure. She could go three octaves, and with some age and training she could possibly go four.

"My momma, she was Irish of course and used to love to sing, now so she did. I know a whole bunch of her songs, and I made some up fer me too. Aye did. When Momma was sad she would sing to cheer herself up, that is until she got herself so sick. My daddy when he got on so bad like and owed all that money, well he got to be really mean and Momma got sad a lot, but then she always got happier when she sang."

Mary Ellen, Maud's piano playing lady, was not exactly a virtuoso; however, she was quite accomplished and had once made a nice living at the piano. Then she married a no-good piano tuner who subsequently took her for all she had, and after she recovered somewhat financially she foolishly let him get to her again. When he showed up the third time, Mary Ellen converted what little she had to cash and headed to the Kansas Territory divorce mill. She got within fifteen miles east of the City of Kansas when the boat hit a snag and sank. Mary Ellen was quite fortunate to escape unharmed, but economically devastated for she had lost everything she owned including her cash. More importantly she lost her fine melodian, an instrument similar to a small piano that was equipped with folding legs for easy transport and which was to have been her living. When Maud spotted Mary Ellen on the docks she was wrapped in a blanket someone had given her. Having sold the jewelry she had been wearing, she had absolutely nothing else except the clothes on her back and two shoes still full of dried mud. She was at the point of a nervous breakdown and at that very moment was looking for the most agreeable man she could spot, to do something disagreeable with.

Maureen now stood by the piano where Mary Ellen quickly picked up as one melody after another poured out of the little redhead's mouth. There was some nonsensical tune about Flan again, Ran again to the Pan again and she also broke into an Irish folk dance a time or two, but mostly she sang beautiful and sometimes haunting ballads.

"Miss Mattie, do you think she is as good as I do?"

Virginia, who had come along for the session, spoke up:

"Maud, I have listened to headliners on steamboats who were not half as good. She is phenomenal!"

Maud continued:

"I'm not sure what that means, but I'm sure all we need now is Miss Mattie's fancy fiddle."

"Oh, do you play, Mattie?"

"Some."

"She is just being nice. You ought to hear her. I only got to hear her one time though."

Mattie protested:

"Well Maureen is simply outstanding."

"Reverend Johnson told me somebody left a very nice fiddle and a whole bunch of music sheets out there with him."

After Maud and Virginia listened to Mattie a bit, an idea was born. They asked her to co-headline a benefit for the house, along with Mary Ellen and Maureen. The other ladies would fill in, Reverend Johnson would be their stand-up-and-talk guy, and there would be a bunch of church songs included too, so everybody would understand these were not a bunch of loose women. They would use the money to brighten up the place and to give the ladies some spending money. Soon the few outsiders who heard a bit of the practice sessions were hurrying to buy tickets and Mr. Majors made a large contribution in exchange for a hundred tickets to pass out. Other prominent people started making contributions far in excess of the advertised price for the tickets they received. If Maud could have found a bigger place to hold the show, she would have sold many more than the 600 seats they had found room for.

Maureen blossomed. She found just the right sized stick and had Bos help her hollow it out with a borrowed spoon auger, and then she cut a notch in one end. He watched as she "worried in" some holes exactly so big and so far apart. Next Maureen slid another stick into the unnotched hollow end and moved it in and out until she heard exactly the sound she was listening for as she blew through the notch. They then fastened the lower end in place:

"Mama used to make these. She called them her shepherd's flutes. She made big ones and little ones and could get just about any sound she wanted, and now let me tell ya that was sure enough a whole bunch of different sounds. Aye. We'll make anothern or two when we get the time. Ya know, a big one and a littler one."

Maureen could play an astonishing number of melodies using the clear notes of her simple flute. Maud shook her head in bewilderment:

"I ain't ever seen nobody play a stick of wood before. That child could get music out of some old gun barrel!"

The violin Reverend Johnson brought in from the mission was a fairly nice one that had been finished to a lighter shade of wood than was common. It looked as though it was especially made to match Mattie's golden mane. After a bit of practice, having given all of those free music lessons paid off, for Mattie's fingers found those old familiar runs that Mr. Julliard had demanded she practice to perfection so many years ago. She was soon playing some fine Irish fiddle as well. Maureen had an uncanny ability to harmonize with the sweet strains of the violin even though she couldn't possibly know a C sharp from an F flat. Mary Ellen was a fine coach and carefully put some of Maureen's songs on paper in order that she and Mattie have a bit of a score to practice with and it became their job to learn Maureen's melodies. Mattie worked hard to get the exact violin tones that would complement Maureen's sweet crisp voice, or her little shepherd's flute.

Mattie was an excellent violinist for who she really was now, an amateur musician who gave some free lessons. Quite actually she was a housewife who could cook a pot roast or make an apple pie with the best of them and was known to have gone out to the chicken house to wring a few necks (although that was admittedly about her least favorite thing to do). Still, with her glowing complexion and dazzling smile, she had only to hold up the violin that matched her hair, and the men folk thought Mattie was show enough all to herself. It was only after she drew the bow it became obvious she was not just in the show for her looks. Majors watched them practice with a completely bemused expression on his face:

"I have never seen anybody do that to a fiddle or use that much of one before. Look at her wrist and fingers. Why they never stop wiggling and see how those long fingers move around way up towards her chin! Mattie Purdy doesn't let an inch of that thing go to waste."

Mary Ellen could cover for about any mistake, although soon there were few to work around. She softly corded the piano for a background, and Mattie would vigorously establish the piece with beautiful clear complex sounds and then fade to a much softer background level. Little Maureen would sing one of her songs or sometimes first pick it up with a short chorus on her shepherd's flute. As this wisp of a young woman's clear Irish brogue was accompanied by violin and soft piano in the background, some of her songs were enough to bring tears to a grown man. Particularly to an Irishman. She broke it up from time to time with a fun song or a folkdance but mostly she sang love songs and ballads. Practicing was a fun thing to do as they waited for any news of Sledge.

Ike was road weary and needed rest, yet he insisted that he hand the letter to her in person.

"Are You Maud? You look like Jeannie said you looked. You must be her."

"Why yes, I am Maud. Do you know Jeannie? How is Jeannie?"

"I promised Jeannie I would hand this to you personal. My name is Ike. Ike Richmond. Jeannie is well and Jess is too. They are doing fair but I think it is about to get a lot better. I have to catch a boat now."

Maud thanked him for his trouble and he was gone without even taking time for a cup of coffee. Maud asked Patty, one of her girls, to read the letter, then snatched it and started for the Harris House in a dead run. She came bursting into the Purdys' room gasping for air:

"We found him, Mr. John. We found him! We know where he is!"

"Maud, for heaven's sake, sit down before you have a stroke!"

"Mr. John we found him! Don't you understand? We found him!"

John grabbed the letter:

Dear Maud,

The man on the poster you sent me is here in the mines, working the claim next to ours. I put a map on the back side of this. It is Sledge for absolute sure. Jess has seen the mole on his shoulder with all the hair growing out and there is no question as to the busted up face and teeth. We have said nothing because there is no law and nowhere to keep him locked up. His claim is doing very well so he will undoubtedly stay here. Somebody will have to come and get him. We will watch best we can. As to other things, Jess treats me like a queen and we are doing well enough to survive but think it is going to get better. If not I suspect we will be going back east where he has some land. We both want a family and this is no place to raise one. He will make a great father. You sure know how to pick one Maud. There are thousands of people streaming in here every week and the place is wild. There are gunfights every day, lots of drinking and as many pleasure women here as there were there down by the river. Jess will not hear to me doing washing or cleaning up after others but I do sew on clothes after someone else washes them and I earn as much as the claim does. We sleep in a wagon but have a tent to set and eat in and I get fixings to make a nice meal from time to time.

Maud you saved me from some awful things that are simply hard to imagine. I will always, always love you and never forget.

Jeannie

It was hard to say who was the most ecstatic, Brown or Blackfeather. John was mainly relieved.

Majors was by far the most trail-wise man around and the thing that made him such an excellent boss and administrator was his own trail experience. He advised John's trio to make their way up through Leavenworth and then north by west out through the Platte valley because there were any number of places where they could trade tired horses for fresh ones, for a fee of course. Some of these horses would be half broke to the saddle but these kinds made good time. Majors knew one man who had made 330 miles in 21 hours but he had killed two horses and ruined another doing it.

Majors continued:

"We just started a stage coach service from Leavenworth to Denver and figure seven or eight days in good weather, but we advertise 12. On horseback you can make it on up north of there to where the mines are in three maybe four days and not kill any horses. You're going to be one tired bunch when you get there, and you'll need horses that are used to the mountains when you get close. A lowland horse can't do you much good at 8000 feet. Take your stuff and catch a boat up to Leavenworth, then go see my friend Peterson. He is right there at the dock and will fix you up with good horses to get started and also send a letter with you and give you kind of a map of where you need to stop. He knows all those people out across there and they will take better care of you and give you better horses if they know you are friends of ours.

John continued to query Majors:

"Would it not be a lot closer to angle up the Kaw Valley to the Blue River?"

"Trust me. You have to get north anyway and you will make better time and have better places to trade horses and eat or rest if you go the way I'm telling you. It is pretty civilized most all the way along there and we have not heard of any Indian trouble up there in a long time. The pro-slave bushwhackers are showing up now and then all along the Kaw, just about everywhere up the valley around Lawrence and Topeka clear out to Manhattan. Some of them are just plain crazy and unreasonable. Besides all that, you know it hasn't rained in this country since June and it looks like 1860 will be the driest year on record. A lot of streams are dry down through here and there is still water for your animals along the trail up north. John, you will be a lot better off up in North Country because about all you will have to worry about is making good time and your rear ends. You better hope they are in good shape."

"Okay! We go your way, but damn that is sure a long trail."

After conferring with Majors, the trio returned to the Harris House and joined the others:

"Mattie, I am sorry we are going to miss the show but you know we have to get gone."

"Of course. You can hear me any time and we will have Maureen sing special just for you men sometime. Now get! That's what we are here for.

Mattie rubbed her tummy:

"John, I am so excited. It seems like we have been here forever and now that we know where Sledge is, as soon as we do the show for Maud I would really like to go home. Virginia and Mammy are heading back south too, so Bos and I could go with them as far as the Ohio River. We could book the boat tickets when we see you off."

John felt comfortable with that arrangement and nodded approvingly. Virginia added:

"The Chester A. Chester is a fine way to travel, so let's take it to St. Louis. It's due by just shortly after the show."

After John and Mattie spent some alone time together, John dressed and went down to the stable. He wished like the dickens he could ride Star, but that was definitely out of the question. John fed the big stallion a treat, took his saddle and other gear and led the trio to the boat to Leavenworth. As they eagerly mounted the first set of horses they would ride to exhaustion, no group ever headed west with more anticipation than John Purdy's trio.

Mary Ellen was an accomplished professional who had shared the stage with the famous and had put a show together with what she had gleaned from all that, and from all of them. As advertised, the entire group of ladies sang a few church songs and drew a bit of obligatory applause; the audience expressed a "what are we in for" mood more than anything else. Then Mary Ellen played a couple of her better pieces of vigorous music in a style that would someday become known as ragtime, and the audience warmed and begin expressing "this may be way better than expected." Mattie was a feast for the eye that surprised them all, for she was far more accomplished than most of her audience was accustomed to. Maud's girls convinced Mattie to wear a dress with a form fitting top and to pile her hair way high on her head, thus making the five-foot-eight and one-half inch tall Mattie a striking figure indeed. Her radiant beauty and the golden violin which accented her hair made Mattie Purdy a statuesque gentlemen's eye candy. It was her wonderfully played spirited classical music that drew the standing ovation.

Next, Mary Ellen begin with the piano and soon Mattie filled the air with the sounds of an Irish fiddle. When little Maureen joined them on stage, a sort of titter filled the air as the crowd wondered about her and her stick of wood. What on earth can this little girl possibly do?

She could do plenty!

The little redheaded green-eyed bundle of raw talent in front of an audience for her very first time became nothing short of astounding. Even those who knew her well watched in amazement as the little girl-woman transformed into a performer with a most incredible presence. Every generation has one or two. A century later the name was Sinatra, a generation after that the name was Elvis, then came Barbra. In 1860, the name inside that magical bubble was Maureen. Anyone who has had the privilege of being inside such a bubble is transported to a different place.

It's a place they never forget!

First came a peppy verse with her homemade flute, then Maureen's beautiful clear Celtic voice filled the air. Her very first song was some nonsensical tune that nobody understood and every one loved, especially when she broke into an Irish folk dance that made it look like her legs had disconnected from her body. The applause was very generous.

Then came the pling pling pling *plung*, pling pling pling *plung* of the piano and this time Mattie's wailing violin was simply haunting. Little Maureen closed her eyes so she might better concentrate, and then, as she lifted her hands to the heavens, every ounce of her gave witness to life as she had seen it.

At five Maureen had sat by her grandmother's body because her starving kin were so weak from hunger they could not carry it out to bury it. (From 1845 to 1855 one forth of all Irish fled to America. About one out of five who stayed behind starved to death.) At age six she had sailed with her desperate parents from the land they loved into this strange place where she had then watched their dream go sour. Maureen did not know all of these numbers, but the facts were that the year she arrived in America, some 52,000 starving Irish had already overwhelmed the 400,000 people then living in the City of New York. She had watched her only older sister be torn from the Irish boy she loved, which seemed to make sister go wild when she reached this new land. When Maureen was nine, her sister had disappeared off the streets of New York City. Maureen also watched as her father got ground down to less than a man by the Irish bosses who were the nastiest of men. He became their white nigger. When she was 11, Maureen was terrified as they slipped away in the middle of the night with Father, to flee his enormous debt to those same bosses. Father then tried life in the highlands, where he failed miserably.

And gave up.

And turn to drink.

And kept moving on.

And got mean.

At 14 Maureen sat by her mother's bed to sing to her.

And watched her depressed mother finally give up.

And get the "sick-lonesome."

And die.

At 15 her drunken father traded her to a devilish old preacher man for some coins....and a barrel of whiskey.

She sang it all.

She sang of leaving the beautiful green hillsides for a place across the sea.

She sang of sailing into the harbor of hope.

She sang of a love that must let go, so the one you loved could have a better life.

She sang of looking at a star that she knew a love 3000 miles away could see, while praying to see that love once again.

She sang of being lonesome.

She sang of a dream gone sour.

She sang of the charity of others.

She sang of goodness.

She sang of continuing hope.

As Mary Ellen and Mattie played softly in the background little girl-woman Maureen stood on the stage with her eyes closed once more, She was slightly weaving back and forth playing her stick for a bit, as the prelude to her third love song.

Then the words came out long and sweet and clear and pure and haunting:

Turn your face to the wind
And look out to the sea.

N'er look back to the place
Where you had to leave me.

A new life awaits
The harbor of hope is o'er there.

At least you'll be safe
Is my heart's only prayer

(Then just a short chorus from the flute.)

Blow a kiss to the wind
T'will find its way home

Love must let go ———

It started over in the corner as murmuring, then rolled across in what one might call a groundswell. Men rose to their feet and the commotion began slowly at first. But then? Then the place came unglued. Bedlam erupted as they hollered and screamed and clapped and yelled and stomped on the risers or beat their palms on the backs of the chairs in front of them. This little green eyed pile of freckles with red hair and a marvelously beautiful Celtic voice was singing their song.

Their dreams.

Their story.

Their life.

Their heartbreaks.

Their hope.

Finally big Tam O'Shanasee hopped up on the stage and quieted the crowd:

"Let the little lady sing, I say."

And so she did.

Until she arrived at Maud's, Maureen had seen very little of people being kind to each other, but this crowd of people were being so kind that she could not help but to love each one of them. Which of course made each one of them love her right back. She stood basking in that love and opened up like a rosebud on a fine summer morning.

600 people stood spellbound.

And she held them in the palm of her hand.

The show of respect had commenced over in the Irish corner again; nevertheless, the entire crowd remained on its feet, thundering applause after each song, then respectfully hushing so she might sing again. The toughest man there had goosebumps, while many of the women struggled to hold back tears. Every one of those 600 felt strongly that at this very moment Maureen was singing just to them and to them alone.

It was .... a Happening.

That night as the John Purdy trio galloped past wagons and herds of cattle that had been in the City of Kansas weeks and weeks ago, the ladies at Maud and Virginia's sat about chattering like magpies. They were basking in Maureen's unbelievable success and wondering how anyone could possibly have their 'tour de force' on their very first performance.

Mattie hugged her and then they sat down beside each other on a sofa, Mattie's hand on Maureen's arm:

"You sang like an angel."

"Well what you did was real special, now it was, cause you sure enough can play that fiddle, Miz. Mattie. But that was a really nice thing of you to say. An angel, eh? Do you really sure enough believe in angels?"

"Why, yes I do. When my mother knew she was not going to be there when I grew up, she promised me she was going to go be an angel. The bible says a lot about angels."

"Aye?"

"Yes. My mother and father had me memorize a great many verses so I would know all about angels. For example Hebrews 13 says:

'Some people have entertained angels and not even known it.'

"That fits Maud's place pretty good doesn't it, Maureen?"

"Aye. Boy it'd sure be different having you pa read the bible with you, now itwood."

Maureen tried unsuccessfully to stifle a big yawn as she asked:

"What other ones do you know? Eh?"

"Well, Mark 1:13 says when Jesus was in the wilderness being tempted by the Satan that the angels waited on him. My mother was really hoping she would get to do that sort of thing. The verse I really like the best is Psalms 92:11:

"For he will command his angels concerning you, to guard you in all your ways."

" Well I'll be jiggered e jigged! It really says that, eh?"

"Yes. It really says that. It's a comfort to know that the angels will be looking out for my John tonight."

"Aye, but where were the angels when you lost your mama and your little boy?"

"Sometimes it is all part of a bigger plan, Maureen, so sometimes we just have to trust something bigger than we are."

"I'd reckon that's right, cause right lately I sure have come to believe in angels too, Miss Mattie."

"Why have you come to believe in angels, Maureen?"

It had been a very, very big day and Maureen tried but failed to stifle another even bigger yawn:

"Well now ever body says you're just an angel and I reckon you must be the way you showed up right on time to fetch me away from the docks. And there was a man who gave me three dollars just cause he wanted me to be safe and right then was when me and Norma needed something to eat pretty bad. Aye. I hear a whole lot of people even call all those women that work some down by the dock 'fallen angels.' Don't you think Maud's got to be an angel the way she looks out for all us every single day? And now you take that Geneva woman that was there tonight. I know she won't ever be one of Miz. Virginia's favorite people but some of them little ones would be in real trouble without her. I go over there to help some and the way I see it, why that is all angel work."

Yawn:

"And you take Miz. Virginia. Lordy she could have closed this whole place down and probably even sent Maud to jail but she didn't cause she's got an angel's heart. Eh? And Mary Ellen, now she found me these clothes. They have been used for sure but they are the best I ever had. And you know what? She is always saving me the good part of the chicken or best piece of pie. That's pretty much guardian angel work now ain't it. Aye? She even got me a bed next to the window so I get the evening breeze. She knows I like that cause it makes me think of Momma, caus Momma she liked the evening breeze and all. Anyway it's pretty hard not to believe in angels when you're setting in a whole flock of em like I am. You are all in cahoots ain't ya? Norma had the hardest job of all you, now didn't she?"

"Why do you say that?"

"Well that guy showed up right on time with them three dollars and you came got me just when them cowboys was a taken me up on the deal and Maud was already out here just waiting. But now Norma, she showed up when I was a running from that old preacher man and she did some pretty tough stuff to keep me what I am. Did you ever think about what I am?"

Mattie was thoughtfully choosing words for her response; however, she need not bother. The little redhead's eyelids were finally just tooooo heavy. She was sitting sound asleep.

Mattie and Mary Ellen stood so they could stretch her out on the sofa, and then Mary Ellen went looking for a blanket.

Maureen roused, yawned again, and was drifting off once more:

"I am a pretty odd duck, Miss Mattie. In fact, I am sure enough a real odd duck. I took a spell at being a whore after I was married and got my divorce. After all that I'm still a virgin. You all did good. Real good in fact, even for bunch of angels. My momma said you never know what the wind will blow through yor window. And it seems like my window is pretty full, eh? And just look at the lot of you all. Maud has gray hair Norma was black headed. Miz. Virginia has both. Yore a blond. Mr. John is white man, Bos is black man and Blackfeather is a red man, and you're all taking care of a red head with a bunch of freckles. Seems like the wind through my window has many colors.

Mary Ellen came back with the blanket and noticed the peculiar smile on Mattie's face and whispered to her over the sleeping girl-woman:

"You look like the cat that found the cream. What are you looking at?"

Mattie whispered back:

"It's a real odd duck and I doubt there will ever be another. It's called a redheaded, golden throated withy girl-woman. It came into our lives on a wind of many colors"

Goat Woman was an ageless creature but probably about 35. Her thin looks could fool anyone, for her muscles were like steel and she made less noise when darting about through the forest than a shadow falling on soft moss. Her eyes were sharper than an eagle's; therefore, along with this uncommon strength, her accuracy with both a knife and bow were the thing legends are made of. Goat Woman was not really a hermit, for on occasion she would visit the Purdy's store in Three Creeks to trade her goods for such things as coffee or a new pot to cook in. She often brought well-preserved soft-spun goat wool, cured goat skins, goat cheese, or young goats that were already spoken for. Most of all, men coveted Goat Woman's magnificently carved walking sticks made of ironwood or persimmon. She was the one who had painstakingly carved the white cedar hands and fastened them to the top of Harvey's small casket, for she also knew the sting of losing loved ones.

The name Goat Woman came from her Indian husband, her second Indian husband at that. As a young girl she was part of the Merrifield clan, three married brothers all living together with their respective women and claiming to be cousins of the Daniel Boones. They lived accordingly. Legend has it that the brilliant Daniel Boone came home after having been gone a year and his wife was suckling a brand new baby so he quite naturally inquired as to "whose baby is this?" When advised it was his brother's he smiled and thundered. "Good! Good! There can never be enough Boones." The Merrifield brothers had much the same view of things and took turns at being first to pick whichever wife struck their fancy to sleep with on any given night. They in turn produced a bewildering array of children, including Goat Woman. She was the first girl.

At the age of 12 she became scared of her father, which ever one he was, and her uncles as they began to look at her and talk among themselves of her as a bed partner. Subsequently she took off and found the Chickasaw who took her in and in due time arranged for a suitable husband who protected and cared for her. She gladly cooked for him, kept his lodge, chewed the leather to make his clothes soft and looked forward to their night times together. He provided well for her. She bore first a son and then a daughter and when they were four and six the fever killed both children plus her husband. She then became the charge of her husband's brother whom she did not care for at all. When asked how she treated him at night he sarcastically replied:

"I would rather sleep with one of the goats she keeps."

Thereafter she was known as Goat Woman.

A few months after her first husband died she begged her leave which his brother gladly granted. Her leaving pleased him so that he allowed her a dozen goats, a dog, and a nearly lame mare. She moved with her menagerie to the Kentucky riverside bluffs, where she became self sufficient and lived in the mouth of a small cave covered by animal skins. It was cool in summer, warm in winter and as peaceful as any place on earth. Dog was good company and she shared fresh spring water with her goats and mare which were sheltered in their own small cave. The critters supplied her with most of all she wanted or required. Along with nature's bounty, she had excellent cured goat skins, fine spun goat wool, goat milk, goat butter, goat cooked in various ways and better company than most. Over time the mare delivered two colts that were now geldings in their prime and followed her around like puppy dogs.

Purdy Mercantile regularly traded with many of their customers, and Goat Woman was one of a large group who used the store for their bank. Locals commonly came in to sign over credit which they held at the store to someone else in payment for an independent transaction. Although Goat Woman was one who always kept a nice balance in her account, Purdy wished she had more to barter, for her goods were outstanding.

Goat Woman kept her mouth fresh and her teeth bright by scrubbing them with a fuzzy stick and regularly used garlic, ginger, and goldenseal, plus any number of bark or root and berry teas for medicine. She was ache free and rarely had so much as a sniffle. On this fine day Goat Woman was relaxing, watching her flock, and enjoying the flowers as the geldings followed her about competing for her to scratch their noses. Dog spent most days trotting circles around the flock but became distracted and started barking excitedly at the riverbank. She was gathering some berries and looking for what other wild fruit nature might be providing when she paused to go the riverbank to see what Dog found so exciting. The man was caught on bank-side tree roots, bobbing in the water.

When Goat Woman pulled Quinton Tooter from the river, he was more dead than alive.

The river always tumbled swiftly through the boulder-lined narrows below the bluff tops where brother had pushed him from. He had bounced off the bluff face on his way down, then the roaring river had pushed him off of the rock he landed on and dragged him down stream, until he finally hit the snag. It held on to him more than he held on to it. Providence alone dictated that his head was held above the water.

Goat Woman waded in and dragged his limp shattered body ashore, then after determining he was still alive, she fashioned a pole skid, and one of the geldings drug him to her cave. Once there she began to splint the broken bones, tend his fresh wounds, and marvel at the older ones. Someone in her old tribe had done a number on this man and she knew immediately that he was greatly despised for they did not often notch ears and nostrils. One look at his genitals confirmed that he had done a heinous thing in their eyes. Her adopted tribesmen were normally gentle souls and made their captives dance and sing to entertain them, as opposed to running them through a vicious gauntlet like the more violent tribes did. Here, however, they wanted the Great Spirit to notice this man as contemptible right off, and also to make certain there were no more of his seed to carry on his traditions.

The Chickasaw would have showed some respect and scalped even a cowardly warrior or cut out his heart if he were brave. If they had wanted him dead, they certainly would never have thrown him in to the river with even the smallest chance to survive; therefore, it had to be the white men who had thrown him in. She easily recognized the other handiwork, so evidently this man was hated by both the white man and the red. Goat Woman was curious. It would be weeks before he could sit up on his own, and even more weeks until he could tell his story.

Goat Woman also knew that among other things the sound of another human was good medicine, so she talked for both of them. Continuously:

"You must be an evil person in the eyes of others. What could you have done that was so evil? Did your mother teach you evil, or was it your father? Few are ever born evil or become evil by watching their brothers or strangers in their clan. It must have been your mother or father who taught you evil ways. Few mothers are evil. What did he do? Your father must have been an evil man. He taught you evil ways, now look at you. You are hard to look at, crushed and scared. You lay crooked and your mouth will never taste the good food, nor will you ever have man's great pleasure of woman again. Were you too weak to pass your father's evil ways? I had to. My people were not noble so I had to find others who were. When I no longer could live among my adopted people in pride and in dignity, I chose to live nobly by myself. Still, my adopted people respect me and there will always be many there who love me. Is there any one who cares about you? Who loves you? You are the age many men die. What is your legacy? Should I find anyone for you? I am rich for I have my pride and no enemies and I have the Great Spirit's gifts of sky and water and his bounty. I am at peace because I like who I am. I like me, but even you cannot like you. You must be in torment because you are hated so. Why are you hated? You must cry over yourself and the thing you are. You could have been noble but you were evil. Now look at what you have become. Even Dog is suspicious and the goats stay away, for they know. You have many strong enemies and it seems no one looks for you. Do you have anyone or anything? Does anyone search for you? Does anyone care? Such is the pay for evil."

For some time Quiton Tooter was able to say nothing, but day after day as she continued these monologues, his eyes never left her face. Finally as she yet again forced the bitter concoction of boiled roots down him, he managed to gasp out:

" Whoo Youut?"

In a few more days it dawned on Goat Woman that the man she was caring for had been one of those caught horsewhipping her friend, Purdy. She knew him as Mr. Tuttoor and had always felt sorry for his woman and their son. Her personal code dictated that it should be a manner of tremendous personal pride to save another human's life; however, Goat Woman could not help but wonder at what she had done.

And what she must do.

Goat Woman sat in Mr. Morris' office at Purdy Mercantile and as always she was pleased with the amount he gave her for the walking sticks. These were some of her very best and she had held them in reserve as they were like money in the bank. Today she needed cash. Plus a lot more things. Morris confirmed for her the balance she held at the store, priced the bundle of fine walking sticks then watched in surprise as she wondered about, picking out two nice sets of men's clothing. She also selected a new Smith and Wesson six shot revolver and some ammunition from the case. It was none of his affair and he made no comment as he watched on, while admiringly running his hand over her exquisite creations.

They were always the same. The lowest carving on the walking stick showed the spirit entering at a baby's birth, then on up there was an adult guiding a youth, then there was an almost erotic scene, then another baby, then a more mature youth holding the baby and guiding an older adult who was stooped. Finally an older adult with their spirit escaping toward the Great Spirit which was perched on the handle at the very top of the stick with the young adults and their child watching on. The complete cycle of life on a walking stick. Mattie's father wanted all of Goat Woman's works he could get his hands on, for he used them as gifts for important business associates all over the world. These were some of Goat Woman's finest, so Morris paid her the equivalent of a month's pay for each of them, and they were worth every dime.

Goat Woman noticed Mr. Morris admiring her work.

"Do you like them?"

"They are absolutely magnificent!"

"I will make one just for you."

Morris sort of wistfully shook his head:

"I am afraid they are a bit much for me, Goat Woman. This is a very good position, but I am just a working man. Those belong in the hands of fine gentlemen"

"You are my friend. You should have one."

She gathered her purchases, took her balance in cash and left.

Morris could never remember her wanting money before and wondered what on earth she would do with it. Or the men's clothes. The Smith and Wesson was the most baffling of all.

Going down river, the boat made about 15 miles an hour plus current speed, and the captain was fearless. Quinton Tooter was amazed at how quickly he found himself in Madison Parish, Louisiana, at the law offices of Vogel and Vogel.

"Yes, Mr. Tooter, we specialize in these kinds of things. I can find those records for you in just a little bit."

"I do noth read wellth but I want to slee them."

"The slave ship Hare made just four trips in here. Lisa was an uncommon name. I will have that for you tomorrow."

"I wanth to slee the bootk."

"Okay. Anybody can look. They are public records. The office is already closed today, but be here at nine in the morning and we will walk across the street.

"I probably neetd you to flind a page in the clensus bootk too"

"Those kinds of records are all in the same place."

"You flind them for me. I canth copy what I slee, but I don't know whereth to lookth."

"Okay, Mr. Tooter, we can mark them. I will show you the pages and exact lines."

"Are thereth other copies of that stluff aroundth?"

"Maybe. I don't really know, but these are the only ones that really count. These are official."

"How much?"

"Mr. Tooter, it looks like you have had some bad luck. I can do this in twenty minutes and I won't need to charge you this time. Who knows? Maybe someday you will need real legal work done."

The next morning Vogel found the records in less than ten minutes and laid them on the visitors desk. Quinton Tooter thanked him profusely, shuffled his pen and paper, and set about the task at hand.

The smaller steamboats would stop anywhere along the river that a customer might wish, sometimes making as many as 50 stops between such towns as Natchez and New Orleans. Later that same morning Quinton Tooter caught one that would drop him off at Island View Plantation. Daniel, who had trotted down to the landing to see who their guest might be, at first thought he was seeing a ghost when he stepped off of the boat. Daniel had seen Coopert's body, so he tried hard not to stare. Miz. Virginia had told them all their old overseer's real name was Cooper Tooter and they no longer need be afraid of him. Still, looking at this man who looked just like him was down right creepy.

"Yo shore looks so much like a man we usta had here."

"Is heth no longer hereth?"

"No sir. He well, he got killed by some hogs, sir."

"You slure?"

"Oh, yes, sir. He be dead. You sure looks like he did before he die though. An awful much like he did."

"You absolutely slure heth dead?"

"Yes sir. I see him dead."

"His flace clut up?"

"Yes, sir. He look just about like you, sir. Awfully much just like you, sir. He be buried up there on the hill by the barn kind of."

"You slee it"

"Yes, sir, I seed it. Mr. Coppert he done change his name to Mr. Tooter and he come driving old Mollie and Bigun back here and he done beg Miz. Virginia to stay and she let him for a while. Then this Mr. Purdy he come on his big white Star horse and dey fight and Mr. Purdy he knock Mr. Coopert in amongst de old sows and dey pigs and they old sows get him fore he could get away. He be dead enough all right. I saw him. Yo could ask Miz. Virginia but she be gone for a while more right now."

The boat captain put the stage back down and Quinton Tooter went back aboard the boat.

Damn. He watched the river flow by and absent-mindedly patted the papers and the Smith and Wesson in his coat. Brother was one score he had wanted to settle for himself, but it sounded as though that score had been settled for him. Now at least he could devote his time to finding Mr. John Purdy.

Virginia and Mammy were both away and Mr. Farout and his Missus were gone right now too. There was no one else around important enough to tell, so Daniel went back to his assigned tasks.

Things would never be better for Sledge. His good luck started just out of Salina where he had requisitioned the strong fast horse that had him to the mines in short order, and where he then traded the horse for a claim a fellow was giving up on. The miner gave up two days too soon. Lighting struck. Sledge's quick and immense riches were the thing of legends, and the very thing that brought men by the thousands from wherever they might be to try their luck in the Gulch. The first four days he became a thousandaire, the first week a ten thousandaire and after that he simply lost track, for it seemed every chunk he picked up would not pass his #10 screen. While others had their little pokes of dust, Sledge had pockets bulging full of nuggets. With those gold nuggets came a life that he never imagined in his wildest dreams.

Even though he had his remaining teeth scaled and polished, as a wealthy man Sledge was even more difficult to like than before. He therefore simply hired some friends whom he called claim guards. His "claim guards" bowed and scraped, laughed at his stories and hung on his every word. In addition to being able to hire friends, another great benefit of his wealth was that the highest-priced, most desirable camp women soon came looking for him by name.

Where $1 a day was considered fair wage on the trail, here $2 or more was the norm and where woman cost $2 or $3 elsewhere, here the average ones were $5 to $10 or a "fair" sized pinch of gold dust. 3,000 years ago in Pompeii, a pretty woman cost three copper coins, which was about the same price as a glass of wine. Centuries later when Rome boasted a population of 50,000, at least 7,000 of them were women turning tricks. Call them what you will. Hustlers, nymphs, chippies, filles de joie, scarlet ladies, bawds, birds, fillies, prostitutes or whores, they always show up where there are lone men with money. In Gregory's Gulch any one of these women could spot a man with gold in his pocket quicker than the miner on the claim next door could.

Often these women traveled the camps with their bed in an enclosed wagon, for no matter how tough and crass a man might seem to be, there are times when even that type wants a little privacy. Some of the legendary whores got hundreds of dollars for an hour and at least one in Colorado mining history, Julia Bulette, charged $1,000 for an overnight stay. Sledge immediately started buying one of the prettier ones by the week for himself, plus a more common one for his guards to share. The three of them always looked eagerly to the changes Monday might bring.

He had a house built, hastily thrown together and not much by normal standards, but a 720 square foot mansion by camp comparison. It had four rooms, two of them measured twelve by twenty-two feet, one of which was complete with a mirror on the ceiling to serve as his bedroom, and the other an eating, sitting, cooking room. The other two eight-by-twelve foot rooms were for his guards and looked out over the claim so they might be most comfortable when they were guarding. The gold on Sledge's claim concentrated into a seam, so he hired men to commence digging one of the 17,000 mine shafts that would ultimately be dug in the Gulch. His miners soon discovered that the incredible seam turned abruptly and went straight into Jess's claim. Sledge's luck had changed and there was no question as to who had the rich vein now, but certainly he was not about to let a little thing like the law slow him down.

In a few weeks Sledge had accumulated enough wealth for him and ten others to live forever in fine fashion, but still he wanted more. He felt he deserved more. He would take more. First off, he offered to buy his neighbor's claim; however, it was fair to speculate there was an immense fortune to be dug out, so naturally Jess and Jeannie politely declined his best offer. Sledge eventually enticed the couple into his house, and shortly thereafter conversation on the claim matter turned in to a heated argument. Sledge's claim guards were now standing their guard at the door.

Sledge sipped his whiskey:

"You best take my offer. $10,000 is a lot of money. We may never get another ounce out of there. My offer is a sure thing and that would get you all a real nice start back whereever home is gonna be, and whereever it is you best get started for right away."

Jess shook his head no:

"You have dug that much out in less than a week. No deal."

Jess set his untouched whiskey aside and started to get up; however, Sledge blocked his way. Jess repeated:

"Absolutely no deal."

"I will go $15,000. That is my best offer."

"No thank you."

"How much you think you deserve, big shot?"

"I deserve to dig my claim."

"Might not be healthy for you or her here in the mines. She's a fine looking woman to be out among all these wild acting men."

"You threatening her?"

"Things happen to a man out here. Women too. Mining is dangerous work."

"That why you have somebody else do all the hard stuff?"

"I am offering you a first class price. You better take it."

"I'm not for sale."

Sledge motioned his friends closer in.

"Mr. Jess here and his fair bride don't want to sell."

Jess started to get out of his chair once more; however, as he was coming up out of the chair one of the goons faked a stumble and fell, with his shoulder striking Jess solidity on the head. Jess hit the floor hard.

"Oh. Excuse me."

Jess got up rubbing his head, and then sat back down beside Jeannie.

Sledge spoke to the larger of his two guards:

"He needs to see things a little different, but it might be hard with his eyes swelled shut."

With that, the second goon whirled and stuck an elbow out which caught Jess hard in the face.

" Oops."

Jeannie did what any miner's wife would have done. She pulled the pistol out from under her apron and aimed it straight for where Sledge's nose should have been. In her fear and excitement Jeannie either forgot herself, or used an unfortunate tactic to protect her Jess.

"For a man with a price on his head you sure are calling a lot of attention to yourself, you arrogant slob! When I show that poster around there will be hundreds of men after you to sell your hide! You are right, $10,000 will buy a lot, Mr. Sledge. It will buy them holding you for that sheriff in Kentucky to come drag you out of these mines like the snake that you are!"

Sledge was thunderstruck! He thought the world had passed him by, but now that rich son of a bitch, Purdy, had chased him all the way to the mines. His goons looked puzzled. Jeannie was headed to the door and Jess was right beside her as Sledge and friends stood frozen, thoroughly convinced she would not hesitate to blow Sledge a new nose hole. The immediate area was always crowded with men anyway, and several quickly gathered around the couple as soon as they heard the hullabaloo. No one who knew Jeannie doubted a word she had to say:

"Let me go get the poster. I will show the rest of you."

There were far too many men gathered around for Sledge to make a break for it, so he ordered his friends to disperse the crowd as they were armed and many of the others were not. Despite the guards waving their pistols around the crowd simply would not give away, particularly after Jeannie came running back with the poster.

Jess picked out two of the miners he knew pretty well.

"Leonard, you and George. We will share the $10,000 with you two if you help me keep this guy until the law gets here."

Both agreed:

"Done."

In the matter of an afternoon, Sledge's little palace of debauchery became his jail as his two hired friends wisely chose not to take on the whole camp, and quietly faded away. Jeanne was absolutely right. There were indeed hundreds of men around who would gladly change out the rich Mr. Sledge for the price on his head.

Up north of the Gulch, John, Brown and Blackfeather swapped horses again, this time for mounts that were acclimated to the altitude. At dawn the fourth day, the bone-tired and trail-weary trio was but a few hours north of one Mr. Sledge.

In that same morning's dawn, Leonard was found with his head caved in. For a good part of the previous night Sledge had lain still as a mouse in the back of Pricilla's wagon as she casually moved through the moonlit canyon. She was still astonished at the size of the gold poke her customer had given her to simply act like what she was.

Just another whore with her bed with her.

Beautiful Pricilla had viewed a week with Sledge as vacation with pay and gladly agreed to keep him company. Instead of having engagement after engagement in her red-wheeled wagon, for a whole week she would service onlyone man who was mostly blow anyway. A week in an honest-to-goodness house was a welcome change and she could keep herself dainty and make it worth his $1,000, even if he were a wanted man with a huge price on his head. Pricilla was smart, stayed off drugs and drank only enough for the client to think she was a wild party girl, which was what she actually was. Most generally Pricilla had her big man Tom close at hand to watch out for rough stuff and to take care of her team. Tom had insisted he should stick close even on this unusual engagement, but she instead had sent him away to relax while she looked forward to her easy week. Sledge was a hot property in the camps, with miners by the hundreds anxious to claim him and the accompanying reward, so when the chance came he paid her extremely well to secret him to the North Canyon Tavern to meet his friends.

Pricilla was one of the more flamboyant ladies of the camps and always wore red shoes, some part of her dress would be red, her jewelry was red, and the wheels on her wagon were bright red to match the large bright red letter P on its white canvas top.

Regrettably, this morning that red matched the bright red blood from her slashed throat, as she lay staring the glassy eyed stare of the dead. Even though they were fairly quiet about it, Sledge had heard Pricilla "do" his two hired friends out front of the wagon. Afterwards she had absolutely refused to turn over the heavy gold poke, and things turned ugly. Remarkably, his friends' shots missed him as he rolled out the open back side of the wagon to plunge headlong into the darkness. Once again his experience in stalking and hiding from large game paid off, for his claim guards failed to find him out in the brushy terrain.

The canyon road was well traveled so at early dawn his pursuers felt compelled to ride on, taking the fortune in gold Sledge had brought along to support them all in style. Fortunately for Sledge, Pricilla had agreed that he had at least one more night coming, and he had heard the entire thing as he lay, mostly sober, so that he might enjoy her when she undressed him. Daybreak now found him alone with the wagon and team.

And her beautiful but untidy corpse.

He still had his boots on.

John, Brown, and Blackfeather finished their early breakfast at the North Canyon Tavern and hustled outside. Brown had shown them the best way to tie themselves into the saddle and one or the other of them had been trying to stay awake at all times. Each had ridden several mounts to exhaustion, having changed horses at Hollenberg Station, Levi Hansel's farm, Ft. Kearney, Mchette's Ranch, Gothenberg Ranch, Scott's Bluff and Old Julesburg. Now, mounted on high altitude acclimated horses they were headed up the road to the mines, having made a hurried stop at the popular tavern. Even after their breakfast break they were still somewhat bushed for had anyone been keeping records for the fastest times on this end of the trail, John Purdy and friends would certainly have been some kind of entry in the book.

"Hey John, look at that wagon over there. You ought to buy some like that for the store."

"That would be classy as the dickens. White horses to match the white top too. I will remember that. Bright red wheels and a red P for Purdy. Wonder what that P really stands for?"

"I hear some camp women do stuff like that. Bet she is headed up canyon to do some business."

"Well I am too tired to even want to look at one. Let's go."

With that, the trio remounted and thundered on to The Gulch.

Later that same day John sat with the small group in Sledge's house, looking completely dejected. Jeannie sat wringing her hands with tears running down her face:

"I am so sorry Mr. Purdy. So very, very, sorry. It just came out. We had been so careful, but when they started on Jess I thought they were going to kill him, or maybe even both of us. I must have panicked and for sure I said the wrong thing. Please believe me, I really thought they were going to kill him and we needed help and it just came out. I am so ashamed. So very ashamed. It hurts so bad, for my slip cost us one of our dear friends. They bashed in Leonard's head and I caused that. Besides, I would climb these mountains on my bare hands and knees for Maud if she wanted me to, and I let her down."

Jess, who had set all this time with a protective arm around his Jeannie, now joined in:

"We have the most promising claim in the area, and we will add to the reward, Mr. Purdy, and do anything else you think might help."

"Do you have any ideas?"

"No. But the whore he had hired for the week is gone too."

"He hired them by the week?"

"Yes. This one was a dandy. The man she had as a bodyguard and to keep her team is frantic. She paid him quite well and gave him personal service if you know what I mean, but I think he really likes her."

"She had a team?"

"Yes beautiful white horses and a fancy red-wheeled wagon. Her name was Pricilla."

Brown jumped up and urged them:

"Come on! We can't be two days behind!"

Blackfeather was already out the door.

The owner of the North Canyon Tavern remembered him quite well:

"Poor fella, had this big blood covered petticoat bandaging his head, couldn't see much of his face at all. He was limping and walked all leaned over to one side. He had gold and bought food like he was going to be on the trail a while and then paid me enough for my old bench rifle for me to buy a new one. Said he was delivering that fancy wagon somewhere but he would not let me look at it very much because he said the old owner was still sleeping inside."

The trio traded horses again at Old Julesburg at the Laughlin ranch where the Colorado mountain trail joined back up with the Oregon Trail. Laughlin had watched the wagon go by and was certain it then headed east for he had sat and watched it disappear into the morning sun. The trio galloped into Corrigan's trading post (where Sledge had seen another poster) and as they saddled their fresh mounts the owner reported the wagon was about a day ahead. The second day they spotted the wagon and rode out around it to set up their ambush. From their hiding spot they watched the tired white team still stepping out magnificently. As the wagon headed directly towards them John Purdy's heart was pounding when he first peered through their telescope:

"That's not him."

The disappointment dripped from John's voice.

"You sure?"

"Yes. I can see his face."

"Could be in the back."

"We're going to find out for damn sure."

The old timer driving the wagon was scared witless when they first descended on him, so he was most cooperative:

"This your wagon? That fella steal this wagon from you'ens? I traded this fella two mules and a bunch of stuff for some gold and this here wagon. It was a honest trade. Must have been crazy for mules though. Kind of crazy anyway I guess from the knots on his head. Had this here bandage with some blood on it covering most of his face. Had hisself a crutch made from a tree limb too but he did'nt seem to need it much. Walked all leaned to one side and favoring a knee though, and I would have thought the wagon would suit him better but he said the mules looked rested and would get him back and forth across the river better and he didn't like ferryboats. I had a good pack made up and them was big mules and could move right on out, and they were in good shape too cause I was just taking it easy. A fella could get by a long time by hisself with just what was on them mules. I got to buy more chuck when I get to Crawford's Lick, and I need some grain for these horses too. Say you got any extra grub? I'm starving cause he took all I had."

"Afraid not much, old timer, we are traveling pretty light. Here is a little jerky."

"Thanks! This here shore is a fancy wagon ain't it though, and with my name being Powell I just had to have it with that P on top. Even got a bed back there. Look it all over good cause you ain't apt to see such as this again. Got some fancy gowns and underwear and there must be a gallon of perfume under that bed. Can you figure? I am a going back to Kentucky to live with my kin and got plenty of time and thing is that fella said that was where he was a heading too, but he was in a big hurry. I think he might have taken a gun to me if I hadn't traded him though, cause he was a wanting to move on out pretty bad. Hey, why don't you men ride along with me? I got to rest these horses up cause they are plum tuckered out and yours look powerful tired too. Sure been meeting lots of wagons and cow herds headed west but ain't many folk a going back this way. I sure like having someone to talk to and you sound sort of Kentucky. You going there too? Don't get to talk to folk mu ... ."

The old timer was talking to himself.

The trail really became a web of trails back closer to Missouri; however, there were three well-traveled ways. The trio got fresh mounts and split up at the Blue River crossing, (Palmetto City, present day Marysville) agreeing on a message center to leave word for each other in the City of Kansas. Brown raced down through Topeka and along the Kaw, Blackfeather headed for Leavenworth, and John galloped towards St. Joseph. They inquired at every point of civilization and John begin pressing his mount extra hard for he had nearly closed the gap as he was approaching the St. Joseph docks.

A steamboat had just cast off shortly before John thundered up, and yes the agent remembered a man with a huge head-bandage carrying a big rifle who bought a cabin class ticket. He also took two big mules aboard.

For weeks John Purdy had listened intently to the best advice he could find, and then planned and schemed accordingly. And planned and schemed. And planned.

In intricate detail.

A lot of Holsher's family had been military people, and he ran his brewery business like it was an army. The older German had convinced John that your soldiers will do exactly what you want done, if they simply know what. Holsher had shared freely the biggest lesson his white hair had earned:

"Always remember this, John. It is not as important for the troops to understand, as it is for the troops not to misunderstand."

Colonel Albin had taught him that any given minute the most important thing for a soldier was a bullet for his gun, and that any given week the most important thing was his devotion to the mission. "And to never forget that any given day, the most important issue is something for your soldier's belly."

Blackfeather had taught him how the Indians used the land to channel their enemy into position.

And then there was Brown. His friend Brown just seemed to have an uncanny ability to think like a man on the run.

In trying to think of every probability John had taken all their advice into account and formed plan after plan, and then given the plan for each happenstance a code name. He immediately sent a wire to his father with the code "Kentucky Girl" to guide his father in precise and appropriate action. This was the code to tell Purdy Sr. that Sledge was headed that way too, for everyone had already been advised that Mattie was starting home and to be watching for her. "Kentucky Girl" alerted all concerned to immediately be prepared for another encounter with Sledge and for chief to re-establish guard camp. Purdy Sr. would move briskly to get the word to everyone in Three Creeks as well as the Chief, for every individual had their very specific "Kentucky Girl" assignments.

Next, John prepared a Kentucky Girl note to be delivered to Colonel Albin at Ft. Leavenworth, for he had shown considerable interest and wanted to be kept fully informed. Albin was now making this a personal concern.

That very day John Purdy learned from gut-wrenching experience what good field commanders have known since the first army charged into battle. When one has a personal stake in the matter, the most precise planning and elaborate preparation, will never trump fear. So now, having made the most exacting plans, John Purdy did the only thing else there was left to do. As the knots in his innards gnawed like hungry rats, he waited impatiently for the second boat of the day to cast off for the City of Kansas.

And prayed fervently that Bos be equal to the task before him.

The Crabtrees had suffered the pain of four children born, with none having lived past the age of two, and now, except for their slaves, the prosperous old Kentucky couple faced their final curtains pretty much alone. Arthur and Ben, the only two prime slaves of the six belonging to the Crabtrees, were well formed sturdy Negro men in their early to mid twenties. Mr. Crabtree now made the assumption that since women were no longer important to him they were not important to others either; so therefore, he had never arranged for these two to have mates. Recently; however, he had made arrangements to do what he considered even better than that, for upon his death they were to go free! This gesture was repayment for an incident where Arthur and Ben stepped forward to place him between themselves and where they took a pretty good threshing, which in turn saved Crabtree from being roughed up by a very angry crowd of Lincoln supporters at a political affair.

The other four older slaves were to stay and tend to Mrs. Crabtree, and at her death they would become property of some distant kin. After Crabtree's death, Mrs. Crabtree immediately called Arthur and Ben to her bedside and bestowed freedom on these young men, and in her own moment of generosity gave each of them $100 and her blessing. The young male slaves were deliriously happy; however, the two were completely unprepared to manage themselves and as newly freed blacks they were unwelcome in Kentucky. Having to move on they quickly bought themselves each a horse, paying far too much for the animals they received. Mostly because the seller had thrown in a couple of gallons of whiskey to clench the deal.

When the pair showed up at Dody's tavern they were near completely drunk.

The Dodys ran a fine place with both rising early each day so they might set a breakfast feast in front of their guests at an early hour. After clearing away the dishes they turned the tavern over to their daughters and retired to get bit of rest, for by mid afternoon they would be in the full swing of preparing a banquet for the evening meal. The Dodys were never certain how many guests to prepare for in the evening, so they prepared an abundance and then daughters, Marie and Mollie, would serve the leftovers next day lunch. The scheme worked well because lunch time was generally for but a few strangers along with a group of friendly locals who offered assistance to the young girls if they got busy tending tavern. Hiram Purdy took lunch there at every given opportunity, for he found the Dody girls both being sweet on him even more compelling than yesterday's delicious pie.

When Arthur and Ben came into the tavern, they were boisterous, more than a little full of themselves, and thinking the girls were left to fend for themselves they got completely out of line. The Dody girls were rightfully terrified, because exactly at the same instant Hiram came through the front door, Ben was grabbing at Marie as she cowered in a corner and Arthur already had Mollie crowded into a table. Both girls were crying and screaming even though Marie had managed to pull the rope that rang the bell in her parents' quarters. The girls were rightfully scared witless but probably never in danger of being greatly harmed, for Mr. Dody burst through the door from the living quarters at about the same instant as Hiram stepped in the front. Dody always kept a pistol close at hand and John insisted Hiram always be armed these days, so Arthur and Ben suddenly found themselves looking down gun barrels from both directions.

White men in such a happenstance would have surely been bound over to the law; however, these were black men in 1860 Kentucky, and thus a completely different circumstance. In short order Ben and Arthur were securely bound, and Dody sent for Mr. Simpson who would surely know what best to do. Simpson reacted with a fervor. After the pair had been thoroughly flogged they were put in chains and a slave dealer was summoned. After only two weeks of being freed men, the pair was sold and summarily sent "down the river" to toil in the rice paddies. Simpson burned their manumission papers in front of their eyes and sent the money from the slave buyer plus the sale of their two horses back to Mrs. Crabtree. He also sent along a letter chastising her severely for setting the likes of those two loose on the public.

Depending on one's point of view, Arthur and Ben might, or might not have been lucky they had not yet harmed the girls. If they had, after the flogging they would have surely been hanged or worse. However, having to spend their remaining lifetime in bondage on a rice plantation might have been the most severe punishment of all. The outcome of Crabtree freeing his two young slaves was wretched on several fronts. Instead of a fairly comfortable life as workmen for Crabtree, the two would now live a miserable existence in the rice paddies. The Dody girls would be scared of black men for the rest of their lives with the Dody family now bitterly opposed to allowing black men to run free.

The other issue was even more gut wrenching:

"Hiram, I have more respect for your father than any man I ever knew, but he is dead wrong about the Negro and this slavery issue. See what happened? It is the white man's duty to keep them in bondage and in check. The freed Negro is a dangerous Negro and you mark my words, son, if they ever get a chance, we will be fighting for our lives."

"Do you really think so, Mr. Simpson? What about those like Bos? He saved my Mother from some white men."

"That Bos needs to be watched too. If he ever thinks it is to his advantage he will turn like a leaf in the wind. My father and his father before him taught me that, and now I am telling you. I have been around the Negro all my life, son. Don't you ever trust a strange one and never, never let your guard down or give one an even a chance at you.

My father's brother was almost killed in a slave rebellion over in Virginia back in '31 by a bunch like those two. Some of his friends and neighbors were. I wish you could talk to my uncle cause everybody over there once trusted this slave named Nat Turner just like you folk trust Bos. His master knew Turner was a real smart one, so he taught him to read and write and treated him real special. Turner thanked him by getting a bunch of slaves to rise up and kill every single white person on 11 farms before they could get em stopped. And you know what, Hiram? Nat Turner's master, along with his wife and children, were the first white people out of 60 the black sons of bitches butchered. My uncle would have probably been next cause his place was the first one down the road from where a couple or three hundred white men caught and hung the whole bunch. All but Turner, they cooked him alive in his own juice! You go read more about that fanatic John Brown; he really believes the slaves will rise up in revolt and in fact he is planning on it. And he may be right because if they have half a chance to do so, they will. Believe me, Hiram, we white men have to stand firm, never let our guard down and keep total control."

"Mr. Crabtree had set them both free. How could you sell them like that?"

"The Supreme Court of the land ruled on that two years ago. A slave has no more legal rights than a cow. This slave named Dred Scott thought he could sue, but the court ruled he could do no such thing. In fact the court also ruled the Missouri Compromise was not legal either, and a slave owner can take his slave anywhere, slave state or not. The federal government has no right to decide what states or territories can or cannot have slaves. That Supreme Court ruling is one of the things that has all the northern states in an uproar, for it pretty much legalizes slavery in all the states, and that's one of the things this Lincoln fellow wants to change. We must never allow the federal government to tell us Kentucky people what we can and cannot do, particularly about slaves or with the slavery issue. If the federal government gets too bossy we should pull out of the Union. We must be strong about that."

"I have read where some states are really upset, Mr. Simpson."

"This Abraham Lincoln thing is enough to upset anybody! He claims his whole deal is to keep the Union together, but if he would get elected it won't be safe for a white woman anywhere. Governor Gist over in South Carolina has already called a conference among the southern states. I understand he and Mississippi, Alabama and Florida are all ready to pull out of the Union right now, but nobody wants to be first."

A fire snorting traveling preacher who was staying at Dodys overheard the older man lecturing Hiram, and added to his consternation. The preacher shouted right into Hiram's face:

"Son, the Bible says 'Servants, obey your master.' It is talking about slaves there! There was slavery a plenty in bible times and not one time ever does Jesus come out agin it; therefore, slavery must be God's natural order of things."

Hiram pondered the advice from these two sages presuming they were both wiser than he, all the while becoming more swayed from his father's points of view. Besides, he could ill afford Simpson's displeasure on this or any other issue right now, for in the very near future he might well wind up totally enraged with him anyway.

Betty Jo Simpson was two years older than Hiram, and young women her age would have ordinarily been looking at more mature young men.

However, after carefully surveying the available crop, she had decided none was worthy of her charms, save maybe Hiram Purdy. His people were rich and Hiram would undoubtedly become well educated which made him about the only one she saw as a gentleman who could maintain her in the style of her parents' home. She reasoned that in fact he could just move out to her family's place and build her a lavish house where she could continue to be cared for by the slave girls who currently tended her every want. Most of the other young men found Betty Jo to be a block of ice, but as of late she had always been warm and sweet to Hiram.

Very warm and very sweet.

Very, very warm and very, very sweet.

Warm and sweet to the point they were now sweating it out.

The tragedy in all of this was that John Purdy was not there for his son, for Hiram needed him now. Hiram loved and respected his father and wished desperately he had listened to his advice about never lying with a woman you would not want to spend the rest of your life with. Betty Jo had got him alone and come on strong, seeming to know exactly just what to do with an inexperienced young virgin. Now he was terrified. He felt completely trapped.

Hiram had always liked either one of the Dody girls a whole lot better than the spoiled and sometimes haughty Betty Jo. The Dody girls were not only pretty, they were sweet, clean, smart, hard working and innocent. He had but to close his eyes to still see the sheer terror in their faces when they were being stalked by Ben and Arthur. It seemed right now about the only thing he knew for certain was that his father must be wrong about the slavery issue, and black people in general. Hiram swore to himself that if need be he would even bear arms for the right of Kentucky people to govern themselves so they could keep every Negro in bondage and in check. And that included Bos.

Thus, the unintended consequence of John Purdy's extended absence was how it soon would impact the Purdy family.

Sledge sat in his cabin on the Chester A. Chester, which was by far the finest steamboat to venture up the Missouri River and a favorite of the military at Ft. Leavenworth. From there it only went another 30 or so miles up river to St. Joseph, where it turned around and headed back down river. It was well over 200 feet long and 44 feet wide but it could "float on a beer" with its very shallow draft. The Chester A. Chester's cabin class accommodations were a floating castle with twin covered paddle wheels set flush with the promenade deck.

He sucked hard on his whiskey and brooded. It was all her fault! (Drunk or sober Sledge's reasoning never made a lot of sense where Mattie Purdy was concerned.) He now thought continuously about that special day when she had backed down the ladder, and when he had his one and only chance to fondle her. He had only the shortest of a moment to hold her close and press his excited manhood against her that day. Still, he vividly remembered the softness of her magnificent body. The scent of mint on her breath. The sweet smell of rose water. Those precious few moments had kindled such a feeling of want he could never get it put out, and now, now, this want was a cancer that consumed every waking moment of each passing day. Sledge rarely had conscious moments anymore where he thought of anything besides those few seconds and that luscious feeling. When he slept he dreamed of nothing else.

Every glance at the wanted posters with his likeness now rekindled his passion to a white-hot fever, for Mattie Purdy was really all that mattered. Even though he now had much to live for, and his gold meant plenty of other women, he must find her and have her for his very own. He would warn John Purdy that if he did not call off the hunt he had the money to have the Purdy family killed, one by one. Sledge assumed that with his wealth he could get a great lawyer to clear his name or even buy off the law. He would then live the life of a gentleman, with Mattie as his pet.

Sledge was definitely a man possessed, for he reasoned if he had Mattie with him, then all of those other people would think he had won, and they would just go away. For these inexplicable reasons, instead of heading into the sunset to disappear with his gold, a few miles north of Pricilla's shallow grave Sledge pointed the red-wheeled wagon toward where he knew Mattie Purdy would be. This burning fixation had already cost him dearly, with the fee including his only irreplaceable friend, his wretched looks, and having been run out of his home in Kentucky. The garden incident when the big Negro had spoiled his plans had really started Sledge over the edge. He was now at the point that even when he was with the likes of poor Pricilla, when he closed his eyes he saw only one thing: Mattie Purdy. He contemplated about Johnson and their botched attempts from time to time, but if truth be told it was Mattie Purdy who seldom left his mind.

He could not shake her.

Sledge finally determined that if he could not have her, then he would see to it that no one else would either. If it came down to that, he would kill her. Then maybe one way or the other he could gain some peace.

In the 1860 travel season on the westbound Oregon Trail it was alive with people and their wagons, teams, and farm animals plus innumerable cowboys driving a great many herds of cattle. A $10 cow in the City of Kansas was bringing $150 in California, so there was lots of beefsteak on the hoof, headed west. There was even one herd of 2,000 turkeys. (Most of them made it.) The north side of the Platte was often called the Mormon side where multitudes of people pulled their high wheeled carts, loaded with every thing they owned. They walked and pulled and pulled and walked and walked and pulled for those hundreds and hundreds of miles. Westward through rivers and mountains and desert. Westward, ever westward. The hard way. The most popular trail was south of the Platte River and fostered many of the earliest points of civilization throughout Nebraska and was where, for now at least, the Indians presented few problems. Sledge took the south side and re-bandaged his head whenever he encountered others up close.

The fancy white horses could only take so much; however, folk would get real curious about whoever traded such fine horses and a rig like this. Furthermore, Pricilla had friends and her man Tom would gather others to help him search, so when possible Sledge steered clear of where some permanent person could report when the wagon had passed by. Or where there might be a poster. He began looking for fresh animals on the trail, and the old prospector had made an excellent choice, for he was headed east in no particular hurry. Both his big mules seemed fresh, plus he also had his tools and lots of grub on the pack mule. One stop shopping had allowed Sledge to avoid most points of civilization and he kept his head bandaged when other travelers could not be avoided.

With incredible cunning and a lot of luck Sledge now sat in his steamship cabin, for the soldiers had been questioning another man about his same size who was also minus some teeth. By sheer luck and a bit of carelessness on the soldiers' part, he walked aboard between the mules and had managed to get his bandaged head past them and their damned poster.

There were other posters. Everywhere. On the dock. On the boat stage. On the promenade. $10,000 they screamed, just like every other poster probably at every other point of civilization on the trail, and certainly on the side of every lead wagon in every wagon train. It seemed there must be thousands more posters of him than there were of this Abraham Lincoln character and all the other political candidates combined! To Sledge it seemed his must be the most recognizable face in the country. Still he must press on.

He slipped his bandaged head down stairs to the lower deck to check the well being of the mules, and then returned to sit on the promenade just outside his room, sipping whiskey as he peeked out from his bandages. He gazed at the City of Kansas passengers boarding the boat, and at first he assumed his eyes were playing tricks on him, or he was hallucinating or perhaps even drunker than he thought! The four of them seemed to be traveling together. There was a heavy set older Negro woman and a tall salt and pepper gray headed white one. Then there was the big nigger dressed up so fine and walking behind.

Sledge sat transfixed!

There was absolutely no mistaking the fourth.

It was Mattie Purdy!

The foursome disappeared and shortly he heard people being ushered into the suite of rooms at the very front of the boat. Sledge cracked his cabin door and peeked out, seeing the two white women standing in an open cabin no more than 50 feet away! His heart pounded, he shook and could scarce get his breath. He could now get even with the big black and he would soon have his way with Mattie. Joy upon joy.

He became so aroused he had to relieve himself.

The Chester A. Chester had the typical layout with the first class cabins between the large dining hall area and the promenade deck, which obviously ran between the cabins and the outside rail. Cabin doors accessed both dining and promenade sides with the Mattie party having the best rooms on the boat, right up front where the cool river breeze was the best. The older black woman and the hated big black were now at the place reserved for servants at the back of the boat, although they were still sitting up in first class. Mattie and the tall woman were being served welcome-aboard refreshments at a table just outside his door! Sledge's elation was boundless. He simply could not believe his good fortune, for providence was still on his side and had delivered.

He began carefully considering his options and in many ways Sledge was a very smart man. He now wisely concluded that trying to capture Mattie and walk off the boat at a river stop would present far too much of a challenge. He also reasoned that as good as he was in the woods his best opportunity would be to get her off the boat in the countryside. He would then kill the big nigger in front of everyone and threaten to kill anybody from the boat who tried to follow them as well. He would then send the boat on its way. It seemed a good scheme, for he had thousands of dollars worth of gold in his boots, and providence was providing not just one, but two good mules.

When in Osceola collecting his money, and again when starting down the Santa Fe Trail he had heard about the goings on down around Ft. Scott, Kansas. Both abolitionist and pro-slaver irregular military units were honoring sort of a safe zone there. Although there were plenty of men and lots of action on both sides of the issue, everyone had sort of an unwritten rule to leave each other alone in the town. He would race there with Mattie and pay this pro-slaver guy, Hamilton, a fortune to hide the two of them right in the town. The bullwhackers had made much about the fact that Hamilton seemingly would do anything for money, so when the time was right he would pay him and his people well to whisk the pair of them away to Mexico. He still had contacts in the mine country that, for a fee, would bring him enough of his gold to live like a king and make it possible for him and Mattie Purdy to simply disappear.

Forever.

The boat got underway after a while, and as Virginia and Mattie sat lingering over their small welcome-aboard dessert Sledge sprang into action.

He burst from his cabin door and jammed a pistol into Mattie's face.

Bos had never taken his eyes off Mattie except to blink, and the moment Sledge ordered Mattie into his stateroom, Bos was bounding over the class divider, counting the number of doors from where he was to where they were. He scared some passengers half to death bursting through their room and stormed into Sledge's room from the promenade side in a matter of seconds. Bos' charging through the door from the promenade side distracted Sledge somewhat as he was tugging at the struggling Mattie. When Sledge momentarily turned his attention to Bos, Virginia managed to jam her foot in the other door and was able to force her way in as well. All at once Sledge's room got quite crowded. He waved his pistol about pointing at first one and then the other, finally aiming it straight into Mattie's face.

"Back off, back off! I'll kill her! I'll kill her!" He snarled.

For just the briefest of instants Virginia's lighting fast mind could not help but ponder: "But a few weeks ago I prayed there be no more Mattie so I would be up next with John Purdy." All this while she continued forcing her way between the two. Sledge was now roughly punching and shoving at Virginia, as he still pointed the gun around her at Mattie. He growled in a most victorious tone:

"Well now Miz. Purdy and wife of the rich son of a bitch who put a price on my head. Tell your friends to back away and you come with me. You have your choice. Come be my woman or stay on this boat and be a dead woman. What's it going to be? Speak up woman!"

Turning to Virginia he demanded:

"Out of the way, bitch! Tell the captain unless he wants some dead people on his boat to put in to shore. Move damn you! I said move!"

Then to Bos:

"Glad you showed up, boy. I got some unfinished business with you. But first, there are two big mules tied at the very back of the lower deck.

Go get them and bring them to the stage. Move! Move or I'll shoot her and you too. Get your butt in gear, you big black jackass, and I mean now!"

Bos was armed, but wisely surmised that if he drew his pistol Sledge might start shooting and that was the very last thing he wanted, so for the moment at least, he kept his pistol concealed.

Virginia did her very best to keep between Sledge and Mattie, but he was very pervasive, and had a death grip on Mattie's wrist as the four of them tumbled out the cabin door to the promenade. First out the door was Bos, then Sledge with Virginia still trying to keep him and Mattie apart. Sledge with Mattie's wrist still in a vice-like hold was now sticking the pistol right into Virginia's gut when several other horrified passengers picked up on the scene.

A couple of the men were starting to press closer.

"Stand aside, all of you stand aside, or a bunch of somebodys is going to get killed!"

Virginia was fearless:

"Be careful, she is carrying a child."

"I didn't see no kid!"

"She's pregnant, you idiot!"

Sledge looked absolutely astonished.

How dare John Purdy!

Sledge suspected that a woman in this condition could probably not travel fast and hard on mule back, no matter what. And now with all of these other people gathering around, somehow this was not working out the way he had seen it in his mind. Looking somewhat bewildered at this new development, Sledge hesitated for just a moment:

Bos saw his chance and took it!

The huge black man was already standing by the rail, so grabbing it with both hands he suddenly vaulted, swinging his feet like a schoolboy clearing the garden gate. He caught Sledge hard in the arms and chest with his ankles, knocking the hand with the gun high into the air where it went off harmlessly. Then both of them crashed through and over the rail, tumbling into the water some 30 feet below.

Virginia moved like lighting up past the Texas deck and found the Captain at the wheel:

"Stop the boat! Stop the boat! Stop the Boat! Stop the boat! There are two men overboard. A crazy one and my slave!"

The captain shouted orders into the talking tube and the engineer went about bringing the big vessel to a stop, then went into reverse to hold the big boat still against the current. A great many of the passengers had rushed to this side of the boat by now and stood craning their necks looking for the two, but the spot where they went overboard was now around a bend and out of sight.

It takes some doing to turn a boat such as the Chester A. Chester around. By the time the captain found a place he considered safe to do so, and got back near to the spot where the incident took place, there was no one to be found. The captain continued upstream looking for another place to turn around when suddenly a group of small fishing boats full of armed men appeared out of the riverside brush, formed a line across the river and hailed the boat. A stick of dynamite went off close to the bow, and two men threw a line with a grappling hook over a convenient spot on the Chester A. Chester's rudder. The line was secured to a large tree on the riverbank, and when it became taunt the boat became untenable and floundered. Two of the small boats, one on either side, bristled with men still at the ready with more sticks of dynamite.

"Let us board or we'll blow you out of the river!"

It was a group of pro-slave guerrillas who were watching for organized groups of abolitionists, but sometimes simply challenged all comers to the Kansas Territory. Anyone who would not swear to vote for slavery when the vote came up and support the pro-slave government was being sent back down river—some of them with a knot on their head. Virtually all organized anti-slave settler groups were now being forced to enter the Kansas Territory across Iowa into Nebraska over what was known as the Lane Trail, to then enter the territory from the north. That trail was well marked (and still is in some places) with sentinels of stone markers piled throughout Iowa over into Nebraska. By 1860 traveling in northern Missouri had become tightly controlled by the proslavers, with both rivers and trails definitely closed to abolitionist groups.

Virginia accosted the guerrilla leader, a redhead named Trotter:

"You damn fools, this boat was headed down river and my slave and a crazy man fell off!"

Although Quantrill had not yet formed up his irregulars, his mindset was the rule of the day. He always demanded of his men they harm no children and respect and protect the ladies from other less gentlemanly types. Trotter used the same rule book, so he graciously removed his hat before he warned her:

"Don't press your luck, lady."

Virginia quickly reappraised the situation and completely reversed her tactics. She placed her hand on the redhead's arm and threw him her sweetest smile as she went plum southern.

"Sir, plaeese, excuuseah mee. I got so exciteeedd I forgot myesslff. My Negro slave man just fell offin thaaais here boat wheena he wasa chasen theiss other man who was a trying to do harm to my frieeendsa."

"So you own slaves?"

Virginia fluttered her dark Spanish eyes:

"About four hundred and sixty five I think mayyybeee. It is just so haaard to keep track and awwll."

"Why I never heard of anybody owning that many slaves."

"Well the one that went over the rail is real important to me. I will pay you two hundred dollars reward just to bring him baacck. Here is a hundeered dollars in gold juusest to let ya awal know I am a serious and I can well afford to pay youaall."

Virginia spotted the large knife Red Trotter was carrying. It was actually a small sword known as a Roman sword, and he insisted all of his men carry one. Red had learned how effective this weapon was from a bloody abolitionist named John Brown who insisted all of his men carry one. It was the perfect weapon for a man on the ground being challenged by a man on a horse. The Romans had perfected exactly the right instrument for the man on the ground to use to gut the horse. And then gut the rider when you had him on the ground.

She pointed to the wicked looking thing:

"That $200 is of course if he don't have no knife marks or whippin marks or such. You know that brings down the price you can get. Whippin marks and such as that makes them buyers think they are hard to handle you awl know, but we really want to keep him and to keep getting lots of younguns out of him. Cause now he is such a big one, well his babies when they get just a little age on em, they are big enough they can sure pick lots of cotton and all ya know. He is real important to me."

Red had heard about plantations in the south having their breeding stock and was immensely impressed because he had never met any slave owner who was that scientific.

"Well, I can see where you stand on slavery, ma'am. Good! Good for you!"

Virginia kept smiling and fluttering:

"That white man he was a chasen now he would be worth a lot more of money to you cause this here Mr. Purdy, he is offering a whole big $10,000 reward for him and awwll, and if you bring both of em back I will see to it that yoall get the monynee. In fact I will just round it up to $ 11,000 if you bring em both back, but now I don't want no hurt marks on my nigger, you hear? They fell off about the second bend in the river back there and I saw them get out past the paddle wheel but my lands, they just, why they just disappeared. They are back there for sure though, and it just might be easy money for you. Let me get you this paper with this other man's picture on it."

"The next stop is Lexington, ma'am. Wait for us there. What is your name?"

She gave him her very best come-on smile:

"Why my name is Virginia. Virginia de Falco and I will be a waiting on you, now you hear."

It took Red about three minutes to round up his band of raiders and move back to their boats. As they departed, Virginia turned her attention to her remaining companions where Mammy was trying to comfort the inconsolable Mattie.

"He is big and strong Mattie, and I saw him clear the paddle wheel. He will be all right."

"Dear God, I hope so!"

The muddy Missouri deserved its reputation of being "too thick to drink, too thin to plow," but a powerful swimmer like Bos could get around in it fine. He had Sledge by the neck and soon was on the south riverbank having scarcely drawn a deep breath. To say the big man was jubilant is the understatement of the century! He held Sledge up by his shirt front with only one hand, like a child scolding his doll:

"Mr. Sledge, Bos done gonna pay Mr. John back for looking out for him. You gonna come with me this time."

They were slimy with river mud, and their boots squished at ever step but Bos could care less. They had both lost their pistols so he now held Sledge by the back of his pants, marshaling him along the ever present river bank telegraph trail. Bos never doubted for a minute that Miz. Mattie would be back for him and he wanted to find a good clear area where they could easily be spotted from the boat. Sledge started cursing Bos and the day he was born, but he could care less; however, when Sledge turned around and hit at him, Bos slapped his face.

It was exactly the wrong thing to do and the wrong time to do it. The two guerrillas Red had left on the riverbank to guard their horses had just noticed the pair. Muddy or not they could tell there was a black man and a white man and the huge black man had just hit the white one. In pre-Civil War Missouri that was a capital offense. The guerrillas were well trained and one continued to stay with the horses while the other galloped up behind the pair. As Bos turned around to face him, the guerrilla struck him in the face with the butt of his rifle, reared his horse to a stop, and jumped off to face the pair, pistol in hand.

"Let him loose, you black bastard!"

The guerrilla cocked the pistol and stuck it right in Bos face:

"Let him loose! Now!"

Bos reluctantly let Sledge loose.

"Sir, he ... ."

The second guerilla could not stand not to be in on the action and rode up behind the group. He cracked Bos across the back of the head with his pistol barrel.

The big man fell to the ground where they commenced beating him unmercifully, one with pistol barrel, the other with rifle butt.

Both then drew their Roman swords.

Sledge just beamed:

Who in hell are you guys? Man I'm glad you are here!"

"We are part of Red's Raiders. We stayed with the horses while the rest of em are busy stopping a steamboat. What's the story here?"

"How do you stop a steamboat?"

"It's easy. Find a spot where they have to watch out for a river full of snags. Get in the clear part of the channel and set off some dynamite in their face. Throw a line on the boat that is already tied to a big tree so it pulls them around in the water so they can't steer. Have some guys with plenty of dynamite in a bunch of small boats talk sense to the captain. Even big ones like the Chester will let us aboard every time. Maybe you didn't hear me. I asked you what's your story, mister?"

"This big black is uncontrollable. I have owned him for years. He did this to my face a year ago, and I was a fool not to kill him then. It's time to get rid of him. Give me a gun!

Raider No 1 growled:

"We really ought to wait till Red gets back. He would want to know about this before we do it!"

Raider No. 2 "Screw em. I am mad as hell cause I wanted to go along and see that fancy boat."

No. 1: "Red and the others will be gone quite a while anyway cause it always takes a while to go through the passengers when you stop a big one like the Chester. Funny thing about today. It's always headed down river this time of week and he was wondering if picking up a bunch of abolitionists is what threw them off schedule. Anyway we got plenty of time for this big boy."

Sledge, knew full well when the other raiders returned from the Chester they then would have the complete story on him and he damned well better vamoose before the others showed back up. That tall salt and pepper haired woman would sic the whole bunch on him like a pack of dogs and although he had quickly realized time was now of the essence, Sledge wanted revenge. He would now get his pound of flesh:

"Let's kill him! I'll kill him right now, right this minute but let me have a knife first. He is mine to do with what I want and he made my face look like this, and the black son of a bitch just hit me again. He hit me! We all know we can't ever have that, and besides look at his size. He's always been a danger to any white man, so don't let him have a chance at you. We need to make an example out of him, so give me a knife and get his pants off! I'll fix him good and stuff em in his mouth before I shoot him. We'll give folk something to look at besides a dead nigger hanging from a tree!"

By now Bos was bound securely, tied to a tree and woozy, fighting hard to maintain consciousness. The raiders untied his legs so Sledge could get at his nigger but as Sledge came close, with his knife at the ready, Bos leg-whipped him and got a cross-legged grip around his middle. With his enormously powerful legs Bos proceeded to crush the air out of Sledge to the point of almost breaking his back. Sledge flailed at the air with his knife:

"Get him off me! My God get him off! Get me looooosee! He's brrreeaaaaaking myyy backackkkccct! Ccchhaawawkelp! Wheezzeelp."

Raider No. 2 hit Bo in the head with a rifle butt. Hard.

Bos regained consciousness with a canteen of water being poured into his face.

Red was standing over him:

"Get him up. Get his pants back on. Damn it! Men, you just cost us $200."

The two raiders had only paused from pistol whipping and clubbing Bos when Red and the others returned so unexpectedly quick. Sledge had followed his instincts and quietly slipped away, for he was furtively watching and noticed the others approaching while they were yet a distance away. In the adjoining woods he did the one thing he did best, and soon the whole bunch of them were wondering how a man can simply become invisible. As the raiders passed the wanted poster around, it became obvious to everyone they had more important things to do than stop a few westbound steamboats.

Red shared with them that the tall salt and pepper haired Spanish looking woman had even added to the reward and he was disappointed they had smacked Bos around, for he was certain it had been a good promise.

"Her name is Virginia de Falco and she claimed to own well over 400 slaves and this big one is her stud. I believe everything she told me and anyway Purdy's $10,000 will finance us for some time to come. Let's go get ol busted nose, boys."

Catching the white man that the big Negro had been marshalling along immediately became their top priority, and after each had a good look at the poster they fanned out to start a door to door search. Looking for a man with missing teeth and with his nose on the side of his face. This man Sledge.

Red turned his attention to Bos:

"Can you set a horse?"

"I don't know, sir, maybe if you tie me on, sir."

Red and another raider helped Bos wobble to his feet.

Lexington, about 7 or 8 miles further on east, was a small town and it took just a couple of queries to find Virginia and her party. Red led the horse with Bos tied slouching forward on its back to where Virginia happened to be sitting on the front porch of the small hotel. He took off his hat:

"I am sorry about your slave, ma'am. They didn't know. They saw him hit a white man, and that is all it takes in these parts."

Red reached into his pocket and handed Virginia back her $100.

"I can't keep this. We cost you quite a bit already. He looks in pretty tough shape but nothing a few weeks won't take care of I reckon. I hope anyway. He had to be worth a lot of money when he was in good shape. I got there fore they cut him though, so you ought to still be able to get some more good ones out of him. We'll go find that Sledge fellow for you, and I'll keep that money."

Mattie rushed down, and in spite of their pleas the hotel owner would only allow a black man who was performing labor of some type to come inside. The three women had to lay Bos out on a thin pallet on the back porch. Mammy, who was forced to stay outside as well, asked at the door for soap and water so they might clean him up. As they did so, Mattie sat on the porch beside him getting blood and water all over a very nice dress. As the women carefully washed, treated, and bandaged the huge black man's grotesque looking head, Virginia watched and listened to the dialog between Bos and Mattie.

Bos was crying:

"I had him, Miz. Mattie, I had him for you and they took him away. They took him away from me. I had him. I had him for Harvey and I had him for Mr. John but most I had him for you, and they just took him away."

"Shh shhhh. Be quiet now. It will be okay."

"I had him, Miss Mattie. I had him."

"Shh shh shh now."

Mattie choked up too, as she looked at the helpless big invalid lying there. He had saved her and her unborn child from Sledge, and who knows what. For his effort his head was now beat to a pulp with dirty bloody cuts covering his face and one eye was swollen completely shut with the other mostly so. He had an ear lobe torn badly, knots and bruises everywhere, plus he would have multiple concussions no doubt. He apparently had also been within minutes of being castrated. And tears were running down his smashed and horribly beaten face; because he had failed her.

Virginia took the scene completely in. There was no doubt Bos and Mattie loved each other. It was a wholesome thing, but they truly did love one another. She found her voice and spoke softly:

"He is in bad shape, Mattie. Really, really bad shape. He can't bend over or lift anything for a long time. It would kill him. His looks will make everyone think he must be really hard to handle. Can't be worth much after all this, but if you want him, he's for sale. I will go see if I can find a doctor to look at him but it will cost more to get him well than he is worth. You can have him for a dollar. You want him?"

The two women's eyes locked.

Sledge finally realized he might be in trouble, and for the first time he pondered if he should have headed the red-wheeled wagon to Oregon or Mexico or somewhere else but here. Still he was confident. He was an undisputed expert and knew these particular woods and rivers as well as anyone ever did. Soon he found an old John boat that some kids had tied to the riverbank and night time found him floating down river. He was tired and hungry, nursing some very sore ribs.

But with a plan.

Red's men searched well into the night but found no trace, so at dawn he organized them into teams of two, ordering them to look in every nook and cranny. In a couple of days one team was down on the Osage River headed toward Sledge and Johnson's old shack, which just happened to be the best place Sledge could think of to go to disappear for a while. He had floated about halfway to Booneville, got lucky and stolen a good horse complete with saddle and a rifle stuck in the scabbard. Sledge assumed there would be a poster on every tree over in St. Louis, and up north along the St. Joseph and Hannibal railroad. He had no idea what else lay farther north of the river than that; therefore, his plan was to hustle down south towards the cabin area where he knew his way around. Meanwhile the raiders did detailed sweeps of Cooper, Moniteau and Morgan Counties and headed on south to Camden and then to Miller county, where the shack was.

Sledge's old partner Johnson had two cousins who had married into some of the largest families in the sparsely populated Osage valley. In fact that was probably why the two of them were allowed to continue trapping so widely there in the first place. Sledge was acquainted with these two families, the Thurmans and the Millers, and was confident one or both families would help him hide out. Any of the numerous caves tucked along the river banks in the 100-mile stretch between the two biggest river bluff sites would be remote and comfy. If he could convince any of Johnson's people to help, he could stay hidden a long time in this no man's land, certainly at least until things settled down and he could make a break for it. Mattie Purdy would have to wait for now. He correctly assumed all of those pro-slavers would now be looking for him him, so he was finally ready to give up on her for the time being. He would head for Mexico or California or anywhere else he could get to that was far, far away.

And regroup.

And come back.

Sledge had a fortune on deposit and would have to figure out how to retrieve it; meanwhile, he appreciated his heavy boots. Sledge had been poor and now he was rich. He liked rich. Being more than a bit paranoid, Sledge had spent some of his alone time back at the mines carefully hollowing out these boot heels and then filling them with pure smelted gold. He had also fashioned a great many coins into easily removable false boot top linings, and now was carrying $1,000 in gold coin, plus two avoirdupois pounds of solid gold. In each boot.

He grinned. The boots might well have drowned him, for with his bad knee he was not a strong swimmer at all, but the big black had drug him safely ashore. Anyway the gold would be a lot of help when it came to convincing Johnson's family folk to help him hide out.

Cousin Rawl Thurman, a good Mennonite and God fearing man, looked at Sledge and shook his head. By now the news of the reward had made it even this deep into the woods.

"Nope. You ain't nothing but bad news for me and mine. You got my wife's cousin killed trying to do meanness before we got his soul saved and that story made it all the way back here. Some Indian took his scalp we heard, and them that told us said it was too good for him. You was the cause of all that. We try hard to be good Christian folk so we don't hold with yore kind, kidnapping women and all. He wasn't a natural mean man and so you had to talk him into that. Cause our blood was involved in the deal we won't hold ya and sell you to that fella looking for you, but we don't want your gold neither. You get. You are welcome to what you just put in your belly but that's all you take Now go. Get on out of here!"

Sledge was incredulous:

"I'll pay you well. I have lots."

"I said get!"

His reception at the Millers' was far less welcoming than at Thurmans', and he had to back away with the stolen rifle pointed at Miller, who would have sure enough sold him for the reward. Sledge was shaken. He swiped some grub at a place where no one was home and retreated to a small cave in the valley along the trail up to the shack. About dusk he was certain he saw a shadow darting along the trail he had come up. He carefully considered making a break for it; however, these hills are virtually impossible to cut through in the dark. Especially so if one has a troublesome knee. Sledge hid the stolen horse back in the little cave, stomped out the fire, then took the rifle and climbed up into a huge oak tree to ponder his next move.

At dawn's first light Sledge slipped up to the top of a ridge and spotted Indians snooping around headed up the valley his direction. He quickly mounted the horse and headed the other way. As he moved along the ridge top trail he was certain he saw a horsemen over on the very next ridge top, and then some more men standing by their horses about three quarters of a mile away

He was starting to panic.

Red's men were working their way south and had come to Millers on yesterday. Miller was still really pissed.

"Yep. He's close by somewheres. Nearly shot me late yesterday, so's I'm helpen ya's look. I got two brothers and they got a couple boys apiece. I got em all started to looking late yesterday. You boys need to listen up. It ain't healthy to point a gun at a Miller around here. Make shore everbody knows that and keeps it in mind."

The team leader sent a man back to Lexington:

"Tell Red we are getting close. He is down here, so get everybody down here to help."

Russell, Waddell and Majors' administrative office remained in Lexington when Majors moved his office some 30 miles west to the Santa Fe Trail's head, at the City of Kansas. From necessity the two locations communicated frequently each day, hence Majors knew within three hours that Mattie and friends were now in Lexington. Majors immediately notified Colonel Albin up at Leavenworth. In a remarkably short time Mattie's little group some 50 miles down river from the Fort would be pleasantly surprised when a goodly number of blue coats climbed off a boat. Most who had volunteered to take up position surrounding their small hotel were the same men who had danced the night away. The soldiers had truly admired the Purdys, and besides, taking turns being up close to this remarkably beautiful woman was incentive enough.

John caught the next boat out of St. Joseph which arrived in the City of Kansas about six hours behind the Chester. He stopped at the Harris House to pick up Star, and when Colonel Harris told him Mattie was safe in Lexington, big strong John Purdy sat for a few minutes with his head in his hands, trembling with relief. He recomposed himself to mount up, and Star thundered out to Lexington. For a few brief hours John and Mattie held on to each other like newlyweds. He wanted nothing more than to stay close and protect her yet he knew full well they were closing in on Sledge.

His job was to lead the chase.

Mattie and John sat on the porch floor and tried to make Bos understand that Virginia had sold him to Mattie, but the big man was incoherent. John finally went to speak to the hotel keeper:

"I need to get my man in a bed, I simply cannot abide having him lay out on the back porch on some quilts like he is."

"Mr. Purdy, I understand you think he is a special nigger, but I will have none of him sleeping in one of my rooms or beds. Why I would feel like I would need to burn the bed. You are fortunate that I am allowing him out there."

"He got bashed up saving my wife and I don't have anywhere else to move him right now. Surely we can make some kind of arrangement."

"No! Now if you will excuse me."

John followed the hotel keeper back into his personal quarters.

"Mr. Purdy, the issue is closed. I said no!"

John walked over and flung the window open wide, then turned and started stripping the bed and tossing the bedclothes through the window. As he took hold of the mattress the hotel keeper physically challenged him.

"Just what do you think you are doing?"

"If I cannot bring him in to a bed, then I am going to take the bed out to him."

When the hotel keeper took a swung at him, John Purdy in turn showed the chap exactly why there were those who thought he should have become a boxer.

Later that same evening Brown and Blackfeather caught up, so the entire trio was formed up again, then, in the middle of the night Red's man showed up with the big news.

Sledge was down on the Osage!

About 2 a.m. John woke up the telegraph operator and broadcast the message:

"Missouri Hilltop, Code 2."

His Father, Sheriff Adams, 'Chief' cousin of Piomingo, the Holsher family, Alexander Majors and Colonel Albin knew immediately and exactly what to do next. About daybreak John received a wire back from Sheriff Adams' office that he would not be coming because the Sheriff recently had a horse shot out from under him and had broken his leg in the fall.

At the break of dawn John held Mattie for a moments embrace and he and Red set out for the bluffs, along with a few of Red's men. At full dawn Majors' bullwhackers who had time off and wanted in on the search set off for Osceola. They, along with some of their Osage Indian friends, would sweep down both sides of the river from the west. A lightly loaded wagon with just enough supplies to meet their needs headed for a rendezvous spot and then followed along. More supplies were loaded on a steamboat in Jefferson City to be dropped off for their benefit at Drake's landing in a town called Warsaw.

The timing was fortuitous as Colonel Albin had recently mustered in almost 80 brand new Calvary recruits, and his superiors readily agreed this would be a fine training exercise. Along with eight veteran sergeants, Albin spread the young cavalrymen out, to sweep from about due north of the Hilltop on around to the Majors' group, joining them at their left flank in Osceola. Their quartermaster supply wagons headed for designated spots.

Brown raced to meet and coordinate with Holsher and the St. Louis German immigrant community. Holsher dispatched men west, where some of them met up with the Calvary and completed the line across Missouri, a few miles south of the river. Another large group of Germans spread on around south to about the Meramec River. Associates in Jefferson City immediately loaded supply wagons to support the Germans.

Blackfeather headed southeast to meet with the Chickasaw who would be racing this way and needed specific orders. The Chickasaw would spread from the Meramec River clear across the southern area. They would live off the land so to speak. From each of their staging points all teams would follow a precision schedule. Mr. Morris and brother Henry would act as coordinators for the rear guard, because Brown insisted that if Sledge made a break for it, he might well head to Kentucky.

The "plus" groups were the Miller clan and a few local mid Missouri Osage Indians who were well aware that the man who cheated them at every opportunity was now in their area with a huge price on his head. They and the Miller clan were already out looking.

John studied his plan carefully. If one presumed the cabin was the center of a clock face, he had organized his resources in this fashion

A. Holsher's Germans had responsibility from 12 o'clock to 4 o'clock.

B. The Chickasaw had from 4 o'clock to about 7:30.

C. Major's men and the Osage Indians were about 7:30 to 9:00, and covering the entire Osage upstream area.

D. Albin's cavalry had from 9:00 back up to 12:00 where they joined with the Germans.

E. Morris and Henry were holding the Three Creek neighbors at the ready in Kentucky.

John truly appreciated the unexpected good fortune of Red's men. They were the commandos so to speak, and Red insisted they would all help John with the "close-in" work.

In an amazingly short time, well over 250 men would be in an irregular thirty mile diameter circle around the bluff top cabin. If no one had found Sledge yet, there would be a two man team holding position about every third of a mile along this circle concentrating on each trail, passable ridge top or any valley with a stream in it. When they came through this area earlier, Brown and Blackfeather had done an extraordinary good job of gathering the intelligence that John now needed.

Robert E. Lee himself would have considered John Purdy's use of this data to be brilliant!

Because it was.

These beautiful mid-Missouri, Osage hills have a very distinct pattern which repeats itself over and over again. The pattern is of a heavily forested large major ridge-top, with many other minor tree-covered ridges falling away at about right angles in both directions. From the air it looks similar to a bunch of crooked backbones and their ribs, scattered randomly about. The backbone ridge-top is generally fairly level and easily traversed; however, 50 yards left or right, and the terrain becomes seriously uphill or seriously downhill, every way one turns. Except for the trails, this country is extremely difficult to travel and almost impossible to cut across as man and beast are soon exhausted if they do not follow the trails along major ridge tops.

The Indians knew, way before the white man ever came, which of the ridge tops traversed the countryside and which of them simply dropped off to dead end in another valley. In the all-out war that soon would follow, the commanders learned the hard way what John Purdy figured out from the get-go. He could seal this land up tightly with a moderate number of men scattered about on the ridge tops that the Indian had used for their trails. All else he needed was a few more sets of eyes positioned where the major valleys came together and along the creek and riverbanks.

The young Miller whom Sledge had watched dart behind the tree found his pa, who in turn got out the word:

"He is fer sure way up on the bluff, there on north side of the river."

Sure enough, a sergeant with a scope soon spotted him moving through the underbrush. The signal was passed and every man knew exactly what to do next. In short order, the circle became a smaller and tighter half circle with the river being the circle's flat side.

John rechecked his weapons:

"Red, he is bound to have a rifle up there, and he is supposed to be damn good with one."

"These men have all seen the wrong end of a rifle before, John. All we need is some daylight."

As dawn cast its early rays, John saddled Star. Once again, he addressed Red straight on:

"Brown and Blackfeather will be back soon. This is kind of our fight."

"I saw your Mattie on the hotel porch, John. I'd take a bullet for the likes of her, so don't piss me off. Besides, we kind of owe you on the big black, so I'm in the game."

Red turned to the goodly number of his men who had gathered around the cook's fire:

"Any you men want out? Now's the time! He's got a rifle up there and we move at dawn."

The general response:

"And miss all the fun?"

To a man, they began saddling up, preparing to head for the bluffs.

Sledge probed the lines again and found armed men waiting at every escape route. He knew better than to try and cut across, for they would hear the horse threshing about in the underbrush. To go on foot would be suicidal, for even a strong man would be completely exhausted in an hour and a half. With his bad knee he wouldn't last half that long. As he crept back to his horse, once again he spotted a 12 or 14-year-old kid on the next ridge over, just as the youngster darted behind a tree. Sledge reasoned that he might possibly shoot the kid, but there was really no point in doing so. Besides the other men would hear the rifle. It seemed there were men everywhere now.

Sledge decided rather than hiding in one of the small bluff-side caves where the Indians were now poking about, he would go back up the short trail and return to the cabin site. He reasoned that if they caught him in a cave he would definitely be trapped, and so he headed to the very highest bluff tops. These jagged pinnacles are very remote and most difficult to reach if one does not know the way. He took comfort in the fact that few people knew their way around up there like he did. At least with the bluffs behind him, his back would be protected and he could see anyone approaching.

It was a learned and good decision.

Every few miles nature crowds up a huge pile of black rock in these hills and leaves a ridge-top spectacularly wide open. These high rock mesa clearings typically command a magnificent and nearly impassable view for miles in most directions. Black oak, white oak, walnut, hickory and dogwood thickets dominate the rest of the forest; however, the mesas have only an occasional clump of sizeable cedar trees at their edges. The rest of the clearing will be covered in huge black-rock formations surrounded by native grassess and a profusion of seasonal wild flowers. Except for the widely scattered clumps of large cedar, from the spot he selected, Sledge's view was virtually uninhibited. He was at home here, for this particular rock mesa was at the very top of the highest river bluff. His and Johnson's old shack overlooked this mesa and sat not far from the bluff's edge.

Sledge had no more than gained his bluff top vantage point when he spotted the white horse climbing up out of a valley's morning fog. Purdy was still slipping among the oak trees at the mesa's east edge for protection. Almost immediately Sledge spotted another rider coming from the north, doing the same. Casting his gaze the other way along the bluff, he saw two more riders approaching cautiously from the west and northwest. The last two horsemen now cut him off from the direction he had just come from. They along with the others formed a half circle north, east and west at the clearing's edge. South was about 225 feet straight down.

Sledge knew it was over. "Damn. Damn. Damn." Why oh why had he just not taken his gold and gone away? Then, he thought about her wonderfully full bosom, her flat stomach, the roundness of her bottom, the softness of her. Her radiant complexion. That beautiful smile. Those blue eyes. Her mane of honey blond hair. The scent of rose water.

He knew full well why he had come back.

He had come so very close.

Men died for less.

It might soon be over, but he wasn't through just yet. Sledge smiled a nervous smile to himself and attempted to draw a bead, wishing all the while that he had his favorite old rifle. Still, he was experienced enough to know that the light from a morning's dawn combined with an open and elevated rifle site are tricky. He waited and gazed past the mesa to the hilltops. He could see little else for the morning fog still hovered in the lower valleys.

Then he saw the white horse again.

Obviously someone had taught Purdy well, for as he and his stallion appeared out of the fog, they moved in an ever changing dance. As Sledge tried to follow Purdy's head with his rifle the horse kept prancing about. While Sledge lay wathing he made a vow: Purdy would pay a price for having the woman he so desperately craved for himself.

Purdy dismounted and somehow instinctively kept the horse between the two of them. Purdy was making it almost impossible to get a good shot

But he would. And Purdy would pay ... the ultimate price.

Sledge continued squinting down the rifle. With this unfamiliar rifle, and the coming light of dawn, he knew from experience that to be absolutely certain, he must patient.

He would let Purdy get maybe a quarter of a mile closer. Even if Purdy were using his horse as a shield, he would then get his shot.

He rarely needed more than one.

This time it had to be perfect.

Sledge lay in wait.

Goat Woman had been genuinely surprised to see Quinton Tooter when he returned so quickly, for they had supposed it would take a much longer time to find brother. Goat Woman filled him in on all the news, for her friend Morris told her John had wired his father about their impending sweep of the Osage valley and they were all hoping and praying they had this guy Sledge cornered. He apparently was returning to his old stomping grounds that he had bragged so much about. Quinton knew exactly their whereabouts from a time when he and Sledge had been drinking over at Dodys. Goat Woman and he had immediately mounted the geldings to race for the ferryboat to Missouri.

"Stop! Pluth down the gun. Stop. Tunith around an flace me!"

Sledge snapped his head in the direction of the voice. A wretched creature of a man had emerged from a large clump of cedar trees about 150 feet away and was holding a pistol with both hands, pointing it at him. As Sledge rolled over to face his ill-timed visitor now silhouetted against the morning sun, the stranger fumbled and lost his grip on the pistol. Sledge was excellent with any rifle and fired from his hip as he rolled over on the ground. The man fell backwards

Goat Woman's arrow was incredible for both distance and force, hitting Sledge in the left shoulder driving its razor sharp arrowhead into the shoulder joint. Quinton meanwhile struggled back to his knees, regained control of the pistol and fired five rounds in Sledge's direction. He then fell face forward into the rocks. The shots went wild except for one. It hit Sledge in the right leg, shattering the bone between knee and hip. Goat Woman bounded over to Sledge and grabbed his rifle, searched about for other weapons he might have, then raced to Quinton's side. He had practiced so very, very hard; however, two fingers on each hand are not much to hold on with. As promised, Goat Woman had only played backup, and per plan, she went into action only when it looked like he might fail. She was so disappointed for him when he lost his grip on the pistol, for he had wanted badly to do this all by himself.

Red was first out of the woods and hustled his horse among the large black stones to the little group. He swung down from the saddle and hunkered down to get a good look.

Sledge pleaded:

"I know who you are. I have money, lots and lots of money. I will double Purdy's reward and pay you $20,000 to get me out of here! The man is down and she's not gonna hurt anybody! I can keep your whole operation in money. Listen to me! You'll not never worry about money if you don't let Purdy get to me. I have gold here in my boots and plenty more. These heels are solid gold and I have more. Lots and lots more. Please help me!"

Sledge pulled the boot off of his uninjured leg and offered it to Red who remained completely stone-faced. Sledge then turned to Goat Woman. Grimacing in pain, he strained at the other boot as he babbled on:

"Please! I have more. Lots more! I will make it $20,000 each for both of you. I will make you both rich! Rich do you hear me? Rich!"

He jerked the false lining out of a boot top and waved it at her. Goat Woman looked at him in disdain:

"I am already rich! I have the respect of all people and the love of a few. I have honor. I have the sun and the sky, the moon and the stars. I have plenty to eat and pure fresh water. I have a warm place when it is cold and a cool place when it is hot. The Great Spirit smiles upon me. I have no need of your gold, Mr. Sledge."

Red responded by getting a rope off of his saddle and was proceeding to tie Sledge up as John and Star picked their way through the rocks. John dismounted, dropped Star's rein to the ground, and stood with his hands on his hips:

" Sledge, I've been looking for you, you murdering bastard!"

Red turned to John:

"John, the son of a bitch says his boot heels are full of gold."

"He won't need gold or boots either one where he is going!"

Goat Woman was now holding Quinton Tooter, attempting to make him more comfortable by leaning him against a big black rock.

"Mr. Purdy, you might well be dead had it not been for Mr. Tooter. You should know he wanted so badly to make things right by you. He crawled on his belly all the way from that tree line over there to these cedar trees, because he knew he couldn't possibly hit Sledge from way over there. Mr. Tooter had to hurry because when Sledge cocked the rifle he was not ready yet, but he thought Sledge was about to pull the trigger. He probably would have shot you.

John Purdy was incredulous. First of all, he thought Quinton Tooter was dead. Second, he could not imagine, of all people, this man he had known as Tuttoor ever trying to help him. John shuddered as he looked at the wretched work of Blackfeather and friends on Tooter's face, now made considerably more grotesque by blood forming in bubbles at the corners of his mouth.

Red examined Tooter:

"He is gut shot bad, John. He won't make it."

Together they carried him to a large walnut tree that overlooked the bluff and then set him leaning against it, so he faced the valley below.

As he slouched against the tree, Quinton Tooter asked of Goat Woman:

"Divd him de plouch."

Goat woman reached inside Tooter's shirt and pulled out a blood covered leather pouch, which was secured about his neck with a rawhide. She handed it to John, and as he opened it, Tooter was gasping:

"Mr. Purdy, I hadth wanted to glive this to Maud and the boy butht It donent lookth like I will slee them. You gid it to dam. Look noweth. Mke sure yo tan read glem."

Tooter struggled for air, and tried to keep talking.

"Tell dey bloy I loved higlem. Recom I dibent kno hlow.

Tell dey woomams I slorry I slo mlean."

John pulled two pieces of paper from the bloody pouch.

The first was page 44 of book 166 torn from the 1850, Madison Parrish, Louisiana, census records. It listed a slave named Pearl and all of her children, including a girl named Maud, then owned by a Mr. Robert Eads. The second paper was a page torn from ships records filed by the slave ship "Tare" or "Hare"; he could not make out just which. It was dated 1756, and concerned names given to the Africans they had brought from Sierra Leone, West Africa, to be sold at auction.

Quinton Tooter sat slouched against the walnut tree, watching as the sun gained full brilliance over the magnificent Osage Valley. Goat Woman tenderly wiped the blood from his chin again and again and put cool water to his mouth. She talked for the both of them yet one last time:

"Mr. Morris almost cried when I gave him his walking stick. Said that he would always cherish it. I used a fine piece of persimmon and fired it hard so it will last way past his children's children. He said the faces on the stick were perfect."

He followed her with his eyes as she spoke:

"Dbid I do glood?"

"You did well. You have been noble. You are now being dignified and gracious and brave. The Great Spirit will be very happy with you."

Goat Woman cuddled him, and Quinton Tooter felt one last time the only gentle hands of someone who really cared since he had been a little boy. He had done a good thing. His enemy now sat respectfully beside him. He was satisfied with himself.

Quinton Tooter coughed up a lot of blood and kind of shuddered.

He smiled.

He was at peace.

Finally.

When they realized it was over, Goat Woman was the first to speak: "White men call that sound the rattle of death, but the Indian knows better. It is the sound of his spirit taking leave. It will be welcomed for he died a noble death."

John helped Goat Woman cover Quinton Tooter with boughs of cedar she hacked from the trees and they searched for large grey stones to cover and further protect the body. He took time to do it well. This man had died protecting him, perhaps even in his stead. His enemy, Tuttoor had become his savior, Quinton Tooter.

John Purdy had never felt this humble in his entire life.

The thought was overwhelming

Surly he thought, surely.

It seems impossible, but I have surely seen a miracle.

I have seen two men live in the same skin.

John then turned his attention from Tooter to the other business at hand. He made his way to the other side of the black-rock mesa where Red and his men were keeping Sledge under guard:

"This guy don't seem to know how to shut up or take no for an answer. I finally hit him up side the head to shut him up. He keeps trying to buy us off."

As John was squatted down on his own heels so as to look Sledge straight in the face, Red handed John the boot linings. Sledge was miserable. His leg was shattered from Tooter's pistol shot, Goat Woman's arrowhead was buried deeply in his shoulder joint, and now he had a knot on his head where Red had smacked him.

He avoided John's eyes and started whining:

"It was not my fault. It's all her fault you know. Yes, all her fault, it was not my fault at all."

"How so?"

"She just drove me crazy. I had to do it. She led me on bad. That's it. She led me on. She made me want her."

"I know better than that. You worried Mattie and she always headed the other way if she saw you coming."

"But you see that was just so I would keep on trying to get close to her. She really wanted me, you know? She led me on."

"She led you on so you would rape her, so you would set fire to our house and kill our boy when you tried to kidnap her? So she would be paralyzed with fear sitting in her own home? She wanted a dirty, stinking, illiterate, worthless sneak? You are a liar or crazy or both."

"It was Johnson. Yes, it was Johnson: he kept saying we had to come back and get even. We never aimed for the boy to get hurt but that was your fault. You both should have run outside where we were to put out the fire. None of that was my fault. Don't you understand. It was not me, it was them. Look, I am a rich man. I will make it all up to you. Those boot linings are worth a lot. The heels are solid gold. What else would you like to have? I will make it right by you."

"Make it right!" John thundered. "Make it right!?"

John barely refrained from drawing his .44:

"You don't make right killing a little boy filled with mischief and wonder! You don't pay someone to sit in the dark because they think they might get shot if they step into the light! You don't ever make a thing like that right, you ignorant bastard. I have one boy at home that I ought to be with and I had to send my other boys away because we were scared to let them stay in their own house. I've scattered my family to the winds and our whole life is in upheaval. My people are scared witless and I have neglected my business for months because of you. My wife has been terrified so many times I lost track. You tried to rape her. You tried to kidnap her. You scared her half out of her mind. You killed her baby. You want to make all of that right with money?"

John Purdy was trembling with rage and had stepped away from Sledge when Brown and Blackfeather rode into the rocky hilltop clearing along with a cavalry sergeant and a big older middle-aged fellow. The four dismounted to join the group.

"Sorry we missed the party, John. Looks like it might have been a good one and it is not even time for breakfast yet."

"Would you believe that Junior's dad was alive and probably saved my skin. Sledge killed him while he was doing it though, and he is lying over there. But then this Indian woman who came up here with him shot Sledge with an arrow. My God, you ought to go over there the other way and look where she shot from. I didn't know anyone could do that. Her name is Goat Woman."

Blackfeather joined the conversation:

"I know of Goat Woman. She is a good and wise woman. She is truly remarkable."

The four newcomers stood looking at Sledge, as Goat Woman walked over and joined the group. Brown then turned to John.

"John, pay somebody that reward so we can all go home."

"Reward? Oh yes. Hell yes! I certainly do owe somebody. I owe a lot of somebodies."

The big fellow was Gerald Holsher's "kid brother" Reimer. He shook his head:

"Rewards. Haa! Vvee ust make a down payment of vot ve owe your vivess family. Yout comes drink beer veeth us sometimes. Looks like you got yore manse. I go tell de others after vee do breakfast vee can go ta home."

"Thank you. Thank everybody. Please get me a list of their names if you can."

The big German nodded affirmatively, mounted up and waved as he rode away.

Just then some of the Millers showed up.

Miller walked up to Sledge and spat a big spurt of tobacco juice in his face:

"That's for pointing a gun at me, you bastard."

John took a good many double eagle coins plus eight single eagles for the younger Miller kids from one of the boot liners.

"That is a lot of money for what we did. Them kids will be plum spoiled"

John glanced at Sledge:

"Keep it. He has plenty."

Sergeant Simms took a good look at Sledge then mounted up:

"No rewards, Mr. Purdy. Colonel Albin's orders. Absolutely no rewards. This is what we get paid to do, and it was a great experience for these young troopers."

John pushed some gold coins at the sergeant:

"Have a party for your men."

The sergeant shook his head.

"Sir, you don't know the colonel as well as I thought you did. If there is going to be a party, you and Mrs. Purdy will have to come and throw it. The colonel sends his best and would like to hear from you when you get a chance. I'll go spread the word and I'll tell the bullwhackers that after we eat they can go home too."

John shouted after him:

"Get me your troopers' names."

Obviously Red was no longer in this thing just for the money, for he had come to really like and admire John. He spoke up:

"Well they had him on the ground when we got here. That ugly cuss died catching the bastard. I guess that about says it all."

"Red, everybody else kept him from getting away, but this morning some of your men pretty much laid it on the line."

"Spose so."

John turned to Goat Woman as if to speak; however, she interrupted him;

"I have no need of your gold. Mr. Sledge wanted to buy me with gold. I said no to him, and I say no to your gold too, Mr. Purdy. I came all this way because it was the right thing for me to do. Mr. Tooter wanted to be a real man. I wanted to help him, so I came. I did not come for gold."

John countered:

"Goat Woman, someday you will be older and may want a more gentle life. You will never want for anything, and I mean anything, for as long as my sons or my grandsons are alive."

Motioning to Red to follow him, John headed over to where Sledge's stolen horse was tied.

"Tooter has a son we call Junior, and I know where he is. How about I split the reward with his boy and Goat Woman. I want to do something for the Osage and Majors' men too. You already know that I think what you and your men are doing is despicable, and I would hate to think I financed any part of it."

Although John and Red had grown to really like each other on the trail, they obviously still harbored extremely different points of view. As he was speaking, John stuffed Sledge's heavy heeled boots into the stirrups and handed the reins of the horse Sledge had stolen to Red.

"You may as well take this horse cause you are going to be blamed for stealing it anyway. Take the boots too; they might fit one of your men."

Red was delighted.

"John, mark my words. In a few months we will all, and I mean all, be fighting for "Slavery without a Union" or "A Union without Slavery." You have to pick your side and take your stand. At least you know mine."

"And you know mine. But that does not mean we cannot be friends, Red. Except for what happened to the big black, I will always be thankful to you and yours for what you have done, and glad we met."

"Speaking of the big black, I sure hope he gets well. And tell Virginia de Falco I might just come see her cause I sure would like to see a 400 or 500-slave operation."

"I will, and thanks again. Make certain I get a list of names."

Red smiled sort of a crooked smile as he shook his head:

"You can't be serious. I'll tell em all you said thanks, but I don't think you will be getting any list. Anyway, good luck, John."

The two shook hands and then embraced warmly. Both of them had the feeling that somehow, someday, somewhere, destiny would bring them together again.

By now several more of Red's teams had found their way to the high rocky clearing, had taken a good look at Sledge, and were congregated over at the edge of the clearing. He joined the group and gave the command:

"Mount up, men. Thanks for the boots, John, they will come in mighty handy."

The horses picked their way off the rocky hilltop, and each man in line looked back and threw John a salute, just as horse and rider found the smooth trail. Then in turn each rider urged his mount to a gallop.

The day was young and they were in a hurry.

They had a steamboat to catch.

Several more men visited the bluff and most were very disappointed when they learned there was to be no hanging. By midmorning the hilltop was down to John Purdy's trio and Goat Woman, plus Sledge, of course. Brown and Blackfeather were watching Sledge, and as John approached, Blackfeather inquired:

"What now, John?"

"Adams couldn't make it, so we probably need to find somebody else wearing a badge I guess."

Brown looked completely astonished:

"A badge?"

"Yes. Can we just take the law into our own hands?"

Brown stormed:

"John, the man tried to kidnap your wife out of your own store, then he tried to rape her in her own garden. After that the first time he tried to kidnap her he started a fire that killed your boy. That wasn't good enough so he tried to kidnap her again, and Mattie lived scared half out of her mind while you were gone. Just for good measure he had that friend of Jess's killed, then came back here after Mattie and tried to kidnap her again. For extra good measure he lay like a snake in the grass waiting to blow your head off, and a man died keeping him from getting his shot. Bos is laying up there half dead; every man you know has dropped everything to look out for you and her, and my butt is sore from riding this horse! And you want a badge? Holy Shit!"

"Are we just an outlaw bunch, Brown?"

Brown became even stormier:

"John, let me give you some advice and you listen up good. Don't ever start something unless you know how you want it to end! Just what kind of a tea party did you have in mind when we rode out of Three Creeks?"

John looked very perplexed:

"Wouldn't it be a sin to just do it ourselves?"

Brown started lecturing:

"Sin is a word that came from the Greek word 'hamartia.' It meant to miss the mark with a bow and arrow and then the word sin came to mean to miss the mark of God's will. You're job is to leave the world a better place than you found it, so that's what you do. Just what do you suppose God's will is right now? I figure he'll be downright pissed if you don't take care of this like you ought to! And you want a badge? Damnation! Let me have him! Mattie deserves her soteria."

"What the hell is that? Another fancy Greek word?"

"Yeah, I guess I'm sounding like a smart-ass, John. Anyway, it means to be taken out of harm's way."

Sledge was miserable. He had been lying there all morning with his shattered leg throbbing, plus the arrowhead buried in his shoulder joint was excruciating. He watched back and forth, first at the trio surrounding him and then over at Goat Woman doing some kind of chant at a smoky fire over by where they had put Tooter's body. Blackfeather followed Sledge's gaze and then stood up:

"I will go be with her. A man should have another man help with that. He turned out to be a real man after all, John, but it looks like it took her to show him how."

Brown walked away muttering to himself, leaving John and Sledge by a big oak tree.

Sledge demanded of John:

"You got anything to write with?"

"I have a poster with your ugly face on one side and a pencil."

"Give it to me."

"I reckon."

Sledge wrote very poorly, but managed to crudely print on the back of a personal wanted poster.

I giv alls I gott to Matee Purdy.
Sledge.

"Purdy, I could never get your woman out of my mind. Every time I was with any woman, I thought about her. I couldn't sleep no more with her on my mind. I had to have her. I needed her so bad. I didn't want nobody else to have her. Not even you. I guess you gotta call that love cause I figured if I couldn't have her then nobody else could neither, and I would have to kill her fore I let that happen no more. I couldn't even stand the thought of you on her. Maybe this will make her like me. Ya suppose she could ever like me? I want her to like me. God, I need her to like me. I got an awful lot of money now and I just give all I got to your Mattie."

John walked away and stood watching Sledge from under a nearby tree. His thoughts were of Mattie and Harvey, but soon turned to Bos lying half dead up in Lexington. There was no doubt Sledge had caused or done all of these things, and in fact he just admitted to setting the fire. Hanging was too easy an out for the son of a bitch. John remembered how paralyzed with fear Mattie had been the night he got home. He blinked hard as his mind went back to Harvey's little red cedar casket with the carved white cedar hands on the lid. He closed his eyes and could still see their boy lying on his blankee and Mattie slipping in the hot cookies, as they were taking their last look. And then fastening down the lid.

John stood with his eyes closed, pressing his thumb and forefinger to the bridge of his nose. There are those who think manly men do not cry, yet John Purdy, who would stand against three men his size, stood blinking away, unable to control the occasional tear that trickled down his face.

He saw the scenes vividly.

She stood like a statue at the head of their baby's grave, composing herself. The wind fluffed her long black dress. The golden sunshine born in the deep blue sky caused her hair to glisten. It brushed over the violin. She fought back the pain as she drew her bow.

John Purdy had dedicated twenty years to protecting his Mattie, yet somehow these ungodly things had happened. Well never again! The next who even considered such a thing would soon find out what happened to such people. Anyone watching John Purdy would have seen him make up his mind. He was resolved. If St. Peter slammed the gates, he would square his shoulders and march straight to Hell.

And besides, there was another thing.

His promise to Mattie.

They dragged Sledge over to the old hunter's shack and put him in a corner, and then Goat Woman joined with Brown and Blackfeather in their search. The three brought back two big timber rattlers. It had taken quite a while, for although there were plenty of copperheads, rattlers were not as common in the area. His three companions seemed to know how to handle poisonous snakes quite well, so John watched on.

Brown seemed to be the expert:

"Rattlesnakes can't see much of anything but they can sense any warm blooded creature 200 feet away, even a baby mouse. This kind of rattler can strike about one-third to one-half its length in a split second, but he'd always rather run than confront a man. They only strike when they are scared or mad. Babies or little kids will die from one strike, but a grown man rarely does. One hit will hurt like hell, and full a grown man has convulsions and can't seem to get his breath. The heart pounds, and a person gets dizzy and has an upset stomach and bad diarrhea and a whole lot of other things. Most men live through one bite. Few, if any, ever live through a whole lot of them."

"Tell me about the rawhide, Brown. How long is this going to take?"

"I hid in the cactus with the snakes for a long time, John. You have a lot of time when you do that. A lot of time to practice. If you only dampen the rawhide down, a piece this long will stretch about six inches in an hour on a good dry day like this. If you soak the rawhide, it takes a long time."

Brown supervised as Goat Woman and Blackfeather carefully poked double holes through the snakes' tails about six inches apart. Next, they unwound and dampened down the thinly woven rawhide cord that Brown had carried some 2000 miles. They completed their task by securing each rattler to a piece of the damp rawhide by passing it through the hole at the top, down to its belly, and then doubling the cord back through the second hole, to the top. The rawhide line was then secured to a small strong cross stick with a notch, so the stick would not slip away, nor could the line pass back out. Along the way Brown explained that it was important to do this correctly. Improperly fastened, the snake may well break its tale off in its frenzy as it strikes time after time after time at any warm-blooded creature it senses.

One of the rattlers was fastened into position at about hip level and the other right in his face. All of Sledge's clothes were piled in a different corner to made certain they did not get in the way, as the rawhide dried enough for the hissing vipers to get at him. Goat Woman and Brown handed the snake-sticks to John, giving him the honor of releasing the little lassos holding the snakes by their heads. The rattlers immediately commenced striking viciously, only to be pulled up short by the rawhide. They were enraged and hissing furiously!

The look on Sledge's face was indescribable.

It was a curious thing. None of them took pleasure or satisfaction from Sledge's hysterical screams and pleadings. It was simply something that must be done. They sat by Tooter's gravesite and visited, mostly about him and what they had witnessed on the chase. As the afternoon wore on, Sledge's pleading became even more hysterical. It was obvious when the snakes reached their prey. After a while, Sledge quieted down and Purdy went to inspect things. It was a gruesome enough sight that John decided enough was enough. He fetched Quinton Tooter's pistol and released the hand at Sledge's unwounded shoulder.

John placed the weapon in Sledge's hand.

"There is one round left. Use it any way you want."

Purdy was brave, but he was no fool. The round remaining in the cylinder was just past the barrel. But he need not have worried. Sledge was sucking frantically on the barrel, as he pulled the trigger time after time.

The sixth pull blew his brains out.

Blackfeather and Goat Woman, (whom he called Eagle Eyes) loaded the horse Tooter had ridden with some of the provisions the Germans had left behind. They were to meet up with the Chickasaw to tell them they could all go home and also to personally deliver a boot lining to Chief. After they had sent the Chickasaw on their way, Goat Woman was anxious to get back to her geldings. She and Tooter had exchanged the exhausted horses for fresh ones down on the Grand Indian Trail at Rolla, approximately halfway back to the Mississippi ferry boat. After she reclaimed her pets, she was not at all anxious to get on home, for she had a trusted friend and Dog watching the goats. On the other hand she was quite anxious to get better acquainted with Blackfeather. She supposed they linger a while in some extraordinary countryside she and Tooter had passed through on their frantic ride from Kentucky. Smiling shyly, she suggested they plan on resting up for a few nights by camping out together.

As John attempted to show further appreciation to the pair, Goat Woman stood aside, and the big Indian faced him and laid both of his hands on John's shoulders, so he might look him straight in the eyes:

"You are my faithful friend. I would lay down my life for you. Say no more."

Before they mounted up he embraced Goat Woman and Blackfeather both. His voice kept cracking:

"I will never accacummm forget any of you, or the trail aacaha mmmn ahum we rode."

Blackfeather took the lead, and she led the packhorse as their mounts picked their way down the black rock mesa. The two were still waving broadly when they passed from view.

John waited as Brown retrieved his rawhide; however, he insisted they leave Tooter's pistol. If anyone became overly curious, Sledge holding the weapon positioned in his own mouth might well save answering a lot of questions.

John then lit the brush which they had piled around the cabin.

There was one more detail to finish. Rainwater, an Osage tribal leader, had taken a serious fall while searching in one of the caves. John wanted very badly to do something for him, and check his well being. Brown insisted on taking care of that chore so John could get started for Lexington, to tell Mattie and the others.

"You get on out of here. I will go visit Rainwater and then see you back in Lexington in a day or two. By the way, John, Virginia said she has a lot of books she thought I would enjoy reading, so you better start looking for another schoolteacher. Said she had this one bedroom, that if she had a little carpentry work done and got rid of some piece of furniture and an awfully ugly picture, then it would be just perfect for me. If you could plan on sending my stuff I'd appreciate it. That way I can just head on south with her and Mammy when they go. I always have liked the South."

As he looked back at his friend the bemused expression never left John's face. Apparently Brown was getting a much bigger reward than John could possibly ever have given him for coming on this sojourn. Star picked his way off the rocky hilltop to the smooth ridge-top trail and sprang to a gallop, for John had already taken off the bridle to let the magnificent beast have its way. John Purdy needed to clear his head.

As the flames from the cabin quickly died down to embers, Brown sat watching from the very edge of the bluff top. Finally he turned his face to the valley and took the golden case from his pocket. He looked at her picture for a long, long time. Next he opened the back and carefully removed the lock of her hair. He sat brushing it gently across his lips.

"It's time to say goodbye, my love.

I got them.

I got them all.

I got every name you gave me.

And a lot more.

But you already know that.

I let his woman and their young son live. I couldn't bring myself to do that. But the rest are dead.

I will always love you.

Always—Always——Always.

You have my heart. It's not fair. I have to make room for her. She is a good woman too. I have to move on. I must. I know you understand. You always did."

With that, Brown kissed her picture one final time. Then, standing at the very edge of the bluff, he threw the golden case with its precious contents as far as he could make it go. Before it fell, it flew far out over the river to twinkle its brilliant approval in the sunlight. As the golden flash then fell into the Osage Valley, Brown whispered a heartfelt prayer:

"God, be with my Bo Lee."

Missouri population was exploding, having tripled in the last three years. A great many people were now moving into the notably rich farm country, which started some 20 miles north of the bluffs and continues north, on past the Missouri River. Eighty percent of these new Missourians lived on farms, the rest in small hamlets scattered along the way. Farmers and village people alike stopped their tasks and watched this man on his horse until he was completely out of view, for big clods were flying up 20 feet behind them. The stallion's tail stood almost straight out and the rider sat as comfortably as if he were in a rocking chair by his fireplace, instead of on his charging white stallion with no bridle. Twilight found John and Star near Syracuse, a small village that one day would be the eastern terminus of the Butterfield Stage Line. John ate at a tavern and bought grain for Star. After a bit of rest, they moved on to a town called Sedalia. The moon was down by now and it was nearly pitch black. John reluctantly elected to spend the rest of night there. He woke up the innkeeper at a place which was already overrun with guests, and where he was assigned a room with two other men who both snored.

John was exhausted, but he lay wide awake.

Waiting impatiently to tell Mattie and the others.

It is impossible to celebrate such a thing by oneself.

He tried to content himself by dwelling on the fact there was risk of hurting Star, and since this odyssey was concluding there was no sense in being foolish. Finally there was enough light just before dawn, and

Star was as anxious to be on the road to Lexington as he was. Four hours later they arrived in Lexington under a brilliant morning sun.

Virginia had gone door to door until she found a widow who lived alone in a large house and she had rented the place. As the homeowner left to stay at her nearby sister's, she was convinced that Santa Clause was a striking, tall, salt and pepper haired lady with a bit of an accent.

It had been a very hard time for Bos. A young doctor had agreed to see him, and while doing so surgically removed a good part of his left ear. Other than that, the doctor told the women where to find ice and gave them whatever advice and medicine he had, which was not much.

Bos started out in bad shape and got continuously worse, as his head continued to swell. He was oblivious to those around him, and they thought they might well lose him. Junior had raced to Lexington when he heard about his dear friend and he too rarely left his side. Meanwhile, Maud brought Maureen along to see if they might possibly be of any help. Maureen sat by his bedside and sang softly to the big man, for somehow that seemed to calm his thrashing about. Bos' first real notable awareness was while Mattie was sitting with him though the night and made some kind of remark which included the phrase, "Bos, I need you." Thereafter, every time he heard Mattie say or use the phrase, he stirred, and finally when she said "Bos, I need you," he would open his less swollen eye and gaze at her for just a bit.

Virginia was amazed at how handy Mattie was in the kitchen and sat in wide-eyed wonder as she separated the whites from the yellows in a dozen or so eggs. She needed the whites to make an angel food cake for the soldiers. The soldiers were quite self-sufficient, but the ladies kept fresh drinks and cookies or cake available which the men appreciated no end. Private Jenkins, who was little more than a boy, was having a birthday, and a birthday without angel food cake was considered sinful at the Purdys' household. Although the slaves back home cooked in a corner of their cabin, Mammy was used to having a whole building to work in and found this little old kitchen downright handy. She almost fainted when she found her Miz. Virginia elbow deep in dishwater cleaning up Mattie' s mess. She also covered her face and looked away when Virginia acted as though she had just made some major medical breakthrough when she brought eggs prepared by her very own hands to the table.

John Purdy burst in the front door as they were preparing to eat those eggs.

"It's over Mattie! It's over! Thank God it's over!"

Mattie threw her arms around him and held on tightly.

"Really over, John? Really, really over?"

"It will never be more over Mattie. We are done. It's over."

"Did you keep your promise?"

" I kept my promise."

She never asked John for details. If Mattie ever knew what happened on that bluff, she found out from someone other than him.

Exhaustion hit hard. Sleepless nights and 280 hours in the saddle in less than three weeks will get to even a big strong man like John Purdy. He collapsed into a chair. Mattie came and sat on his lap and put her arms around his neck, pulling his head to her chest. She started to cry just a little, and the longer she sat the more tears there were.

She sobbed quietly as memories of her blue-eyed little boy with his golden tassels overwhelmed her.

Mattie got a faraway look in her eyes, and between sniffs she mused, more to herself than to John or anybody else:

"I miss him so."

"I've been so worried for you."

"I have been so scared"

"So very scared."

"It's been a horrible dream."

"A nightmare."

"I want to go home."

She took John's face in her hands:

"John, please take me home now."

John wanted to look in on Bos, so they stopped by his room; he was coherent.

"When somebody ask me about this ear, Miss Mattie, I'll have quite a yarn to spin. Sides that, when I look there, it will just make me think of you. I always like thinking about you, so don't you worry none."

Mattie bent over and kissed Bos on his bandaged ear like a momma kissing her child's hurt.

"Bos, you will always, always be my handsome hero."

The soldiers thanked the ladies for all the treats, especially the angel food cake, and then headed back to post. John took their names for they would certainly hear from the Purdys again sometime soon.

John freshened up for the first time since he had passed through Lexington before. Mattie hovered close by. At this alone moment John queried Mattie:

"Had you picked up on this Virginia and Brown thing?"

"Men are so blind."

"So you say. Really now, did you see this coming?"

"All you had to do was watch them at the Harris House, besides, I even heard her call him Horaticus."

"Well I'll be damned."

"Watch your tongue, Mr. Purdy. There is a lady present."

"There shore is ma'am. And a right pretty one at that." He pinched her bottom, then started rubbing out the pinch.

She flashed her best come-on smile.

"Now mister, I'm gonna give you less than a half day to quit that."

After a brief interlude, John Purdy fell asleep and slept the clock around.

Mammy stood with Virginia and Brown as they hovered together on the cabin deck, waving as their boat churned back out onto the Mississippi. Brown actually had choked up a bit too as the group was splitting up at the river city of Cairo where the Ohio joins the Mississippi. It had taken several days to get there from Lexington, giving them plenty of time to reminisce and plan.

The Purdys and Bos were taking it very easy because of Bos' continuing convalescence and planned on spending time in Paducah with John's family as they were waiting for their boys. Henry and Harold were already headed back down the Ohio and besides waiting for them, it would take a lot of time to give Grandmother Ella the detailed report she would expect and demand.

Virginia and Brown were going to take it slow to make certain this thing was real, but Mammy and Mattie both agreed that anybody with eyes and a brain knew that it was.

"I done raise that girl and dis be what ought to have happen when she be eighteen. She be plumb moon struck."

Even so, the others felt compelled to politely look the other direction as Virginia held on to John for almost toooooo long as they said their goodbyes. She hugged him tightly about his neck and laid her head on his shoulder, brushing her lips against his check as she spoke softly:

"You opened up my heart, John, so there will always be room in there for you. I will always love you."

John's eyes twinkled:

"Oh, I'm not so sure about that. He is the right size, smart, good looking, the right age, loves music, is well educated and is a great conversationalist. However, I do see one small problem?"

"Oh really?"

She leaned her ear to his lips to hear him whisper, and then turned scarlet red at his answer.

"I think he dresses right."

Epilogue

By the time, Virginia and, Brown disembarked at Island View she had briefed him completely on her instructions to Steven Farout. Virginia was losing her heart to Brown because he was her kind of a man; however, she could now think of no one she would rather have at her side if the other slave holders became restless. Island View was going to be the best place a southern Negro slave could hope to be, their lives more akin to prosperous share-croppers than slaves. Virginia's plan looked like a modern day co-op with its members under her protective wings where all of them would be allowed to accumulate money. When, and if, she ever thought the slaveholding community would stand for it, she planned to let the Negroes buy themselves. With the 1857 Louisiana laws pertaining to such matters, that was apt to be quite a while, and her radical long term thinking would incense some of the locals. Virginia did not want to get run out of the South, so currently, only Farout, lawyer Rawson and now Brown knew about that part of her plan.

And just maybe Grandfather "Spinner" de Falco.

Virginia sold the painting and in a couple of months she also had the furniture rearranged and a little carpentry work done. And sent for a Priest. She and Brown were delighted at how intimate the master bedroom suite became. It soon became her favorite place.

Brown had rescued the poster where Sledge had written his last will and testament when Sledge had spat it out on the ground after John had forcefully stuffed it into his mouth. Brown was being pragmatic; there was a fortune involved here and that fact could simply not be ignored. When emotions had cooled enough he would give the poster with Sledge's last will and testament on its backside to Mattie. And ask John to let her decide for herself what to do. They would visit about that when he and Virginia went up to Kentucky to see the new baby.

After John presented Maud and Junior with details of what had happened, plus the genealogy records and a bank draft for half of the reward, Junior tore the bank draft in two:

"You don't take money for something like that from people you love."

Young Tooter decided to take his father's real name, for his father had indeed given him something to admire after all, and he would honor that memory by carrying on his name. Instead of attending Transylvanian College, Quinton Tooter II quickly became a star pupil at William Jewell College in Liberty just north of the City of Kansas. Little Maureen was impressed with the manner in which he looked after his mother and soon decided the young man was different than most she had known. Best she not let him get away.

Mary Ellen convinced everyone that with two Irish fiddlers plus a few more instruments to back her, and someone to sing harmony from time to time, Maureen could fill any house in the country. Virginia and John both decided to invest in an entertainer and bought a small house close by Maud's where Mary Ellen and Maureen moved in permanently. For their engagement present, Quinton Tooter II found a craftsman to help his new fiancée make a fine set of shepherd's flutes. At first they preformed on Captain Mac's boats, riding down the river and catching the next one back up. They were fabulous and "Maureen and Mary Ellen" were soon playing to standing room only in the largest theaters in America's major cities. At a time when word was either by newspaper or mouth, they soon became household names. Although they stayed an entire extra week in both places, the police had to be called to manage the disappointed throngs unable to get tickets when they appeared in New York and Philadelphia. Quinton II managed to continue somewhat with his book learning and still shoulder the task of business manager, for they were overwhelmed with dates to keep. Mary Ellen was simply devoted to Maureen, becoming the perfect mother hen who accompanied her on stage and then spent the balance of her time arranging and producing. And protecting. They asked John and Virginia to devise the formula in which to disperse and manage the considerable flood of funds, and Mary Ellen was exacting in defending Maureen's interests.

Almost overnight Jess and Jeannie became famously wealthy and set about finding Leonard's family, so as to take care of his widow and children. Jeannie also immediately set about founding a home in current Denver for abused women. She named it "Maud's Other Place."

Janice and Alfred went to the City of Kansas to visit Geneva, and Alfred decided to stay a while; however, Janice felt somewhat estranged and returned quickly to Island View as she now preferred Virginia's council to her mother's.

Mattie gave Sarah to Bos; however, even smiling "full dazzle" the best Mattie could do was to get Simpson to agree to accept a premium price for Sarah, but only after Bos worked for him as a blacksmith for three years. Part of the contract was that Bos and all children born of Sarah would be owned by the Purdys; however, Bos and Sarah could always keep any of their children with them, including the one she now carried. After the three years it would be up to Simpson to see to it they wanted to stay, and the Purdys could not set them free so long as they chose to live in the home Simpson was to provide. Simpson needed a blacksmith and Bos was outstanding; however, Simpson was very uncomfortable with the idea of a free black out on his place. As far as Mattie was concerned, the most important part of the contract specified that she be allowed unrestricted access to her slave and that any time the slaves had time to themselves, he and his family could come see her at will. Furthermore she would be present in the unlikely event, and then only John would be allowed to administer any discipline or punishment deemed necessary.

The spring of 1861 was indeed noteworthy.

A big Frenchman by the name of Terhune said it was the God awfulest thing he ever saw. He was poking around in the charred ruins of that old shack at the very top Osage bluff. He had been out "sorrying around," just looking for some of his cows that had strayed. He had been poking around in the ashes of that old shack when he found the human skeleton, with two rattlesnake skeletons hanging to it. The fellow still had a pistol in his hand where he had shot himself in the head. It gave Terhune the creeps, for it appeared the chap could get to his gun, but couldn't get away from the snakes.

"Sheriff, that fellow reached into the bag of life and drew out a black ball."

The Sheriff agreed that the fellow's luck had run out. And that he was going to watch more carefully for snakes when he was up on the black-rock.

Almost everyone knows Lincoln was elected and about Ft. Sumter and how the union really started to collapse.

Edith Virginia Purdy came in at about six and one half pounds, and by seven pounds had her father completely wrapped round her little finger.

Bos and Sarah asked if they might name their boy Harvey. He came in big and bigger. Sarah was a large woman and handled it well; however, she readily admitted that the baby sure was a chunk. He was Bos all over again.

Virginia de Falco Brown caused quite a stir in the slave holding community by partially disclosing Island View's brilliant new business plan. The plan greatly improves their slaves' lot. Some saw this as progress while many others saw it as a blight that best not be allowed to get hold, even if the economics were indisputable.

Mammy and her staff outdid themselves preparing a huge wedding for Janice and a fine young man who was a neighboring plantation owner's son. Virginia made an exception and allowed Geneva on Island View for just this one day, to attend the spectacular event.

Mr. Simpson started forming up a confederate unit and he and John had an honest-to-goodness fight, coming to blows when Simpson demanded that Hiram join as his adjunct. Colonel Albin was promoted to General and sent a captain all the way to Three Creeks with a confidential message to John that the Union had room for a full colonel on his staff, and it was his for the taking. Lincoln himself had heard of John's tactical abilities, and Albin assured him in his letter that a generals' star for John Purdy was a given. John Purdy well deserved his reputations as a business visionary and also as a genius when it came to organizing a manhunting special force. He had always enjoyed being looked up to for his business acumen; however, being looked upon by Washington and the neighborhood as a logical military leader was quite another thing.

The young man John had put in the photography business became famous over the next five years for the pictures he took of Americans fighting and killing each other.

John and Mattie had long talks with their boy Hiram. Mattie had also gone one-on-one with Betty Jo who begged at the time that her parents not be told she was pregnant. If indeed there was to be a first grandchild about the same time as Mattie delivered, the Purdys expected both of them to act like adults and take full responsibility for what supposedly was happening. Betty Jo got quite a surprise proviso from the Purdys; it was as Grandmother Ella always said:

"The truth will out."

That however, is a story unto itself, best saved for some other time.

Sample Populations (in Thousands)

	1840	1850	1860
New York	312	515	813
Baltimore	102	169	595
New Orleans	104	116	168
Philadelphia	93	169	565
Boston	93	136	177
Cincinnati	46	115	161
Brookline	34	96	*
St. Louis	16	77	160
Chicago	*	29	112
Buffalo NY	*	41	81
U S Total	14,195,695		31,433,321
Slaves	2,487,453		3,953,760

Slave State Population (in Thousands) 1860

	White	Slaves
Arkansas	324	111
Delaware	90	2
Florida	90	77
Georgia	591	462
Kentucky	919	219
Louisiana	357	351
Maryland	515	87
Mississippi	353	436
Missouri	1063	114
North Carolina	629	351
South Carolina	291	402
Tennessee	826	275
Texas	420	182
Virginia	1,047	490

Ambrose & Brinkley
Witness to America Lou Reda Productions 1999

Angus, Fern
Down the Wire Road T & I Publishing 1992

Bailey, John
The Lost German Slave Girl Grove Press N Y 2004

Butruille, Susan G
Women's Voices From the Western Frontier Tamarack 1995

Carnegie, Dale
Lincoln the Unknown Carnegie and Associates 1965

Clinton, Catherin
Fannie Kemble's Civil wars Simon & Shuster 2000

Dary, David
The Santa Fe Trail Penguin Books 2000

Dary, David
The Oregon Trail an American Saga Oxford University Press 2004

Davis, Kenneth S.
Kansas a History. Norton and Co. 1976

Dean, Virgil W.
Movers and Shakers in Kansas History University press of Kansas 2006

Den Dooven
Pony Express K C Publications 1999
California Trail K C Publications 1996
Oregon Trail K C Publications 1992
Santa Fe Trail K C Publications 1994

Erbsen, Wayne
Log Cabin Pioneers Native Ground Music 2001

Flansburg, Scott
Math Magic Harper Perennial 1994

Fleischner, Jennifer
Mrs. Lincoln and Mrs. Keckly Broadway 2004

Fradkin, Philip L
Stagecoach Simon and Schuster 2002

Gandy & Gandy
The Mississippi Steamboat Era Dover Publications 1987

Goodwin, *Jason*
The Almighty Dollar and the Invention of America Picador, of N Y 1964

Hallmark Creations
Kansas City, an Intimate Portrait Hallmark Publications 1973

Hamilton Adam, Sr. Pastor
Villa, Yolanda Exec. Pastor
Various Sermons Church of the Resurrection 2005,6,7

Howe, Charles C.
This place called KANSAS Univ. Of Oklahoma Press 1952

Kalman, Bovvie
Life on a Plantation Crabtree Publishing 1997

Kennedy, Billy
The Scots-Irish In the Shenandoah Valley Ambassador Productions 1996

Krakauer, Jon
Under the Banner of Heaven Anchor Books 2003

Mobley & Parkinson
Kansas City Community Publications, Montgomery Ala. 1994

Montgomery & Kasper
Kansas City an American Story Star Books 1999

Phillips, Charles
Missouri, Mother of the American West Windsor Publications 1988

Richmond, Robert W.
Kansas a Land of Contrasts Forum Press III 1974

Schirmer & Mckinzie
At the River's Bend Wilson Publications 1982

Schultz, G.B.
Gully Town Shadow Mountain Press 1981

Stratton, Joanna L.
Pioneer Women Schuster and Schuster 1981

Wilcox, Pearl
Jackson County Pioneers Jackson County Historical Society 1975

Williamson, E.W.
The Man from the Brazos Brazos Novels 2002

Wilson, R.L.
The Peacemakers-Arms and Adventures in the Early West Cartwell Books 2004

Zaner
Those Spirited Women of the Early West Zanel Publications 1989

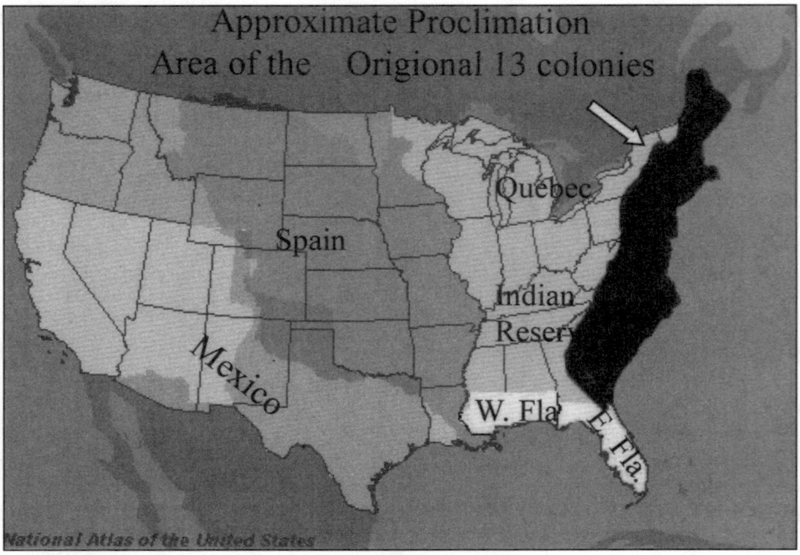
Approximate Proclimation
Area of the Origional 13 colonies
Quebec
Spain
Indian
Reser
Mexico
W. Fla
E. Fla.
National Atlas of the United States

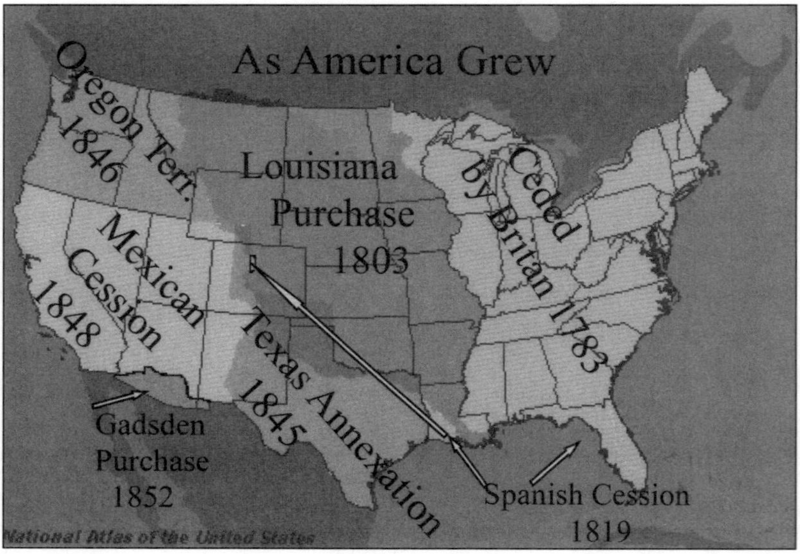
As America Grew
Oregon Terr.
1846
Louisiana
Purchase
1803
Ceded
by Britan 1783
Mexican
Cession
1848
Texas Annexation
1845
Gadsden
Purchase
1852
Spanish Cession
1819
National Atlas of the United States